Books by Tim Powers

The Skies Discrowned
An Epitaph in Rust
The Drawing of the Dark
The Anubis Gates
Dinner at Deviant's Palace
On Stranger Tides
The Stress of Her Regard

Fault Lines Series
Last Call
Expiration Date
Earthquake Weather

Declare
Three Days to Never
Hide Me Among the Graves
Medusa's Web

Vickery and Castine Series
Alternate Routes
Forced Prospectives

Short Story Collections
Night Moves and Other Stories • *Strange Itineraries*
The Bible Repairman and Other Stories
Down and Out in Purgatory: The Collected Stories of Tim Powers

To purchase Baen Book titles in e-book form, please go to www.baen.com.

↓FORCED↓
PERSPECTIVES

↓FORCED↓
PERSPECTIVES

BY
TIM POWERS

BAEN

A Baen Books Original

Baen Publishing Enterprises
P.O. Box 1403
Riverdale, NY 10471
www.baen.com

ISBN: 978-1-9821-2440-3

Cover art by Adam Burn

First printing, March 2020

Distributed by Simon & Schuster
1230 Avenue of the Americas
New York, NY 10020

Library of Congress Cataloging-in-Publication Data

Names: Powers, Tim, 1952- author.
Title: Forced perspectives / Tim Powers.
Description: Riverdale, NY : Baen Books, [2020]
Identifiers: LCCN 2019051640 | ISBN 9781982124403 (hardcover)
Subjects: GSAFD: Mystery fiction. | Occult fiction.
Classification: LCC PS3566.O95 F67 2020 | DDC 813/.54--dc23
LC record available at https://lccn.loc.gov/2019051640

Printed in the United States of America

10 9 8 7 6 5 4 3 2 1

To my wife, Serena

With thanks to:
Tony Daniel, J.R. Dunn, Ken Estes, Russell Galen,
Tom Gilchrist, Becca and Mike Rottiers, Bill Schafer,
Joe Stefko, Toni Weisskopf, Bill and Peggy Wu,
and Michael and Laura Yanovich

↓FORCED↓
PERSPECTIVES

PROLOGUE, 1928:
Before the Shadows Crept In

"It was on the south wall of the Pharaoh's city."

The man had to speak loudly over the onshore wind, and in spite of the rushing veils of sand he had taken off his goggles to see the dunes more clearly in the twilight.

Apart from the shivering figures of his four hooded companions, one of them dutifully blowing into a smoking coffee can, the only features in the desolate landscape were the black rocks that stood up here and there like islands in the infinite rippled expanse of sand, and the fragments of broken plaster that littered the area all the way down to the surf line. The random arrangements of the rocks were no good as landmarks—for all he knew, they had shifted during the five years since he had last been here.

"Boundless and bare," called Mrs. Haas, the High Priestess of the coven, "the lone and level sands stretch far away."

Wystan fitted the goggles back over his eyes and shifted the bulky knapsack on his back to a more comfortable position. His nearly-new 1925 Model T Ford pickup truck was stalled and stuck in the sand half a mile inland, and that was half a mile from the dirt track that led east to the new extension of Route 56 connecting Pismo Beach and Las Cruces. He wondered how he might find somebody in nearby Guadalupe with a truck and block and chains who would come out here at this hour. He didn't need old women quoting Shelley at him.

3

The three other witches were talking among themselves, probably speculating that Wystan wasn't a very effective High Priest, and that perhaps they didn't need a High Priest at all—especially one who drank liquor, in blatant defiance of the Volstead Act. Mrs. Haas' shiny new Model A sedan was parked way back there on the paved road, and the four old women had sat in the bed of his pickup for the last leg of the expedition until the truck had got stuck. They had all then walked the last half mile, with much grumbling.

"It's unlikely we're even in the right place," said the witch holding the coffee can in her gloved hands. "One little movie set, out here in these miles of nothing?"

"Keep blowing on it," said Wystan. Then, "It's here—all these plaster fragments were part of it. It wasn't a little movie set." He waved around at the empty miles of dunes, and went on more loudly, "The Pharaoh's city alone covered ten acres, and the walls were a hundred feet high! And DeMille built a whole city here, besides, with medical tents and kitchen tents—even a kosher kitchen!—for all the cast and crew, all 25,000 of us. Altogether the production covered twenty-four square miles! We took over the town—you'd see Egyptian chariots parked in front of the bars, and DeMille hired every local person and horse and steer for the crowd scenes."

Wystan turned away from his tiresome companions, and he took the opportunity to pull his flask from an inside pocket of his overcoat. He quickly unscrewed the cap and swallowed two liberal mouthfuls of what his bootlegger swore was English gin, then twisted the cap back on and tucked the flask away.

The witch with the coffee can had resumed blowing into it; her face glowed with each puff, and smoke flickered away in the gathering darkness. The wind smelled strongly of the ocean.

"It was a fine movie," allowed Mrs. Haas. "I never saw anything like when Moses parted the Red Sea."

Wystan laughed, so softly that the women probably didn't hear. "You should have seen us all wading into the sea one day to get seaweed. DeMille had put up fences to show where the walls of water would be matted in later, and he had to shoot at exactly noon, or the fences would throw shadows, and at the last minute somebody pointed out that the path through what was supposed to be the Red Sea bed was dry sand. So DeMille and everybody else went rushing into the surf to drag up kelp and spread it out on the path. And he got the shot before the shadows crept in."

And a hundred people suddenly and spontaneously agitating the sea, thought Wystan, and them dragging a lot of living stuff out of the sea onto the land, roused my *Ba* hieroglyph sigil. It pulled its nails nearly all the way out of the Pharaoh's south wall, and I had to hammer it back flat and repaint it to match the painted plywood wall before anybody noticed.

He took a few unsteady steps in a new direction across the sand, and his boot scuffed something that wasn't a pebble or piece of plaster; and when he had bent down to pick it up and shake the sand off it, he held it out for the witches to see. It was a rusty metal disk, and by the fading light over the ocean it was possible to read *Eastman Film* stamped on the surface.

"This is the lid of a film can," he said. "We're in the right place. If the cameras were about here . . . the wall would have been east of us. Best we set up right here, between the wall and the sea."

"Where *is* the wall?" quavered one of the witches. "Did it . . . erode away to dust? In just five years?"

"No." Wystan shrugged out of his knapsack and set it carefully on the sand. "DeMille, interfering son of a bitch that he was, hired bulldozers to dig a big deep trench and then damn well knock down the whole Pharaoh's city set and push it into the trench, and then bury it." Wystan had got the knapsack open, and now lifted out of it a lantern, an unwieldy two-foot-square cardboard portfolio, and, after groping around, a pair of needle-nose pliers. To the witch with the coffee can, he said, "Bring that over here."

When she had crouched beside him in the cold sand, he pressed the thumb lever to raise the lantern's glass globe, and with his free hand picked up the needle-nose pliers.

"You're going to light that lantern?" asked the witch. Wystan recalled that her husband owned an Italian restaurant in Whittier. When he nodded distractedly, she went on, "So why did I have to bring these coals?"

"Not coals," he said, reaching into the coffee can with the pliers, "embers. And you brought them to light the lantern with." He caught a glowing piece of punkwood with the pliers, and carefully held it under the bottom edge of the glass globe.

The woman sniffed and said, archly, "Watch you don't set your breath on fire."

Shut up, thought Wystan.

In the kitchen of the High Priestess' house back in San Pedro stood a four-foot tall Paschal candle; it had recently been stolen from a Catholic church in Redondo Beach, but its wick glowed with a flame whose combustion had been relayed—via a long, difficult succession of torches, locomotive fireboxes, ship's lanterns, and even, for one anxious half hour, the bowl of a briar pipe—from the eternal flame at Baba Gurgur in Iraq.

Wystan held the glowing ember of punkwood to the lantern's wick, but the oil-soaked fabric didn't catch fire. He bent down to blow on it, gently.

"But you could have lit the lantern back at Mrs. Haas' house," said the witch; he couldn't see her face in the shadows under her hood, but she sounded irritable, "it'd still be lit from the eternal flame, and I wouldn't have had to keep dropping bits of rotten wood into this can for four hours while we drove up here."

"You noticed," said Wystan tightly as he prodded the recalcitrant wick with the ember, "that Mrs. Haas had to send Cassie out to get coffee this afternoon. Her stove won't work, with that candle flame pre-empting all the . . . *flamehood* in her kitchen. Smoldering, it's what you might call asleep, but if it had been a flame in this lamp back in San Pedro, I doubt she'd have got ignition in her car's cylinders. Ah, there we go," he added, for a bright inch-high flare now enveloped the lantern's wick.

The woman's face was sharply visible now in the yellow glow, as was the sand for a dozen feet around. Wystan quickly untied the ribbons holding the portfolio closed and flipped open the cover.

"Don't look at this," he said as he lifted out a square of one-by-eight pine board, onto which he had painstakingly glued little wooden carvings—three pots, three wavy lines, and a stylized bier. He had arranged their pattern very carefully, following a precise description provided in a letter from Aleister Crowley, the British ceremonial magician.

Wystan didn't look at the board either. Even while putting it together, he had looked at only one corner of it at a time, and always in a mirror.

For more than twenty years, Claude Wystan's goal had been to find a way out of himself, and drinking provided only partial and temporary escape. He had studied in secret occult colleges in Leipzig and Beirut,and read a suppressed text of *The Book of Enoch* in the Ge-ez language, and had found and opened a lost tomb in the Umm El Ga'ab necropolis by the Nile and taken from it a five-thousand-year-old scroll that had escaped the destruction ordered by the Pharaoh Horus Aha. Ultimately Wystan had traced to Oslo a photograph of the *Ba* hieroglyph, and blackmailed the owner into allowing him to carve a high-relief copy.

And DeMille had buried it.

This hieroglyph he had brought to the burial site tonight was a rare variant of the name of *Nu*, the Egyptian god, or force, of negation and dissolution; just as the lost panel he was seeking here tonight was a variant but still valid—dynamically valid—version of the name of *Ba*, the god or force that made identity and consciousness possible. The two were opposites, and he was confident that the buried *Ba* image would be drawn to the *Nu* image, now illuminated by an extension of the Baba Gurgur fire.

He set the *Nu* board upright in the sand in back of the lantern, facing inland. He flexed his fingers and sat back, watching the sand. The lost board with his *Ba* sigil on it was a yard tall, and its motion should be easily visible.

For several long minutes, while the witches of the San Pedro coven shivered and shifted in their blowing robes, nothing happened. Streamers of sand whirled past in the lantern's glow.

Then, "Behind you!" called Mrs. Haas, pointing toward the dark ocean.

Wystan turned and saw a point of agitation in the sand on the seaward side of the lantern; something was making the sand hump up, and it was moving slowly, laboriously, away from them.

"That's got to be my sigil!" he exclaimed, and he leaped up and began running after the moving tumble of sand.

But why, he thought desperately, is it moving *away* from the *Nu* hieroglyph?

He knew he'd lose it forever if it got into the sea, to which it was apparently being drawn; and it was moving faster, its long edges visible now as it tossed up bursts of sand that blew away on the wind.

He dove forward onto the sand, his hands grasping the sides of the retreating wooden board, clinging to it even though one of its old nails dug into his right palm.

"I've got the bastard," he gasped, rolling over with it on top of him; then, more loudly, "Kill that damned lantern!"

He heard a clank behind him, and the glow of the lantern became brighter; then some hasty scuffing, and the light was gone.

The board's tugging toward the sea stopped. Wystan sat up, and as his breathing and heartbeat slowed, the fingers of his unwounded hand were feeling the damp board, tracing once again the figure of a hawk with a bearded man's head, which he had carved in Oslo many years ago . . . and which in 1923 he had surreptitiously attached to the south wall of the Pharaoh's City set, in among a cluster of other, inert hieroglyphs.

He had understood that DeMille would film a fairly lengthy scene with that section of the wall in the background, but as it happened the scene was shot in front of the main, west-facing wall. If it *had* been filmed in front of the south wall . . . Wystan believed that everyone who watched that scene in the eventual movie, and thus kept the hieroglyph image in their attentions for the better part of a minute, would unknowingly allow the force that was *Ba* to enter their minds, and would thus unite with Wystan in a transcendent *group-mind*.

More misfortune followed the relocation of the scene. DeMille had arranged for religious services to be available to the crew, and a Catholic priest and an Orthodox rabbi had together approached the director and told him that certain dreams their congregations were having had led them to believe that some genuinely dangerous sigil had been incorporated into the otherwise innocuous hieroglyphs on his set. DeMille had affected to scoff at the idea . . . but when filming was finished he buried the entire set, including even the rows of twenty-five-foot-tall sphinxes he had trucked up from Los Angeles.

And so Wystan had tried to replicate the variant *Ba* hieroglyph, from memory—but he no longer had any hope of seeing the original photograph, even if it had still been in Oslo, and when he stared at his attempted replications, none of them had given him the remembered ringing in the ears and quiver of mild electric shock.

But Wystan was still determined to rid himself of his own

individuality; *not* to have it end in death, in which event he might find himself facing some afterlife judgment and be held accountable for his past actions—but to exist instead, in at least some attenuated way, *past* the death of his body, perhaps for centuries, in an entity so big that his individual sins would be effectively negated.

The worst thing he had done was known only to himself, unshared with anyone, and loomed bigger in his mind because of that. He had ignored his father's deathbed command to acknowledge a previously unknown illegitimate half-sister; and when, years later, Claude Wystan had idly traced her, he had found that she had eventually fallen into poverty and killed herself. No one besides himself knew about his betrayal of her, and of his father, and his greatest wish now was that he might lose the awareness of it himself.

Ba could provide that. Wystan had needed to recover the buried hieroglyph sigil, and he needed at least a few credulous minds to combine with his, once he had found it—and so he had joined Mrs. Haas' coven and, by default, had become its High Priest.

And now he had finally recovered the *Ba* hieroglyph, the sigil. The *Nu* hieroglyph that had called it out of the sand would be inert, now that the extension of the Baba Gurgur fire in the lantern was extinguished, but even so, he didn't want to let the two sigils get within several yards of each other.

"Pull that smaller board out of the sand," he called to the witch who was standing over the dark lantern, "and put it back in the portfolio—that cardboard folder!—and close it and tie the ribbon. Now we all walk back to Mrs. Haas' auto, and you stay out in front with it, away from me."

He got to his feet, shivering, and clasped the recovered *Ba* hieroglyph board firmly under his arm. With luck, he thought, by midnight we'll be back at Mrs. Haas' house on Paseo del Mar in the Point Fermin area of San Pedro. And we can finally blow out the sacrilegiously employed Paschal candle and make some coffee and then sit down around the kitchen table and all have a look at *Ba*. The minds of these few women and himself would not be enough to engender the sort of autonomous, transcendent entity in which he yearned to lose himself, but they were a start.

CHAPTER ONE:
Some Kind of Hobo

The enigmatic ad in the Los Angeles *Times* classified section had read, in its entirety, *"Skeet thrower for sale, October 29, 2018, 2 PM,"* and at 1:30 PM Sebastian Vickery was sitting on a bus bench across the street from Canter's Delicatessen.

There was a plexiglass roof on struts over the metal-screen bench, and he had taken off his faded tan bush hat and set it beside him. His hair and graying beard were clipped short these days, and aviator sunglasses hid his eyes. The breeze down Fairfax Avenue was cool on his damp forehead.

He had spent the previous fifteen minutes in the Council Thrift Store across Oakwood Avenue, to all appearances giving close scrutiny to a dining table and a china hutch and several chairs, all of which stood by the window that gave a good view of the parking lot and entrance of Canter's. In another ten minutes he planned to cross Fairfax and take a while sorting through the various sizes of shipping cartons at the FedEx Print and Ship outlet, from the window of which he would be able to watch the Canter's parking lot and sidewalk and the rooftops of the nearby buildings. At 1:50, if he still saw no signs of surveillance, he would go into Canter's and take a seat at the far end of the counter, by the back wall.

Apart from a couple of brief, furtive visits to certain clearings beside the 710 and 405 freeways, Sebastian Vickery hadn't been to Los Angeles in eight months, and he was glad that Canter's, at least, was still in business. The FedEx outlet was new, replacing a bar, as he recalled, and the thrift store had been called Out of the Closet when he had last been down here.

His car, an oddly angular bright blue sedan, was parked across the street, only a dozen yards from the Canter's front door. While waiting for a curbside spot to open up, he had driven around several blocks, noting alleys and unevident parking lots.

No one was likely to bump into him on this bus bench in the next few minutes, so he decided to risk a look back in what he thought of as echo time.

Most of his echo time intervals were brief, and he could afford to lose nearly half an hour here in apparent catatonic oblivion. He would at least feel it if any Good Samaritan were to touch or shake him, and though he wouldn't be able to see what was going on, he'd be able to say reassuring things to dissuade any unwanted help.

His attention, though, would be elsewhere. Elsewhen.

Last year he and a woman named Ingrid Castine had been driven to cross over, alive, from ordinary reality into a nightmarish afterlife, known as the Labyrinth, populated by deceased or never-born spirits. The two of them had managed to return, still alive, and close the leaky conduit between the two worlds—but, among other things, they had learned that the moment of "now" is not a discrete instant, as irreducible as a point on a line in geometry.

What normal people perceive as the instant of "now" is in fact just the blanket average of an infinity of time-spikes that spring up and disappear at the interface between the fluid future and the crystallized past. The spikes are quantum extensions of the past into the future, but they're far too brief to have any effect on the world's smooth continuity.

But those traumatic experiences of last year had left him able to drop himself—his perceptions, at least—into whatever flickering time-spike he might at some moment be in contact with; and time tends to be especially spiky in populated areas, so in a crowded city like Los Angeles it was unlikely that any spot would be absolutely chronologically flat.

Leaning back on the bus bench, he looked at his watch: 1:35. He memorized the cars at the curbs and in the deli parking lot, then took off his sunglasses and sat back and let his eyes unfocus; and when the street and buildings in front of him seemed to be no more than a flat collage of shifting random colors, he made himself look *past* it, as if trying to see the image hidden in the confetti dots of a stereogram print.

Lately the echo view had been alarmingly unreliable, but today it worked as expected, and abruptly he was seeing parked and moving cars and pedestrians in three dimensions again, but in a sepia twilight; the faces and swinging hands of the human figures glowed with a color he never saw in real time, a sort of silvery bronze. The grumble of traffic was muted, almost inaudible.

What he was seeing now, dimly, was the recent local past.

He looked carefully at the cars parked along the street and in the lot. Colors were virtually indistinguishable in this echo view, but he noted that a pale Honda Accord was parked over there in front of Canter's; a moment ago, in real time, he had seen an apparently identical white Honda on this side of the street, to his right.

All at once the buildings and cars and people sprang into color again, and the rattling tremolo of car engines resumed. His eyesight was back in alignment with real common time, and the cars and pedestrians he saw now were actually present.

He put on his sunglasses and looked to his right, at the white Honda parked three spaces up the street. Sun-glare on the windshield made it impossible to see any occupant or occupants, but by echo vision Vickery had seen that it, or a car very like it, had been parked on the other side of the street not long before. The extents of his echo visions were variable, but he had never been able to see his surroundings as they had been more than a couple of hours earlier.

The Honda might belong to somebody who had moved it to avoid a parking ticket; Vickery was asking for a ticket himself, leaving his car parked where it was. Or there might simply have been two light-colored Hondas parked on Fairfax Avenue this afternoon.

Or it might be that Ingrid Castine had been careless, and unwittingly led *them* to this meeting, and to himself.

Whoever *them* was, exactly. At least this wasn't the Ford van he had seen parked in front of his apartment on a cold February morning eight months ago, triggering his flight from the city and the adoption of this new identity.

He had spent these eight months of exile covertly trying to find a way to retrieve a uniquely precious book that had been stolen from him on that morning—a worn paperback copy of Frances Hodgson Burnett's *The Secret Garden* that contained, fossilized in its unliving but organic pages, the spirit of a little girl. He and Castine had encountered her in the Labyrinth afterworld—ghosts' memories often fell out of their insubstantial heads and were scavenged by other spirits, and this wraith had picked up a memory of the Burnett novel; and, lacking a name of her own, had taken to herself the name of the book's heroine, Mary Lennox. The small spirit had told him at one point that a robin had shown Mary Lennox where to find the key to a secret walled garden, and it had seemed that the spirit, too, was hoping to find a key to some enduring refuge.

The girl-spirit had followed Vickery back from the turbulent afterworld last year, and even before being subsumed into that copy of the book, the spirit had been especially frail and evanescent—for it was not even the ghost of a deceased person, but just the unfulfilled likelihood of a little girl who had never actually been conceived, whose chance of existence had gone by, unrealized.

It was, in fact, the shade of a girl Vickery would have fathered, if he had not, long before, taken steps to ensure that he would never have children—it was, or was to have been, his daughter, whom circumstances had cheated of life.

She was inert in the pages, but, driven by guilt and a love whose object had tragically never existed, he had daily read aloud sections of the book, and imagined that his unconceived daughter might somehow be aware of his voice, her almost-father's presence.

These days his main concern was trying to find a clue to where the book was now, and his researches didn't depend on his location— but he had felt bound to come back to Los Angeles today.

Before parting last year, he and Castine had agreed that if she put an ad having to do with skeet shooting in the *Times* classifieds, the two of them would meet at Canter's at the date and time specified in the ad. *October 29, 2018, 2 PM.* Now, in retrospect, the scheme seemed foolhardy, and he was tempted to get into his car and drive back north to his trailer in Barstow.

The driver's-side door of the Honda opened—and it was Castine herself stepping out. She closed the door and began walking this way, toward the corner and the crosswalk. Vickery put his hat back on and faced straight ahead, watching her peripherally.

Her auburn hair was longer now, bouncing around her shoulders as she walked, and she was wearing tan slacks and a matching jacket and white sneakers. She didn't have a purse, and her jacket seemed too short and close-fitting for her to be wearing a holster.

Vickery himself had a Glock 43 behind his belt buckle, under his untucked shirt. The gun was six inches long from backstrap to muzzle and only an inch wide, but it held seven 9-millimeter rounds.

He let Castine walk past the bus bench and stop at the corner, waiting for the green walk signal. He wasn't surprised that she hadn't recognized him. His dark hair had been longer last year, and he had been more or less clean-shaven; and spending a lot of time outdoors lately had given him a deep tan.

She's thirty-one now, he thought. Standing straight, shoulders back, slim and graceful—she seems to have brushed her hair over the gunshot scar above her right ear, or maybe she had got hair implants.

Vickery recalled that she had been engaged last year, and that her fiancé had been murdered. The last time Vickery had seen her, last August, she had said she was on paid leave from the Transportation Utility Agency . . . which had pretty clearly been responsible for the fiancé's death. He wondered, not for the first time, how she had reconciled herself to going on taking the agency's paychecks, and what her situation was these days.

He had first met her five years ago, when he had been a Secret Service field agent and onetime Los Angeles Police officer, and she had been an active agent of the TUA. He had broken protocol during a Presidential motorcade on Wilshire Boulevard, and stumbled onto the TUA's top-secret clandestine use of ghosts as a security measure, and she had arrested him and turned him over to a couple of higher-ranking TUA agents. They had taken him away in handcuffs, intending to summarily execute him in the desert out by Palmdale, but he had managed to escape by killing both of them . . . and for the next five years he had led a furtive, covert life as the fictitious Sebastian Vickery.

And then last year he and Castine had been thrown together again in fleeing the lethal attentions of a rogue regional TUA director . . . and they had wound up fleeing together right out of the normal world into the Labyrinth afterworld, and back.

Vickery and Castine had become allies, during it all—friends, even.

The rogue director had decisively disappeared, the TUA had undergone a drastic reorganization, and Castine had stayed on the TUA payroll.

When the walk signal came on, he waited until she was halfway across the street before he stood up from the bench and followed her. Glancing from side to side behind the lenses of his sunglasses, he didn't see any car doors opening or anyone who seemed to be watching her.

On the west side of the street, he paused as if to look at the display in a mattress store window while Castine walked on and pulled open the steel-framed glass door of Canter's. When she had gone in, he followed and caught the door before it had quite closed.

The air inside was cool and smelled of corned beef and pickles. Castine was already past the cashier and being shown to the left, where Vickery remembered a row of orange vinyl booths by the stairs that led up to the restrooms. He paused as if to look at a display of eclairs and brownies on the street side of the cash register; before joining her, he wanted to see who else might follow her in.

Canter's is a busy restaurant, even after the lunch rush. A couple in their twenties, wearing shorts and probably tourists, pulled open the door and crossed to the cashier's desk to ask if they could get their parking slip validated; a middle-aged red-haired man in a black turtleneck sweater and red cowboy boots came in after them and stepped directly to the "Please Wait To Be Seated" sign, and a waiter escorted him straight ahead, toward the back of the restaurant; he was followed a few moments later by a goateed teenager in a black Bob Marley T-shirt, who waved familiarly at the clerk behind the bakery case before making a beeline to the right, toward the lunch counter. None of them glanced to the left, toward where Castine was presumably sitting.

Vickery had just turned to step past the cash register into the dining room when the front door was pulled open again, and a young man in round black-frame glasses and a white shirt with red suspenders stepped quickly in from the street. His hair was now long and styled on top and shaved close over the ears—but Vickery recognized him.

Vickery's chest was suddenly cold and his pulse was pounding in his ears, though his expression didn't change as he let his gaze shift unhurriedly to the tables in the dining room—and the man hurried past him with no sign of recognition.

Did my beard and sunglasses fool him? Vickery wondered. He knew me eight months ago, when he and his accomplices stole *The Secret Garden* and nearly grabbed me too. And now he's after Castine? What the hell's going on?

The man paused to glance around at all the tables and the counter along the right-side wall; when he looked to the left he seemed to stiffen, and then started in that direction.

Vickery followed him, closely, and saw Castine sitting alone in a booth ten feet ahead.

The young man lifted a dish from a table he passed, and he tossed it past Castine's booth; and when the thing shattered loudly on the linoleum floor, and Castine had turned a startled glance in that direction, the man crowded close to her table—and Vickery saw him surreptitiously shake the contents of a tiny envelope into her water glass and then without a pause move on toward the restroom stairs.

Vickery quickly stepped forward, but was shouldered aside by the red-haired man in the black turtleneck, who reached across him and slapped Castine's water glass right off the table onto the seat across from her.

"Stop Elisha, damn it," the man snapped at someone behind Vickery. "We've got this."

For just an instant Vickery looked anxiously after the man disappearing up the restroom stairs; then he leaned in and grabbed Castine's shoulder. "Up," he said, "we're out of here."

She tried to throw herself back in the booth, but Vickery's grip was unyielding. "Get *away* from me," she said, as hands from behind clamped on Vickery's left arm and the back of his neck.

"It's him!" said one of the people holding him. "We've got both of them!"

"Stun-gun if you have to," rasped another, "just get 'em both into the car, quick."

Vickery felt a blunt object bump across his back—evidently a stun-gun, and he knew that in a moment he might be knocked down by millions of volts of electricity.

Instantly, old training took over. He sprang back away from Castine and spun to his right, sweeping his arm around to knock the hand away from his neck—it belonged to the man in the turtleneck, his white teeth now bared with effort—and in the same motion pistoned the heel of his left hand very hard into the goateed chin of the teenager who was holding his left arm with one hand and gripping a black plastic stun-gun in the other. The incongruous pair tumbled backward onto the table behind them, overturning dishes and glasses. People at other tables were getting to their feet.

Turning back to Castine's booth, Vickery leaned in and grabbed her by both shoulders. "It's me, Vickery!" he hissed at her. "Come on!"

Castine stared into his face for a moment, then nodded and slid out of the booth, and together they ran to the entryway and past the cash register. Several people hurriedly stepped out of their way, and Vickery noticed a moustached man in a tan-and-orange plaid sportcoat, whose brown eyes seemed to widen in surprised recognition at the sight of them—and then they were out the door and on the sidewalk. Vickery pulled Castine to the left, toward his blue sedan.

"I've got a car across the street," she said breathlessly, but a moment later he had pulled open the passenger-side door of his car and shoved her in.

As he got in on the driver's side and started the engine, the man in the black turtleneck and red boots came slamming out of Canter's, shouting into a cell phone; and a couple of men were now shoving past the pedestrians on the sidewalk to the north. Glancing that way, Vickery caught only a quick impression of gray hair and a dark windbreaker.

Castine had locked her door just as one of them grabbed the outside handle, and Vickery clicked the gear shift into reverse, backed into the car behind them with a jangling crash, and then shifted to drive and swerved out into traffic. From the corner of his eye he saw the young man in red suspenders burst out of the restaurant and stare after them for a moment before dodging his way across the street.

Vickery gritted his teeth at having to let him get away, and fervently hoped to see him again.

The traffic light at Oakwood was red, but Vickery leaned on the horn and edged through, glancing quickly left and right; then he was past it, and accelerating south on Fairfax.

Castine pulled her seatbelt across and clicked it into its slot.

"Who," she said, and took a deep breath, "were *they*?"

"They weren't yours?"

Vickery flexed his right hand on the wheel. The wrist ached—he had reflexively hit that teenager pretty hard.

"What," said Castine, "the TUA? They don't do this sort of stuff anymore."

Vickery nodded. She had mentioned last August that the functions and personnel of the Transportation Utility Agency had been cut way back, and its days of unsupervised ruthlessness were long past. So who was this crowd, and what did they want?

Castine shifted in her seat now to look out the back window. "They must still be behind that red light. Where are we going?"

"Parking lot up here on the right," he said. "We only need about a twenty-second window, if you help."

"I think I see 'em behind us now, changing lanes. Two cars. Or three." She looked at him. "Help with what?"

Halfway down the next block Vickery stomped on the brake and swung the wheel to the right, and the car bounced up a curb and he drove fast between two rows of parked cars to an alley at the far end of the lot. He steered left into the alley, but braked to a jolting halt in front of a big delivery truck that blocked the way.

"Shit!" yelled Castine, blinking at the obstacle, but Vickery was already out of the car and crouching by the front bumper.

"Out!" he yelled. "Help me!"

He had peeled up the edges of a blue plastic film from around the left headlight, and he was tugging it up off of the fender, where a wedge-shaped chunk of styrofoam came away with the thin, sticky film as he peeled it back toward the driver's-side door. Castine quickly followed his example on the right side, and within seconds they had stripped the blue film from the sides and the roof of the car. Two children watched them wonderingly from behind a chain link fence.

"You get the hood and the doors!" Vickery yelled, standing on the trunk now and wrestling with the bundle of crumpled blue plastic and styrofoam blocks. He leaned back, and the rest of the thin sheet came free from around the taillights with a ripping sound, and then he was sitting on the pavement. The rear license plate frame was secured only by two snaps, and he pulled it open and snatched out the blue Santa Ana dealer's plate, exposing a red Anaheim one, and snapped the frame back into place.

He rolled over to the right and shoved the sticky blue-and-white bundle under the car, just forward of the right rear tire, as Castine slid to a crouching halt beside him, a somewhat smaller bundle in her arms. She pushed it too under the car, rattling fragments of a broken beer bottle on the pavement.

The car blocked their view of the parking lot they had just driven through, and Vickery couldn't see under the vehicle because of the masses of crumpled plastic and styrofoam. But he heard a car, and then another, come rocking into the parking lot from Fairfax.

"Move to the front," he said hoarsely, "and slide around to the bumper when they pass this."

The roar of car engines quickly grew louder, and Vickery waved at Castine and began crawling toward the front of the car; and they had both scrambled around to crouch by the front bumper when two cars turned right and gunned away up the alley away from them.

"Are there any more?" gasped Castine, sitting up on the cracked cement pavement. One bloody knee showed through a rip in her slacks and she pushed her tangled hair back from her face. "There's broken glass all over the place."

"Give 'em a minute." The breeze on his scalp let him know that his hat was gone. "I think they were following you. One of them shook some kind of powder into your water glass, and it was another of them who knocked it over."

Castine was getting to her feet, cautiously. "They couldn't have followed me! You're not the only one who's been trained in this stuff, you know."

Vickery stood up, wincing and rubbing his hip. "Then they knew when and where we were supposed to meet," he said, looking north along the alley. He didn't see any moving cars. "We've got to get clear of the area."

Vickery's sedan was now visibly a white 1990s Saturn, with dented fenders and a primer-red driver's side door. He and Castine got in, and he backed it off of the tangled mess of blue plastic and then drove sedately out of the lot and turned right on Fairfax. The interior of the car was hot from sitting in direct sunlight, and he switched on the air conditioner. Dust and hot air blew out of the vents, then cooler air.

Vickery took off his sunglasses and waved them toward Castine. "Put these on," he said, "and there's a blanket in the back seat—pull it around yourself."

The blanket was bright yellow, and Vickery hoped that the changes in their appearances would deflect the attention of any very attentive pursuers.

He caught a green light at Beverly Boulevard and sped through the intersection, watching his rear view mirror; but no cars seemed to be following them.

"This is a Saturn," said Castine, gingerly tucking the old blanket around her shoulders. She peered out through the windshield. "White. It looked like some kind of . . . caricature sky-blue Mercedes a few minutes ago. And *I* never told anybody that we were to meet at Canter's."

Vickery pursed his lips. "I believe you. I—"

"Oh, thanks!" A box of Kleenex was wedged between the dashboard and the windshield, and she pulled a sheet free and dabbed at her cut knee.

"Well, I do," said Vickery. "But there they were." He glanced at her. "Did you recognize any of them?"

"*Damn* it—I thought we were through with this kind of stuff! Have you . . . *done* something?"

Vickery made himself keep the nervous irritation out of his voice: "I've been living very low profile in a trailer park outside Barstow, under a new name, since February."

"Well—I haven't done anything either. No, I didn't recognize them. I hardly saw them. Something broke, and some guy knocked over my water glass, and then you threw him and some kid onto a table."

"I," Vickery said heavily, "recognized the one who put something in your glass."

"So you do have some connection with this!"

"It was before I went dark. It was *why* I went dark. Eight months ago, in February, that guy and a couple of other people cornered me. Tried to." He started to mention the stolen book, but said instead, "I'd had a new identity prepared and ready to assume since September of last year—"

"I should have cooked up an escape identity myself!"

Vickery rocked his head judiciously. "—And I stopped being Sebastian Vickery altogether."

"And you only ran as far as Barstow? What's that, a hundred miles?"

"A hundred and fourteen." Vickery made a left turn and drove east on Third Street, past the old Farmer's Market clock tower. "Why did you place the ad?"

"Oh. I guess I got you into this, didn't I, with that ad? Back into it, anyway. Sorry, I guess. Why did I put the ad in the paper." She was silent for a moment, then shrugged. "Because I was scared."

"Well, yeah, I've been scared too," Vickery admitted, alternately watching the traffic ahead and glancing at the rear view mirror. The sun was bright on chrome and windshields, and he wished he hadn't given Castine his sunglasses. "Before I went into the restaurant just now, I tried the look-in-the-past trick to see the street a little while earlier—and for once the trick still worked, I *did* see that."

"You were lucky." She shivered. "I never even try it anymore, and I drink gallons of coffee to stop it happening spontaneously. All I see now, when it happens, is—"

He nodded grimly. "That solitary wrecked house."

"*Ooh*, I'm glad you see it too, Sebastian! Right, a two-story Victorian house, all dilapidated, in some kind of little valley, right? And you can't move, not voluntarily, anyway. In the—hah!—*ordinary* visions of the past, I could at least *decide* whether I walked in some direction, or held still."

"True. These intrusive new ones are like watching a video."

"And," she went on, "have you noticed that each time you see that terrible house, it's always later in the day? A month ago I'd see it with shadows, but lately they're gone, like it's noon, there." She was hugging herself now, gripping her elbows. "I don't want to see it when the sun's down. If I even *could* see it much, in that murky light."

Vickery decided not to ask her yet if she'd noticed the man's face that he had sometimes seen peering out from an upstairs window of the hallucinated old house.

"Yeah," he said, "I've noticed that it's later in the day, in *some* day, when I've seen it."

"Do you think that has something to do with—" She waved behind them.

Vickery briefly spread his fingers on the steering wheel, then gripped it again.

Castine hitched around to peer out the back window, then relaxed back into her seat. "Where are we going?"

"For now, just—away."

She nodded. "Away is good. Do you think it was arsenic or something? In my water glass?"

"Whatever it was, the guy in the turtleneck didn't want you to drink it."

After a moment of silence, she said, "I'm glad you were there. It's sort of good to see you again, Sebastian. Though I'm not sure I like the beard."

"My name's Bill Ardmore now." She raised her eyebrows, and he went on, "The real Bill Ardmore was a grocery clerk in Oshkosh, Wisconsin, and he died last May, single and childless."

"You . . . liked the sound of the name?"

"It'll do. Are you watching traffic?"

"The only car that's been steady in view for the last thirty seconds is that old Chevy with kids in it that you just passed. Ah—and they just turned into the Ralph's parking lot anyway." Her knee had apparently stopped bleeding, and she rolled down the window and threw the blood-spotted Kleenex out.

"I got the name from an obituary," said Vickery. "All the states cross-index death and birth certificates these days, but Wisconsin didn't start doing it till '79, and Bill Ardmore was born in '78; so I'm officially forty now, instead of thirty-seven."

"Oh." She rolled the window back up. "I hope I don't have to do that myself. I'd be adding nine years. Did he have a beard?"

"Probably not. But I grew it because Sebastian Vickery didn't have one." He squinted at the traffic ahead. "I'm going to circle some blocks, so keep watching traffic. Then we can stop at MacArthur Park and catch up on—everything."

"I never did get lunch."

"We can probably get a couple of hot dogs or something there."

"Of course." Her smile was faint, but he felt at last that this was the same woman he'd known last year. "I forgot about your dining style," she said.

Back at the Canter's parking lot, two men stood on the sidewalk, blinking in the sun.

"Where's the cars?" one asked. He appeared to be in his early forties, and was dressed a bit too young in black skinny jeans and a faded blue denim shirt buttoned to the top. His head was entirely shaved and gleaming with sweat, and he wore sunglasses with a little leather wedge snapped over the bridge. "I'm going to go to that thrift store and see if they have any decent hats."

"When Harlowe shows up," said his companion, "he's not going to be happy. Pratt got knocked out back there, with his jaw dislocated, and now the Castine woman knows somebody's after her. You best not be off hat shopping." His brush-cut hair was gray, his tanned face was deeply lined, and his olive-green windbreaker and blue jeans were calculatedly unmemorable.

"Damn it, Taitz, what were we supposed to do? The car didn't even *have* a license plate, just a dealer's plate!"

"Harlowe didn't say you should try anything like *opening her door*. This whole thing was supposed to be just . . . let her meet Vickery and then follow them, and grab them somewhere less crowded. But I guess it was Elisha that really screwed it up."

The other man nodded. "What, he broke some dishes?"

An old woman who had just finished laboriously pushing a shopping cart to this end of the Oakwood crosswalk paused and said, as if talking to herself, "Harlowe says he tried to poison her."

The younger man stared at her in alarm, and as she hobbled past them he took a step after her.

Taitz caught his arm. "Steady, Foster. You think *she* knows anything? It's just the black hole effect. We're lucky somebody across the street didn't say it."

"For all we know somebody did! Maybe half a dozen people did." Foster shook his head and wiped his bald scalp. "Shouldn't our guys have caught up with them by now? Shit. That didn't look like any powerhouse car Castine drove away in."

"It was Vickery driving, if that guy was Vickery."

"And he's what, some kind of hobo?"

Taitz shrugged, scanning the cars east and west for some sign of Harlowe's gray Chevrolet Tahoe SUV. "He showed up in L.A. about five years ago, and nobody seems to know where he came from. Eight months ago Elisha and Agnes tried to snatch him, and blew it, though they did get that book Harlowe wanted. Then Vickery totally dropped out of sight—until today, maybe—but before that he was working for a Mexican woman in East L.A., driving some kind of tricked-out *santeria* stealth cars for people scared of ghosts."

"And, uh, he and the Castine woman both *died* last year, I understand, and came back from the dead."

"That's the story." John Taitz waved toward the old woman with the shopping cart, who was still visible making her way up the Fairfax sidewalk. "That's why we need them, *both* of them."

"There's Harlowe." Foster stepped to the curb and waved at the westbound lanes of Oakwood Avenue, and a few moments later a gray SUV surged across the Fairfax intersection and swerved to a stop beside them. Taitz hurried to the curb and opened the left rear door and got in, with Foster right behind him.

The middle pair of seats had been reversed, facing the third row, where Simon Harlowe sat. The sleeves of his turtleneck sweater were rolled back, and his probably-dyed burgundy red hair was disarranged, but he looked a good deal more alert and purposeful than he had this morning, when they had lost track of Castine. He crossed his left red boot over his right knee and waved Foster and Taitz to the facing seats as the vehicle moved forward.

"Elisha has gone rogue," he said, and added in a businesslike tone, "one of you is going to have to take his blood pressure." Taitz repressed a wince; he had got along well enough with Ragotskie, and he hoped it would be Foster's task to kill the young man. "The *Black*

Sheep is being moved to a different marina," Harlowe went on, "and I've told Biloxi to vacate the office on Sepulveda—put everything in a couple of U-Haul trucks and park it somewhere till we can move it to another property I've got."

Taitz shifted uneasily. "Any luck following Castine?"

"No," said Harlowe. "That blue car, whatever it was, simply turned in to an alley and disappeared. We had four cars circling fast around all these blocks, and up and down Beverly and Third—no sign of it."

"We had a black hole incident here a minute ago," said Taitz. "An old woman walked by us and said Elisha tried to poison Castine."

Harlowe nodded, rubbing his chin. "Were you two holding hands?"

"*No*," said Taitz.

"Well, you were standing close to each other, I imagine, and not moving. It's not premature." He raised his hand to preclude any objection. "Castine and Vickery are apparently traveling together, and," he went on, patting a polished wooden box on the seat beside him, "we've got the bloody sock to see where she goes. Unless they get on a plane real quick, which isn't likely, or that wasn't Vickery she met, which also isn't likely, we should have them both in the mix within the next few hours."

"We'd better," said Taitz. "Halloween's only two days off, and if you haven't got a pair of . . . *communicators* by then—do you think it's even still *possible* to damp the whole show down and try for next year?"

Harlowe sat back and gave Taitz a benevolent smile. "Well, John, I tell you what. No, it's not still possible. This thing is gonna take wing on the thirty-first whatever we do, and if we don't have the right couple of people incorporated—our routers, our switchboard operators, our *thalamus*—then we're all gonna be facets of one big cosmic imbecile. But," and he eyed Taitz with something like cautious amusement as he went on, "if we don't get Vickery and Castine for it, we can use the twins."

Taitz squinted at him. "The twins? You mean your nieces?"

"I've had them in mind all along—lately as a fallback. They're a bit—"

"Crazy," said Taitz flatly.

"Now now. They're neurotic and deluded, but in directions that make them very suitable. I'd rather have Vickery and Castine, but the twins can do it."

"You think everybody will . . . go along with that idea?" asked Taitz. "They're all real serious about this thing."

Harlowe's genial expression slipped for a moment, and Taitz forced himself not to flinch at the blazing eyes in the momentarily slack face; then the serene smile was reassembled, and Harlowe said, softly, "I'm more serious than any of them, and I know more about it than any of them."

Foster, looking out the window, had missed the momentary glare. "The twins," he echoed wonderingly; then added, as he turned to his companions with a visible shudder, "At least Lexi and Amber *want* to be something besides themselves."

Taitz sat back, still watching Harlowe. "Huh. I think we'd better find Vickery and Castine."

Harlowe tapped the polished box on the seat. "The bloody sock has worked fine so far."

The bloody sock. Taitz had seen Harlowe working the old white sock in the office on Sepulveda this morning, and it hadn't so much looked bloody as just very dirty; but the brown stains on it were supposed to be Ingrid Castine's blood, and she and Sebastian Vickery had experienced *something* last year—death and resurrection, according to some stories, or just a brief corporeal trip to the afterworld and back, according to others—something that made their souls oscillate irregularly, in a way normal souls did not, like a couple of Frequency Modulation radio transmitters in a world of Amplitude Modulation. And any samples of Castine's FM blood would resonate in tune to the metaphorical transmitter, which was Castine herself, and be drawn to it.

Harlowe's ambitious Singularity project required the participation of a nearly unique sort of pair, and, because of their crazy history, Ingrid Castine and Sebastian Vickery were ideal.

They were so desirable, in fact, that Harlowe had waited a dangerously long time in the hope of getting them. Constant monitoring of Castine had not been difficult—she worked in a government office in Washington D.C. and had an apartment in Gaithersburg—but after Elisha's unsuccessful attempt to snatch

Vickery in February, the man had effectively disappeared. The Singularity project was already in perilous gestation, but Harlowe had maddeningly postponed finding some other pair—because, it turned out, he had had his nieces in mind as an option all along. A dubious option, Taitz thought.

And then, just three days ago, Castine had placed the ad in the Los Angeles *Times,* and Harlowe had guessed that it was a message to Vickery, stating the time, but not the place, of a proposed meeting. The guess had been effectively confirmed when Castine booked a flight for today to Los Angeles: the city where she and Vickery had reportedly died and somehow been resurrected last year, and where Vickery had last verifiably been living. On her arrival at dawn, Castine had rented a car from Hertz at the airport . . . but had then unexpectedly done a fast lanes-crossing exit from the 405 freeway, shaking off the Singularity cars that had been following her, and she had not used her credit card since.

At that point the bloody sock had been the only hope of tracing her. Harlowe had bought the unsavory thing months ago from a freeway-side gypsy who claimed to have inherited it from another of that furtive tribe, and this morning Harlowe had wrapped the stiffened white sock around a stapler, for weight, and tied a string around it and, holding the free end of the string, dangled it like a pendulum over his desk.

It had consistently swung away from vertical toward the northeast.

And so four cars had set out at noon, driving up Venice Boulevard, with Harlowe right here in the Chevy Tahoe holding the string and calling directions to Tony, the earnest young driver.

The pendulum had begun swinging more northward as they drove through Culver City, and at the Fairfax intersection the four cars had turned north; the pendulum had been tilting steadily northward then, but when they passed Melrose it had abruptly begun straining to the south, so they had all made U-turns.

And the pendulum had swung to the right, and then backward, as they passed a white Honda parked at the curb near Canter's Delicatessen, and Taitz had recognized Ingrid Castine's profile in the Honda as they had passed it.

Tony had managed to park the Tahoe SUV at the curb only a few spaces ahead of her, and the three other cars had sped on to find parking spaces nearby.

Castine had been an hour early for the probable 2 PM assignation, and after sitting in her car for twenty minutes she had started it again and driven south; but before Tony had been able to steer out into traffic after her, one of the men in the other cars reported that she had simply turned right on Oakwood and done a U-turn at the next street—and when she had got back to Fairfax she had turned left and found a space to park on the east side of the street, across from Canter's. And after another fifteen minutes she had got out of her car and walked to the crosswalk.

And it had all been going as planned until Elisha got out of his surveillance car and went into the restaurant.

"*Did* Elisha try to poison Castine?" asked Taitz now, as the SUV crossed Third Street.

"I don't know," said Harlowe. "He put something in her water glass, and I knocked it over." He opened the wooden box and lifted out the string-wrapped sock and stapler, and handed it to Taitz. "You track her for a while, my hands are shaky."

Taitz reluctantly took hold of the bundle and unwound the string. The sock and the stapler were perceptibly warm, though the interior of the vehicle was nearly chilly; and of course the sock had never been washed, and he made a mental note to wash his hands at the earliest opportunity.

He held it up by the free end of the string, feeling both ridiculous and uneasy, and stared at it as it swung with the movement of the car. "I dunno, chief," he said, "it seems to be swinging east more than anything else."

"Take a left on Third Street, Tony," said Harlowe, "and call the other drivers, tell them to catch up."

CHAPTER TWO:
A Lot of M&Ms and Cigarettes

"Whoa!" exclaimed Taitz as the sock bundle swung around on the end of the string he held. "We just passed her, to the right!"

"That was Sycamore," said Tony from the driver's seat, signaling for a lane change. "I'll loop around the block."

"Quickly," suggested Harlowe.

"I'm on it."

Tony made a right turn and sped down a narrow street of well-kept old houses set back from the sidewalks, the SUV's windshield flickering between direct sunlight and the shadows of curbside trees, and at the next intersection he turned right, and then right again, and then he was cruising slowly up Sycamore while the three men in the back alternately peered at the dangling sock and looked out the side windows.

"To the right," Harlowe muttered, "now directly to our right—I don't see anybody—is she in that house? Where's their car?"

The sock jerked backward on its string. "She's moving!" exclaimed Foster, hiking forward on his seat and opening the door. "Tony, stop the car!" A hot breeze smelling of cut grass broke up the cool interior air.

The SUV rocked to a halt. Harlowe was snapping his fingers and frowning. "You'd better both grab her—and get Vickery too!"

But Taitz stayed seated, glancing from the slanting sock-string to the pavement outside the open door. "Uh, Foster," he said, "pick up that tissue paper on the sidewalk. Quick, it's blowing away."

"I don't see anybody!" Foster called back.

To Harlowe, Taitz said, "Tell him to fetch it."

Harlowe raised his eyebrows, but said loudly, "Foster! Bring me that tissue paper!"

A moment later Foster was standing on the pavement outside the SUV, still squinting up and down the street, while Harlowe sat back and gingerly uncrumpled the sheet of Kleenex and held it up by one corner.

Red spots on the tissue paper were evidently blood. Taitz sighed and laid the sock-and-string on the seat beside him.

"Get back in here, Foster," Harlowe snapped, and when Foster had climbed back in and closed the door, Harlowe said to Tony, "East on Third again."

"Rightie-O." The vehicle sped forward.

"Rightie-O," echoed Harlowe softly, with evident distaste.

Foster was panting, and he swiped his sleeve over his bald head. "What," he said, peering at the tissue paper in the relative dimness of the SUV's interior, "she got a nosebleed?"

"Or something," agreed Harlowe, handing it to Taitz. "Burn this, will you? The effect apparently diminishes as the square of the distance, and this small thing was close enough to us to eclipse her signal."

Taitz took the tissue paper from him and with his free hand dug into his pocket for a lighter. He flicked the flint wheel, and the tissue readily caught fire. The SUV had no ashtrays, so when the thing was flaming out he looked around and then dropped it on the instep of his right shoe and ground it out with the heel of his left.

Harlowe nodded, and Taitz blew on his fingers and then picked up the weighted string. Soon the sock was detectably pulling away from vertical again, distinct from the rocking of the vehicle.

"You should have cut the sock into three pieces," said Taitz. "We could triangulate her location."

"Of course I thought of that," snapped Harlowe, "but the stains are so faint and dried out—I was afraid a third, or even a half, of the sock wouldn't get a perceptible pull." He frowned at the dangling sock. "I didn't expect her to throw *chaff*."

Wilshire Boulevard cuts MacArthur Park in half from east to

west, and Vickery found a parking space alongside the southern half, within sight of the park's broad lake glittering in the sun. He and Castine got out and made their way across the grass to a curling lane lined with tarpaulin-roofed booths, tables under umbrellas, and even just blankets spread out on the grass, all decked with merchandise for sale—fruits and vegetables, toys, clothing, cell phones, Spanish language CDs—and the breeze was redolent with the smells of salsa, teriyaki and marijuana.

Vickery bought a gaudy Hawaiian shirt and another pair of sunglasses for himself, and a baseball cap with "Hollywood" stitched on the front for Castine. The yellow blanket was still draped over her jacket and the right knee of her trousers was torn and spotted with blood, and altogether they didn't look much like the couple who had fled Canter's less than an hour earlier.

Food vendors pushed shopping carts, equipped with coolers or little ovens, across the open area beside the lake, and from one of them Vickery bought a couple of tamales in waxed paper and two plastic cups of *agua de tamarindo,* and he and Castine carried them across the grass to a cement bench. Only a few yards away a flotilla of ducks patrolled the shore, and seagulls whirled in the blue sky overhead, and the bench proved to be nearly whitewashed with bird dung old and new. Vickery and Castine sat down on the grass.

"This is nice, actually," said Castine, looking around as she pulled a rubber band off a paper napkin wrapped around a plastic fork. "I hate it that I'm—back in trouble in L.A. again!—but I wish I'd known about this park when I was working here."

"It's nice now," Vickery agreed. He had already freed his fork, and, after glancing back toward the car, he began digging into his steaming tamale. "Ten years ago it was rough. When I was in LAPD, I was mostly assigned to the Hollywood and Wilshire Divisions, but for a while I was out here in Ramparts. It was all gangs here in those days, the 18th Street Gang and MS-13. This was where you came to get crack or heroin, or fake green cards and driver's licenses. Or to get killed."

"But you quit that, and became a Secret Service agent."

"Sure did. And *that* nearly got me killed."

"Don't look back," she said. Then, seeing him again glance toward the street, she added, "What did I just say? Why do you keep looking at the car?"

"They can't sneak up on us here," he said, "if they're tracking us somehow. And I've got a gun."

"How can they be tracking us?" Castine looked around in alarm, then frowned at him and took a forkful of her tamale. "Even if they," she said, chewing, "I don't know, followed me from the United terminal and put a GPS tracker on my rental car and followed me to Canter's, they can't have put one on *your* car, and you made sure nobody followed us here."

She paused, then looked away over the lake. "Maybe—God help me—maybe they were after *you*, all along, and figured I'd lead them to you. Which I did!"

He nodded. Certainly her notice in the *Times* had brought him out of hiding. "I think they want both of us. That guy with the red boots that I threw onto the table said, 'It's him, we've got both of them.'"

"But I busted your anonymity for them! Now even if you go back to your Bill Ardmore life in Barstow, they at least know what you look like these days." Guilt appeared to make her irritable, and she faced him and added sharply, "Why Barstow, anyway? That's not very far from L.A. What was wrong with . . . Las Vegas, New York, London?"

Vickery started to crush his plastic cup, then made his hand relax. "Partly," he said in a carefully level tone, "to be close enough to L.A. to get to Canter's quickly and cheaply, on the specified date, if you gave me short notice."

"Oh. Sorry, again." She took a deep breath and let it out. "Both of us. You said these people tried to corner you, in February—what happened?"

"Yeah." He sat back and set his half-eaten tamale aside. "Well. For a week or so I'd had a sort of itchy feeling that I was under somebody's surveillance. I seemed to pass too many people with earbuds, and my phone battery ran down quicker than usual, and twice I didn't get my phone bill. Altogether it wasn't enough to make me jump ship, but the echo vision was still working consistently then, not just showing me that terrible old house in the canyon like it does lately—"

She huffed one syllable of a mirthless laugh. "'Echo vision!'"

"That's how I've thought of it. A time-spike, a replay of the recent past, right?" He shrugged. "Echo. So I started checking on how long cars had been parked on my street. And early one morning I saw a Ford van parked for a while down the block with its engine running, and when I walked toward it, it drove off. But when I stepped back and focused into echo vision to look at the street as it had been an hour or so earlier, I saw the same van at dawn, parked right across from my apartment, so I walked across the street—"

"Sebastian! In . . . in echo vision? You're lucky you weren't run over by a car in real time!"

"Well, I looked both ways first, and as it happened I only saw the past for a few seconds. Anyway, I was able to walk to where the car had been earlier. I couldn't make out the license plate number in that monochrome echo light—couldn't even crouch and try to feel the embossed numbers, since the van wasn't actually there anymore!—but I could see the driver through the windshield. And it was that guy that put something in your water glass today. Different haircut, but it was him, I could see *him* clearly. You know the way people kind of glow, when you see 'em in the past?"

She nodded. "I remember. Something like brown, but bright."

"Yeah. I think it's infrared, and in echo vision we get it directly in the primary visual cortex, not through the narrow-band retinas at all." Again he peered across the grass at the parked car, and then around at the people walking along the lakeside pavement, but saw nothing out of the ordinary.

"So as soon as I was back in real, common time, I got in my car and drove off," he went on, "aiming to scout the surrounding streets in real time and then—parked, of course!—in echo time. But at the first intersection, a woman was pushing a baby carriage across the crosswalk, against the light, and I had to stop—and when I did, two cars behind me stopped too, and their doors opened and four guys got out and started sprinting toward me. One of them was the guy from the Ford van, having switched vehicles—"

"You sure it was the same guy? You only saw him in your echo light, and he'd have had to switch vehicles awful quick—"

"Well, they knew I'd spotted the van. Yes, I'm sure it was him. The woman kept her baby carriage right in front of my bumper, not moving, and she wasn't looking at me."

Castine's eyes were wide. "Did you . . . run over her?"

"Hah. No. I reversed hard into the car behind me and did a sharp U-turn. The car whose radiator I hadn't wrecked tried to follow me, but I got away from him with no trouble."

"I'd be surprised if you didn't." She finished her tamarindo drink and looked around for a trash can. "And so you became Bill Ardmore."

"Well—not that instant. After a couple of hours I snuck back into my apartment, through the bedroom window, from the next street over."

"You did?" she asked in surprise. "Why?"

Vickery was staring past her. "There's a gray Chevy Tahoe," he said thoughtfully. "It just drove by my car without stopping . . . but it's moving way slow." He got to his feet. "Up. Face me, not the street."

"Just a minute, let me gather up our trash. Probably a lot of cars drive slow." She balled up the cups and waxed paper and stood up.

"Let's move around the south side of the lake," he said, "and keep facing east."

"We should find a trash can. You don't want to go back to the car?"

"No, I don't want them connecting the car with us. If they show up, we'll evade them and come back later for the car."

"*Evade* them. Okay." She was looking past him, evidently scanning the clusters of people nearby. "You said you went to Barstow partly to be close to L.A., in case I signaled for a meeting. Why else?"

Vickery hesitated, then said, "You remember that old guy, Isaac Laquedem. When we last heard of him, he was in Barstow, and I wanted to find him and ask him if he knew anything about that attempt to snatch me."

Apparently having satisfied herself that nobody in their vicinity was a threat, Castine was unfolding the wax paper, peering at it. "Did you find him?"

"No. A couple of times I thought I had a kind of intuition about where he might be, but it didn't lead to anything I was able to track down. He may be back in L.A., but I haven't been, except for a couple of furtive sneaks. And I've had no luck with internet searches, and he wasn't the sort to be traceable online anyway."

"But you stayed on in Barstow." She poked at the remains of his tamale. "Why him? He mostly knew about ghosts, and the—the Labyrinth."

Vickery looked away, toward the ducks out on the water. "The Labyrinth," he said, and forced a laugh. "The afterworld! By the time I left L.A., the story among the freeway gypsies was that you and I *died,* to get there, and were resurrected from the dead, when we came back."

"Well, most people did have to die, to get there." She had freed some fragments of Vickery's tamale, and tossed them out over the water toward the ducks. "So why did you want to talk to Laquedem? Grouchy old guy, as I recall."

"There's signs that say don't feed the ducks."

"You're not a cop anymore. So why?"

He stopped walking and turned to face her. "Oh hell. You'll think I'm crazy. There's a trash can over there, if you want to pitch that stuff."

Castine waved her fistful of litter. "It can wait."

He exhaled and shook his head. "Okay. When I snuck back to my apartment, about five hours after the attempted snatch with the baby carriage in the crosswalk, there was a guy waiting there, standing by the street-facing living room window. But I had climbed in through the bedroom window, silently, and I made sure he was alone and then came up behind him and got him in a blood chokehold—as opposed to an air one—and when he lost consciousness I tied and gagged him. These guys aren't pros, whoever they are."

"Oh, Sebastian," said Castine with a look that was both pitying and exasperated, "I bet I know what you went back for."

"I—well, damn it, I bet you do. That copy of *The Secret Garden.* And it was gone. It was the only thing missing, as far as I could tell. The only person besides you and me who knew about that book was my old boss—"

"Lady Galvan," said Castine, nodding. "With her supernatural-evasion car service."

"—And I went straight to her garage and braced her about it. It turned out she had told somebody about the book, some guy who claimed to collect such things and asked if she knew of any for sale. He left her a business card, but it was fake. So *then* I drove to Barstow and became Bill Ardmore."

"And that's the other reason—the main reason?—that you didn't want to get too far away from L.A."

He shrugged and nodded. "I want to get the book back. I don't want them to have it—and maybe," he added, "*use* it, somehow."

"It's not a real person," said Castine, wearily. "You *know* that. She never existed! She's imaginary."

"Right," said Vickery, his voice flat. "Imaginary. My daughter times the square root of minus one. But when the conduit to the Labyrinth was open, we were able to see her. *Speak* with her, even. She talked about the robin who showed Mary Lennox the key to the secret garden, in that story."

After a moment, Castine nodded, making even that concession with evident reluctance. She walked to a nearby trash can and dumped the lunch remains, then walked back, wiping her hands on the blanket draped over her shoulders.

"So what have you been doing?" she asked, "in Barstow?"

"I've got a little nest alongside the 15 freeway, outside of town, and I've been—well, I've been calling up ghosts from the freeway current, and asking them if they can sense her. I think fresh ghosts can sometimes sense . . . fossilized spirits, the ones that are subsumed forever in some organic object. The ghosts seem to hear them as a subsonic note, if they can be persuaded to listen for it." He smiled, not happily. "I go through a lot of M&Ms and cigarettes, bribing them."

Vickery took a look back the way they'd come, but he couldn't see the street from here. He turned to Castine.

She was staring at him wide-eyed. "I thought the ghosts were all gone now! Since we closed the conduit to the Labyrinth!"

"People still *die*, Ingrid, and as long as particles of indeterminism— that is, free wills, which is to say, people—move rapidly past non-moving particles, like on freeways, the current is going to be generated, and ghosts can . . . *manifest* themselves! They do still crop up."

"And you a Catholic! Consulting the dead!"

Vickery spread his hands. "I don't consult dead *people*! They're in Heaven or Hell or someplace. I consult their ghosts, which aren't *them*."

Castine gave him a disapproving look. "They're pretty dead, though."

"Lively sometimes, you gotta admit."

"But—you don't talk to them in complete sentences, do you? They'll get a fix on you, try to switch places with you!"

Vickery shook his head. "They're not as substantial, not as powerful, as they were last year, when they were plugged into the crazy dynamo of the Labyrinth. It's like dropping a radio into your bathtub—if it's just working on its own batteries, not plugged into 120 volts, you're okay."

Castine shook her head. "Well, remember your math anyway. Jeez."

Vickery smiled and nodded. "Two plus two is four and nothing else. I remember." The field in which ghosts could appear was one of gross indeterminism, irrationally expanded possibility, and the hard, unyielding logic of mathematics could drive ghosts away—if they paid attention.

"And don't let them stick their tongues out at you," she added, for the ghosts they'd encountered last year had been able to quickly extrude their tongues, which were freezingly, incapacitatingly cold.

"I've got a chicken-wire screen there, to keep them away from me." Like the screen in a confessional, he thought—except in this case the figures on both sides of the screen are looking for absolution. "And what have *you* been doing, back east? Why are you still with the TUA?"

"Oh." The question seemed to have startled her. "It's not the same TUA now, it's been merged into Naval Intelligence—it's not the agency that killed Eliot, anymore." Vickery recalled that Eliot had been the name of her fiancé, murdered last year by the TUA when it had still been a rogue, autonomous agency. "I do clerical work there. I—after last year, I just want the rest of my life to be . . . humdrum. Boring, even." She laughed without smiling. "Socrates said the unconsidered life is not worth living, but that's what I want. Wanted."

She walked slowly to the trash can and dropped the crumpled wax paper into it, then looked around at the lake and the grass as if to reassure herself that she was still in the blessedly ordinary world. "But then," she went on in a harsh whisper, "the visions of that terrible old house started intruding, and I—I can't—I hardly dare *sleep* anymore, thinking that it's leading up to something—that I might one day soon see it for real, be standing in front of it!" She turned to him, her eyes frightened. "Do we die there?"

"I—" Vickery paused, looking past her.

On the other side of the lake, two men were walking swiftly along the shore-side pavement, and to Vickery they seemed to be looking closely at the people they passed. The dark windbreaker one of them wore reminded him of the two men who had rushed at their car on the sidewalk in front of Canter's.

He took Castine's elbow and turned her south, away from the lake. "Don't look back," he said, "and don't visibly hurry—but hurry."

She nodded and took long steps off the pavement and across the grass to keep up with his stride. "Bad guys?"

"I'm pretty sure."

"No—*how?*"

"Dunno. We'll try to get on a bus or something before they see us."

Past a cluster of acacia trees and a couple of tall palms, he could see traffic moving from left to right on Seventh Street, which lay at right angles to the street on which they had left the car. He tried to remember if there was a bus stop on Seventh along this block. A free taxi, or any taxi at all, would be very unlikely.

Then his view of the street and cars seemed to flatten. He clutched her arm and whispered, "Oh *no!*"

He heard her say, "What—" and then the light dimmed and all sounds faded away to silence.

He could still feel the grass brushing past under his shoes, and Castine's arm in his gripping hand, but what he saw was a dilapidated two-story Victorian house fifty yards in front of him, with an eroded dirt slope rising behind it. In the coppery echo light he couldn't make out the color of the house, and it seemed to crouch out there in front of him like a huge, ragged spider. Several of the downstairs windows were broken, and the broad porch slanted down sharply to the right, its farthest extent partly buried in the sand. A motorcycle, an old Harley Davidson panhead, leaned on its kickstand close to the porch railing.

Castine was palpably leading him now. They were stepping more slowly but with evident deliberateness, and he hoped she understood that he was—briefly, God willing!—experiencing an involuntary time-spike echo vision.

From his point of view he was striding quickly toward the old house, and the difference between his real, felt pace and his visually perceived one brought back memories of treading moving walkways at airports. He reminded himself that he was in no sense physically present in the scene he was seeing, and that he couldn't be sensed by any people who might appear in it.

And in fact he saw a man step out of the front door, onto the porch. Vickery knew that Castine must have felt his shudder when he recognized the lean face—it was the same face he had seen in an upstairs window, in previous episodes like this.

Vickery's view of the house stopped expanding, as if he had halted, though he could feel that he and Castine were still trudging forward; the sensory confusion almost made him stumble, but he concentrated on the texture of the real MacArthur Park grass under his pacing feet.

He knew that in real time he and Castine must be approaching the edge of the park and the lanes of Seventh Street, but what filled his vision was the porch and the man standing on it. The man's face was framed by tangles of long dark hair that hung down to the shoulders of his open Nehru jacket, and when the man moved to the porch rail and gripped it, Vickery glimpsed the curved grip of a revolver in the man's belt. The man looked left and right, and then stared with clear recognition directly into Vickery's point of view.

Then the sounds and sunlight of present-day MacArthur park washed over Vickery and he could peripherally see Castine in the yellow blanket to his right—and he found himself looking straight at another face, also alarmingly familiar.

The eyes behind the round black-framed glasses met Vickery's for a moment and then swept past him, toward the crowded lawns of the park. Sweat was now trickling down the shaved areas over the young man's ears, and the white shirt under the red suspenders was darkened across the chest.

Vickery pushed Castine past him, blocking the man's view of her and wishing he had bought her a garish head-scarf in addition to the baseball cap.

Ahead of them, a pearl-white Nissan sedan pulled in to the red curb at the same moment that a voice from behind called, "Hold it, you two."

Vickery's hand was on the grip of his Glock as he spun toward the speaker; it was the young man in red suspenders who had spoken, and he was now facing them and holding a pocket-sized semi-automatic pistol.

"Turn around, lady." The young man's voice was tight with evident tension. "And take off the shades."

Vickery's gun was out and pointed at the man's chest, but before he could speak, a voice from the street behind him said, loudly, "*I will shoot you—*" and then went on more quietly, "through the heart, if you do not drop your gun."

Several pedestrians had exclaimed and stepped back, and a woman screamed—not loudly, but as if the situation seemed to call for it.

Gritting his teeth, and relying on the fact that the voice had said "through the heart" rather than "in the back," Vickery held his own gun steady.

Behind the lenses of the round glasses, the young man's eyes were wide; he lowered the little gun and then let it fall to the grass. "I was only—" he began.

Vickery stepped quickly to the side so that he could see both speakers, and he noted the moustache and the plaid sportcoat of a man standing now beside the white car that idled at the curb—this man had been in the entry at Canter's when Vickery and Castine had run out of the place, and he was now holding a big-caliber stainless steel revolver pointed toward the young man in red suspenders.

"Go!" he shouted now, waving the gun, and then stepped back and opened the rear door of the white sedan. To Vickery and Castine he said, "Inside, quickly! They must not have you."

The young man hesitated, then went sprinting away east down the Seventh Street sidewalk.

Vickery almost started after him—he was one of the people who had stolen *The Secret Garden*!—but the gray-haired man in the dark windbreaker and his companion were closer, and moving quickly this way.

"Let's do it," said Vickery to Castine. He crouched to snatch up the gun on the grass and toss it to Castine, and then he shoved his own gun back under his belt and scrambled into the back seat after her.

Their apparent rescuer tucked the revolver under his sportcoat and ran around to get in on the driver's side. The car's interior smelled of licorice.

In moments the car had sped away west on Seventh Street, but not before Vickery had glance out the back window. The young man in the white shirt and suspenders was hurrying away up the sidewalk, and Vickery noticed something like a bulky white handkerchief stuffed into a rear pocket of his black jeans.

The man behind the wheel raised his right hand. "You needn't touch your weapons," he said. "I am employed by the Egyptian Ministry of Antiquities, doing work from the Consulate on Wilshire Boulevard." He waved ahead vaguely. "You must both leave the Los Angeles region, far, immediately. Funds if necessary can be provided." He glanced at Vickery in the rear view mirror. "I think," he went on, "you do not know why those various men are pursuing you."

Vickery was breathing carefully and focusing through the windshield at the sunlit cars in the lane ahead of them, forcing his eyes to comprehend volume, depth of field; he didn't want to fall into another involuntary echo vision.

"No, we don't," said Castine. "Do you know why?"

"Guesses based on guesses are of no value. My concern is the recovery of an artifact that was negligently curated long ago." He lifted one hand from the wheel in a dismissive wave. "I will drive you now to the LAX airport, and you will get a flight, do you understand? These men are following you by some means, but they no longer have time to chase you in a distant city. Do you have money, and identification, for tickets?"

"Uh," said Castine, giving Vickery a bewildered, questioning look.

Equally puzzled, he just shrugged. At least this is getting us away from the guy in the dark windbreaker, he thought. Just so this fellow doesn't insist on seeing us actually buy tickets.

Vickery cleared his throat. "Well—yes."

"Good," said their driver. "In a few days their project will have become ended, willy nilly, and you could safely return, no matter what their intentions toward you have been."

"Why will their project be ended in a few days?" Vickery asked.

"I will have retrieved the artifact by then, and taken it back to Cairo."

The man had hesitated very slightly before the word *taken*, and Vickery was certain that he meant in fact to destroy the artifact, whatever it was.

Castine might have noticed it too. "What sort of artifact is it?" she asked.

"Very new and very old. If you have cell phones, you can arrange a flight even now."

"We don't," said Vickery.

"No matter. It is a large airport, there will be many flights available."

Harlowe's men had all fanned out across the park, circling the lake, and Elisha Ragotskie now just needed to get away. The white car had disappeared into the westbound traffic, taking his Beretta Pico with it, so he sprinted across the lanes of Seventh Street to the sidewalk on the south side and began walking rapidly east, his head down. After a few steps he pulled his conspicuous red suspenders off his shoulders and tucked them messily into his black jeans. He was panting, and afraid to look across the street. Harlowe would certainly have Taitz kill him, if they saw him.

Ragotskie looked down at his right hand, which was still visibly trembling. Would I, he wondered, have been able, actually, to shoot the Castine woman? My finger was on the trigger, the gun was pointed at the middle of her. She was wearing sunglasses, so I couldn't see her eyes—I wonder if I'd actually have been able to pull the trigger, if I'd seen her eyes. It was so much easier, so much less *momentous*, to shake cyanide powder into her water glass!

And who the hell was that man in the midtown orange-plaid sportcoat? If I hadn't burned my bridges with Harlowe, I'd tell him there seems to be another player in the situation.

Ragotskie ached to talk to his onetime lover, Agnes Loria, but, as she was now, she might very well just turn him over to Harlowe.

Ragotskie had cautiously followed Harlowe's three-car procession to MacArthur Park, and when two of the cars had split off to loop around the north half of the park, Harlowe's SUV had stopped at a red no-parking curb on Wilshire. Harlowe and Taitz and Foster had all climbed out and gone loping away across the grass, leaving only Tony the driver in the vehicle.

Ragotskie had stopped his Audi right behind it, and then left the motor running while he grabbed a heavy flashlight and ran up to the rear passenger-side door of the SUV and with three rapid blows smashed the window. Tony had quickly got out on the driver's side, shouting; but Ragotskie had leaned in through the ruptured glass, grabbed the polished wooden box off the rear seat, and raced back to his own car.

He had gunned away in reverse, bouncing up the curb for a few yards and then thumping back onto the street again, while Tony had run after him; but Tony had jumped out of the way when Ragotskie shifted into drive and sped forward.

Ragotskie had then driven around the park and left his car at a bus stop on the south side—he could see his green Audi now, and he was grateful that it had not been towed.

He was hurrying past a storefront church and a clinic now, and he peered left and right past cars parked at the curb. Before running back across the lanes of Seventh Street to his car, he patted his back pocket to make sure the bloodstained sock had not fallen out. He couldn't even remember now what he had done with Harlowe's wooden box.

The sock was stiff, and he grimaced and wiped his hand on his damp shirt as he crossed the street to his car.

Maybe Harlowe, for all his insectile cleverness, had no way of tracing Castine or Vickery besides the sock. Or even if he did, maybe they would have the sense to flee L.A. very fast and far, right now. Without those two, Harlowe's Singularity project would surely fail, and Agnes Loria would not lose her identity—even if losing it was what she wanted. In that case, Ragotskie would be fortunate in having failed to kill Castine!

He peered back over the top of the car as he unlocked the door. He didn't see Taitz or Foster, and he exhaled and relaxed as he got in.

But Castine and Vickery might hang around. How much did they know? They might have, they probably had, plans of their own. They might even want to approach Harlowe, in some mutually secure location.

Ragotskie's face was cold with the realization that he might have to kill Castine, or Vickery, after all.

The thought nauseated him.

They had driven away west with the man in the plaid jacket. Luckily Ragotskie's car was facing that way. He could drive west a few blocks and find a place to park, and then try to make the sock pendulum do its trick.

CHAPTER THREE:
Is Supergirl Thirsty?

Lateef Fakhouri steered his rented Nissan around the curled onramp onto the northbound 405 freeway, and he was troubled by the way he had handled the pair of fugitives. He had dropped them off at the Delta departures terminal, but he had very little confidence—none, in fact—that they would actually buy tickets and fly to some distant city. He really should have detained them, somehow.

His present posting with the Ministry of Antiquities was temporary; ordinarily he was employed as a clerk in the research division of the General Intelligence Directorate, in a branch office in Lazhogli Square in Cairo, and his duties until recently had consisted mainly of cross-referencing reports of illegal tunnels between Sinai and Gaza. But while tracing the origins of some wooden *ushabti* statues looted from a tomb in Saqqara, he had come across a disturbing, decades-old file—it was marked as property of the State Security Investigations Service, which had been shut down shortly after the 2011 revolution. The SSI had purged most of its records in the turbulent days before its official dissolution, but this file, labeled *Austria, 1855*, had somehow escaped the hasty shredding of files.

Some of the papers in the file had been very old, having to do with the gift of a number of Pharaonic antiquities to Archduke Maximilian of Austria in 1855; those items had eventually found their way to the Kunsthistorisches Museum in Vienna, but notes in the SSI file indicated that one particular item, designated *Ba: World*

Soul: Restricted, had disappeared between the initial indexing and a later inventory conducted in 1862. The item was described as a fired clay panel of Third Dynasty hieroglyphics, four or five thousand years old. A report dated 1922, badly translated from the French, indicated that the artifact had been destroyed in Paris, but noted—with evident disapproval—that a Norwegian Egyptologist had photographed it beforehand.

Lateef Fakhouri had been ready to consign the file to the vast records archive at Heliopolis when he noticed newer pages on blue-lined notebook paper tucked into a pocket at the back of the file. These proved to be handwritten notes made by the assembler of the file, an SSI agent named Khalid Boutros, who had died in the 1990s.

According to these notes, Boutros had become concerned about the Norwegian Egyptologist's photograph of the lost artifact after viewing some—Fakhouri had had to read the words twice—some *coloring books* published in Los Angeles in 1966. A page cut from one of the coloring books was paper-clipped to Boutros' notes; printed on the page was a complicated stylized design, and in the margin someone had written, in blurred and faded ball-point ink, *Acid test, Cinema Theater, Hollywood, February 25 '66.*

From the description in the 1855 transfer index, the SSI agent Khalid Boutros had known that the clay panel of hieroglyphs had originally been taken from a particular tomb in Saqquara, the ancient necropolis twenty miles south of Cairo, and he had driven out there in 1967. According to his notes, Boutros had spent two days picking his way among the weathered walls and tumbled stones of the necropolis until, in a sand-clogged corridor near the pyramid of Djoser, he had found the recessed rectangular patch that the clay panel had once occupied. It was high up on a shadowed wall, and Boutros had piled up stones to reach the spot. A corner of the missing panel had still been clinging to the wall, and from the state of that fragment Boutros had somehow come to conclusions that impelled him to fly to Los Angeles.

The only notes which might have referred to that trip, and which apparently concluded the file, were a few words scrawled on the back of the last sheet of lined paper: *Chronic egregore, neutralized by Nu hieroglyph,* and below that, *Saqqara fragment inert, as of 31/10/68.* In Christian cultures, 31/10 was All Hallow's Eve—Halloween.

And behind the last page of notes was a photograph of a hieroglyph depicting three pots, three wavy lines, and what appeared to be a bracket laid on its side like a table. On the back of the photograph someone, presumably Khalid Boutros, had scrawled *NU.*

Fakhouri had looked up the word "egregore," and found that it was used in Eliphas Levy's book *Le Grand Arcane,* posthumously published in 1868, to describe ancient quasi-angelic beings dangerous to mankind; though in the writings of the later Hermetic Order of the Golden Dawn, the term referred to a kind of group-mind, arising from a number of strongly aligned individual human minds but existing independent of them, autonomous—a new and superior category of being.

For a week Fakhouri had brooded on the enigmatic old file, and then he had done two things.

First, he had put an aluminum ladder in the back of his car and driven south to the ruins of Saqqara, and, following Khalid Boutros' old account, had found the section of wall from which the ancient panel had been taken. He had to roll aside the stones Boutros had stacked there fifty years earlier in order to set up his ladder. Crouched with a flashlight at the top of it, Fakhouri had seen the fragment of fired clay that remained on the wall, as Boutros had described; but when he touched it, his hand sprang away. It was vibrating, and as hot as a pan over a high flame. Anything but "inert."

Then, back in his office, Fakhouri had put through an official research request for any recently published American coloring books, especially any that might originate in or around the city of Los Angeles. The request must have struck the consulate and embassy staffs as peculiar, but there had been no indignant replies.

While waiting for results, he had dug out some research volumes on the gods of ancient Egypt, and found that *Ba,* represented in hieroglyphs by a hawk with a man's head, wasn't a specific god, but was a "world soul"—something analogous to a magnetic field or carrier wave—that defined, and even permitted the existence of, gods. And *Nu,* he learned, was the oldest of the ancient Egyptian gods, and was likewise more of a force than a person—it embodied profound absence, lack of form, the ultimate welcoming void. It was represented by the sea.

And when a bundle of new coloring books had eventually been delivered to his office, he'd found in several of them the same intricate, stylized pattern that Khalid Boutros had found in the coloring book from 1966. These new coloring books, in both English and Spanish, were apparently aimed at adults, consisting mainly of diagrams of people sitting yoga-style or standing with spread arms and rays emanating out of their heads, but the mysterious pattern occupied the first and last pages. These coloring books had been printed in 2017 by a company—ChakraSys Inc.—that was located in Los Angeles.

Fakhouri had noticed that the many curved and straight lines in the center of the repeated pattern formed the profile outline of a hawk with a spike-bearded human head.

After he had put all the flimsy booklets away in a desk drawer, he had tried to recall the profile outline—and it seemed to him that it had differed, in some lines, from the illustrations of the *Ba* hieroglyph he had seen in the reference books. And he was obscurely glad that he had not stared at it for more than a few seconds.

The patchwork data he had assembled so far was troubling:

A variant depiction of *Ba*, the World Soul, on a hieroglyph panel—restricted, eventually destroyed, but photographed some time before 1922—appearing decades later in coloring books in California, in connection with some enterprise—some egregore?— that Boutros had believed he had stopped in October of '68 by somehow using the contrary *Nu* hieroglyph. And Boutros had confirmed the closure of the affair to his own satisfaction by again visiting the wall in Saqqara from which the panel had originally been taken, and finding the remaining fragment of it reassuringly "inert."

Saqqara fragment inert, as of 31/10/68

Boutros had stopped it then, at any rate.

But when Fakhouri had recently touched the fragment on the wall in Saqqara, it was hot, and vibrating—no longer describable as *inert*. And now the image-concealing pattern was again appearing in coloring books printed in Los Angeles. Whatever phenomenon it was that old Khalid Boutros had discovered and stymied in 1968— *Ba: World Soul: Restricted*—*Chronic egregore*—it was evidently happening again.

Nobody in the General Intelligence Directorate was likely to take these vague and outlandish suspicions seriously, so Fakhouri had told his chief that he had discovered some possible irregularities in the "King Tut: Treasures of the Golden Pharaoh" exhibit at the California Science Center in Los Angeles, and requested a temporary transfer to the Ministry of Antiquities, which had organized the exhibition. The transfer had been approved by both agencies, and Fakhouri had been assigned to the Los Angeles Egyptian Consulate.

And he had begun his investigation by tracing the source of the new coloring books—ChakraSys Publications.

When the pearl-white Ford pulled into the parking lot and slowed, and then stopped fifty yards away from the back side of the ChakraSys building, a boy who had been sitting beside a bicycle in the shade of a camphor tree stood up and got on the bike and began pedaling across the hot asphalt. His gray hoodie was thrown back, and the wind fluttered his uncombed black hair.

Within the last half hour, three U-Haul trucks had driven into the lot and backed up to the rear entrance of the ChakraSys building, and people were carrying desks and lamps out and wrestling them up the ramps of the trucks.

The boy halted his bike by the rolled-up driver's side window of the Ford. This car had driven into the parking lot several times over the last couple of days, and had always parked this way, far from the ChakraSys building but in a position to watch it.

The window buzzed down, and the boy noted for the first time that the man behind the wheel had a moustache and black hair—perhaps he was Hispanic too.

"Can I help you?" the man said in a harried tone.

"You're afraid of them," the boy said, "but you watch." The man just blinked out at him in evident confusion, and the boy went on, "I watch them also."

"Them? What them?"

The boy nodded toward the U-Haul trucks.

"Uh . . ." The man scratched his nose. "So why is it that *you* watch them?"

The boy squinted speculatively at him, then said, "I mean to stop them. I think you do too."

The man laughed weakly. "How have they offended *you*?" He

raised one hand and flipped his fingers toward Venice Boulevard. "Go home, young *bey*."

The boy sighed and glanced at the trucks. "They mean to make a monster, did you know that?"

"A monster." The man sighed, looking at the trucks. "You could say so."

"And Simon Harlowe's people killed a man I loved, who knew about them and tried to fight them." The boy braced one foot on a pedal, ready to ride away quickly; then pulled at the back of his hoodie, and when the fabric over his right pocket was drawn tight, the raised outline of a pistol was visible. "I want to finish my friend's work, and avenge him."

The man recoiled in the car seat. "Ach, so many guns here! Even a child! And Simon Harlowe is not in that building now—he is off pursuing two people he wants for his, his monster. Go *home*, forget this, leave it to others . . . and throw that thing *away*."

"My home is wherever I am. What people?"

The man laughed again, no more strongly than before. Perhaps to himself, he muttered, "Two people who drove a taco truck to Hell, and came back, in this mad country. Go away now, boy."

The boy nodded. "Sebastian Vickery and Ingrid Castine."

The man was staring intently at him now, and twice he opened his mouth and closed it without saying anything. Finally he asked, "Who *are* you?"

"Santiago." The boy went on, "I watch and carry messages—I keep track of things. Vickery and Castine owe me money, they are not for Harlowe's monster."

"And you know—*you* know?—about Harlowe, ChakraSys, what they are doing?"

Santiago nodded solemnly. "I know what my friend told me, and what the freeway gypsies say."

After a moment of hesitation, the man waved toward the trucks and spoke quickly: "Harlowe is obviously moving his base of operations, and I need to follow them. But—*ya allah, saa'edni!*—how can I get in touch with you?"

Santiago recited the number of one of his disposable phones, and as the man scribbled it on a receipt from the console, the boy asked, "And who are you?"

"Oh—it is best that you don't know. What you—"

"I won't work with someone whose name I don't know."

The man looked at him and laughed in surprise. "But how can you know I'll tell you my real name?"

Santiago waved toward the ChakraSys building and the people carrying furniture into the trucks. "You work against the Harlowe *pulgas,* so you are like my friend, who they killed. And he was honest."

The man barked one syllable of a laugh. "A street urchin compels me! Well, so be it, *inshallah.*" Carefully he said, "I am Lateef Fakhouri."

Santiago nodded. "Call me if you think you can help me in this." He nodded, then stepped up on the pedal and rode away from the car toward Venice Boulevard.

Sebastian Vickery and Ingrid Castine, back in Los Angeles! Santiago wished his surrogate father had not been killed—old Isaac Laquedem would have known what to do here.

At the airport, Vickery and Castine had waited inside the Delta terminal until their enigmatic rescuer had steered his white Nissan back into the flow of traffic. When the car had disappeared in the one-way current of taxis and shuttle buses, they had walked to the International terminal, got into a taxi there, and asked to be driven to MacArthur Park. They didn't speak during the twenty-minute ride except to make absentminded small talk; Vickery remarked on the resemblance of several downtown L.A. office buildings to rocket ships, and Castine noted that modern cars all used to look like computer mouses and now all looked like trendy athletic shoes.

At the street on the west side of MacArthur Park, Vickery told the taxi driver to halt a few car-lengths short of his old Saturn, which was still sitting where he'd parked it, and he looked around before opening the taxi door; but he didn't see anyone in a dark windbreaker or red suspenders. He stepped out onto the pavement and paid the driver.

"At this point," he said to Castine as she climbed out and hurried with him toward the Saturn, "I think we may have lost our friends from Canter's. Neither of us can have anything as big as a GPS tracker stuck to us, and a radio frequency tag's only good for a hundred yards or so."

"I don't have a tag on me," she said. "You think I wouldn't notice one?—stuck on, I don't know, the rental car's key fob?"

He opened the Saturn's passenger-side door for her. "It might be the fob itself," he said. "You should throw it away. For all I know, they can—"

"What happened to you, there," she interrupted, "just before that guy pulled a gun on us? It was like you were blind for a few seconds."

"Get in. I—I had a vision of the old house. Spontaneous, obviously I wasn't trying to see by echo vision when it happened. It just—"

He paused and looked past her. A teenage girl who had been riding a bicycle down the sidewalk had braked to a sudden stop six feet away, and visibly shuddered. She mumbled something, then said clearly, speaking to no one, " . . . to Canter's in her rented Honda. We could have taken her blood pressure any time."

The girl shook her head as if to clear it, then glanced around and gave Vickery and Castine an embarrassed smile, and pedaled away.

Castine stared after her for a moment, then got into the car and pulled the door closed, and Vickery hurried around and got in on the other side.

"You've got a billfold or something?" he asked as he closed the door and quickly started the engine. "For ID and credit cards?" When she tapped her jacket and nodded, he went on, "And a return airline ticket, I assume. Why didn't you stay at the airport?"

He had backed the Saturn out of the parking slot and now clicked the engine into drive and accelerated north toward Wilshire Boulevard.

Castine was facing him, and her eyes were wide. "She was talking about me, wasn't she? My rental car is a Honda."

"Yeah, I think she was. Damn."

"Like she was talking in her sleep!"

Vickery turned right on the boulevard, driving now along the curve of Wilshire between the north and south expanses of the park, with the lake on the right. "I should loop around and get you back to the airport, fast," he said. "Why the hell didn't you stay there, after Omar Sharif dropped us off? You've only got trouble in L.A."

Castine slumped in her seat and looked straight ahead. "Oh shut up, can't you? My flight's not till tomorrow."

He rocked his head back and forth as if her answer settled the question.

"And Omar Sharif is dead," she added. She pulled a keyring from her pocket and began sliding the single key off the ring.

Vickery sighed. "True." Absently, watching the traffic, he said, "He was great in *Doctor Zhivago*."

Castine just muttered, "She was talking about me!"

"Look," Vickery said, "I'm going to reconnoiter, at my place in Barstow. You can come along, or I can take you back to the airport."

She rolled down the window and tossed the keyring and fob out, and pocketed the key. "That probably wasn't it, was it? The key fob?"

"Probably not. But it was a good idea to get rid of it anyway. It wouldn't hurt to get you a whole fresh set of clothes, from the skin out, though that might not help either."

"You really think they can still track us?" she said, rolling the window back up. "Or specifically me?"

"God knows. With luck their method isn't very long-range, *whatever* it is. And Barstow's separated from L.A. by a twelve-thousand-foot height of rock." When she gave him a haggard, incredulous look, he explained, "The Cajon Pass is four-thousand foot elevation, and the plain-old curvature of the earth adds another eight or nine thousand feet to that. And the curvature is shallow at either end obviously, but from here to Barstow it's a hundred and fourteen miles wide."

"Let's go to Barstow. Fast."

"Are you sure? The airport's—"

"I said Barstow! I—dammit, my flight's not till tomorrow, I *told* you."

He just nodded. And in spite of his concern for her, he was glad she was staying. Last year, when she volunteered to accompany him in a terrible-odds dive into the Labyrinth afterworld, old Isaac Laquedem had told Vickery, *You'll need help. Respect her choice.*

"Okay," he said finally, shifting to the left lane to pass a slow-moving bus. "I'm glad." Then he added, diffidently, "We do have to make a slight detour on the way. To, uh, Hollywood Boulevard."

"*What?*" She slapped the dashboard. "Why, for God's sake? Just drive straight out of here to Barstow, right now!"

"I think we need to find out about that old wrecked house that's been pre-empting our usual echo vision. Why it's closer, and later in that day, every time we see it. I can't believe it's a coincidence that it started happening right before these guys decided to grab us. There's—"

"Grab *you*. With the baby carriage."

He waved a hand impatiently. "I'm part of us. There's somebody we need to consult."

"Who, that Laquedem guy? You said you couldn't find him."

"No. Um—a superhero, actually."

Castine had been craning her neck to look behind them, but now she flopped back in her seat again and closed her eyes. "You're all I've got," she said. "You're not going crazy, are you? Superheroes, curvature of the earth?" Now she was giving him a worried look. "Say something sane."

He smiled bleakly, his eyes on the cars ahead. "You and I are not normal people."

"Huh." She shook her head. "That's not sane, that's just true."

"I'm going to catch the 110 north, up here. If you want to think sane thoughts, you should probably close your eyes again."

It had been from a spot on the northbound 110 that Castine and Vickery had exited the real world last year, and found themselves in the nightmare Labyrinth afterworld.

She rubbed both hands over her face, and pushed her hair back and exhaled. "Oh, I remember," she said. For a while she just swayed in her seat as Vickery swerved from lane to lane, passing slower vehicles, and she might have been thinking about their time in that savagely counter-rational world. "Do you still go to church?" she said finally. "Latin Mass?"

"They don't have Latin Mass in Barstow, but yes, I still make it to Mass on Sundays. I went yesterday." He spared her a sideways glance. "Last year, when it was all over, you told me you got a rosary. Do you still have it?"

"No. No, I moved to an apartment in Gaithersburg, and it must have got lost."

"Ah."

She quickly went on, "Do you think that guy, your *Omar Sharif,* is really with the Egyptian Antiquities Patrol, or whatever it was? It's weird he just told us to get out of town."

"He's really from Egypt, at least," said Vickery, "that's a Masri Arabic accent. What was it, 'an artifact that was negligently curated'?"

"'Long ago,'" agreed Castine. "I got the idea he means to destroy it. Do you suppose he was following us too?"

"My impression was that he was monitoring the other crowd, and stepped in quick to stop Red Suspenders from shooting you. You've still got his gun, I trust."

"You were pretty quick there yourself, especially just coming out of a vision. Yes." She pulled the little gun out of her jacket pocket and held it in her lap. "How soon till we're on the 110?"

"A few more miles yet. Say ten minutes."

"I *might* shut my eyes when we drive by that spot." She stretched and yawned, and Vickery knew it was a yawn of tension rather than fatigue. "So are we allies again? Like last year?"

"Looks like it."

"Friends, even, as I recall." She found the magazine release button on the gun and popped the magazine out, then pulled the slide back, ejecting a .380 round. "I didn't really lose the rosary," she said, staring down at the gun as she let the slide snap back. "I've even been to Mass, a couple of times." She pulled the trigger, and with a click some part of the gun flew out onto the floor.

She bent down and picked up a tiny metal rod, and held it out on her palm.

Vickery glanced at it. "The firing pin. I guess you weren't supposed to dry-fire it. Never mind, I've got a couple of spare guns at home."

She dropped the firing pin in the ashtray, and seemed relieved that the gun had changed the subject.

Vickery parked in a lot off Highland Avenue, a block south of Hollywood Boulevard, and he and Castine walked up to the crowded black sidewalk with its inset pink stars, and paused in the recessed entry of a store called Souvenirs of Hollywood. A cold wind was blowing straight down the boulevard from the west, and Castine pulled her jacket tighter and gripped her elbows.

"She'll probably be out in front of the Chinese Theater, across the street," Vickery said. Castine still hadn't asked, so he explained, "The person we're looking for is one of the costumed superheroes that tourists pay to have their picture taken with."

Castine rolled her eyes but didn't say anything.

The traffic light ahead of them switched from red to the green silhouette of a walking man, and masses of pedestrians in bright T-shirts or tank tops or grimy overcoats stepped out onto the pavement, moving simultaneously straight ahead across Hollywood Boulevard and to the right across Highland, and even diagonally to the far corner, since the crosswalks at this intersection formed a big square with an X in the middle, and all motor traffic faced red lights. Vickery and Castine moved with the northbound stream of the crowd, glancing cautiously around at the brightly dressed tourists and bearded street lunatics jostling them, and on the sunny north sidewalk Castine hurried out of the crowd to stand beside a wide window in the shade under an awning. Over the awning, Vickery had noticed tall letters on a higher row of windows spelling out LIVE YOUR LIFE.

Castine had seen it too. "I'd *like* to live my life," she said crossly. "We should have picked a different city to meet up in. Does *everywhere* in L.A. smell like marijuana?" She glanced left and right at the bobbing heads of the people moving in conflicting eddies in both directions on the sidewalk in front of them.

More quietly, she asked, "Do you think any of these are ghosts?"

"Among all these—sure, a few, though not as many as there would have been last year, before you and I closed the afterworld conduit." He looked away from the rocking parade of now-questionable profiles to look at her. "I imagine there's one or two who'll soon spin away to nothing, which will startle any tourists who're able see them. But the ones who attached themselves to us then are gone."

She tugged the cuffs of her jacket and pulled the bill of her Hollywood baseball cap further down. "I'd like to get home without picking up any new ones."

"Right. We shouldn't hold still anyway, in case everybody's following our trail of breadcrumbs or whatever. Let's see if we can find Supergirl."

"Supergirl." Castine's voice was flat.

Vickery just nodded and took her arm. Rejoining the pedestrian stream, he led the way west along the broad, glittering black sidewalk, past curbside evangelists and pirated-CD sellers and plain beggars, choosing paths where the crowd ahead opened up for a moment, and soon they stepped out of the flux into the more static crowd in the Chinese Theater forecourt. Here the stiller air smelled of car exhaust and sunblock and chocolate from the Ghirardelli's ice cream parlor on the other side of the boulevard.

A Captain Jack Sparrow, in full pirate costume and beaded beard, was standing between a couple of girls while an older woman took their picture with a phone, and when the tourists had hurried off toward a towering yellow Transformer figure, Vickery caught the Sparrow's eye and held up a palm with a twenty-dollar bill crimped in it.

"Not a picture," Vickery told him. "I'm looking for Supergirl."

"Got a couple of such, mate," said the Jack Sparrow.

"I mean—" Vickery paused; Rachel Voss might not want her name known to just any superhero on the boulevard. "She used to be Wonder Woman, but she was really too short for that."

The Jack Sparrow nodded and reached out and took the bill. "She was over by the Ghirardelli a few minutes ago. Can't have got too far."

Vickery nodded and took Castine's elbow again as he eased and sidestepped back out to the sidewalk. As they pushed their way through the crowd to the right, toward a crosswalk, she leaned in close to him to be heard over the multilingual babble around them.

"Supergirl?" she said again, more insistently.

"When I was an L.A. cop," he said, "she was what they call a CRI, Confidential Reliable Informant. You're supposed to register all your CRIs with a central database, but I kept a few of them secret, and she was one of those. She was very good with some ATM fraud cases I handled, but she was always—"

He paused while they separated around a Captain America.

"She was always," he went on when they had rejoined on the far side, "telling me about occult activity in Hollywood. When I was a cop I didn't pay much attention to that stuff, but last year I looked her up because I needed to get in touch with somebody who could allegedly talk to ghosts."

"Laquedem."

"Right," he said, pausing at the crosswalk. "She steered me to him. Of all my old contacts, she's likeliest to know who to ask about our haunted house visions."

At the curb below a towering Madame Tussaud's wax museum sign, a man was hunched over a smoking grill, turning browned bratwursts and sliding them into split rolls.

Castine nodded in that direction. "I once thought we were going to get lunch at that deli."

The light turned green, and Vickery stepped into the street. "You had a tamale," he said. "And I've got stuff in Barstow."

"Stuff," she said, falling into step beside him. "But you're right, we shouldn't slow down any more than we—maybe—have to."

"There's a good chance that Rachel's worth the delay," he said, standing on tip-toe to scan the crowd to the east. "I just wish she were taller."

They had sidled and edged their way past the ornate foyer of the El Capitan Theater when someone tapped Vickery on the shoulder, and when he quickly turned around he saw the short, blonde figure of Supergirl, still trim and fit-looking in her red and blue Krypton suit.

"I think you're Herbert Woods," she said, using his nearly forgotten real name. She had stepped back, apparently leaving herself room to duck away if he was not.

"Hi, Rachel," he said. He pulled Castine back and said, "This is Ingrid, a friend of mine."

Rachel nodded politely. "Jack Sparrow sent a relay hand-jive signal that somebody was looking for me and coming this way, so I was waiting behind the box office here to see who it was. You're lucky I recognized you again—a beard now? And where have you been? I've heard some weird stories."

"Out of town," he said. "Is Supergirl thirsty?"

"What do you think? It's got to be after four, Boardner's should be open."

The crowd thinned out when they had walked the two blocks east to Cherokee Avenue, and Rachel was able to stop explaining to tourists that she was on a break and not open to posing for photographs. Vickery led the way around the corner and across the narrower street, and as he held open the door of Boardner's he looked back and scanned the 180-degree view, and sighed with relief to see no sign of pursuers or watchers. He stepped inside after his two companions.

The interior was dim, lit mainly by the glow of blue lights under the glass shelves behind the bar, but Rachel led the way to a booth at the back. Vickery and Castine sat down on one side, facing Rachel.

"I bet," Rachel began, then paused when a waitress stopped at their booth to take drink orders—a large Coke for Castine, a Coors beer for Vickery, and a sidecar for Rachel; "I bet," she went on when the waitress had moved away, "you're the woman this guy is supposed to have gone to Hell with!"

Castine looked at Vickery, who nodded. "Yes," she said.

"I'd like to hear that story sometime," said Rachel, scratching at her scalp under the blonde wig. "I heard you flew out in a hot-air balloon."

"A hang-glider, actually," said Vickery. "I'll tell you about it another time. Right now we need a pen and paper."

Castine slid the billfold from her inner jacket pocket and unclipped a pen from one side. "You can draw on the back of the rental contract for the Honda," she said, pulling that free. "I'm afraid I'll never return it."

"Okay," said Vickery, beginning to sketch on the back side of the stiff paper, "we'd like you to ask around among your witchy contacts, Rachel, to see if—"

Castine was watching him draw. "Leave room for two gables on the roof," she interjected.

"Oh yeah," said Vickery, nodding.

The drinks arrived, and he paused to take a long sip of the cold beer. "I think I'd be wise to have another of these," he told the waitress.

When she had smiled and nodded and withdrawn, he went on, "Ask your people if they know anything about a house that looks like this." He inked in the ground floor verandah, tilted and partly sunk in the ground on the right side. "This is sand," he said, writing the word below. "And the whole building is dark—brown or gray." He drew wavy lines behind the drawing of the three-story house, then decided that they just looked like smoke, and wrote "dirt slope behind the house" to make it clear.

Rachel put down her drink and craned her neck to see the picture. "It looks kind of wrecked."

"Yeah, there's sand piled up on the left side here too." He drew some bumps there, and wrote *sand* below them. "I think the whole ground floor was flooded sometime, and it's probably full of sand all the way through."

"And—" said Castine, hesitantly touching a rectangle that represented one of the left-side ground floor windows, "there's a spiral staircase inside."

Vickery frowned. "I never saw that."

"Somebody was going upstairs once," Castine said. "I could tell."

"It'd help if I knew where it is," said Rachel.

"We don't know," Vickery told her. "We think it's probably in the L.A. area."

Rachel was staring at them. "But you've seen it; seen people moving in it. What, in a movie?"

"In . . . visions, sort of," said Vickery. "And I think it involves a group of people who tried to grab us a couple of hours ago."

Castine had been crunching an ice cube from her glass of Coke, and now swallowed it and said, "And maybe an Egyptian artifact."

"Oh, right," said Vickery, "these guys may have some sort of artifact that the Egyptian government wants back. We've got to run, but could we meet here again tomorrow? Say four o'clock?"

Rachel gave him a suspicious look over the top of her glass. She set it down and said, "Is your 'group of people' still after you?"

"I don't think they can trace us," said Vickery, "and anyway we got here fast—but yes, I'm sure they're still after us. So we really should go. What sort of donation to the Justice League of America do you think would be appropriate?"

"Am I going to get in the middle of something, even just asking about this place?"

"I—don't know," said Vickery. "I don't know the shape of this situation at all."

"You always were honest, and you did keep my name off the LAPD snitch list. A long time ago." Rachel stood up and drained the last of her drink. "I think this is a thousand bucks, Woods. Even if I come back here tomorrow with nothing for you—even if I plain stand you up."

Castine had squeaked when she heard the amount, but Vickery hesitated only a moment before nodding and reaching into his pocket. Before becoming Bill Ardmore, he had cashed out his old

Secret Service 401k and a settlement from the Transportation Utility Agency, and divided the cash and hidden it in several locations; and he had brought five thousand dollars with him today when he had driven down from Barstow.

"You've always been honest too, Rachel," he said. He pulled the roll of hundred dollar bills from his pocket and peeled off ten of them.

Castine gave Rachel a wide-eyed look. "You can at least pay for the drinks!"

Rachel smiled and adjusted her wig and cape. "I got it. You two split."

CHAPTER FOUR:
If You'd Just Try

Leaving Los Angeles at last, Vickery and Castine drove east to San Bernardino, then up through the Cajon Pass into the Mojave Desert. They stopped for half an hour at the little town of Hesperia, thirty-five miles north of San Bernardino, then they were on the freeway again.

During the straight forty-mile drive up the 15 freeway north of Hesperia, Vickery eventually realized that it wasn't the few other cars on the sun-baked lanes that Castine kept hitching around to look at, but the flat expanses of the desert itself, dotted with star-thistle and saltbush weeds, stretching away to distant foothills.

"Civilization again soon," he told her finally. "Just a bit more curvature."

She nodded. "We should have got some Cokes or something," she said absently, "when we stopped in Hesperia." She slid lower in her seat, as if to avoid being seen—though the nearest car was a hundred yards ahead of them. "The sun's going down," she said faintly, "but I'm glad the sky is still blue."

Vickery nodded sympathetically without looking away from the onrushing pavement. The Labyrinth afterworld had had the appearance of a desert ringed by low hills, with a highway curving through it, but the turbulent sky there had been various shades of brown.

"I know what you mean," he said. "When I first moved out here,

I liked to drive with the windows down, so I could be sure it was fresh air outside." At the moment the car's air-conditioner was set to the maximum, and he was keeping an eye on the temperature and battery gauges.

"What if we were to see that house," said Castine, with a visible shiver, "now, way out there in the desert?"

Vickery's lips pulled back from his teeth. "With a figure standing on the roof—beckoning."

"Shut up! Where the hell do you live, anyway?" She plucked bewilderedly at the denim jacket she was now wearing. "Yesterday I still had a—an identity!"

In Hesperia they had found a Ross Dress for Less store, and she had bought entirely new clothing and shoes; they had stashed her old things, including her billfold, in a locker at the Greyhound bus station. She had kept only her driver's license, which was now in the front pocket of her new jeans. The Hollywood baseball cap she had left in a shopping cart.

Eventually a little cluster of buildings became visible on the flat horizon ahead, and within a few minutes Vickery was driving past it—an outlet mall, with Target and Skechers and Old Navy stores and broad parking lots ringed with young camphor trees.

"Barstow in just a couple of miles," he said, "though you can't see much of it because of the concrete-block sound walls. Not that there's much to see anyway."

And in fact tan sound walls were virtually all there was to be seen of Barstow, and Vickery drove through it in only a couple of minutes. Out past the east end of town, the view on either side of the highway was nothing but tumbleweeds and a few anonymous buildings in the distance, and low hills on the horizon.

Castine looked back. "We're in the desert again," she said uneasily. "I think you passed it."

"Nearly there."

Soon an overpass loomed ahead, and Vickery eased the car into the right lane. "That's Old Highway 58, coming up," he said. "When we pass under it, look at the little shelf up where the slope meets the underside of the bridge. That's where I've got my nest. We'll drive out to it later."

"To talk to ghosts, I suppose," said Castine as Vickery steered the

Saturn around the offramp and under the freeway bridge, heading north now. The sun was above the remote bumpy horizon to his left, and he swung the visor to the side to shade his eyes.

"There's a few things I want to check," he agreed.

"Ghosts are all idiots."

"True, but they do love to talk."

The highway curled around to the northwest for half a mile, and then there were widely spaced houses visible ahead, and Vickery made a left turn onto a two-lane road flanked by occasional old trailers and houses set well back from the narrow pavement.

Having traced a long loop, Vickery drove under an overpass of the 15 freeway that they'd traversed a few minutes earlier, and soon steered right, into the driveway of a small trailer park. His own single-wide trailer was around to the rear of the fenced-in area, its back side facing a mile of empty scrub with railroad tracks beyond.

He stopped the Saturn beside a set of wooden steps that led up to a narrow wooden porch and the trailer's front door, and at last switched off the engine. In the ensuing quiet, he could hear country-western music from a nearby radio mingling with the rustle of dry wind in the bordering trees.

Castine had opened the passenger-side door and swung her legs out onto the gravel, but paused to stretch before climbing stiffly out. The warm air smelled of heated stone and creosote.

"Eight hours in a coach airline seat, and now two hours in a car," she said. "I'll never stand up straight again." She stepped unsteadily away from the car and shut the door. "I hope we're not going back to L.A."

Vickery closed the driver's side door. "Not today."

Castine looked over the top of the car at the trailer, probably noting the row of spinning pinwheels mounted on the roof. "Have you got a spare room?"

"The couch in the living room opens to a bed," he said as he started up the steps. "I'll take that."

"Oh, I can take the couch. You've already—"

"You're the guest, no arguing." He unlocked the door, and it opened with a squeal when he tugged on the knob.

She spread her hands in wry surrender and followed him in.

They were in the dim kitchen, with a round formica-top table and the refrigerator six feet ahead. He switched on a ceiling light and said, "I'll get the air going," and hurried to the left, past the table. A moment later a light came on there in a small living room, and then the clatter of an air conditioner started up.

"Come on in," he said. "It'll be cool in a couple of minutes."

Castine stepped around the kitchen table into the living room, and Vickery imagined her response to the old couch and pair of easy chairs, the coffee table with a couple of issues of the *New Oxford Review* on it, the two standing lamps with yellowed parchment shades, the mismatched rugs partly covering the linoleum floor, and the bookshelves around the windows and over the back door. The place, he realized for the first time, smelled of coffee and motor oil. Could be worse, he thought.

"Get you a drink?" he said. "Sit down, or sprawl on the couch if you'd rather."

"I think I'll sprawl." She lowered herself onto the couch, resting her head on one arm and her ankles up on the other. "This is the first time I've relaxed in . . . lots of hours. Are we for sure safe here, from . . . whoever?"

"I think so. Drink?"

"Oh . . . whiskey, if you've got any, with ice. Bourbon, rye, scotch, whatever. You *think* so?"

Vickery stepped into the kitchen. "Well, we've certainly got no electronic tags on us now," he called as he opened a cabinet over the sink, "nothing *rational*. As for *irrational*, each of those pinwheels on the roof has a bit of organic stuff—wood, bone, leather—"

"—With a terminally subsumed ghost in it," guessed Castine.

"Right. Mounted at the hub. When they're all whirling—and it's always windy here—they project definitive nullity, *nobody here,* to most kinds of supernatural scanning." He fetched down a bottle of Maker's Mark bourbon and a couple of glasses. "At least I'm pretty sure they would, if anybody were to come snooping around with dowsing rods or a ghost guide or anything like that."

He opened the freezer and took an ice-cube tray to the sink and banged the cubes out into a bowl. "I've even got Jack Hipple's pinecone in one of them."

"Hah!" came Castine's voice from the living room. "He's doing some good at last."

Last year they had learned that frightened or exhausted ghosts—or even animate potentials-of-persons that never quite achieved actual existence—could be fixed forever into organic objects, as Vickery had saved his never-conceived daughter in a copy of *The Secret Garden*. And the ghost of a magic-dabbler and blackmailer called Jack Hipple had at one point collapsed itself into a pinecone, and Vickery had kept it.

"I hope he gets termites," said Vickery now.

He shook ice cubes into the glasses, sloshed a liberal measure of bourbon into each, then picked them up and carried them into the living room.

"I've seen several of Hipple's ghost portraits on eBay," said Castine as she took a glass from him. "Thanks! They go for a couple of hundred bucks, usually. People collect this stuff."

Vickery sat down in the easy chair closest to the couch. "I remember he thought the paintings were tethers, to keep a ghost from dissipating. I doubt they still work, if they ever did."

Castine took a big sip of her drink and then set the glass on a magazine on the table. "And now you want to go talk to some ghosts—in your *nest* under the 15 freeway. That's still possible, I gather."

"Sporadically, these days." He took a liberal sip of his own drink. "There's a dirt road that takes you to the overpass, and I drive out there a couple of times a week, and the freeway provides enough rapidly moving free wills to generate the old current."

She waved her hand in a circle indicating the surrounding area. "Your neighbors wonder about that?"

"There's a lot of dirt roads that lead out into the desert in every direction from here, and I make sure I'm seen taking them all, at one time or another. I get in a good deal of shooting practice in real remote spots. That's covert, but I always conspicuously take a metal detector, and I've dropped a few hints about Roswell and the Von Daniken books."

"So Bill Ardmore is a saucer nut."

"If anybody was to wonder about him, sure. A UFOlogist. I'm going to cook us up something to eat, and then we can drive out to my freeway nest. I've got eggs, bacon, onions, cheddar cheese—how about a big old omelette?"

"Drive out tonight? It's—it'll be dark."

"The 15 has a fair amount of traffic at all hours, since it's the way from L.A. to Las Vegas and back, so there'll be current. And the ghosts come through clearer after sundown—I think ultraviolet interferes with their composition."

"And they don't attack you?" she asked, clearly remembering one they had encountered last year in the Hollywood Forever cemetery.

"I dragged a roll of chicken wire to the shelf under the bridge, and made a barrier, like a Faraday Cage. It's an old trick I learned from the freeway gypsies in L.A. Does an omelette sound good? Or I could do scrambled eggs, fried eggs—"

"But you just had a, an *episode,* a vision of that awful house, a couple of hours ago! What if it were to happen again, out—" She waved toward the window, clearly meaning: *out there in the desert, at night*!

"I'd come out of it again pretty quick," he said stolidly. "Either one of us would." He tipped up his glass for another sip and got one of the ice cubes as well as a mouthful of bourbon.

"I'll go with you," she said firmly, "in the morning."

For several seconds neither of them spoke. Vickery chewed the ice cube.

Then, "You'll be safe here," he said gently. "Lock the doors, and I'll give you a gun. And when I come back, I'll knock—" He reached out and rapped *knock-knock-knock, knock* on the table, "—before I put the key in the lock, so you'll know it's me. I shouldn't be more than two hours."

"Oh, damn you, I'll go along," she said angrily. "Omelette, cooked through, not runny. And I want a gun anyway."

Vickery nodded respectful acknowledgment and stood up to go back into the kitchen.

Only a few surfers still bobbed on the darkening waves out past the surf line, and a chilly onshore breeze had driven most of the beachgoers to pack up their towels and coolers and head for their cars, and the parking lot was a good deal emptier now than when the woman with the two pre-teen girls had arrived. The three of them scuffed quickly now through the loose sand around the volleyball nets, their shadows stretching out in front of them to the parking lot pavement. The woman wore a blue cotton dress that fluttered around her legs, and a leather purse swung on a strap over her shoulder; her eyes were hidden behind sunglasses and her mouth was a tight line. The girls wore identical Batman T-shirts and denim shorts, and they glanced at each other and bit their lips to keep from giggling.

"Oops!" whispered one of them to the other, and then they both looked away, shaking as they hurried to keep up with the woman.

Six notes of Strauss' *Death and Transfiguration* chimed faintly in the wind, and the woman snatched a phone out of her purse. "This is Agnes," she said, angling the phone through her disordered chestnut hair, "speak up, it's windy." Then, "We're leaving right now, as a matter of fact." She nodded emphatically as she walked. "Yes, I think you could call it that! A big black hole event on the beach. Yes—yes, a whole family, six people, at least, all babbling in unison. Something about Dr. Zhivago, and buying clothes in Hesperia. What? I said *Dr. Zhivago*—How should I know? No, this family was drunk, they didn't connect it with us. Yes, all of them, they had a jug of wine under a blanket, I should have called the cops."

The three of them had reached the pavement, and the woman paused to take off one of her flat canvas shoes and knock sand out of it. The girls were barefoot. "No," snapped the woman, bracing the phone awkwardly between her ear and her shoulder, "I wouldn't really have called them. I'm not an idiot." She took off her other shoe. "No," she went on, "just therapy wading, not even up to their knees! I know—" she glanced at the girls, "—their history. Here, I'll let Amber explain."

She thrust the phone at one of the girls.

"I'm Lexi," the girl said, but she pushed back her wind-blown brown hair and took the phone. "Hello, Uncle Simon." After a few seconds she said, "Well, we were wading, and Lexi slipped—"

"I thought *I* slipped," said the other girl.

"And so I caught her, to keep her from falling. Yes, by the hand, but we were just holding hands for a second! We didn't mean to start that family all squawking away!"

She nodded several more times, blinking away tears. "Don't let Agnes leave us here! We won't do it again!"

The other girl was now wringing her hands and glancing anxiously back at the sparsely populated shore and the sea beyond.

"Make her promise not to leave us here!" said the girl with the phone. A moment later she held it out toward Agnes Loria. "He wants to talk to you."

Loria was shaking sand out of her other shoe, and now took the phone impatiently with her free hand. "Agnes again," she said. "Elisha? Yes, he's texted me a few times, but I haven't had time to reply." She frowned then, her shoe evidently forgotten in her hand. "He *did*?" She listened intently, then said, "Of course he will. I'll let you know where." Again she was silent, and Lexi and Amber exchanged nervous looks.

"And the twins," Loria went on, "should I—oh! Okay. Holiday Harbor Marina now? Where's that?" She dropped her shoe to dig a pen and an envelope out of her purse, and she scribbled briefly on the envelope. She lifted the pen and didn't speak for a few seconds, then glared at the girls. "No, I was far enough away, but I felt the black hole effect—like I was a big super centipede. Right, we'll see you there."

Loria tucked her phone and the pen and envelope back in her purse and put on her shoe. She was frowning.

"The sun's going down," wailed one of the girls. "We'll die out here!"

"Ass—asphyxiate," sobbed the other.

Suddenly the thoughts in Loria's mind all collapsed, replaced by an impression of frightened fluttering, like a bird helplessly falling in vacuum. She could feel that her hands were extending, fingers spread, and after a few seconds she was aware that she was holding two other hands.

Then her thoughts flooded back, and she took a quick step to catch her balance. She saw that she was holding the twin's hands. At least they weren't touching each other.

Loria mentally replayed the recent conversation. "Don't be silly," she said, a bit breathlessly, "I'm not going to abandon you. You're both part of the big family, right? Come on." She let go of their hands and started toward the car, which was parked at the back of the lot, by the narrow road that separated the beach from the big waterfront houses. "But I think I'm going to make you two wear gloves, all the time."

"We can't wear gloves," objected the one that Loria was pretty sure was Amber. Tears still streaked the girls' faces, but their momentary despair was evidently forgotten. "Without fingerprints, there'd be no difference between us, and we'd melt."

Loria's face was still chilly with a dew of sweat. It was them, again, she thought. They were in my mind for a moment, and this time they made me hold their hands because they were afraid of being abandoned. A week ago I found myself violently tearing open a bag of Doritos, after I had told them they couldn't have any. I wish their identities—identity?—would stay in their heads!

"Did your *boyfriend* do something *wrong*?" asked the probable Lexi now.

"Is Uncle Simon mad at him now?" piped up the other girl.

"How cheerfully he seems to grin," said Lexi, "how neatly spread his claws!"

That was a quote from *Alice's Adventures in Wonderland*. Loria wished the girls had never got hold of a copy of the book.

"Oh, shut up, shut up," she breathed, "poor demented things." More loudly, she went on, "Get in the car, we're going to spend the night on the *Black Sheep*. It's berthed somewhere down in Wilmington now."

"It's birthed!" said one of the girls. "Uncle Simon has to slap its ass, make it cry, or it won't breathe."

The two of them ran awkwardly ahead toward Loria's yellow station wagon. I'll have to tell Simon about it, she thought. He hates hearing alarming news about the twins, but I'll have to tell him.

A hundred yards away, at the other end of the parking lot, Lateef Fakhouri stood beside his pearl-white Nissan, watching the woman and the two girls get into the station wagon. He shrugged out of his tan-and-orange plaid sportcoat and tossed it across the front seat, then hurriedly got in and started the engine. The station wagon drove to the parking lot entrance and turned right onto Pacific Coast Highway, and Fakhouri followed at a discreet distance.

For the past two weeks, Fakhouri had been exploring the occult subculture of Los Angeles. His knowledge of Khalid Boutros' visit fifty years earlier—and Fakhouri's own Egyptian name and Ministry of Antiquities credentials—had led to a few confidential, nervous referrals, and at last, a few days ago, he had managed to purchase the privilege of igniting some sticks of punkwood from an "eternal flame" that was maintained in a garage in San Pedro.

The flame's caretaker was the self-described High Priestess of a local coven. She had told Fakhouri that the flame was a direct continuation of the Baba Gurgur fire that had been burning for thousands of years in Iraq, and that her grandmother, a previous High Priestess, had acquired the relayed combustion from it in 1928. The flame had been carefully kept burning ever since in an oil drum in the grandmother's garage.

The grandmother had died in the '40s; the man who had originally acquired the flame, one Claude Wystan, had gone blind from drinking bootleg gin and killed himself in the '30s; and this current High Priestess had been in a hurry because she worked as a waitress in a nearby Denny's, but she gave him an old coffee can to carry the smoldering punkwood in.

Fakhouri had driven quickly back to the Egyptian Embassy on Wilshire and used the smoldering sticks to light an oil lantern, and the junior staff had been strictly ordered to keep the oil replenished in the lantern so that the ancient combustion wouldn't go out.

Then Fakhouri had found a bottle of Bic Wite-Out and drawn random white squiggles on Khalid Boutros' old photograph of the Nu hieroglyph, and got a Staples store to make a four-foot-tall cardboard blow-up of it. He trusted that the random white lines would prevent the symbol from having any effect on the Staples employees, and he would be able to "erase" the lines later with a gray felt marker.

He had looked up ChakraSys Incorporated, the source of the new coloring books, and had then researched its CEO, Simon Harlowe: the man's vagabond past, his troubled family, and, most of all, his current pursuits, associates, and activities; and it had become clear enough that Harlowe intended to consummate the interrupted egregore of 1968, on the fiftieth anniversary of that aborted attempt.

And on Halloween night, when Simon Harlowe would try to complete the long-delayed birth of the *Ba*-enabled egregore, Fakhouri intended to be present, and to illuminate the potent *Nu* hieroglyph with the ancient flame. It was the method he believed Khalid Boutros had used to defeat the quickening 1968 egregore, and he was cautiously confident that it would do the same for Harlowe's, two days from now. The *Nu* hieroglyph would surely negate the *Ba* one.

Streetlights had come on at some point. The yellow station wagon turned inland at Beach Boulevard, and Fakhouri let a couple of cars merge into his lane ahead of him as he made the same turn; the station wagon was still clearly visible, and not going fast.

But Boutros' use of the *Nu* hieroglyph in 1968 might not be effective now. Fakhouri suspected that this launching of the egregore would be more powerful—people on the streets, who had no connection to it, had in the last few days begun helplessly speaking the thoughts of Harlowe and his cultists. Fakhouri had heard nothing about such an effect occurring in Los Angeles in 1968. The victims recovered their own consciousnesses within seconds, with only momentary disorientation afterward—but might that possession soon become irreversible?

What if Harlowe's revitalized, *Ba*-quickened egregore could simply roll over the *Nu* sigil, now, even when that sigil was illuminated by the primordial Iraqi flame?

And what if it had been some other factor, unrecorded or completely unsuspected by old Boutros, that had stymied the egregore in 1968?

As a precaution, Fakhouri should really have some other tactic in readiness too, to prevent the egregore from attaining coherence, agency, mentation—irresistible dominance.

According to a neurologist to whom he had described the matter as a theoretical hypothesis, such an entity would need the equivalent of a switchboard or computer router, a communication nexus, analogous to the two cooperating halves of the thalamus in the human brain. And since the egregore was to be made of human minds instead of physical neurons, it would probably require a reciprocating pair of minds that suffered from something like what psychiatrists called dissociation. This idea seemed to be borne out by Harlowe's pursuit of Vickery and Castine, who were said to have fallen into the afterworld and come back with a compromised connection to normal sequential time; but Vickery and Castine were in the wind now. Perhaps they had taken Fakhouri's advice after all, and got on a flight to a distant city; in any case, Harlowe had not caught them and didn't seem likely to.

The yellow station wagon had sped up, and Fakhouri passed a slower-moving Volkswagen to keep it in sight.

But Harlowe had adopted his brother's two pre-teen daughters, after their parents' puzzling suicide, and it was a matter of public record that the girls had been treated for psychological ailments. Depending on what sorts of ailment . . . could Harlowe be planning to use those girls as replacements for Vickery and Castine? They seemed to be part of his inner circle, in spite of their age, so they must certainly have been initiated by now with the *Ba* figure in the coloring books.

Today he had watched the two girls through binoculars, and he had been bothered by an old memory. For no discernible reason, Lexi and Amber had reminded him of two Coptic girls he had seen many years ago in Manshiyat Naser, the Garbage City of Cairo, east of the El-Nasr Road at the base of the Mukatam Hills. He had been there on official business, tracing Pharaonic artifacts believed to be smuggled out of Egypt by way of that trash collecting district; and the two Coptic girls, perched on top of a load of malodorous bags in the back of a battered old Chevrolet pickup truck, had appeared to be in no more peril than any other of the *Zabaleen,* the "garbage people," the untouchables whose lives were spent sorting through Cairo's refuse. Undoubtedly the girls had had families, which had probably specialized for generations in salvaging some particular categories of stuff from the collected trash of Cairo—broken glass, or plastic bottles, or old discarded food for the ubiquitous pigs of the district. Undoubtedly they were Christians, with the blue cross tattooed on their wrists. But after he had returned to his office in Lazhogli Square, three miles to the west, he had been troubled by the thought that he should somehow have saved them from their inherited predicament, and to this day his sleep was sometimes disrupted by a nightmare in which those two *Zabaleen* girls figured.

The yellow station wagon slowed for a moment by a Starbuck's, then sped up and caught the last seconds of a green traffic light at the intersection, and Fakhouri had to step on the accelerator to cross after them before the yellow light turned red.

Within the last few hours Harlowe's ChakraSys team had vacated their office on Sepulveda, and Harlowe's boat, the *Black Sheep,* had been moved from its berth at a Santa Monica marina. Fakhouri told himself—firmly!—that he was following the Loria woman this evening only to discover Harlowe's new center of operations.

He would not even *consider* making any plan to abduct the twins.

He quailed even at the thought of committing such a perilous felony, in a foreign country. He reminded himself that Harlowe's nieces were entirely unlike those two Coptic girls, who in fact were probably mothers of children of their own by now.

It was foolish to imagine that abducting the twins—even though it would be saving their souls, really—would relieve him of the troubling memory of two girls sitting on top of trash bags in the back of a pickup truck in Manshiyat Naser.

But he might get a smaller, more easily portable facsimile of the *Nu* hieroglyph.

The dirt road that curled away to the northeast from Vickery's trailer park was just a flattened track across the desert, paralleling the 15 freeway and a line of power poles to the left. The sun had set, and their path was only discernible as a consistent gap between sparse weeds, but Castine didn't suggest that he turn on the headlights. The dry wind from the south was still warm, blowing sand against the passenger side window until she rolled it up.

"So what do you, you know, *do*," she asked, "in Barstow?" Her voice was resolutely light. "Besides talk to ghosts?"

"Oh," he said, not looking away from the dim path, "under-the-table handyman work and car repair. And I, uh, manage events for the St. Joseph Catholic Church. Retreats, carnivals. Picnics, mostly. And I read a lot."

"No . . . girl?"

"Oh." The question had taken him by surprise, and he didn't look away from the path. "It wouldn't—well, no, nothing serious. I don't think it'd be fair to get a girl involved with . . . "

"Somebody like us."

"Well—right, exactly." He went on quickly, "And I hit the library pretty often, use their computers. I've got the TOR browser on a flash drive, so I can check the deep and dark webs to watch traffic in ghost-inhabited objects—which there's a lot of, actually, and my . . . my copy of *The Secret Garden* might show up on one of those." He smiled uncomfortably. "It's been eight months since I've been able to read to her." He took a deep breath and let it out. "And I'm always careful to delete any traces afterward, and then click through a lot of general news or UFO websites, in case somebody should get curious and look at the computer's history. But I keep searching."

He saw Castine shake her head.

"*And*," he went on stolidly, "yes, I do ask the ghosts about it. I told you they can sometimes sense subsumed entities, personalities— even ones that never—"

"Never actually existed," said Castine.

Vickery nodded. "Pencil notes that never got inked in, on God's ledger. I have to get the ghosts to look past the pinwheels on my trailer roof, but when I've done that they've told me several times that they sense one near the ocean. I've tried to track that one more closely by setting up impromptu nests down south beside the 405 and the 710, but the ghosts there haven't come up with anything more precise—just 'by the sea,' with no details."

He shifted his hands on the wheel—the path slanted away from the freeway here, and a branching path ahead would take them straight to the south side of the overpass.

"Almost there," he said, watching in the dimness for the path. "And now I know a bit more about the people who stole the book. I can ask different questions."

Castine huffed air through her nose. "Sure, you know how a couple of them dress." After a moment she went on, grudgingly, "And, okay, you know it may involve some sort of Egyptian artifact."

"And—maybe—a wrecked old house in a canyon, with a panhead Harley Davidson parked out front, and a long-haired lean-faced guy who stands on the porch."

Castine shifted on the seat to face him. "I never saw that! Was that what you saw when you blanked out in the park this afternoon?"

"Yes. And I was closer to the house than I've been in past visions."

"Oh shit. That means I will be too, next time I see it."

She was silent as he carefully steered to the left onto the side path, toward the freeway, and braked the car to a stop between the weeds, far enough from the bridge so that it wouldn't show in any headlights circling around the offramp.

He picked up a pack of cigarettes from the seat beside him and tucked it into his shirt pocket, then opened his door and stepped out onto the shadowed dirt. The dry wind that stirred his hair smelled faintly of sage.

Castine had got out on her side and plodded around to stand beside him. "Lead the way," she sighed.

Back at the trailer, Vickery had left the little Glock and tucked a Colt Government Model .45 semi-automatic into the pocket of his old corduroy jacket, and had given Castine a .38 Special revolver; and when he pulled his gun out now, she did the same.

"You threaten ghosts with guns?" she whispered as they began walking toward the freeway bridge.

"Sometimes," replied Vickery quietly. "They still know what guns are. But it's always possible that some living person has crawled up onto my shelf, and any such are likely to be as crazy as the ghosts."

The sweep of the curved freeway offramp was up an embankment, and when no oncoming cars were visible, Vickery led Castine around it to the underside of the bridge. They stepped carefully up the dark dirt slope, and Vickery caught Castine's denim-sleeved arm to stop her when they were still a couple of yards short of the shelf at the top. With his free hand he dug a little LED flashlight out of his pocket, and, after glancing back to be sure no cars were in view on the freeway, played its bright beam along the length of the shelf. The only thing visible was a wooden frame halfway along the length of it.

"That's my chicken wire barrier," he said, switching off the flashlight and putting it back in his pocket. All that could be seen now was the dimly starlit pavement out on either side of the bridge. "You can put the gun away," he added, pushing his own .45 into his belt and leaning forward to feel the slope as he climbed. "If you're still hungry," he added, "I've got an old peanut can full of M&Ms up there."

"I'm good," said Castine, following him up to crouch on the narrow strip of flat dirt in almost complete darkness. Their heads brushed the cement underside of the freeway bridge until they sat down.

An eighteen-foot-wide load-bearing wall stood down there at the edge of the freeway, blocking their view of any car that might stop directly below them, but the occasional cars that flashed past were only momentarily eclipsed by it. Vickery dug the cigarette pack out of his pocket.

The close cement slab overhead and the dry dirt they were sitting on were suddenly visible when he snapped a Bic Lighter and lit a cigarette . . . and then lit another, and another. The flame went out, and by feel he pushed the cigarettes through the hexagonal gaps in the chicken-wire barrier; they fell to the dirt on that side and made three glowing red dots in the darkness. He handed Castine the lighter, then groped to the side until he found a can propped against the wall. He popped the plastic lid off it, shook some M&Ms into his hand and tossed them through the wire.

"We could do with a few more cars before we start singing," he said quietly. "A sustained current."

He heard Castine shift around, and then she said, "*Singing*?" Her voice echoed under the bridge, and she went on more softly, "Are you kidding? Singing what?"

A pair of headlights appeared in the west, and shortly another pair was visible behind it.

"The song that works best is 'What a Wonderful World.' You must know it, everybody does."

"Sure, Louis Armstrong, but—what, ghosts like it?"

"Come on, before the cigarettes go out."

Vickery began to sing the wistful, half-melancholy song, and after a few syllables Castine joined in. Vickery couldn't see her face, but her contralto voice blended smoothly with his tenor, and she was evidently enjoying it in spite of herself. Vickery found himself wishing that no conjuring would happen, that they could sing the old song uninterrupted, just the two of them out here in the lonely Mojave Desert.

The cars flashed past under the bridge, briefly hidden behind the wall, and as they reappeared on the other side and receded to the east, something bumped into the chicken wire barrier from the other side.

Their song stopped abruptly, and Vickery heard Castine scramble back away from the barrier.

"I thought you said they weren't substantial now!" she hissed.

"I said less!" whispered Vickery.

And from the other side of the barrier a woman's hoarse voice said, "Don't look at me! I'm dead!"

Vickery made the sign of the cross and took a deep breath. "We can't see you," he said. "Have a cigarette—I lit it for you."

In the darkness, one of the coals on the other side of the chicken wire rose into the air, and when it brightened for a second, Vickery glimpsed a high forehead and glittering eyes between locks of dark hair; then he felt smoky air brush his face and there was nothing to see but the bobbing coal.

Vickery frowned. This was the first time out here that one of them had been able to *pick up* a cigarette; much less actually draw smoke though it. Previously they had just rolled them around in the dirt.

"Thanks," came the voice. "You could be dead too, if you'd just try."

"Not today." He could hear Castine breathing behind him, but aside from the puff of smoke a moment ago, there was no breath audible from the ghost. "Can you see," he went on, "if there are any strings attached to either of us? Or any kind of flags, beepers, beacons? Can people see where we—"

"No, Steve," said the ghost, in a new, breathy voice, "there are no strings tied to you. Not yet."

Vickery recognized the line—Lauren Bacall, in *To Have and Have Not*. He had noticed before that ghosts often quoted bits of dialogue from old movies. Scraps of memory somehow retained.

"There's people trying to find us, this woman and me," he went on. "Can you see them?"

There was silence from the other side of the barrier for so long that Vickery believed the ghost had dissipated; and he jumped when its voice quavered, "Ba ba black sheep, have you any souls?"

The wood-frame barrier creaked, as if the ghost were leaning on it from the other side. Vickery hiked himself back, trying to remember how sturdily he had built it.

We should get out of here, he thought—but if this ghost is more *present* than the others have been, I do have to ask it more questions.

"They have—" Damn, he thought, this would be hard enough with a living person; "—some connection to an old house in a canyon, two stories, and the bottom story is full of sand—"

"Spiral staircase!" called Castine breathlessly.

"Right, it's got a spiral staircase—"

"Spiral is right-twist rifling," said the ghost, speaking more rapidly now. "They fired that once, you know, and they're gonna fire it again. Shut up about it."

"Do you know where it is—"

The scratchy ghost voice interrupted: "I said shut up! If you want to be dead, you better get busy quick."

Again the frame creaked. Move on, Vickery thought.

"Okay," he said as the breeze under the bridge chilled the sweat on his face, "listen, there's a fossil spirit, in a book, *The Secret Garden,* somewhere in the L.A. area. Can you catch any sort of . . . *vibration* from it?"

"I always see the fossil spirits," said the ghost, "dancing on the roof yonder. They only know one dance."

The bottom of the frame slid forward an inch in the dirt, and Vickery braced his foot against it.

"Past them," he said desperately, "by the sea. Can you make out where it is?"

For several second there was silence, except for the windy rush of a car, and a few moments later another, speeding past under the bridge.

Then, "The whole world is lit up," said the ghost with something like a gasp, though the night beyond the bridge was as dark as ever. Then a man's harsh voice, somehow familiar to Vickery, said, "It's on a boat, among a lot of boats, and . . . a crowd of people falling into the black hole, a shape with a hawk body and the head of a man, a gaze blank and pitiless as the sun . . . "

Castine leaned forward and gripped Vickery's shoulder. "Some people in Los Angeles," she said quickly, "have an Egyptian artifact—"

A scream like a circular saw biting into sheet steel sent Vickery lurching back against Castine. The scream broke up into shrill, imbecilic laughter that echoed back from the close cement surfaces, and now there seemed to be a number of figures on the far side of the chicken-wire, all thrashing and grunting. The wooden frame fell right over onto Vickery, and he tried to shove it back in place as irregular impacts from the other side pushed it toward him.

"Math," said Castine in the darkness; then in a louder voice, "Two and two is four!"

"Four subtracted from four," shouted Vickery, "is nothing! Check it out!"

But the ghosts clearly weren't listening.

"*Ba, Ba!*" another voice was yelling, and a woman's voice, not the one that had been speaking a few moments ago, wailed, "Quoth the raven!" followed by a mumbled word that Vickery thought might have ben *Nevermore*, and then wailed "Its hour come round again!"

Again the frame creaked.

Over the increasing tumult Vickery could hear wet things slapping against the chicken wire, and he knew it was the elongated, ice-cold ectoplasmic tongues of the maddened ghosts. He was still holding the chicken-wire barrier in place, and before he could pull his fingers free, one of the tongues touched the knuckles of his right hand; his hand was suddenly numbed and aching, and he lost his balance.

He thrashed convulsively, brushing long, tangled hair away from his somehow sunken face, and his right foot slipped off the ledge and bent like putty on the dirt slope—and the realization crashed in on him that he was now *on the other side of the barrier*, while his body was still over there beside Castine. Soft, grunting shapes crowded against his back and shoulders.

His breath was now rasping in an insubstantial throat that was not his own, but he managed to choke out the syllables, "*Skeet shooting, help!*"

Over the bestial cries of the ghosts around him, he heard Castine gasp. Then the lighter flame flared up, and he saw that she was holding up her free hand with two fingers extended.

Vickery quailed to see his own body over there with her on the other side of the chicken-wire; it was crawling clumsily past Castine, away from the light.

She didn't glance at it. "Two," she said loudly, then raised her other two fingers in the light, "plus two, is four, and nothing else! See?"

The flame wavered as her hand shook, but she closed her free hand in a fist and said, "Minus four—is nothing! Look! Nothing!"

And then, with a mental and physical jolt, Vickery was on his hands and knees behind her. He looked over his shoulder and saw Castine's crouching silhouette against the glow of the lighter.

"I'm here," he gasped, "it's me, Vickery. Down the slope, back to the car. Fast."

"Thank God." The light went out, and when, above the groaning and weeping of the turbulent ghosts, he heard her sliding away below, he dove down after her as things snatched ineffectively at his heels.

As he slid head-first down the dirt incline, the wall and the underside of the bridge were suddenly lit with a yellow glow, and he guessed that at least one of the ghosts up on the ledge had burst into flame.

He hit the base of the wall with his outstretched hands and let his flexing elbows absorb the impact, and then he had rolled over and got his legs under himself and was running out from under the bridge, following Castine, who was sprinting away across the open dirt a few yards ahead of him. He was panting, and the cold air stung his throat.

When he caught up with her he grabbed her hand to lead her toward the car—

And all at once the world was bathed in coppery light, and Castine squeezed his hand tightly as they both slid to a halt.

The freeway bridge was no longer visible to Vickery's left; and he could feel Castine's hand, but he appeared to be standing by himself in a narrow valley, once again facing the crooked old two-story house. Its porch steps were only a few yards away.

The motorcycle was now parked off to the left, and the shadow of it was longer. Three people were standing on the wide porch this time, and Vickery's field of vision swiveled involuntarily from side to side to see each of them: at the left end stood a woman in a long robe, and at the other, two men. One of the men leaned against the slanted railing, his face hidden in the shadow of a cowboy hat, and the other, in the familiar Nehru jacket, was the man Vickery had seen here before. That man's right arm was extended toward the woman, and he was holding a revolver.

Vickery yelled and started forward, dragging the invisible Castine by the hand, but the house didn't draw closer, and of course none of the figures on the porch could hear or see him.

CHAPTER FIVE:
Regressively Indiv

By feel, for he had no visible body in this hallucination, Vickery pulled the .45 out from behind his belt with his left hand and flicked down the tight safety lever. He couldn't see his arm or the gun, but the textured grip felt solid as he extended his invisible hand in the direction of the porch, between the woman and the two men, and the ridged trigger was pressed firmly against his finger as he squeezed it.

The grip punched back into his palm in recoil, but there was no sound, and the three people didn't react.

The arm of the man with the revolver jerked upward, and Vickery did hear that shot—as a stuttering rumble—and the woman at the other end of the porch rocked her head back and then collapsed.

Castine's hand twisted free of his own. He turned his head, but the scene didn't shift from in front of his eyes—he was still helplessly staring at the house; peripheral vision showed him nothing but trees and the close hills in the sepia light.

The man in the leather jacket had lowered the gun, and now said something. The words were muffled—something like *haddock tucker lud bishop*—but in this dim interlude the gunshot had been no louder. The man laughed, which sounded like someone trying to start a car with a nearly dead battery, and turned away, toward the front door of the house.

And then the world went dark, with a flickering glare off to

Vickery's left. He swung his head that way, and now his view matched the way he was facing; he saw the freeway overpass, with a few flames still visible at the top of the slope underneath it. He looked in the other direction, out across the dark desert, and hoarsely called, "Castine!"

"Here," came her voice from ahead of him. His night vision was not impaired by the just-closed hallucination, and he saw her silhouette standing among the weeds a dozen yards off. She added, "Are you okay?"

Vickery took a deep breath and let it out, and spat to get rid of the imagined taste of ghost saliva. Two and two is four, he thought. "I guess so."

"Where the hell's your car?"

He gingerly tucked his hot gun back into his belt and trudged up to her and extended his hand.

She shied back and glanced toward the weakly underlit bridge. "I don't think you should touch me skin-to-skin. Look what just happened."

Vickery closed his hand. "You may be right." He yawned widely enough to creak his jaw. "The car. Right, the car's over here."

He led the way across the weeds to his old white Saturn; the flames under the bridge had subsided, and the car was now the most visible thing in the nighted landscape. Castine hurried around to the passenger side, but stopped abruptly and drew her revolver, ducking below the rear fender.

Vickery had seen her and heard her cock the gun, and he drew his own gun again and crouched, looking around and groping in his pocket with his free hand for the flashlight. He was breathing deeply, forcing alertness.

He heard Castine's harsh whisper: "Somebody's shot out your rear side window!" After a moment she added, "Both of them, left and right!"

Vickery had got his flashlight out when he paused, and then relaxed.

"It's okay," he said, straightening up, "I think I did it myself."

"No, they weren't broken when we drove out here! Stay down!"

"Were you—in that vision, just now? The old house, the people on the porch?"

"Yes! That man shot that woman! Will you get *down*?"

"I pulled my gun and shot at the house door—as best I could—to get his attention—make him drop the revolver. But of course it had no effect *there*."

"Oh!" She stood up from behind the car, lowering the gun. "I didn't hear your shot . . . no, of course not. I did hear his." She was facing him over the car's roof. "Are you sure you're okay? Some ghost *switched places* with you, for God's sake!"

"Yes, I'm fine, or okay, at least. Thank you for the . . . visibly empirical math."

"You're welcome." She opened the passenger side door, glancing back at the rear side window. "In one and out the other. Lucky you didn't hit the gas tank." She slid onto the seat and pulled the door closed. Vickery heard a rattle of glass falling out of the rear windows.

"Too bad I wasn't able to save that woman," he said as he climbed in on his side and started the engine.

"I think it was a long time ago," Castine said as Vickery carefully backed the car around and then drove forward along the dirt track. "And the visions aren't time travel, just—like you said, echoes." She dropped the revolver onto the floor and wiped her hands on her new blouse. "I *hate* ghosts!"

Vickery's hands were sweating too, and he knew they'd be trembling if they weren't clamped on the steering wheel.

Castine was peering ahead. "Still no headlights?"

"Especially now, if somebody reports a fire under the bridge. I think at least one of the ghosts got excited to the point of ignition."

Castine's breathing gradually slowed. Finally she burst out, "*Not substantial!*"

"They weren't like this before, not anything like this." He gulped against a surge of nausea. "It's as if they've found a fresh 120-volt socket to plug into."

"Or a black hole. Did you hear what the leather jacket guy said, after he shot that woman?"

"I couldn't make it out."

"He said, 'Had to take her blood pressure.'"

Vickery was concentrating entirely on seeing the faint path. "Let's talk when we're back in the trailer."

She nodded, staring ahead. "Where the fossil spirits dance on the roof. I want to go *home*."

The trailer still smelled of fried bacon and onions, and Vickery decided the pan and the dishes could wait till morning. He saw Castine sniffing as she stepped into the living room and sat down on the couch, and he hoped she found the familiar domestic smells as reassuring as he did.

He dropped ice cubes into two fresh glasses and carried them and the bottle into the living room and set it all down on the coffee table. "Help yourself," he said as he lowered himself stiffly into an easy chair.

Castine was frowning at him. "I don't think you should go to your damn freeway nest anymore."

"Two minds with but a single thought," he said, leaning forward to pour bourbon into one of the glasses. "All we learned about the echo-vision house—"

"If we learned anything."

Vickery bobbed his head in acknowledgment. "If anything," he went on, "is that it was 'fired' once, whatever that might mean, and will be again. Right-twist rifling refers to the grooves—"

"In a gun barrel, I know."

"Okay." Vickery leaned back. "That was Yeats, sort of, what that first ghost was quoting." He handed her the bottle.

She went on frowning at him for a moment, then relaxed. "I know that too. 'Somewhere in sands of the desert'—but it's supposed to be 'a shape with a *lion* body and the head of a man,' not a hawk body— 'is moving its slow thighs, while all about it reel the indignant shadows of the desert birds.' And it's supposed to be, 'What rough beast, its hour come round at last, slouches toward Bethlehem to be born.'" She had poured a good two inches into her own glass, and drank a third of it in one swallow. "*Whew!* And—something about a crowd of people falling into a black hole."

"It was a man's voice, that said that." Vickery lifted his glass and swallowed a mouthful of the bourbon, and sighed as he felt it begin to relax him. "Did you recognize it? I think I did."

After a pause, she said, "That old guy, Laquedem." She sat back and stared at the stained ceiling. "So he obviously died, sometime in this last year. Well—God rest his soul."

"Wherever it is," agreed Vickery.

"So," Castine went on, "you've found him in Barstow after all. Your think he knew he was talking to us?"

Vickery shrugged, remembering the gruff old man they'd met last year. "Poor old Laquedem. Setting fires under a freeway bridge in the desert now."

"His ghost isn't him."

"I know, it's just a thing that thinks it's him." Vickery looked around at his modest living room and wondered if some freeway gypsy might one day summon *his* ghost—a half-wit revenant believing it was still Sebastian Vickery, trying in its imbecilic way to meet uncomprehended goals, straining uselessly to convey broken thoughts to actual, living people.

Castine might have been thinking along the same lines. "It's a bad deal, for sure," she said; and when Vickery raised his eyebrows, she added, "Death."

In a fruity, affected voice, he said, "Death is a *natural* part of *life*."

"It's not, though," she said. "According to Genesis, we weren't originally meant to experience it . . . that sundering, cleaving . . . soul and body torn apart . . . ghost fragments spinning away from the wreckage. If Adam and Eve hadn't screwed up, it wouldn't happen to us."

"At least we get to exist," said Vickery, thinking of his never-conceived daughter.

Castine took a breath, then just let in out in a sigh.

For half a minute neither of them spoke, and the hum of the air conditioner was the only sound.

Vickery stirred and said, "My daughter is on a boat. Among a lot of other boats. That sounds like a marina."

"Your nonexistent daughter. Fossilized now in a paperback book. Yes." Castine set down her glass and looked around the room. "Do you even have a TV?"

"In the bedroom. No cable, though, I just watch DVDs." He stretched, and said, "Your friend with the red suspenders was outside my apartment when that copy of *The Secret Garden* was taken. Why would they take that?"

She spread the fingers of one hand. "Ransom, I imagine—coercion—to get you to do something you wouldn't want to do. But you evaded them and then disappeared, so they weren't able to tell you their terms. And so you didn't have to do something you didn't want to do."

Vickery nodded and took a deeper gulp of his drink. "I do wonder, though, if they wanted it for *its own* sake, somehow. I told you I made another stop before I left L.A. eight months ago and became Bill Ardmore."

Castine set down her glass and laid back on the couch. "You went to see your old boss, Galvan."

"Right. I was still occasionally driving for her then, taking such supernatural-evasion fares as still came along . . . and doing occasional retro-surveillance jobs . . . even working in her fleet of taco trucks, sometimes. Anyway, I asked her if she knew anything about my book being stolen, and she got all huffy and said she didn't know my *Secret Garden* was any more a secret than it was a garden. And she told me—"

"Some guy who collected fossilized spirits asked if she knew of any for sale. And she told him about your book. I remember."

Vickery idly moved his glass in a circle on the table. "And Galvan was the only one, besides you and me, who even *knew* about the book."

"Along with some of her family, you recall."

"Well, yeah . . . and Galvan was known to have dealings in supernatural stuff, so I guess it makes sense that a collector of such things would approach her. But the guy was clearly, or probably, with this group that was after us today. Galvan pointed them to my book."

"Innocently—"

Castine had started to say the word as a statement, but the last syllable went up in pitch, making it a question.

"She kind of blew it off," said Vickery, "when I asked her about it, like I'd lost a souvenir pen or something. I assumed she was embarrassed at having told a thief where to find it." He laughed briefly. "Especially without her getting a cut."

"Unless, I suppose, she did get a cut."

Vickery drained his glass, and it clanked when he set it down on the table. "She gave me a description of this alleged collector. Now I think she was just describing Harry Dean Stanton. She was a big fan of *Repo Man*."

Castine yawned. "Doesn't matter either way, now. She told the guy, and they've got it. On a boat, maybe."

She reached across for her glass and tipped it up to her mouth. The ice cubes rattled against her teeth as she finished it, and she caught one and began chewing it.

Vickery shivered. "I wish you wouldn't do that. Chew your ice cubes," he added when she gave him a blank look.

"I wasn't," she said. "Anyway, you do it yourself."

"I never—" he began, then remembered doing it right here, less than an hour ago, before they'd set out for the nest under the bridge. "Must be a nervous habit," he finished lamely.

"Whatever." She put the glass back and wiped her face with the sleeve of her jacket. "It seems to me," she said, "that taking somebody's blood pressure must be slang for killing them. And you remember that disoriented girl on the bicycle at the park? She said, 'We could have taken her blood pressure any time.' I think she was channeling one of those people who were at Canter's, and I think that person was pretty clearly talking about me."

Vickery pursed his lips and nodded.

"I wonder," said Castine, "if Omar Khayyam would still give us those funds he mentioned."

"Omar Sharif," corrected Vickery with a tired smile. "We never did learn his actual name. But I know where the Egyptian Consulate is. I picked up a few fares there, when I was a driver for Galvan."

Castine sat up. "Let's just go. Away. Get on a plane tomorrow and fly to Maryland, and there'll be a huge curvature of the earth between us and all this dreadful stuff. We were lucky today—guys were waving guns around! A ghost possessed you!"

"We'd still have the echo-visions. Or old-house visions, as they are these days."

"Those are bound to stop, eventually, and it's long ago stuff anyway." She looked straight at him and spoke clearly. "Your daughter, the daughter you didn't even have, is oblivious to everything, you *know* that. Even if they, I don't know, *burn* the book, it won't change her situation one bit."

"That *is* true," he conceded.

She looked down into her empty glass. "I could even put you up, till you found an apartment."

No . . . girl? thought Vickery. "I might even be able to hold your hand without setting off hallucinations."

"Worth a try. Then." Hurriedly she went on, "Omar did say he had the situation well in hand, didn't he?"

"Over in a few days, he said." Vickery shrugged. "If we stay, we'd probably only get in his way, mess up his plans."

Castine waved around at the furniture and the peel-and-stick *faux* wood paneling. "I hate to ask you to give up all this."

"My space rent's paid up through next month. I can come back after it's all blown over, if I want to." He yawned. "We can stop at Hesperia on the way to LAX, and pick up your clothes and billfold."

Castine got unsteadily to her feet. "I said I could sleep on the couch."

"You're the guest, you get the bed. I'll put fresh sheets on it." He stood up and walked down the narrow hall to the shelf that served as a linen closet. Behind him he could hear Castine humming "What A Wonderful World."

The tall windows in the bottom three floors of Clifton's Cafeteria were outlined in red and yellow neon, and the marquee projecting out over the Broadway sidewalk held back the Los Angeles night with a white glare that was reflected in the roofs of passing cars. Looking down on the pillars and cornices from a fire-escape balcony on the fifth level of the parking structure across the street, Elisha Ragotskie thought the place looked like one of the movie palaces of the 1920s.

He stepped back through the broad window opening, into the humbler glow of widely-spaced lights in the cement ceiling. Not many cars were parked on this level yet, and he wheeled his bicycle into the shadows behind a van parked next to the north wall. It was a second-hand Schwinn ten-speed bicycle, with canvas pannier bags, that he had bought for cash four hours ago, feeling safer away from his too-recognizable Audi. His white shirt was still damp with sweat and he was shivering in the evening breeze that whispered through the big open windows in the street-side wall. He had thrown away the red suspenders.

He was carrying two cell phones: his Samsung and a new prepaid TracFone. By touch he pried open the back of the Samsung and took its battery out of his shirt pocket; and when he clicked the battery into place in the phone, snapped the cover shut and thumbed the phone on, the screen soon glowed sky blue in the shadows behind the van. When he touched the Messages icon, the top text was from Agnes—she had finally replied to his several texts.

OK, read her text from an hour ago, *where? And what did you do?*

He entered the words, *You pick—one of our places—familiar—food, drinks—whatever you've heard, I can explain. Trust.*

Her reply was immediate: *OK—n/naka on Overland.*

Sweating in spite of the cold, he tapped in, *Feeling more occidental—the Rose?* The Rose was in Venice, and he knew she had been to the beach with the twins today, and wouldn't relish driving back out there.

Occidental, you mean, came her reply. *Too far. Tesse, Clifton's, Pizzana?*

He exhaled in relief, and tapped in, *Pizzana sounds good* and sent it; then immediately typed in, *No, Clifton's is better. Drinks at the 2nd floor bar—alone, off the record!*

He had first kissed her in that mellowly lit cathedral of a bar, just a few steps from the huge redwood tree that extended up through all the floors, at a table beside a stuffed deer in a glassed-in diorama.

Agreed, came her reply. *When?*

I can be there in half an hour.

See you then.

He turned off the phone and leaned back against the wall, breathing hard. She *might* come alone, he told himself, as she agreed to. Maybe I still mean a bit more to her than oblivion does.

Agnes Loria had been a philosophy major at UCLA when Ragotskie met her, and she had already been inclined toward the pragmatic sorts of mysticism—she had progressed from the psychic training methods described in Alexandra David-Neel's *Magic and Mystery in Tibet* to Guillaume Cendre-Benir's *Technomancy* and the post-modern techniques of chaos magic, and claimed to have seen the future through the Burroughs method of reading random reassemblies of cut-up texts. She said the future was blurry.

They had met at the Conscious Life Expo at the LAX Hilton in February of last year. She had been standing outside by the valet parking line, smoking a cigarette—"I've moved past any concern for my individual body," she had told him when he asked her about the cigarette. He had found her individual body compellingly attractive, though—she was tall, her figure willowy and athletic, and her green eyes under chestnut bangs seemed deeper and more expressive than those of anyone else he'd ever met.

He had lately moved down to Los Angeles from San Jose, along with the rest of Harlowe's ChakraSys team, and he dropped a few hints about their work and their goal—and Agnes had seized on it. She had described their meeting as synchronicity, and within a week the two of them had moved into an Echo Park apartment together.

And at first Agnes had found him fascinating. Many of his interests were in fields new to her, and she was a voracious pupil. Poetry and painting left her baffled, but semiconductor electronics and the formal logic of computer coding excited her enormously. The only classical music she had ever heard had been snippets in movie soundtracks and advertisements, and she gratefully followed Ragotskie's guidance into the works of Tchaikovsky, Beethoven, Rimsky-Korsakov, Wagner . . . though she hadn't cared for the austerity of Bach or Vivaldi. She told him one time that the great symphonies were superior to any literature, since they were emotional but not discernibly about people, and didn't involve the language and vocabulary of the listener.

But she had progressed in the Singularity disciplines faster than Ragotskie himself. Ego-death, the dark night of the soul, was something she seemed to crave; unlike Ragotskie, who, despite his best efforts, still clung to a lot of affective aspects of his particular existence—especially his growing affection for the particular person who was Agnes Loria.

She had soon come to find his feelings for her, and her own feelings for him, "regressively indiv," and a week ago she had moved out of the apartment, and wouldn't tell him where she was staying now. She yearned to subsume herself in the Singularity, the big egregore that was taking form from the minds of the group— "gestating and gestalting," as Harlowe put it.

Ragotskie had been resolutely willing to let his own personality be dissolved in the transcendently greater entity which would be the egregore, but he had found that he could not bear the prospect of Agnes Loria ceasing to be specifically and fascinatingly herself.

And so today he had broken ranks—and how. He had thrown away his chance at a kind of immortality, not to mention his career with ChakraSys, and possibly his life—and made himself the enemy of Simon Harlowe and probably of Agnes Loria too. And for nothing—he had used up his cyanide and lost his gun, and when he had tried to use the bloody sock pendulum to find the Castine woman again, he'd discovered that the job really called for a second person, to navigate; the necessity of pulling into a parking lot every few blocks to consult the thing had made it hopeless.

Now he shook off those uncomfortable memories and pocketed his phones and stepped out from behind the van. He crossed the cement floor and stepped over the window sill and stood again in the chilly breeze on the fire-escape balcony, looking down at the traffic on Seventh Street and the glowing façade of Clifton's. He would recognize Agnes' station wagon when it turned in to the parking structure entrance on the street directly below; he would recognize Harlowe's gray Chevy Tahoe SUV, too, if it were to show up, but Harlowe would surely still be pursuing Castine and Vickery, even without the bloody sock as a pointer.

But with any luck Castine and Vickery would elude Harlowe— Harlowe had certainly lost what he liked to call the elephant of surprise, and those two seemed adept at running and hiding—and then Ragotskie's clumsy attempts at assassination would have accomplished his purpose after all, without his having to kill anybody. The egregore would fail without the IMPs, and Agnes would surely be able to free herself from it then, and remain the precious individual that she had always been—even though she'd have preferred it otherwise.

In order to emerge as a rational, self-consistent entity, the egregore would need to incorporate a reciprocating pair of special people—what Harlowe fancifully referred to as a couple of IMPs. IMP was an acronym for Interface Message Processor, which, in the early days of computers, was a kind of mini-computer that allowed many different sorts of computers to function together as a single network, and maximized internet communications. Routers served the purpose now.

The various minds that would constitute the emerging egregore would need to be able to function together as facets of a single entity, pulses that could be applied anywhere in the system at any time. The structure, the entity, would need IMPs.

Castine and Vickery would have been ideal. Their psychic foundations had been shifted by whatever it was that happened to them last year—Harlowe's man Foster said they died and came back from the afterlife—and it had left them insecurely moored in *now*. Unlike normal people, Castine and Vickery were at least potentially in several moments at once, like figures in a time-lapse photograph. Integrated together into the egregore, they might very well have been able to operate across several seconds simultaneously, anticipate thought-signals that hadn't even been sent yet, and make the egregore's mentation instantaneous.

Ragotskie wished them well in their continued evasion of Simon Harlowe.

A car that looked like Agnes' station wagon swung into view on the street below, and the breath caught in Ragotskie's throat—but the car drove on past the parking entrance, and before it disappeared around the Seventh Street corner he saw that it was white, not yellow.

She might not appear at all, he thought. She might simply have called Harlowe and told him to find me at Clifton's and deal with me.

But five minutes later a yellow station wagon slowed directly below, and it disappeared into the parking structure entrance. Ragotskie waited until he could hear the car's tires squealing on the polished cement as it rounded the turns from one level up to the next, and then he hurried back to crouch beside the bicycle, between the van and the wall.

Soon he heard the rumbling of a car engine echoing on this level, and after a few seconds it switched off and he heard a door clank open. He raised his head enough to see through the van's side windows, and it was Agnes, alone, closing the door of her car.

Ragotskie had to force himself not to stand up and speak to her.

She looked toward the fire escape, then turned and scanned the several parked cars; Ragotskie ducked down before her gaze swept the van. He heard her walk to the elevator in the far corner, and after a few seconds he heard the elevator doors open and then close.

She was about twenty minutes early.

Ragotskie stood up. He was actually considering wheeling his bicycle back into the elevator and going down to meet her at the restaurant after all—he had bought a cable and lock, and could secure the bicycle to a lamp post—when he heard another car coming up the ramps.

He hesitated, then crouched behind the van again.

The engine noise expanded out of the ramp tunnel, and then a car idled to a halt on this level, and this time he heard two doors open and close, and the unmistakable knock of Harlowe's cowboy boot heels.

"He won't be here for a while yet," came Harlowe's well remembered voice. "Taitz, wait here, you know his car—watch this level and the ones immediately below and above, and taser him if he shows up. Foster, you come with me."

Ragotskie heard footsteps knock across the cement floor in the direction of the elevator, and soon he heard its doors open and close again. He managed, an inch at a time, to shift his feet and sit down without making a sound. After a while he was wrinkling his nose at the scent of cigarette smoke on the breeze that found its way to the space behind the van.

Ragotskie imagined Taitz standing out there in the middle of the floor, or leaning against the balcony rail with his back to the street, the olive-green windbreaker tight across his shoulders, his narrow eyes watching the ramps and the stairs and the elevator doors. His right hand might be in his pocket, holding the pistol-grip of the taser.

Ragotskie shivered as he recalled breaking the window of Harlowe's SUV and stealing the wooden box with the bloody sock in it. Taitz must certainly be angry.

By his estimation ten minutes passed before Taitz moved to the stairs; and the scuff of his footsteps was diminishing downward.

When Ragotskie judged that Taitz had reached the bottom of the stairs and was looking around at the cars and the ramp on that level, he quickly pulled out both of his phones, and he tapped the number of the TracFone burner phone into his Samsung; sweat made rainbow sparkles on the screen. When the burner phone jingled, he hastily swiped the screen to open the connection, then stepped out from behind the van and hurried across the floor to Agnes' car.

It was locked, but he scuttled around and crouched by the front bumper, and he held both phones in one hand while he groped under the bumper—whispering curses—until he found the magnetic box that contained a spare key.

His breath was rushing in and out through his open mouth as he scrambled to his feet, and he had to stab the key at the door lock twice before it rattled in; and as he turned it, the sound of the lock post snapping up was immediately followed by the tap of footsteps on the stairs.

Ragotskie levered open the car door and dropped the TracFone burner into the map pocket, then eased the door shut and darted back to his refuge in the shadows behind the van. Sweat ran into his eyes, and the effort of keeping his breath slow and shallow made his throat ache. Planting the phone had been a risky move, but, with a call in progress, it was a good microphone—Agnes always used the Waze app on an iPad to know what route to take when she was going anywhere, and he hoped to overhear the Waze voice's directions as it guided her to wherever she was living now.

The soft tap of shoes had reached this level, and moved out across the floor.

A sudden thought made Ragotskie's ears ring—in his haste a few moments ago, he had left the empty magnetic box on the cement floor by the right from tire of Agnes' car.

But the cool breeze again carried the smell of cigarette smoke. Ragotskie let his muscles relax, very slowly.

And he jumped when he heard Taitz's voice say, loudly, "What?" For several seconds Ragotskie just held his breath, and even closed his eyes; then Taitz said, "He probably saw you guys." Evidently Taitz' phone had been set to vibrate, so there had been no ringtone for Ragotskie to hear. "He would have called her if he was just delayed . . . yeah, ten more minutes."

With his teeth clenched and his eyes still closed, Ragotskie began mentally counting seconds; and he had counted off fifteen minutes' worth before the elevator doors audibly slid open and the footsteps of several people advanced across the cement floor. The rap of Harlowe's boot heels raised echoes.

Ragotskie winced to hear Agnes' voice, but he couldn't make out the words, and he hoped fervently that she would walk straight to the driver's side door of her car and not notice the empty magnetic box on the cement floor on the other side.

But he heard her car door slam, loudly in the air and more muffled from the speaker of his Samsung phone. He hastily covered the speaker slot with his thumb. Both cars started up, and tires squeaked as the drivers backed and filled to turn toward the descending ramp.

When the sounds of the car engines had diminished away below, Ragotskie slid the phone into his shirt pocket and stood up. There was no one to be seen on this level now. He thought about crossing to the balcony and peeking over the rail to see the cars exit onto Broadway, but the idea of Harlowe glancing up and seeing him made him shudder and discard the idea.

He stretched, rotating his head on his stiff neck, then finally wheeled his bicycle out from behind the van—but before he could start toward the elevator a cheerful voice spoke from the phone in his shirt pocket.

"Are you going home?" it asked. Ragotskie recognized it as the automated voice of the Waze app, and he hastily fumbled the phone to his ear. "Turn right on Broadway," the voice said. "In one hundred feet, turn right on Eighth Street."

Two seconds later he heard the chime of Agnes' phone.

"Yo, Simon," said her voice then. The burner TracFone in the map pocket of her passenger side door was picking her up clearly.

The calm voice of the Waze app interjected, "Turn right on Eighth Street."

"That's just Waze," said Agnes' voice. Ragotskie could clearly hear th ticking of her turn signal. "Listen, I could text him. Even if he did see Foster, he'll still agree to meet me. I'll make up some explanation, and he'll believe it. He's in *love* with me." Her tone was only amused.

Ragotskie carefully laid his thumb over the tiny microphone slot. Then he let himself take a hitching breath.

"In one mile, turn left to the 110 freeway south," advised the Waze voice.

"I know," said Agnes' voice now, "the sock. I'll get it back from him." After a few seconds she said, "The *twins*? Instead of Vickery and Castine? Uh—hah!—are you *sure*?" She was silent for several seconds, then went on, "I know, but—well, okay, you're our Pygmalion here. How's young Pratt? I hear Vickery knocked him out, at Canter's." For several seconds she didn't speak; then she said, "Good God. Open his skull?" Again she was silent, while Waze droned on about the freeway. "Okay," Agnes said at last, "bye for now."

Ragotskie heard her phone thump on the passenger seat, and then the rasp of a cigarette lighter.

The twins? he thought in dismay. No, he can't—if he uses *them* as his IMPs, I have no hope of having accomplished anything. I've only made it worse—Agnes will still lose her identity in the egregore, but now its IMPs will be the delusional and capricious Amber and Lexi. Imps for real.

He could see Harlowe's reasoning. The twins did have the useful quality of diffraction—nobody, including the girls themselves, could tell which of them was which, or where one personality ended and the other began. Merged into the egregore, they should in theory find no difficulty in rapidly switching the group-mind's theses and antitheses back and forth through their uniquely open-ended identity.

But they weren't sane.

The Waze app spoke up, advising her to make a left turn onto the freeway. Ragotskie made a mental note of the route she was taking, though it would be the last couple of turns and street names that would be important. And when he had learned what street she lived on, he would again take the battery out of his Samsung.

After more than a minute her voice said, "Move it, shithead!"

Apparently she was addressing another driver. Waze continued to indicate directions, but it occurred to Ragotskie that *Move it, shithead* might be the last words he would ever hear Agnes Loria say.

More than a hundred miles to the northeast, out in the desert beyond the Cajon Pass, Ingrid Castine finally fell asleep in Vickery's single bed.

For an hour she had lain awake in the darkness, listening to the faint buzz of the pinwheels on the trailer's roof, and listening too, in her mind, to what she had said to Vickery this afternoon: *Socrates said the unconsidered life is not worth living, but that's what I want. Wanted.*

She wondered where the old house in their visions might be, and she tried to remember what echo vision had been like, before the views of the house had pre-empted it. Even then, she had resented the intrusion of the past.

She didn't like to consider the past at all. Nor the future, really.

Last year her deceased fiancé had knowingly directed her into a trap, because he'd been threatened with disbarment and possible tax-fraud charges if he did not. He had reacted as her pursuers had known he would—he had thought to save himself a lot of bad trouble by betraying her—though in fact they had killed him in spite of his contemptible cooperation.

She fell asleep thinking of him, wondering if his ghost had been in the afterworld Labyrinth when she and Vickery had been there alive. The two of them had escaped in a makeshift hang-glider and closed the conduit between that insane world and the normal one—had they sealed his ghost in, on that side?

Would she have wanted instead to subsume his ghost in some unliving organic object on this side, like the bits of bone or wood in the hubs of the pinwheels, or the book in which Vickery's nonexistent daughter was fossilized?

In her dream she hovered over an enormous open book, and she could see that its pages were filled with columns of what she knew were names, though their letters were too blurred and overlapped to be readable. And she knew that she could relax and merge into the pages, and that her name, itself safely indecipherable there, would be all that remained of her. Not just the unexamined life, but the unconscious life; the *un*life life, in fact.

The book's pages fluttered as if in a randomizing wind, and it rose upright and was a pinwheel, spinning in bright moonlight. She drifted toward its hub, knowing that she could dance unaware in it forever, but she glanced sideways—other pinwheels stood nearby, and though they were spinning, she was able to recognize faces in the hubs—Jack Hipple, yes, . . . but also the girl who had stopped her bicycle and spoken a cryptical phrase at MacArthur Park this afternoon, and Supergirl . . . and the faces were all contorted in imbecilic grimaces.

She recoiled into wakefulness, and after a few panicky moments remembered where she was. She though of getting up and going to the living room and waking Vickery, but the memory of the dream had faded to a few meaningless images. She fluffed the pillow and rolled over and went back to sleep.

CHAPTER SIX:
How You Get Out of Your Way

At 6 AM Vickery had tucked the .45 into his belt and trudged around the trailer park and looked up and down the road, but the cars in the park were all familiar, and there were no vehicles stopped alongside the road for as far as he could see. The October wind had still been cool over the desert, and he had gone back to the trailer and opened all the windows and turned on fans to blow the stale air out. Finally he had carried gloves and a whiskbroom and dustpan out to the Saturn and punched out the remaining glass in the two back windows and swept out the interior, and had then gone in to wash the dishes and make breakfast.

He was standing by the stove, turning sizzling strips of bacon in a pan, when he felt warmer air puff in through the kitchen window, so he took the pan off the burner and closed the window, then went around taking fans down and sliding windows shut in the utility area and the living room. The bedroom door was closed, and he was reluctant to knock, though he would have to as soon as the bacon and eggs were ready.

But Castine came shuffling into the kitchen as he was using the rim of a tumbler to cut disks out of the middles of two slices of sourdough bread.

"I smell coffee," she said, squinting at him.

He poured a cup and stepped past her to set it on the table. "Milk and sugar are already out. Silverware is in the basket by the condiments."

She stirred two spoonfuls of sugar into the coffee and took a sip. "What are you cutting holes in bread for?"

"It's Guy Kibbee eggs." He forked the bacon strips out onto paper towels, lifted the pan and poured most of the grease into a jar, then laid the slices of bread in the pan and broke an egg into the hole in the middle of each one. "I'll flip 'em in a minute. You get your egg and toast all in one piece, see."

She nodded grudgingly and had another sip of coffee. "You've looked around?"

Vickery refilled his own cup from the pot. "Yes, just after dawn." He shrugged. "Evidently nobody could see us over the curvature of the earth."

"The way you live out here," she said. "It's as if you've been marking time. Waiting."

He was mildly startled. "It could look that way, yes."

"I suppose I've been doing the same, after all." She set down her cup and ran her fingers through her disordered hair. "It's a long drive to LAX."

"Ontario airport is just eighty miles south. Hour and a half drive, even with a stop at Hesperia to retrieve your stuff from the bus station locker."

"Oh." She yawned. "We should check flights, I suppose."

Vickery flipped the slices of bread. The top sides now were browned, and the eggs in the middles were white with yellow centers. "Can't do it here. I've got no computer or smart phone."

"Time yet for a hundred indecisions," she said, "and for a hundred visions and revisions, before the taking of Guy Kibbee eggs and coffee." She looked up at him. "That's T.S. Eliot, except for the eggs and coffee."

Vickery laid bacon strips on two plates, then slid the egg-and-toast slices alongside. He carried them to the table and went back for his coffee, and when he sat down he said, "Indecisions?"

"And visions!—and revisions." She had found a knife and fork in the basket of mismatched silverware, and cut into her fried bread. "What was it Laquedem said last night? Right after 'it's on a boat'— something about 'a crowd of people falling into the black hole.'"

"That's what he said. He didn't say anything *about* it."

Castine nodded and shook Tabasco and then salt onto her cut-up egg. "That guy shot that woman, in the wrecked-house vision last night."

"Echo vision. A time-spike. As you said, it probably happened a long time ago."

"Imagine if we tried to tell the police about it—'In a hallucination we saw a woman get killed somewhere, sometime.'" She took a bite and chewed thoughtfully. She swallowed, and said, "But it did happen. I wonder who she was. Who *he* was."

"No way of telling."

"Probably not. Old betrayals." Castine glanced past him at the kitchen counter, where the bottle of Maker's Mark still stood, visibly depleted. "It would be a mistake to fortify this coffee."

He rocked his head, considering. "You don't need to be very sober just to get on an airplane."

"If we do get on an airplane." She put down her knife and fork. "Last night we were closer to the old house than we've ever been; and did you see the motorcycle's shadow? It was longer, it's late afternoon on that day now. That long day. And the killer said he took that woman's blood pressure, which is the same phrase that poor girl on the bicycle used—and she was pretty clearly channeling the crowd that was chasing us yesterday." She gave him a quizzical look. "And they've got your daughter."

He smiled wryly across the table at Castine. "My fossil daughter. You don't want to get on an airplane."

"Do you? I was awake a long time last night, thinking. Why do we keep seeing that old house, now, instead of our recent local pasts like before? I *don't* want to see what happens there when the sun's down. And I'm afraid I will, if these things are allowed to take their course. And—a lot of people falling into a black hole."

Vickery turned his head to look at the bottle, then looked around at the interior of his trailer, noting the crowded bookshelves and the framed Maxfield Parrish prints in the living room, and the hole in the wall over the washing machine where he'd had to get at some pipes, and which he'd been meaning to patch. "I guess I wasn't really considering leaving—not really. I guess I pictured escorting you to a departure gate and then . . . "

She nodded. "Driving back to L.A."

"Well, yeah, I do want to talk to Galvan."

"And we've got a date at four with Supergirl. You gave her a thousand dollars!"

Vickery tore off a piece of the fried bread to mop up some egg yolk. For several seconds he just chewed, then took a sip of coffee and said, "Okay. We don't fly away, we go back down into L.A. and try to get a handle on this stuff. That's about a two-hour drive."

"We've got plenty of time. I'm glad to see you've got a shower in your bathroom, and—if I can borrow some money?—I'll want to stop at that outlet mall below town for some fresh clothes."

Vickery was chewing a strip of bacon, and nodded.

After they'd finished eating and the breakfast things were cleared away, Vickery went outside to check the tire pressures and oil and coolant levels on the car. When he came back in, Castine was washing the dishes.

She looked up. "Okay if I hang onto your .38?"

The question made their plan immediate, and depressed him. "I guess you may as well. Get a big purse. The gun's registered—to Bill Ardmore—but you're on your own if a cop should catch you with a concealed gun and no CCW permit."

"That's a misdemeanor, as I recall. I think we've got bigger worries."

"I guess we do." Vickery looked out the kitchen window at the desert, then back at Castine. "I'll fill a couple of speed-loaders and magazines and put 'em in the trunk. And I should crawl under the trailer and get another pocketful of cash."

Out past the Long Beach breakwater, the 45-foot Hatteras increased her speed, surging west across the twenty-mile expanse of glittering blue sea between Santa Catalina Island and Point Vicente, and her shallow keel cut smoothly across the low waves. The twin V-6 diesel engines hummed in perfect synchronization, and the hull was cored with balsa wood between the fiberglass layers, so in the boat's interior the engines and the water rushing past the hull outside were muted enough that the passengers had quickly stopped being aware of them.

In the lounge, the view forward was blocked by cabinets Harlowe had installed, and Lexi and Amber were kneeling on the long couch, sipping from plastic cups of root beer and peering out through the starboard windows. They were absorbed in the view, communicating only in excited squeaks and brief, sung bass notes. Simon Harlowe sat on a padded bench below the windows in the opposite bulkhead, staring at the girls.

They were his brother's twin daughters, and Harlowe had adopted them after the death of both their parents in what the district attorney had concluded was a tandem suicide.

For decades the brothers had had no contact at all, and although they had renewed their acquaintance two years ago, they hadn't ever been close. Chris Harlowe had graduated respectably enough from Cal Poly and ended up doing tech writing for Apple. Simon Harlowe, on the other hand, had been a boy genius who got involved in computers in 1972 by way of the computer center at Stanford University. He enrolled in the university in 1973, at the age of sixteen, and for a year he had even worked at the Stanford Research Institute—but his theoretical extrapolations, linking computer networking with neurology and occult philosophy, had isolated him, and he had left without getting a degree. By the '80s he'd been living on the outskirts of Salinas, subsisting on food stamps, in an old trailer equipped with a TRS-80 computer and stacks of books and charts and floppy disks.

The only intimate contact he'd had with anyone during that period had been when he had killed a vagrant who broke into the trailer one night. The incident had been ruled a justifiable homicide, but the effect on Harlowe had for a number of reasons been devastating, and when he had eventually found a psychological equilibrium it was by means of projecting a personality that was constructed, artificial—almost theatrical—though he pursued his researches even more monomaniacally for the next twenty years.

His mother had died at some point, and his long-estranged father died, somewhere, in 2015, when Simon Harlowe was fifty-eight; and, because they had invested widely in real estate, he was suddenly a millionaire.

The inheritance had led to a reunion with his brother—and had also led to Simon's fortuitous discovery of Chris' twin daughters. Simon chose to imagine that his manipulatively avuncular relationship with the girls had been, or would ultimately be, beneficial to them. Even the traditionally-horrifying crime he had

subtly encouraged them to commit would, he believed, prove to have
been a step in their salvation.

"You girls feeling . . . all right?" he asked them now. They had
both been seasick the first time they'd been out on the boat, though
he later concluded that it had only been because he had warned them
that it might happen.

They ignored him, humming and squeaking in unison now as
they stared out the window at the sea. Harlowe shivered.

The girls had apparently always been difficult. They had been
tentatively diagnosed as borderline personalities, and after the deaths
of their parents a doctor had put them on Prozac; after which they
had immediately attempted to drown themselves off Little Coyote
Point in the San Francisco Bay.

Harlowe had very soon guessed at their possible usefulness as
IMPs in his planned egregore—and he really believed that
incorporation into that transcendent group-mind would be the best
possible resolution of their problems. They were more one person
than two—hardly even one, really—and their moods changed as
often as winning numbers on a roulette wheel. In the group-mind of
the egregore, they would, like himself and Agnes Loria, and even
rogue Elisha Ragotskie—and ultimately everyone!—be just
semiconductors in the mind of God.

Eventually he had initiated the twins, using the costly fifty-year-
old coloring books.

Harlowe leaned back on the bench, rocking with the motion of
the boat, and closed his eyes. Tomorrow night the long-delayed
apotheosis would happen, and he would lose his unwanted identity
forever.

For decades he had been tracing indications—in early issues of
Stewart Brand's *Whole Earth Catalog,* and the Los Angeles *Free
Press*—that a group-mind egregore had been attempted in Los
Angeles in the '60s. It proved to have been the project of a
charismatic young hippie musician known as Conrad Chronic, who
had got hold of a suppressed hieroglyph embodying the Egyptian
god—or force, or psychic polarizer—called *Ba.* Chronic had printed
the hieroglyph, surrounded by disguising random lines, on a back
page of *Groan,* an underground coloring book otherwise full of
satirical black-and-white cartoons with captions like *Color Him*

Racist and *Six Uses For My Draft Card*. The *Ba* image in the coloring book had been Chronic's covert recruiting tool. The cult had reportedly included some never-named celebrities among its mostly itinerant and drug-addled membership; but it had failed to achieve coherence, and had violently fallen apart at a gathering in 1968, an event commemorated in a B-side ballad, "Elegy in a Seaside Meadow," by the rock group Fogwillow. On a morbid-nostalgia website Harlowe had seen a couple of photographs of Chronic at a place called Rodney Bingenheimer's English Disco on Sunset Boulevard in 1967, but he was unable to find any other pictures of the man.

Harlowe knew little more about the Chronic group than that, but he had recognized the coloring-book *Ba* image as a clever initiator of minds, and over the course of several months he had succeeded in buying half a dozen copies of *Groan* from various rare book dealers. The image differed slightly but crucially from the image of *Ba* in reference books on Egyptian mythology, and was segmented like a figure in a stained glass window. It was necessary that an initiate spend at least a minute staring at the image steadily, concentrating on it, for it to fully replicate itself in the initiate's mind—like installing software that took a while to load—and a person who colored in all the spaces on that page would inevitably have stared at the image for at least the necessary amount of time.

Harlowe had stared at the image himself, and after no more than a minute had felt what he had only been able to describe as a faint electrical current in his mind, and it had proved to be as persistent as tinnitus. He had given his Singularity team only the sketchiest account of the old failed egregore, and had never mentioned Conrad Chronic to any of them, but he had made them, too, look at the image on that page of the coloring books. The only other after-effect any of them had noticed was that the scarcely-perceived mental vibration was stronger if two or more of them stood in close proximity to one another.

And then Harlowe had given copies of the coloring book to the twins, along with a box of crayons. The twins had taken to the task readily, though they had insisted on coloring all the pages of the book in order, and had wasted a day meticulously coloring caricatures of people like Lyndon Johnson and Earl Warren. But at last they had arrived at the page with the *Ba* image on it—and when they had simultaneously colored in the last segment of it and dropped their crayons, they had been silent for the rest of that day.

They were different, after that.

Even before that initiation with the coloring books, they had sometimes been able to induce actions in people around them: Harlowe had sometimes found himself fetching Cokes they had wanted but not asked for, or unable to speak if they were absorbed in watching a movie on TV; . . . and when encouraged, he had discovered, they could even force two people at once to do something they would never voluntarily do.

And after their initiation, they had seemed to expand, psychically—he was always aware now of their mercurial mentation as something like a shrill, indecipherable twittering in a corner of his mind—and they had sporadically been able to describe people and events far removed from their own experience.

They had, in fact, made him aware of Vickery and Castine.

"There's two strangers tangled up in your spiderweb," one of them had remarked nine months ago, in January. "They drove a truck into Hell and flew a glider back out, and now their clocks are no good." The other twin had added, "Their kite strings are looped around yours."

Uneasy, Harlowe had put out inquiries among a few of the occultists in Los Angeles, and had soon learned that two people, Sebastian Vickery and Ingrid Castine, had reportedly driven a taco truck, of all things, into some sort of afterlife in May of last year, and had come back, alive; though without the truck. From other sources he had learned that at least one LAPD detective had covertly consulted Vickery on a few cases, because Vickery was apparently now able to step out of the present moment and see events of the recent local past.

And it had occurred to Harlowe that, if Castine too had acquired this ability, the pair of them would be better IMPs than the twins—and would almost certainly be more rational.

The twins were still looking out the starboard window, now humming two sustained, unharmonious notes; the faint perception of their jiggling thoughts, usually ignorable, was like an itch at the back of his mind. Harlowe frowned and looked away.

At least the attempted capture of Vickery in February had secured the unique copy of *The Secret Garden*.

He had tracked down Vickery through the man's employer, Anita Galvan, who ran fleets of taco trucks and supernatural-evasion cars; but from her he had learned, too, of that book. When she had demanded five thousand dollars to deliver Vickery, and Harlowe had refused to pay it, she had said, *Maybe it's worth it to you since he has a book with a never-born spirit fossilized in it? It's a daughter the* eunuco *never had the balls to beget. The* brujas *say there's uses for such things.*

Harlowe had gone away and had in fact consulted a Hispanic medium. And then he had gone back and given Galvan the five thousand dollars.

It seemed likely that Harlowe would be able to subsume the ghost of an *actual* person, too, into the book, blend it there with the . . . spirit? failed likelihood? . . . of the daughter Vickery never had. The resulting irrational juxtaposition of that "pair" should, it seemed to Harlowe, compellingly attract any ghosts that might otherwise be drawn into the emerging egregore, where their animate absences would psychically cripple it. The augmented book would ideally function like cadmium rods in nuclear reactors, which absorb excess neutrons and prevent meltdown.

The five thousand dollars had not been wasted, even though Vickery had got away.

And Vickery and Castine *could still* be the reliable communication organ of the egregore gestalt; and their "kite strings," incorporated into it, would surely provide added strength to the whole. Ragotskie stole the bloody sock yesterday, but Harlowe had long ago covertly installed in the car of each member of the ChakraSys staff a GPS tracker, charged from the car's battery, and Taitz and Foster were even now out following him. Their instructions were to wait until, ideally, Ragotskie located Vickery and Castine with the aid of the sock, and then kill Ragotskie and capture them. No stops or delays.

That was admittedly a long shot—but Harlowe had taken the twins out on the boat this morning in the hope that they might themselves be able to locate the fugitive pair.

Nine months ago Lexi and Amber had sensed Vickery and Castine, but hadn't been able to tell where they might be. But that had been when the twins were in a city, among hundreds of people whose free wills were always distorting the moment of *now*. Out here on the empty face of the sea, though, the chronocline plane would be pretty genuinely flat, not the usual averaging-out of an infinity of fractal time-spikes. The five people on the boat, especially with the twins practically being one person, shouldn't appreciably distort the flatness of local time. If the twins *could* determine the actual location of Vickery and Castine, it would most likely be from the psychic calm out here.

A crunching noise from the other side of the lounge now caught Harlowe's attention. The twins had grown tired of peering out the starboard window at the ocean and had tipped up their empty cups to get the ice cubes,and were chewing them vigorously.

"Welcome little fishes in," said one of the twins, "with gently smiling jaws!"

More *Alice in Wonderland* stuff. Harlowe wasn't sure what to make of their obsession with that passage from the Lewis Carroll book; Harlowe had never been able to make any sense of the *Alice* books himself.

"When do we touch the two people who drove to Hell?" said the other.

"Touch?" said Harlowe. "Oh—soon. When we stop the boat. And you'll look around then, right? See what they're seeing, see where they are."

"Uh huh." The girl set her empty cup on the deck. "Uncle Simon, can we go up to the bow? We want to see what kinds of fish fly."

Harlowe opened his mouth, but his tongue wouldn't move. He nodded emphatically so that they'd release him, and then said, quickly, "If you put on life jackets!" Sweat had broken out on his forehead.

"*Semper ubi sub ubi.*" It was a joke of theirs, apparently learned from their late father: Latin for *Always where under where*. Ho ho.

They scampered out onto the cockpit deck, and a moment later he saw them run along the narrow side-deck past the starboard windows.

Tony was up on the fly bridge, and Harlowe sighed and picked up the intercom microphone. "Tony, see that they put on life jackets, okay?"

Tony's reply came over the speaker: "Rightie-O."

Rightie-O. Shit. Harlowe stood up and stretched. He could see Agnes Loria out in the cockpit, bundled up in a blue nylon parka. She was leaning against the transom and squinting into the eddying headwind, and he buttoned his wool coat and stepped out onto the broad fiberglass deck. The smell of the open sea on the wind was a pleasant change from the climate-controlled blandness inside.

He crossed the deck and stood at the rail a few feet away from Loria, and he too turned to face forward, for the rising sun over Seal Beach was directly astern.

Loria was wearing sunglasses now, but Harlowe remembered that her eyes had been red, with dark circles under them, when she had joined him for coffee in the little breakfast nook below. She had spent the night with the twins in the forward vee-berth cabin, and evidently the girls had had a couple of nightmares. At least they always had them together, he thought, and didn't stagger them.

"They could," Loria said now, "have made me jump over the side. In the middle of the night." She pulled a pack of Marlboros and a lighter out of her jacket pocket and hunched over, cupping her hands around the lighter.

"Oh, don't be melodramatic." Harlowe frowned impatiently. "Make you walk down the hall, up the steps, through the lounge—" He waved at the white deck they were standing on, "—across the cockpit to the rail? And over?" He chuffed an exhalation and shook his head, trying to express more skepticism than he actually felt. "So okay, once they made you open a bag of tortilla chips—"

Loria had got her cigarette lit, and smoke fluttered out of her mouth as she spoke. "They were angry. Those chips went all over the place."

He raised his hand. "—And then they made you hold their hands yesterday. Those are momentary—"

"Hijackings."

"*Momentary.*"

For several seconds neither of them spoke. The roar of the engines was louder out here.

"You could have Tony kill the engines any time," Loria said. "This is as unpopulated an area as you'll find."

Harlowe looked out at the rippling expanse of blue sea. Loria was right. The irregular line of Catalina Island was easily ten miles away, and the mainland waterfront lay at about the same distance to the northeast. The nearest boat, a catamaran under full sail, was several miles off and tacking toward Catalina.

"Maybe Vickery and Castine drove all night," said Loria. "Maybe they're in Salt Lake City or San Francisco by now." She took a long drag on the cigarette and then pitched it over her shoulder, into the boat's spreading wake. "I don't think Elisha could follow them all that way, just with that silly sock. You think the twins will be able to perceive them clearly enough to . . . I don't know, see what they see, share their space?"

"It's worth a try. I think our fugitive pair is partly in alignment with Lexi and Amber already."

"Oh?"

"Yesterday the twins caused a black hole incident at the beach, by holding hands—do you remember what that family said?"

"Uh—no."

"You told me they were babbling about getting new clothes in Hesperia. That's north of here, on the way to Las Vegas or Salt Lake City, and it would make sense for Vickery and Castine to think of ditching the clothes they were wearing, in case we'd managed to plant radio frequence tags on them."

"You think it was *their* thoughts that drunk family picked up? But if—"

"I think it's possible. Likely, even. The twins pointed them out to us in the first place, remember—sensed them. And if it *was* their thoughts that the twins were picking up yesterday, it means Vickery and Castine are impinging on us, but uninitiated. They're—" He frowned, then waved at the deck under their feet, "—they're like a boat on an intersecting course with our luxury liner, as it were. We've got to get them to line up parallel—and permit boarders."

"Or sink them?"

Harlowe shrugged, irritably. "If necessary. If possible."

"The Vickery guy did kill Platt."

"Who's got time for vengeance? I hope they can still be an asset."

"How did," Loria began, but a yell and splash from up by the bow interrupted her—and the faint, shrill agitation at the back of Harlowe's awareness abruptly ceased.

Loria stepped away from the transom to grip the starboard rail with one hand. "*Man overboard!*" she yelled, pointing out at the water; her arm was moving from left to right. "Both twins overboard!" she added.

From up on the fly deck came a yell from Tony: "Hang on everybody!" The engines roared as the boat sped up, leaning to port.

Salt spray stung Harlowe's eyes. He slipped on the fiberglass deck and grabbed the transom rail, and he frantically probed his mind; but the ordinarily-constant awareness of the twins' thinking was gone.

Harlowe blinked around at the sea and the shoreline. "He's going the wrong way!" he gasped.

"He's looping around to come back," said Loria, her arm still extended. "Go up and show him where I'm pointing."

Harlowe scrambled across the deck and started up the ladder to the fly bridge, and nearly swung off it when the boat shifted ponderously over to starboard and spray from that direction blinded him. Up on the wet fly bridge deck at last, he crawled on his hands and knees to the back of the pilot chair, then stood up and squinted down over the rail. He couldn't see two heads in the water at all, but he saw Loria down on the cockpit deck and pointed in the same direction that she was.

"They're there!" he yelled at Tony, who was hunched over the wheel. "Are they wearing life preservers?"

"No," said Tony, "I told 'em—"

"Hurry."

The deck vibrated under Harlowe's tennis shoes, and the bristly Long Beach skyline was crawling from right to left across the horizon. Loria's arm swung like a compass needle as she hurried across the deck to the port side, and now she was pointing exactly abeam. Tony pulled the shift lever to neutral, and after a few seconds he switched off the engines and clicked the shift lever into gear.

Harlowe gave him a furiously impatient look.

"Stops the propellers," Tony explained breathlessly. "And we're between them and the wind—we'll drift closer."

Tony ran back and slid down the ladder to the cockpit deck. Harlowe followed carefully; and he was dizzy with relief when the faint chatter of the twins' mental activity was suddenly restored.

Loria had sailed a life ring like a frisbee out across the water, and now threw another. Light nylon lines snaked behind them.

When the rings slapped the water, Harlowe could see the twins' heads, a dozen yards away; and he began to relax, tentatively, when the saw their hands grab the rings. Evidently this had not been another suicide attempt. The nylon lines sprang taut, throwing bright drops, as Tony and Loria began pulling the twins in.

"Fetch the ladder!" called Tony over his shoulder. His sunglasses had fallen off, and sweat glittered in his brush-cut blond hair. Harlowe could see the man's shoulder muscles flexing under the white T-shirt, and Loria had one knee braced against the gunwale as she pulled her line in.

Fetch? thought Harlowe; but he ran halfway forward and lifted the hook-topped aluminum ladder from its bracket and hurried back to where Tony and Loria stood.

The twins were only ten feet away now, their legs and bare feet kicking behind them, and Harlowe hooked the ladder over the railing at the point they seemed to be approaching; and within no more than a minute they had both climbed up and swung over the rail, and now they stood dripping and shivering on the deck while Loria hurried below to get blankets.

Harlowe stared at both of them as his heartbeat slowed down, and at last he turned to face Tony.

"I told 'em," Tony protested again, but one of the twins interrupted.

"We needed," she said haltingly, "to be all the way under, and life jackets don't even let you get your hair wet."

"You're lucky you didn't *stay* underwater!" said Harlowe. He took a deep breath. "You think you could have joined the egregore from the bottom of—"

"It was," began one of the twins; "new," finished the other. "It's how you get out of your way," added the first, with a look of reproach. "We had to give ourself away to it, just for a minute."

Loria had reappeared with two blankets bundled in her arms, and she draped one over each of the twins. "Now go below," she told them, "and get into some dry things."

The twins padded through the door into the lounge, and Harlowe waited until he heard their feet thumping down the steps to the lower deck, and then turned to Tony.

"I'm sorry, Mr. Harlowe," the young man said hastily, "you know how they—"

"*I* know how they," said Loria. "Get back up on the bridge, Tony."

"You want me to start up again? We could—"

"No," said Loria. "This is perfect. Let's just sit a while."

With one last anxious look at Harlowe, Tony turned and clambered back up the ladder.

When he had disappeared forward, Loria said, "He's more loyal than you deserve, you know."

"Oh, he's a good man, beyond doubt," admitted Harlowe, stepping back to the transom rail. "A devoted member—if a bit simple. He does feel terrible about Elisha stealing the bloody sock out of the Tahoe yesterday, when he was left to guard it." Harlowe absently rattled the transom door. "It *was* damn negligent of him."

"But all are welcomed in," Loria reminded him. "All *compelled* eventually, right? Everybody into the black hole."

"Why do you talk this way, Agnes?" Harlowe was still shaky from the long moments when the twins' mentation had seemed abruptly to stop. "You know the egregore won't be predatory. I wish that term, *black hole,* had never gained currency among us. It'll be inclusive, benevolent—ultimately it's the God that people have looked for, and a million times thought they'd found."

"I know, I know. I agree!" She nodded toward the lounge. "I'm just thinking about those poor girls." The boat was rocking in the swell now, and Loria stepped carefully to the rail beside him. "I started to ask you something. How did her parents—hah! I'm falling into their point of view—how did their parents kill themselves, anyway?"

Harlowe was aware that if he'd been able to feel guilt and shame, he'd feel them now. "Damn it, Agnes," he said, "it's not helpful to talk about old individual concerns! Tomorrow night the thing which will be all of us will be able to . . . transcend such stuff. Apotheosis. Everything it does will be right, by definition." He nodded; then glanced at her. "They pulled plastic bags over their heads."

Loria rocked her head back, her eyes on the lounge doorway. "How did they restrain their hands?"

Harlowe suppressed the remembered image: the bodies of his brother and sister-in-law, sitting in two chairs on their patio deck. The plastic had been desperately indented over their gaping mouths. The twins had been in the house.

"It doesn't matter now," he said, affecting a grave tone.

"No," agreed Loria. "But—how?"

"They—I don't remember, and it's not—"

"Their hands *weren't* restrained, were they?"

Harlowe didn't answer.

Loria nodded. "Huh."

Through the open door of the lounge, Harlowe saw the twins mount the steps from below. They both wore blue corduroy overalls now, and their brown hair was pulled back in stringy wet ponytails. They shuffled awkwardly out onto the cockpit deck, squinting in the sun.

"You wanted us to look for that man and that woman," said one of them sulkily. "Not just know they're out there, but touch them, see what they're seeing."

"We had to close all apps, first, didn't we?" demanded the other. "Clear the task bar."

"It's a *new* thing," said the first girl, and Harlowe felt his scalp tighten and the hairs on the back of his neck stand up.

They weren't saying *new*, they were citing the name of *Nu*, the Egyptian god represented by the sea, the personification of the abyss, the absence of all activity and awareness, the void from which identity had been made—the ever-patient universal identity-sink. *Nu* was the eternal counterpart of *Ba*, which, or who, was the essence of distinct identity.

The two forces had to be kept apart!

"The twins," he said thickly, "can't go in the ocean anymore, understand? No, not even wading." Had it been, in effect, *Nu* that they'd been seeking when they had nearly drowned themselves off Little Coyote Point?

He stared at the two little girls as if he'd never seen them before.

"At least they resurfaced," said Loria. "And now they've closed all their apps, whatever that means! They should have bandwidth free to locate your fugitives."

"I think," Harlowe said quietly to Loria, "we'd better re-initiate them—have them color in the picture again." He was sweating, but he forced a smile and turned to the twins. "Sit down, Lexi, Amber. You were right to . . . *close the apps*. I was just—worried about you!" When the girls had sat down together on a lidded cabinet that contained a bait tank, he stepped to the starboard gunwale and leaned on it. "Yes, I would like you to look for that man and that woman. Can you sense them? Buy new clothes in Hesperia. Doctor Zhivago."

One of the girls lifted her hand—Loria opened her mouth in alarm, but before she could say anything the other girl clasped the hand.

And Loria and Harlowe fell to their hands and knees on the deck.

Harlowe could feel that his palms were flat on the fiberglass deck, and he knew that his knuckles were only a foot from his face—but what he saw, as if through heavily tinted sunglasses, was a *level* view of a decrepit old two-story Victorian house. A man holding a revolver stood on the long, sagging porch while another man dragged a body—a woman in a long robe—down the steps to the dirt. The body left dark, gleaming streaks on the steps.

Harlowe turned his head, but the image stayed central in his vision; he lifted his hands to wave in front of his face, but they didn't appear in his sight and he felt his forehead strike the cockpit deck. His hip and shoulder hit the deck then, and he rolled over, but there was no shift in what he was seeing.

Then he had to squint against a sudden blue sky and sunlight reflecting off the deck and the chrome ladder. He was lying on the wet deck, but the first thing he did was raise his hands and flex them, and he coughed in relief to see his fingers clearly.

"Fuck," croaked Loria behind him. He rolled over and sat up. Loria was sitting against the transom gunwale, her head between her knees; the twins still sat on the sink cabinet, though they were no longer holding hands.

"We got that from them," said one of the twins defensively. "Honest."

"I think we pushed them a little, crowding in," added the other.

Loria raised her head and gave Harlowe a haggard stare. "Did you . . . *see* that, too?" When he nodded, she went on, "We just saw a woman murdered somewhere."

"It was," said Harlowe as he laboriously got to his feet, "a long time ago."

Loria slowly stood up, bracing herself against the gunwale. "What do you mean? How do you know?" She stared out at the broad sunlit face of the sea, as if to confirm that the vision had ended.

Harlowe just shook his head. How do I know? he thought. Because I recognized the face of the man holding the revolver. Conrad Chronic looked the same in this vision as he did in those old photographs online, and those were taken fifty years ago.

We got that from them, one of the twins had said. *Honest.* Vickery and Castine were somehow a connection to Chronic's 1968 egregore, which had failed—spectacularly.

He pulled Loria to the rail and whispered, "I think—no, I'm sure—Vickery and Castine have to be killed too. Along with Ragotskie. All three. Damn."

His head was only inches from hers, and he was aware of the increased mental vibration that he always experienced when standing very close to another initiate.

"Well don't tell *me*," she said, stepping away from him, "I'm the spiritual type. I've never taken anybody's blood pressure, and I'm not going to start."

"No, of course not, I don't mean you. But—yes, get on the radio and tell Taitz."

She was frowning at him. "I thought you wanted those two. For your IMPs."

"They're—no, they're linked to—something I don't see how we can incorporate, safely. I can't take the chance."

"Is it that old egregore? Those fifty-year-old coloring books?"

"The—dammit, the coloring books are neutral, but Vickery and Castine are apparently . . . tainted. Get on the radio. I—" He touched his bruised forehead. "I don't think we should try again with the twins."

"You're being impulsive. We've spent all this time and effort trying to get Vickery and Castine—and now, if we find them, you just want them killed? You think the twins will *do*, as your IMPs?"

"The twins have disadvantages too," Harlowe conceded, "but they're already initiated—or if that app got closed,we'll initiate them again to reopen it—and they're willing participants, and they're here. Vickery and Castine we'd have to catch, alive, and transport, and initiate. And I think they're hostile."

"I can see how they might be, at that." Loria exhaled through pursed lips in a silent whistle. "Okay."

She started to turn away toward the cabin, but Harlowe caught her arm, making them both wince. "Wait—for the next forty hours all of us have to be ready for the possibility of violence." He reached into his coat, where he carried a small .22 revolver in a suede holster; he unclipped the holster and pulled it out, and, facing away from the twins, held it out to Loria. "Keep this with you."

She looked down at the curved wood-sided grip protruding from the tan suede flap, then up at him. "No."

"Damn it, it's for self-defense! If one of these unsecured *dramatis personae* should kill you, you'd miss the apotheosis—you'd just be plain dead."

She frowned at the little gun.

"You want to go on to some judgmental *afterlife*," Harlowe went on, "or plain oblivion?—or live big, forever, here?"

She sighed and took the gun from his hand and slid it into a pocket of her bulky nylon jacket.

Even as he had helplessly watched the two men drag the woman from the porch in the penumbral dimness, Vickery had been aware of the car bucking and shaking, and the steering wheel jerking powerfully under his gripping hands. Now the car had evidently stopped, and was just rocking from side to side, but though Vickery swiveled his head toward where the windshield and rear-view mirror should have been visible, his vision showed him nothing but the men pulling the woman's body down the last steps onto the dirt.

When light sprang up again, he was reassured to at least see the dashboard, for nothing showed through the windshield but whirling dust.

"Fuck!" exclaimed Castine. He glanced at her, and she seemed startled at having spoken.

The engine had stalled, and Vickery quickly started it again in case he was still out in the lanes; but in moments the dust blew away, and he saw that they were a dozen yards off the pavement, among sand and dry weeds. The car was at right angles to the highway, pointed out toward the desert.

Vickery just breathed in and out through his open mouth and waited for his heartbeat to slow down.

"Obviously," said Castine, then paused to clear her throat. "Obviously you saw it too."

Vickery nodded. "God knows what that did to the suspension. Anyway, how do I dare drive, anymore?" He shook his head, carefully. "We weren't even touching each other!"

Castine opened her door and stepped out onto the sand. "I think a couple of people were," she called, "somewhere." She leaned in. "It's kind of nice to step out—stretch and smell the breeze—after nearly dying."

Vickery unclenched his fingers from the steering wheel. "Okay." He levered open the door and swung his feet out onto the sand. "I was doing better than seventy!" he called.

"So drive slow from now on. We don't need all that wind from the two missing back windows anyway."

"We keep going?"

"Sure. You'd rather stay out here?" She got back into the car and pulled the door closed. "That was provoked in us. Just at the beginning of it, I got the impression of two girls, on a boat, holding hands. Did you sense that?"

"I—" Vickery thought about it. In the instant before the vision had eclipsed his view of the highway, there *had* been a sense of a couple of people—young people—and yes, rocking, though that had been nothing compared to the way the car had begun jumping and slewing a moment later. "A boat, you think."

"In a marina, maybe? This *won't* leave us alone—we've got to find a way out of it."

The engine was running smoothly, and Vickery pulled his feet back into the car and glanced around, wondering how best to get back onto the highway. "Okay. But yeah, I'll drive slow, and I'll be ready to stand on the brakes."

CHAPTER SEVEN:
Two and Two Is Four

During a one-minute-interval update on his iPad, Don Foster tapped back to the All Events page.

John Taitz was driving Harlowe's Chevy Tahoe slowly north on Normandie, past more of the apartment buildings which, it seemed to him, made up most of Los Angeles.

They had just received Harlowe's order that Vickery and Castine, as well as Ragotskie, were to be killed. Taitz briefly wished he'd had a drink or two before setting out.

"Where's Ragotskie now?" he asked. Ragotskie's car had been located in a parking lot yesterday afternoon, but by midnight he had not returned to it, and Harlowe had concluded that Ragotskie must have abandoned it; early this morning, though, the GPS tracker had been registering movement.

"As of thirty seconds ago, he was a block east of us," said Foster, "on Mariposa. But check this out—at nine-thirty last night he was parked in the Holiday Marina lot for ten minutes! I thought he wasn't supposed to know where the *Black Sheep* is berthed now, since he went rogue yesterday?"

"That's right," said Taitz, "he's not." *I'll have to tell Harlowe he has to move it again,* he thought. *He'll love that.*

"You think he followed the Castine woman there, with the bloody sock? How would *she* have found out about it?"

"I don't think—no, he must have actually been at that weird restaurant on Seventh last night, and we just didn't see him. He probably followed Loria to the marina. He's obsessed with her."

Foster settled back in the seat and tapped the iPad screen to get back to the one-minute-interval updates. "He's only moved up half a block. I bet he's parked."

"Consulting the sock, probably. It's a good sign that he's driving around L.A.—Harlowe was afraid Castine and Vickery just ran straight east, like to Vegas." Taitz steered the SUV to a strip of empty curb and shifted to park.

"I wonder if they're still in that blue sedan," said Foster. "What was that, some kind of foreign thing?"

"It looked like an old East German Trabant. Maybe Vickery drove it back from Hell last year."

"Maybe he drove it back there again. He sure disappeared yesterday." Foster scratched his bald scalp. "I'd still like to get a hat. And not just some tacky fishing hat bag thing." He shifted around to look up and down this street, then said, "You think they'll . . . offer resistance?"

"We'll have no problems." Right after getting Harlowe's newest order, Taitz had swung through a parking lot and taken a pair of licence plates from a parked car and put them on the Tahoe, and the windshield and windows were fortunately tinted against the ubiquitous street cameras.

"Ragotskie's nothing," Taitz went on. "He's got that little Beretta, but he couldn't shoot anybody. And Ingrid Castine's just an office clerk for some transportation agency back east. Vickery—he was a driver for that Galvan woman's ghost-evasion car service, which didn't look like a real carriage trade operation. He's some kind of rootless loser. I don't anticipate any problems."

In killing three people, he thought. What kind of apotheosis is to be found at the end of this sort of road?

"Vickery's good at evasive driving, for sure. And he got out of that deli pretty smooth. Bam! Bam!"

"Big deal," said Taitz, "he sucker-punched poor Pratt and ran out."

To Taitz's annoyance, Foster drew his Glock 40 from the shoulder holster under his shiny new six-hundred-dollar black leather jacket, and pointed it at the floor. After he worked his hand on the grip for a moment, a luminous green dot appeared on the carpeting between his sneakers.

"A three-bet before the flop!" said Foster. "And this flop's gonna be dealt face-down, *oh* yeah."

"Put it away," said Taitz, restraining himself from adding, *idiot,* "and watch your iPad."

Foster was always using poker slang, which Taitz believed he got exclusively from YouTube videos; and using it now, breezily, minutes after they had received the order to kill Vickery and Castine as well as Ragotskie, was—if nothing else—shallow.

Taitz glanced with concealed distaste at Foster, who had put the gun away and was again peering at the iPad. And, *Not just some tacky fishing hat bag thing.* Oh, God forbid. And what is Foster going to contribute, Taitz wondered, to the egregore? Sophomoric self-satisfaction? I can't blame him, though, for wanting to subsume his glib, shallow self in the godhead.

I'm counting on it too.

At fifty-five, John Taitz had been the oldest employee of ChakraSys when Harlowe had bought the company in 2016. Until Harlowe's arrival, the chakra therapy salon had occupied a space in a strip mall in San Jose, offering counseling on diet, and "workshops," and exercises to keep the clients' seven "chakras" functioning smoothly. Taitz had been privately skeptical of the whole affair—deep breathing and rainbow diets and forever tightening the Kegel muscles, which he gathered basically meant a person's rear end—but Harlowe had brought a vastly bigger and more ambitious perspective to the whole business.

The egregore, the living cauldron into which they would all dump their unattractive selves.

John Taitz wondered what his own personality could contribute to the transcendent egregore. Before getting the job at ChakraSys, he had served time in Soledad State Prison for murdering a woman he had believed—still believed—he had loved.

They had been living together in an apartment in Santa Clara, and in the midst of a drunken argument in 1986 she had grabbed her car keys and stormed out; when she drove away in her car he followed her in his, and on the 101 freeway he had caught up with her at eighty miles per hour and swerved to force her off onto the shoulder. But his right front bumper had struck her car, which had skidded sideways and then gone tumbling right over the freeway embankment, into a parking lot below. Hannah had not been wearing her seatbelt. Two other drivers had witnessed the incident and pulled over, and their eventual testimony had led to his conviction for murder.

He lived each day now in stoic confidence that he would soon be able to cease being the person who carried the intolerable memory of yanking the steering wheel to the right, and the boom of the impact, and the glimpse of her car in the first of what must have been several rolls. And he had killed two other men since, for reasons that were incomprehensible to him now. Perhaps the egregore would need a capacity for weathering guilt.

"Flop's gonna be dealt *face*-down," said Foster again, nodding and grinning.

Taitz crossed his arms and looked at him. "I thought you liked Ragotskie."

"Like?" said Foster. "I guess I don't *like* anybody."

"Just watch your damn app, and let me know when he moves."

Vickery parked the Saturn in a lot on Irolo Street, around the corner from Galvan's yard. He rolled down the front windows to match the empty back ones, remarking that it was common practice in San Francisco to leave all windows open on parked cars, so that thieves could ransack the interior without having to break any glass. He and Castine then walked up to Eighth Street, where they paused by a couple of barbed-wire-enclosed dumpsters behind a Jon's Market. The noon sun was bright on the downstairs shops and upstairs apartment windows across the street, and the wind from the west smelled of the distant sea.

"I wish we'd brought Omar Khayyam along," said Castine. "If those bad guys show up, he could rescue us again." Since their stop in Hesperia this morning she was wearing a long suede coat over a white cotton blouse and blue jeans. She had not bought a purse, and Vickery's .38 was in her right-hand coat pocket.

"We should be okay if we keep moving around," said Vickery. He had bought a Dodgers baseball cap and a black nylon bomber jacket, and he had followed Castine's example and carried the flat 9-millimeter Glock in the right jacket pocket. "And this business with

Galvan shouldn't take long. She probably owes me a few favors, and it's been eight months since she—"

"Told a bad guy where to find your *Secret Garden.*"

"Yeah. And she'd probably like to have me around for the occasional echo-vision job. She doesn't need to know that it . . . generally doesn't work right anymore."

"Were there a lot of those? Echo-vision jobs?"

Vickery yawned widely. "Excuse me. I probably could have made a living at it, even with Galvan taking forty percent, as she did. It seemed almost natural at first—remember when it first started happening, you seemed to have a body, in the visions? That turned out to be just a projection, like a visible phantom limb, and it wore off, but it did make the visions less disorienting. Yeah, I got sent to offices to see documents that had been on a desk an hour earlier, and rushed into empty restaurant booths to try to read a number off the cell phone of some guy who'd just left—one time some guys with guns grabbed me off the street and took me to a corner in South Central, and just wanted to know if a certain car in a parking lot had been there for more than an hour. It had—I could tell by the shadows—and I said so. I wonder if I saved somebody or got 'em killed."

"Good lord." Castine shook her head. "I never let anybody know I could even do it. People just thought I had mini-strokes sometimes." She was looking east down Eighth Street, and she shivered. "I should just wait for you here. She doesn't like me."

The crosswalk light had turned green, and they started forward.

Vickery glanced at her. "Who, Galvan? Well, no. I'm not sure she likes *me.* But we saved her nephew or cousin or something, a year ago, remember?"

Castine smiled in spite of herself, and nodded. "He was going to jump down into the Labyrinth, try to close the hole between the worlds, but lucky for him we'd already closed it." She actually laughed. "He had a parachute."

They stopped, waiting to cross Irolo.

"And what," said Vickery, "holy water grenades? And a gun with silver bullets."

Castine shook her head pityingly. "Much too conventional for that place."

Galvan's yard had no sign, but Vickery could see the green netting over the chain link fence ahead, and as they drew closer he saw that the gate had been slid back from across the driveway.

"She's still in business, at least," he said. "Or somebody is, anyway."

"Last time I was here," said Castine nervously, "we stole one of her taco trucks. And left it in the Labyrinth."

"And she only ever carried liability insurance on her vehicles. But we did save her damn nephew—and probably her and all of her family that lives in L.A."

Castine nodded. "According to poor old Laquedem, anyway."

They had reached the driveway, and Vickery let his gaze sweep from the rows of cars to the old Silver Airstream trailer at the far end of the lot on the left, and on to the long car-maintenance bay, and finally to the two-story office building with its windows painted over white. Galvan's office was in there, and he led Castine across the asphalt in that direction.

The door of the trailer on the other side of the lot was open, and a heavy-set bald man in a sweatshirt leaned out. "Can I help you?" he yelled, not in a friendly tone.

"Tom! It's me, Vickery!"

Tom was the yard manager, and his round face was puckered sternly now as he plodded down the steps to the pavement. He squinted at Vickery for five seconds, then burst out, "You got no pay coming, so forget it—you still owe her heaps for taking that truck." Then he visibly recognized Castine. "You brought *her* here? You better just get lost before the boss sees you."

Several drivers and mechanics had stepped out from the shade of the maintenance bay and were watching curiously. Vickery could see one of Galvan's super-stealth cars, guaranteed to keep passengers invisible to all supernatural attentions, parked in the bay.

"We want to talk to her," said Vickery, with a wave toward the office building.

Tom hesitated, then stepped back toward the trailer. "I'll call her. You wait right there, and when she tells me to throw you out, I'll get the guys to do it."

He climbed the steps again and disappeared into the trailer.

"Now we get beat up, I think," said Castine quietly.

"She'll see me. I've been as much profit as loss to her, over the years. Probably. You want to go over there in the shade and get some coffee?"

"No! He said stay here!"

"Suit yourself." Vickery began walking toward the maintenance bay, and Castine hurried to catch up. A cart with a coffee urn and a stack of styrofoam cups on it stood by one of the big steel door frames, and Vickery nodded to one of the mechanics and filled two cups. Castine rolled her eyes, then took a cup and shook sugar into it from a greasy canister on the cart.

The familiar smells of gasoline and Mexican food, and the burnt taste of the coffee, made Vickery almost relax.

"This wasn't a bad job, actually," he remarked to Castine.

Castine, who had worked for Galvan one day last year, said, "I never cared for it." She sipped the coffee and made a sour face.

"Vickery!" came a call from behind them; "and Betty Boop!"

Vickery recognized Galvan's voice, and he remembered that Castine had used the name Betty Boop in their dealings with her last year. He turned around with a smile, and there was Anita Galvan, just as he remembered her—not tall, but stocky, with a broad brown face and short-cropped black hair. She was dressed, as usual, in cargo pants and a khaki jacket, and her protuberant and piercing brown eyes twinkled with unpredictable merriment.

"You two come to steal another one of my vehicles?" she called as she strode across the asphalt to where Vickery and Castine stood.

Vickery waved toward the office building. "I wanted to ask you about something."

"You can talk out here. I don't like hallways sometimes."

"Uh . . . " Vickery glanced around—none of the drivers or mechanics were nearby. "Okay. You remember that guy that came in here eight months or so ago, asking about objects with ghosts fossilized in them—"

"Oh, Vick," said Galvan, with an almost pitying look in her big eyes. "For this you came here?"

"I need to know more about him. I know he left you a business card that was a phony, but—" He paused, wanting to give the woman a plausible excuse for knowing more than she had told him in February. "I was thinking maybe he got in touch again, after I went away, and gave you some contact information for him."

Galvan shook her head, then said, loudly, "*Contrata.*"

Vickery's heart sank as he heard steps behind him, and Galvan went on, "Both of you put down the coffee. With your left hands you will take out any guns you carry, and lay them on the coffee cart. After that, Ramon will frisk you, and I'll be angry if he finds a gun then."

Vickery had twice seen this *contrata* move before, and participated himself in one of those times, and he knew that at least one of the men behind him was standing to the side and pointing a gun at him and Castine.

He set his coffee cup on the cart, then pulled the flat little Glock out of his jacket pocket and laid it down beside the cup. "What the hell, boss?"

Castine gave him a wide-eyed, accusatory look as she clanked the revolver next to it. A pair of hands from behind them quickly and expertly patted down Vickery, and then Castine.

"Guess," said Galvan. "And step back behind that Honda."

"You're selling us to somebody again," said Vickery.

"Yup," she said.

Vickery recalled that, because Galvan's drivers weren't supposed to be armed, he had left a .45 semi-automatic on a shelf against the back wall last year, with his name on a tag tied around the trigger guard. It was a spare, with a dubious legal history, and he had never picked it up, and in any case other drivers sometimes carried guns and left them checked and tagged on that shelf while they drove fares.

When he walked into the bay and around the back end of the tan Honda, he took a few extra steps, and was now within reaching distance of the shelf. Castine seemed to guess that he had some sort of plan, and stepped wide.

He glanced over his shoulder to check Ramon's position and balance—and saw that the shelf was empty.

Vickery's mind raced. "You're selling us to the guy who you told about the book, back in February, right? Maybe you sold him the information then, but that's blood under the bridge. You know why he suddenly right now wants to get hold of me?" The story was taking shape in Vickery's mind as he spoke. "Why I showed up here within, I bet, days of when he contacted you?"

"I just care that he's paying me."

Vickery let out a bitter laugh. "You called him as soon as Tom told you we were here, didn't you? I bet he's not paying you a million-four."

"No," said Galvan cheerfully, "he's not. Neither are you."

"No. But the reason I came here today, hoping you had a line on the guy who has the book, is because a collector in London just lately learned about the existence of it, and he wants it real bad." Vickery was cautiously pleased with this story; it seemed fairly credible. "He got in touch with a number of people who deal in such stuff."

Castine had caught on that he was up to something, and gave him a good imitation of a warning frown.

"Ruben is gonna gag you and tie you up," said Galvan. "The buyer will be along in a minute, and right now neither of you has any broken bones."

"Dammit, boss," said Vickery, "listen to me! That book isn't just another object with a ghost sunk in it, like Hipple's corncob pipes— it's an object *with a never-born in it*. Remember? My daughter who I never had? You know how rare that is? Well, 'rare' doesn't cover it— it's absolutely unique. Ask your *bruja* pals what that's worth."

Galvan's smile was skeptical. "And this London guy is willing to pay a million-four for it?"

"That's right. I heard about him, and called him, and I was able to tell him enough to convince him I have it. And I worked him up to that figure."

"So why does Harlowe need you? He can sell the book to the collector in London and leave you out of it."

"Who's Harlowe?"

Galvan pursed her lips. "The guy I just called."

"And I bet the money he gets from selling the book to the guy in London will be just about pure profit," said Vickery while he tried desperately to come up with a convincing answer to her question. "Is this Harlowe paying you a lot for me today?"

"Five thousand, same as he paid me for steering him to the book itself, in February."

"He's getting off damn cheap."

"But why does he need *you*, now?" persisted Galvan.

Vickery hesitated, and Castine spoke up, in a tone of weary resignation.

"This buyer who just cropped up," she said, "is what you might call a celebrity clergyman. You'd know the name—books, his own TV show. He can't afford to have people find out he's interested in witchy stuff, which would probably happen if Sebastian were to make a stink about the book being stolen from him. The London guy would deny ever having heard of the book—he wouldn't buy it at any price, much less the million-four he's willing to pay Sebastian right now."

"But if I'm verifiably out of the picture," Vickery said, gratefully picking up Castine's story, "like if it's reported that I've killed myself, for instance, your man Harlowe will be free to sell it to this buyer with no risk of a counterclaim . . . and probably for a whole lot less money that what I've got the guy to agree to."

Galvan ran her tongue along the edges of her teeth. Then, "Get in the Honda, quick," she said, nodding toward one of her ordinary cars. "Back seat, and get down on the floor. Ramon, give me your gun, and you drive."

"Ramon," added Vickery, "fetch our guns along."

The man glanced at Galvan, who rolled her eyes and nodded. Ramon handed her his revolver and sprinted back toward the coffee cart.

Sixty seconds later, Ramon was steering the Honda out of the driveway onto Eighth Street, heading west. Vickery and Castine were crouched head-to-head on the floor in front of the rear seat, and Galvan sat in the front passenger seat, holding three guns in her lap.

As Ramon picked up speed, she reached out through the open window and twisted the mirror. "Stay down," she said. "A gray SUV just turned in to my lot." To Ramon, she added, "Around back of that 7-Eleven, and park it."

As the Honda swung to the right and rocked up a driveway, the top of Vickery's baseball cap bumped Castine's head; he caught her eye and winked, and she gave him a brief, impatient nod.

When Ramon had stopped the car and put it in park with the engine still running, Galvan turned around in the front seat. She was holding Ramon's revolver, but pointing it at the headliner for now.

"I get half," she said to Vickery, "If we can get the book away from Harlowe and sell it to your London preacher. You get the other half." She raised her eyebrows and whistled, miming appreciation of how much that would be.

"You get a third," said Vickery, hoping that disagreement about the nonexistent payment would make the story more convincing. "Can we sit up now?"

Galvan looked around. "Yeah, just be ready to duck again. A third?"

"Four-hundred-sixty-six thousand," said Castine, straightening up.

Galvan looked amiably baffled. "Why should Betty Boop get a share? It wasn't her book."

"She . . . helped." Vickery hiked himself up onto the back seat, where he was joined a moment later by Castine. Both of them peered cautiously around at the parking lot. "The guy said his name's Harlowe?"

"No," said Galvan, "he didn't give me a name, so I ran his license plate. He's from out of town. You don't need to know any more than that. I can fix up a meeting with him, and then—I don't know, we could bug his SUV, or frame him for a bad felony bust and blackmail him, or just get rid of his guys and grab him and torture him till he gives us the book—"

"I'm supposed to call my buyer every day before the British banks close," said Vickery, "and in London it's already—"

Castine gave him a quick, anxious look, then raised her arm and glanced at her new watch. "you've got half an hour," she said tensely.

"So we gotta run," said Vickery. "I'll call you later, or tomorrow."

"We'll drive you back to your car," said Galvan.

Castine shook her head. "We like to walk."

"And I can call him while I'm walking," said Vickery, who in fact was not carrying a phone.

Galvan was silent, then said, flatly, "Walk."

"Sure," said Vickery. "Pedestrians have right of way everywhere. Eventually I imagine we'll get on a bus." He slowly opened the door on his side, and Galvan didn't object when he stepped out onto the parking lot pavement. Castine carefully did the same on her side.

"A *bus*," said Galvan.

"I'm just visiting L.A.," Castine explained. "I want to take one of those tours where you see the movie stars' homes."

Galvan laughed softly and shook her head. "Okay, go. Remember, I'm the one who knows who Harlowe is, and how to contact him!"

Vickery smiled at her. "That's what I was hoping for when we came to see you. Oh," he added, "our guns?"

Galvan squinted up at him. "Sure, Vick." She gave the revolver back to Ramon, then lifted Vickery's Glock and Castine's .38 and held them up by the open window. Vickery handed the .38 to Castine and tucked the Glock into his jacket pocket.

"It would be purely dumb," said Galvan as Ramon clicked the Honda into gear and stepped on the brake, "if you were lying to me about this London buyer." When Vickery shook his head, she went on, "I thought you liked having your phantom daughter around."

"I did. But she *is* fossilized, inert. Not even as present as a picture. And she never actually existed anyway." He shrugged. "I like four-hundred grand better."

Galvan gave him an unreadable look. "You used to be more sentimental."

Ramon lifted his foot from the brake and steered the car toward the street on the other side of the parking lot.

Vickery took Castine's suede-sleeved elbow and followed, and then led her quickly north along the sidewalk, away from where he had parked his Saturn. Old brick apartment buildings with fire escapes lined both sides of the street, and the bushy curbside trees were easily a dozen feet tall.

"We'll turn left on Seventh," he told Castine quietly, "go through a few stores, take a taxi or two. Make sure we're not being followed."

He was breathing deeply, still shaky from the tightrope they had just walked with Galvan.

"That story about a London buyer saved us," said Castine. "Oh— and it was nice of you to put me down for a third."

"I had to sound serious." He flexed his hands and stretched. "Your celebrity clergyman was a good touch too."

"But England is eight hours ahead! All the banks closed hours ago."

Vickery was looking up and down the street, noting cars and alleys; there were no unbarred ground-floor windows, and all doors were presumably locked, but a U-Haul truck was parked at the curb a few yards ahead, and near it an apartment gate stood open, braced by an upended couch. "She doesn't know that."

"You better hope she doesn't check it out. She seems thorough."

Castine was looking around too. "God help us when she eventually learns you made the whole thing up." She glanced at Vickery. "You figure you can get a taxi?"

"If I can find a pay phone. A taxi'll come if we call and say we want a long trip, like to Universal Studios. And if we ask nice, the driver'll do some checking and evasion moves."

"I've never been to Universal Studios. I hear it's fun, lots of cool rides."

"Well, we won't be doing any of that today. We'll just get out of one taxi, duck around a couple of corners, and then get in another."

"Oh well." Castine glanced up and down the street. "If you do get your book back," she said, "and if there were a buyer." She looked up at him. "Would you sell it?"

"What, for a million-four?"

"Let's say."

"You'll think I'm crazy, but . . . " His voice trailed off.

A bright green Audi with a bicycle strapped on the roof had passed them slowly, and now its brake lights came on. "You watch around and behind," he told Castine.

The Audi was stopped in the middle of the street, and two empty hands appeared over the bicycle's front wheel. "Let me talk!" came a yell from the car. "I can help you!"

Vickery caught Castine's eye and jerked his head toward the open apartment gate, and they hurried forward to stand by the upended couch. Vickery's hand was in his jacket pocket, and both of Castine's hands were in the pockets of her suede coat.

"Step out of the car," called Vickery.

"Let me park it." The driver's hands withdrew, and the car swerved forward and stopped at a red curb a few yards ahead. The hands waved out of the window again, and then the driver's side door opened and a young man stepped out, his arms raised.

He wasn't wearing the red suspenders, but Vickery recognized him by the round glasses and the eccentric shaved-on-the-sides haircut. After a moment, Vickery beckoned him over with his free hand.

A goateed teenaged boy in a black T-shirt had stepped out of the apartment doorway, and his narrowed eyes switched from Vickery to the young man in the street and back.

"My brother," Vickery told him. "He's going through a bad divorce."

Castine nodded sadly.

The young man from the Audi was close enough to hear Vickery's explanation, and visibly wilted—a touch Vickery admired.

The teenage boy nodded and stepped to the back of the U-Haul truck and rattled the latch on the roll-up door.

Vickery motioned the young man to follow as he and Castine walked a few yards down the sidewalk.

"My name's Elisha Ragotskie," said the young man quietly when Vickery halted. He looked left and right nervously. His white shirt was wrinkled, as if he'd slept in it, and he hadn't shaved recently—but that might have been just a fashion statement. "I can tell you what's going on, if—"

"Tell us first," said Vickery. "What does Harlowe want with us?"

"How do you know his name?" When Vickery impatiently waved the question aside, Ragotskie went on, "You know about the twins? He's going to use *them* as imps for his egregore now, since you two didn't work out. I—I'm sorry, I was stressed!—I tried to—yesterday—"

"Kill this woman," said Vickery quietly. "Go on." He remembered one of the ghosts under the bridge last night saying something like *Quoth the raven nevermore.* Had that last word been this *egregore*?

"Well, either of you, really," said Ragotskie, "to break the pair. I'm sorry, Ms. Castine! I just wanted to stop the egregore, and it looked like you two were going to be the necessary imps. I never imagined he'd go with the twins!"

The boy in the T-shirt was still yanking at the latch on the back of the U-Haul truck, and Ragotskie peered in that direction. Turning back to Vickery, he asked, "Is somebody stuck in that truck?"

"He's just trying to open it," said Vickery. "You were there in February, when Harlowe's people stole a book from me. Do you—"

"But he must be stuck inside! We should—"

Vickery just frowned at him in baffled annoyance, but Castine grabbed Ragotskie's arm. "Do you," she asked urgently, "see the boy in the black T-shirt standing by the back of the truck? Dark hair, got a little beard?"

Ragotskie blinked at her, then looked again at the truck with the rattling latch. "Uh," he said, "no?"

Castine turned a frightened look on Vickery. "You spoke to it in a complete sentence, with not even any Faraday cage chicken-wire in between."

Vickery's face was suddenly cold. "Don't look at it. There's an alley back this way—come on, both of you."

The skinny figure in the black T-shirt, still idiotically yanking on the truck's door handle, was evidently a ghost—a spontaneous, unsummoned one.

Ragotskie opened his mouth but shut it when Castine glared at him, and he followed her and Vickery further down the sidewalk toward the opening of a narrow alley.

Vickery was looking back over his shoulder, and he muttered, "Shit," for the ghost was now lurching after them. Its shadow on the sunlit sidewalk was just a churning blur.

A picture of Bob Marley was visible printed on its T-shirt; Vickery abruptly realized whose ghost it must be, and his steps faltered—and he felt bound to look at it. I *made* it, he thought.

The thing was only a couple of yards away now; it opened its mouth and said, "You think you're so big. I don't *need* a stun-gun— I can take you."

Its mouth opened wider then, and its features began to curdle— and its chameleon tongue, hardly visible in the direct sunlight, looped out of its mouth-hole and struck Vickery in the chest. And then for a prolonged moment Vickery was staring into his own gray-bearded face, six feet away and getting closer, or bigger.

"*I can take you.*" Either it spoke those words again or they replayed forcefully in Vickery's mind.

There was no breeze, but he was suddenly cold all the way through his flesh to his bones, and though the lines of buildings in his peripheral vision remained vertical, he felt himself tipping into a fall that would not end when he hit the pavement—

As if from a distance, he heard Castine's voice call, "Two and two is four, and nothing else!"

The elongated tongue fell away, or evaporated. Vickery was able to hop back, regaining his balance, and glance at her. Just as she had done last night, she was holding up four fingers. She's right, he thought dazedly. It *is* four.

Vickery shook himself and didn't look again at the ghost's face. "Six and six is twelve," he said hoarsely, "and squared is—"

He paused, for at the moment he had no idea what twelve squared was.

"A hundred and forty four!" said Castine. To Vickery, she muttered, "Give it stuff we can do on our fingers! It's got to *see* it."

The ghost had halted; its mouth was closed, and it was swaying back and forth. It seemed less tall than it had been a moment ago. "I'm as good as you," it muttered angrily. "And I'm gonna be in your book, mixing it up with your daughter, what do you think of that?"

"Five and five!" said Castine loudly, holding up the spread fingers of both hands.

"Is ten!" called Vickery, pointing at Castine's hands.

"Isn't either," grumbled the ghost.

Vickery held up his own hands, with his fingers stretched out— it must look as if he and Castine were surrendering—and said, "And ten is twenty, see? Look! There's no place for you here."

For a moment the very air seemed bent, stressed.

Then the ghost turned around, turned again to face them, and then began spinning rapidly, so rapidly that in seconds it was just a blur; and then it disappeared with a *whump* that stirred dust on the sidewalk.

"Terminal z-axis spin," whispered Castine.

CHAPTER EIGHT:
Last Bus to Oblivion

Ragotskie was blinking around in evident confusion.

Vickery rubbed one hand over his face.

"You okay?" asked Castine anxiously. "This is twice in less than twenty-four hours for you."

"Sure." There was a taste like pennies and sour milk in his mouth, and he turned and spat into the gutter. "Excuse me. Sure. Yes." He noticed that his shirt was damp, and clinging to him. "We can talk in the alley," he added, and he was careful to walk steadily as he led the way. His heart was thudding rapidly and he concentrated on breathing in and out.

"It looked like you, for a second!" said Castine, who was walking close beside him, evidently prepared to catch him if he should stumble.

"I know," said Vickery shortly, "I was there."

When all three of them were in the narrow, shaded passage between high brick walls, Vickery looked down the length of it and saw that after about a hundred and fifty feet it opened out at the far end onto a paved lot. He sighed deeply, then turned to Ragotskie. "You didn't see that thing?"

"No. Was there a ghost? I've never—"

"We're miles from any freeway current, and I don't know why it should have appeared here, now. Have you got some kind of mobile hotspot on you?"

"I—oh!—I guess I do. Heh. I had it hooked over my rear-view mirror."

He reached around toward his back pocket, and Vickery caught his arm. "Very slowly."

"I don't have a gun. You took my gun yesterday." Ragotskie fumbled at the back of his black jeans, then held out a dirty white sock.

"What the hell is that?" demanded Vickery.

"Oh my God, Sebastian," said Castine wonderingly, "I think it's the sock I wiped the blood off my face with, last year, right after we came out of the Labyrinth!"

Ragotskie nodded jerkily. "Right, I stole it out of Harlowe's Chevy Tahoe yesterday, at MacArthur Park. It tilts toward you," he said, nodding to Castine. "It's how I've followed you."

She took it out of his hand and stuffed it into her left coat pocket. Ragotskie just bobbed his head, obviously anxious to please.

"I recognized the ghost," said Vickery, feeling sick. "It was that kid I hit in Canter's."

"Pratt?" said Ragotskie. "I heard they had to open his skull. He was nineteen."

Nineteen, Vickery thought. I made that shambling travesty out of him, and I can't apologize, explain.

"I should . . . check the street," he muttered; and with a vague wave he stumbled to the mouth of the alley and just blinked up and down the sunlit street, breathing deeply. I've now certainly killed four men, in the course of my life, he thought. Three men and a boy, rather.

He made himself pay attention to the moving cars—and saw a gray SUV turn onto the street from Eighth. It might have been a Chevy Tahoe.

Over his shoulder, he said, "Ragotskie, does Harlowe have a way to track you?"

Immediately Ragotskie was standing beside him, staring south; then he stepped back quickly, pulling Vickery with him. "They must have had a *tracker* on my car all along! Agnes can't have known about it. She'd have told me."

The SUV was moving slowly up the street. Within seconds it would be in sight of Ragotskie's parked Audi and in line with the alley.

Vickery waved toward the far end of the alley and said, "Walk casually, and don't look back. He won't be looking for three people together."

"He might be," said Ragotskie miserably. "He might have held off on grabbing me in hopes I'd lead him to you two."

"Swell," said Vickery. "Walk casually anyway."

Vickery took Castine's elbow, and as they walked he scanned the doors and windows that faced the alley. The windows were all set in behind iron bars, and the doors were either padlocked or had two keyholes, indicating deadbolts. There was not even a trash can to hide behind.

"You got g-guns?" whispered Ragotskie. "If he sees us, shoot the lock off a door."

"A handgun won't do it," said Vickery. "It'd just lock it worse."

"You'd need a slug out of a shotgun," said Castine, stepping carefully and watching the parking lot ahead.

Vickery heard a car engine in the alley behind him, and then the sound stopped and he heard car doors clunk open.

"Don't speed up," he said. He reached into his jacket pocket and closed his hand on the narrow grip of the Glock. To Ragotskie he said, "Do *they* have guns?"

"Taitz does."

"Is he any good with it?"

"He's killed people." Ragotskie was walking with his head tilted back, as if wading through chin-deep water.

"Excuse me," came a call from behind them, "you three? Police. We'd like to speak to you."

"Keep walking," said Vickery.

More quietly, in a voice just loud enough to carry down the alley, the voice at their backs said, "Stop or we'll shoot."

Castine had thrust her hands into her coat pockets, but what she pulled out wasn't the revolver. She was holding the dirty white sock.

"I think we stop," said Vickery.

Castine raised the somewhat white sock over her head and waved it back and forth; and to Vickery she said, "Call Pratt."

Vickery winced, but had to concede that it was as good an idea as any. He took a breath and opened his mouth.

"I'll do it," said Ragotskie, though he didn't look happy with the idea either. "I knew him." He turned toward the street with his hands raised and said, "Hey, Pratt, come here, dude."

A sourceless groaning cough,echoing between the close brick walls, might have been a reply.

"Let's see everybody's hands," called the voice from the street.

"Pratt," said Ragotskie again, hoarsely. "We forgot to tell you something."

Vickery was about to turn around, but a shiver in the air made him pause. Again the stressful cough sounded in his ears.

"Pratt?" came Ragotskie's oddly muffled voice. "Are you—lonely?"

"Pratt," Vickery said, "it's me."

The air was suddenly cold, and Ragotskie stepped back and gave Vickery an uncertain look.

Vickery and Castine both turned around then, and Vickery's incredulous gasp was simultaneous with Castine's.

A human head was bobbing in mid-air only a couple of yards in front of them, the eyes rolling in the sockets and the beard-fringed mouth rattling open and shut more rapidly than Vickery would have believed possible; then with a sound like somebody vigorously flapping broken glass out of a blanket, there was a body below the head. A blur on the front of the black T-shirt resolved itself into the image of Bob Marley.

The mouth jiggled to steadiness, then pronounced, "Sick, so sick, call 911 . . . "

Beyond the suffering figure, two men stood in front of the SUV at the mouth of the alley, and Vickery saw them step back into the sunlight. One of them was gray haired and wearing an olive-green windbreaker.

"Stay—where you are!" that one called; the other, a younger man in a leather jacket, stood in the one-foot-forward Weaver stance with a pistol at eye level, clearly ready to shoot.

"Tell it," grated Vickery, "to go after them."

Ragotskie blinked at him. "He's here? Okay. Those guys, Pratt," he said more loudly, pointing at the two men, "Taitz and Foster, they left you to die on the street. Look—can you see them?"

"I want to go," said the ghost. Its mouth wasn't moving in synch with the sound of its words. "It's too bright here, crowded. Where is no people?"

The man in the leather jacket called, "On the ground, face down! Now!"

Vickery spoke urgently toward Pratt's ghost. "Behind you. Get in that van. Quick, they're going to leave!"

"Yeah," said Ragotskie, wincing as he looked toward the man with the pistol, "Pratt, you gotta catch the van! Last bus to oblivion!"

With a whimper, the ghost of young Pratt twisted toward the street, and a moment later it was crouching—and then it was loping on all fours, awkwardly but quickly, toward the SUV.

"Jesus God," whispered Castine.

The man in the dark windbreaker, at least, could obviously see the thing—he grabbed his companion and they scrambled back into the SUV and slammed the doors. When Vickery heard the starter whine, he drew his gun.

The bottom curves of the front tires were visible against the sunlit pavement beyond, and he quickly fired twice. The gunshots echoed between the close walls like powerful hammer blows on a metal door, and dust blew out to the sides of the SUV and the front end sagged. The windshield wipers were working rapidly.

Forward or back? thought Vickery. "Crowd up, fast," he said.

He and Castine sprinted toward the street, their guns raised and the sock flapping in Castine's left hand. The ghost, perhaps frustrated at being locked out of the vehicle, had extruded a filament of glassy tongue that was now stuck to the driver's window of the SUV, and the window was opaque white; but the driver had got the vehicle into reverse, and the vehicle rumbled backward in a sharp turn on its two flat front tires.

The ghost was jerked off its feet; its head went down and its feet came up, and then it was spinning in mid-air like a pinwheel, wailing. Its tongue had disappeared. Vickery watched in sick horror as it spun faster, until it was a blur, and then with a wail and a windy implosion it was gone.

At the mouth of the alley Vickery had stepped aside to keep Ragotskie in his peripheral vision, and now that young man came puffing up to where he and Castine stood. He smelled sharply of sweat.

The SUV rocked to a thumping, uneven halt, and the passenger side door opened cautiously.

"Get in my car!" said Ragotskie, running toward his Audi.

But a gun muzzle appeared in the gap between the SUV's opening door and the windshield frame, and Vickery's own gun was instantly in line and he fired at it—the hard *pop* was less loud out here on the street—and over the ringing in his ears he heard a hoarse bark of pain, and the gun clanked to the pavement.

Vickery backed toward the Audi, keeping his gun leveled at the SUV's windshield. "I'll drive," he said over his shoulder. "Ingrid can keep an eye on you in the back seat."

Vickery fired one more shot, squarely through the center of the windshield, then turned and hurried to the car. Ragotskie tossed him the keys over the roof.

Vickery got in and started the engine. "Get down," he snapped as Castine and Ragotskie piled into the back seat, and then he shifted to reverse and stamped on the gas pedal. Castine and Ragotskie were both flung against the back of the front seat, and then they were tossed back when the Audi's rear bumper struck the SUV's front left corner with a resounding crash. Pieces of red plastic skittered across the pavement.

In the back seat, Ragotskie yelped, "My car!"

Vickery shifted to low gear and floored the accelerator again. The Audi tore away from the Tahoe with a rattling clatter, and then it was speeding north. Vickery was hunched over the wheel, his teeth clenched, but there were no gunshots from behind.

At Wilshire Boulevard he ran the stop sign and swerved between honking traffic to make a left turn. Glancing in the mirror, he didn't see any vehicles following them. He shifted to drive.

"You can straighten up," he said. "Are your tags up to date on this? On the license plate?"

"Of course," said Ragotskie. He was sitting up now, blinking through his round glasses at the white high-rise apartment buildings rushing past. He turned to peer back toward the street they'd been on, then rubbed his eyes. "Are you guys some kind of pros? You shoot like . . . if you can see it, you can hit it."

Vickery thought of the intensive and continuous training he'd got while he was a Secret Service agent, which had required that all Protection Detail agents be able to hit one subject, and no others, in a shifting crowd; and he reflected that his more recent hours of shooting practice in the desert had maintained at least some of his skill.

He didn't answer Ragotskie. To Castine he said, "You still got that sock?"

"Yes. I should pitch the filthy thing."

"Tuck it in your pocket."

"You could have killed them both," she said in an accusing tone.

Vickery slowed and made a right turn onto Western. "So could you," he said. "I—killed a guy yesterday." He glanced in the rear view mirror. "Ragotskie? That *ghost* back there said 'I'm gonna be in your book, with your daughter.' What did it mean?"

"I don't know. We took that gardening book from your apartment in February, and we were going to grab you too, but you disappeared. Listen, you've got to—"

"And what do you mean—twins—imps—Ecuador?"

"You've got to help me get my girlfriend away from them, her name is Agnes Loria, okay?" When neither Vickery nor Castine said anything, he exhaled audibly and took a deep breath, and Vickery guessed that it was difficult for him to tell secrets that he had been committed to keeping until recently. Finally, "Egregore, it means a group-mind," Ragotskie said rapidly, "people pour their identities into it like . . . I don't know, like different kinds of liquor in a Long Island Iced Tea, and it becomes a way-bigger entity, orders of orders of magnitude, independent of the people in it, just made out of them like a body is made of cells. Shit. It can live forever—new identities get absorbed and old members fall away like sloughed-off skin. And Agnes is—dammit—"

Vickery caught a green arrow and turned left on Western, still watching the rear-view mirror.

"Take it easy," said Castine to Ragotskie. "You wanted to break up the pair of us, you said. And yes, something about twins."

"Okay," said Ragotskie. "Okay. The egregore will need, damn quick, a pair of Interface Message Processors, that's IMPs, see, to let the various minds all work together as one network, and you two would have been perfect because you—what, died? And came back? And so you're not exactly stuck in the discrete increments of now, like the rest of us. Harlowe says you're FM radios in a world of AM. And you'd have worked like superconductor IMPs. But I managed to screw that up, even without killing you . . . uh, ma'am. So the egregore should have misfired, miscarried, and Agnes wouldn't be able to *sacrifice herself* to the damned thing. She could come to her senses, see?"

"But," prompted Castine.

"But he's got these twin girls, his nieces, they're schizophrenic or something, they fall in and out of each other's minds all the time, and Agnes says they can get into other people's minds too, make 'em do things—anyway their identities are a kind of open-ended relay—and so I guess they'll *do*, as his IMPs."

He was silent for a moment, staring blindly at the buildings rushing past outside, then said, "Can I borrow some money? I went to a Versatel machine yesterday, and my accounts have been deleted. Harlowe's a wizard with computer stuff, hacking and all that. I slept in this car last night, but I can't do that again, now that they've obviously got some kind of *tracker* on the poor thing."

"So far you've told us about twenty bucks' worth," said Vickery. "If they've got these twins now, and don't need Ingrid and me anymore—and it sounds like they don't need you anymore either—why did those guys threaten us? Why has Harlowe offered Galvan five thousand bucks to hand us over to him?"

"About you, I don't know. Maybe he wants you on hand for backup in case the twins flip out. As for—"

Castine shook her head. "They acted like they were ready to kill us right there in the alley."

"I think they would have," agreed Vickery. The guy in the leather jacket, he thought, had seemed positively eager.

"Okay," said Ragotskie, "that's true, so Harlowe must have decided you're toxic in some way—"

"Jeez," muttered Castine, "I could make you a list."

"—and he's determined to use the twins. Me," Ragotskie went on, "I'm initiated but renegade now, so I guess they want to—take my blood pressure, as they'd say. Hah. That means—"

"We know what it means," said Castine.

"How do we stop him from trying to kill us," asked Vickery, "and how do I get my book back?" He turned left again on Olympic, past the monolithic Koreatown Galleria.

"Your book! What the hell *is* it?" When Vickery didn't reply,

Ragotskie went on, "He—I don't know, he keeps it locked away somewhere. But he wants to kill all three of us, now, see? We're in this together!" He paused, and when he again got no response he went on, "If the egregore were to fail, then there wouldn't be any point in killing any of us . . . except you, about Pratt, I guess." He laughed briefly, unhappily. "And Agnes won't be able to lose her self. We can get her away from them, safe, even if she doesn't love me anymore."

"Get her away," echoed Vickery, not looking away from the traffic ahead and keeping his voice level. "So how do we kill this egregore thing?"

"Would we be okay if we just left town?" interjected Castine. "Fly to the east coast?" Vickery tilted his head and flicked a glance at the rear view mirror, but she avoided meeting his eye.

Ragotskie's answer was nearly a monotone: "When the egregore does come online, it'd find you. Strangers who were part of it would kill you." Vickery heard him blow his nose, and hoped the young man had a handkerchief or Kleenex or something. Good thing Castine had taken the sock. "And," Ragotskie went on, "it's already started spontaneously gathering people into itself—Agnes calls it the black hole effect, when random people suddenly fall into it and start speaking our thoughts. I've seen it happen."

"So have we," said Vickery, thinking of the girl on the bicycle yesterday at MacArthur Park.

"It's just a temporary possession now," said Ragotskie, "like for a minute, and they're just disoriented, after. But when the thing is actually born, it'll be taking them permanently, like a worldful of dominoes falling, and when they're down they won't ever be getting up again—all their personalities and memories and skills will be dissolved, dispersed through the whole egregore thing. And God only knows what it'll want to do. Harlowe says it'll *be* God." He laughed again, again not happily. "You should hear him talk about it. He'd convince you. He convinced me . . . until he convinced Agnes."

Castine too may have been thinking of the girl on the bicycle. "What," she asked hesitantly, "becomes of the people who get taken by it?"

"They'll be like . . . just the egregore's fingers, or toes," said

Ragotskie. "Or eyes or ears, anything, fingernails. Bloodstream, really. They'll probably wear out pretty quick—Harlowe says the big entity probably won't waste a lot of attention on getting each of its seven billion members to eat or sleep. Though it will want them to reproduce a lot, so there's new cells to replace the ones that drop out of it."

"Drop out of it meaning die," said Vickery. He slowed to a stop for a red light at Harvard. The signs on all the nearby buildings seemed to be in Korean.

"Or just, you know, wander around," said Ragotskie, "too crazy and malnourished to be any further use to it. But yeah, die, probably, pretty quick."

Castine's voice shivered as she said, "So how do we kill it?"

"A guy tried to start an egregore in the '60s," said Ragotskie, swaying as the car started forward again. "Some kind of hippie rock musician, I think. Harlowe doesn't like to talk about that, though he had Taitz and Foster question a bunch of old folks who were around then, and offer them money if they hear of anybody lately looking into it. He won't say who the hippie was, but he's using at least some of the guy's methods."

Vickery tensed as Ragotskie's hand waved over the passenger seat, but he was just pointing at the floor. "Down there's an envelope, some stuff I stole and printed out on Sunday, day before yesterday, at Harlowe's office on Sepulveda. A coloring book the hippie had printed up in 1966, and a couple of copies of a coloring book Harlowe published and distributed last year, in Spanish and English, with a picture in it reprinted from the 1966 one. Uh—don't stare at the picture for more than a few seconds, okay? Concentrating on it is the initiation, that's why the picture's so detailed—it takes a person at least a minute of focusing on it, to color it all in." Ragotskie inhaled with an audible shudder. "And," he went on, "I printed out a file of Harlowe's, where he wrote some stuff about that old egregore, though he doesn't give the hippie leader's name or any traceable details."

Vickery lifted one hand from the wheel and spread his fingers.

"Right, okay," said Ragotskie, "the thing is, something went bad wrong for the hippie's egregore. This was in 1968. When he tried to quicken it, launch it, cut the umbilical cord, some people reportedly got shot or went nuts, and the whole program crashed on him. It got hushed up, nobody called the cops and everybody who was there said afterward that they were someplace else, far away. So—you two seem pretty smart—figure out what went wrong in '68, and make it happen again now."

"Which will save your Agnes from emptying her mind into the worldwide soup," said Vickery.

"Right, but you still need to help me get her away. You help me, I help you."

"How do you help us?" asked Vickery. He had driven back past Irolo now, and was looking for a section of empty curb.

"Well, shit, man, I just told you a lot of stuff, and I'm giving you that file, and—there's more I could tell you."

After a few seconds, Vickery said, "Okay, we'll try. Where's this office of Harlowe's on Sepulveda?"

"I don't remember the street number, but it's at Sepulveda and Venice, out by the Santa Monica airport, a little office building with a sign that says ChakraSys, *sys* with a *y*. And he's, uh, got a boat at a local marina. I—" Vickery saw him shake his head; "—tracked Agnes there last night, with Waze. I drove away before anybody could see me."

"Waves?" said Castine.

Vickery noticed belatedly that he had lost his Dodgers cap at some point. "Waze," he said impatiently, "it's an app that navigates traffic." To Ragotskie he said, "What's the name of the boat, and where's the marina?"

"Excuse *me*," put in Castine.

"I don't remember—right now," said Ragotskie. His voice was flat with defiance. "And he'll have cleaned out the office on Sepulveda, since I went rogue, but I can still establish contact with them. You help me, and I'll help you. *Agnes*."

Vickery looked at him in the rear view mirror. Ragotskie's weak mouth was set firmly for once. Vickery found himself reluctantly admiring the young man.

"Okay," said Vickery finally. "You got a phone?"

"Yes, but I took the battery out of it. They could GPS me if it was working." He exhaled through clenched teeth. "And I gotta ditch this car. Well, you already bashed it up, didn't you?"

Vickery glanced at Ragotskie in the mirror. "I'm going to drop you off here, pretty quick." Ragotskie began to protest in a panicky tone, but Vickery talked over him: "I'll give you five hundred bucks. Take the bike off the roof of this, and get yourself a burner phone and meet us tonight at . . . " Vickery paused to think about it. "Okay, go to where Estes Street dead ends against the north side of the 10 freeway, right? There's a thrift store and a closed bowling alley there, and behind them is a dirt slope that leads up to the freeway shoulder. Go up the slope, and there's a clearing among the shoulder trees— probably a couple of chairs, cigarette butts, beer cans. If there are a few guys there, just tell them that you're supposed to meet a kid named Santiago, can you remember all that?"

Ragotskie repeated the instructions haltingly. "Is that a freeway gypsy nest? Harlowe said they're dangerous."

"If Santiago is still around, they won't mess with you. They'll assume you're connected. And if they say he isn't around anymore, just—wing it. It'd be a good idea to bring a lot of sandwiches and beer, too, share 'em around. Good sandwiches, not the little triangles in plastic boxes."

"Out of my five hundred?" Getting no reply, Ragotskie went on, "Meet you there when?"

"I can't be sure. Be there by sundown, and wait for us."

"What if this Santiago kid is *there*? Who is he?"

"Oh hell, tell him you're both to wait there for us. He's a sort of freelance courier and watcher."

"And thief," added Castine.

"Sometimes. Anyway, he knows us." Vickery swung the car to a vacant curb space and put it in park. He hiked up to reach into his pocket, and peeled off five hundred dollars bills and passed them to Ragotskie. "Now get out."

Ragotskie's eyes were big behind the round lenses. "You'll be there for sure?"

"Unless we run into trouble."

Ragotskie opened his door and stepped out onto the sidewalk. He unbuckled the straps on his bicycle and carefully lifted it down onto the pavement, and spent a few seconds anxiously looking it over. Apparently satisfied that it hadn't sustained any damage when Vickery had backed the car into Harlowe's SUV, he hiked it around so that it was facing back the way they'd come, then swung one leg over it and took hold of the hand grips.

He bent down to peer through the open door at Vickery. "I do know where your book is!" he said loudly. "Trade! Agnes for the book! Be there!" And then he was pedaling rapidly away down the sidewalk. In the side mirror, Vickery saw him disappear around the corner of some office building.

Vickery waited for a gap in traffic, then swung the car into the right lane.

"You just let him go," observed Castine.

"Sure. We've got to get away from this car, and I don't want him knowing about our Saturn. At that freeway nest we can sneak up from the shoulder side, make sure he's alone."

Castine nodded. "He *might* try to re-establish himself with Harlowe—or his Agnes!—by turning us over to Harlowe."

"He doesn't know which way he's facing," agreed Vickery. "He may work with us, but he's no ally."

"He mentioned twin girls," said Castine, "and a boat."

"And two girls holding hands on a boat seemed to send that old-house vision to us this morning, and ran us off the road. What do you bet it was the same two girls?"

"A lot," said Castine. "And it connects this Harlowe person's group with that awful house."

"Maybe. Probably." He glanced at the manila envelope on the floor by her feet. "We might as well drive by Harlowe's office on Sepulveda, once we're back in the Saturn. We've got time before we meet Supergirl."

"Then dinner, I hope. And not some hot dog stand."

"I think we'll be going to the Central Library on Fifth, and Philippe's is right by there. Great French dip sandwiches."

"I'm ready for that. Don't crash us before we get there."

Taitz and Foster had found their way to a Lavanderia, and in the steamy, fluorescent-lit interior, over the noise of the washers and dryers and the Spanish-language chat of the customers, Taitz had got Harlowe on his cell phone. He was holding it in his left hand; his right was wrapped in a now-blood-blotted towel he had bought for five dollars from a woman at one of the dryers. The place was fragrant with laundry detergent and bleach.

"And you're going to have to report your Tahoe as stolen," Taitz was saying into the phone. "Vickery shot out both front tires and put a round through the windshield—in addition to shooting my hand. No way Foster and I were going to hang around and talk to cops. No, listen, we're at some kind of Mexican laundromat at Eighth and Mariposa, you gotta send a car here to take me to an emergency room." He listened for a few moments, then said, "What? I don't care, I want real doctors! Yes, Ragotskie led us to both of them, he sure did, and a lot of good it did us. He's *with* them now, somehow—they all three drove off together in his car."

He took a deep breath and let it out shudderingly. "Who *is* this Vickery guy? He could have killed both of us, but he just . . . *disabled* us. Oh, and he sicced a *ghost* on us! Yes! I think it was Pratt, the damn thing froze my window with its tongue, broke the glass. I don't know, when we cornered Ragotskie and Castine and him, he just conjured the thing out of thin air! It came at us like some kind of mad dog! And then he started shooting!" Taitz listened for a few seconds, then said, "Yes, it did seem to be Pratt. What? It didn't *go* anywhere, it just spun around in the air and disappeared!" Taitz moved his injured hand from his chest to his knee. "Shit, this hurts. Get somebody here quick. Oh, another thing—you better move the *Black Sheep* again, Ragotskie was at that marina last night, according to Foster's tracking app. I guess he tracked Loria somehow." Taitz barked one strained syllable of a laugh and said, "Yeah, you too."

He touched the screen with his thumb, then switched the phone off and slid it into the pocket of his windbreaker.

"A *ghost* did that to your window?" said Foster, wide-eyed. Sweat was running down his bald scalp. "I thought Vickery shot it. *Pratt's* ghost? Jesus, I didn't actually think ghosts were real."

Taitz leaned back and wiped his sweating face with his left sleeve. "You were no help. After he shot me, he turned around to go to Ragotskie's car. You had a clear field of fire. You could have—" He hissed as he moved his wounded hand. "You could have got all three of them."

"He shot the windshield! I couldn't see out."

"Shit. You told me—bragged to me!—that last year you killed a guy who tried to steal your winnings, in the parking lot of the Commerce Casino. That's right by the 5 Freeway, definitely inside the current. But—you didn't see Pratt's ghost just now."

"Oh. Yeah, well—everything happened so fast—and Vickery was in the way—"

"You've never killed anybody, and I bet you've never even been to that casino."

"The freeway was closed down that day—yeah, remember, a big semi jackknifed—"

Taitz was about to give a scornful reply, but paused when the woman who had sold him the towel came shuffling to the chairs he and Foster were sitting in.

"For a ghost that follows you," she said diffidently, "you need to change how you look, to it. You are right-handed? Good, the bandages will make you do everything different from usual. Get shoes that belonged to someone else—"

"Get *lost,* chiquita," snapped Foster, but Taitz raised his good hand.

"Shut up," he said to Foster; and to the woman he said, "Go on."

"Shoes from a thrift store," the woman said, "so the ghost won't know your footsteps. Wear your shirts facing backward. You wear no rings—get a ring, two rings, from the thrift store—the ghost will maybe see only the shadows of who had them before."

She said nothing more, and after a few seconds Taitz said, "Thank you."

She nodded, and cocked her head as if to see him better. "You saw it?" It wasn't really a question.

"Yes."

"Because of the death of someone?"

Taitz thought of Hannah's car tumbling over the 101 freeway embankment in 1986.

"Yes."

"May God have mercy on you."

Taitz sighed. He and Foster knew, as this woman apparently did too, that people who had committed homicide in the freeway current acquired a certain expanded perspective: the generally unwelcome ability to see ghosts. There were other ways to fall into that ability, but the woman had clearly guessed that murder had been the cause of it in his case; what she had said had been a prayer.

"Thank you," he said again, quietly.

CHAPTER NINE:
A Splendid and Effective Insanity

Vickery parked Ragotskie's green Audi on Normandie, right under a TOW AWAY—NO PARKING ANY TIME sign, hoping it would be towed soon, and then he and Castine walked quickly down an alley and through a parking lot to Irolo Street, where his Saturn was parked. The only consequence of having left all the windows down was that a half-full bag of french fries had been tossed into the back seat.

Vickery opened the trunk and laid Ragotskie's envelope beside the jack, and Castine tossed in the old bloodstained sock; and though they rolled up the front windows, they still had to talk loudly when Vickery had got onto the westbound 10 freeway, because of the headwind buffeting in through the two glassless back windows.

When he found his way to Sepulveda and Venice, the building Ragotskie had told them about was on the northwest corner of the intersection—a one-story stucco structure with a cement ramp up to the front doors, and the *ChakraSys* logo in bold sans-serif letters between two windows above the doors.

The parking lot behind the place was empty except for a couple of abandoned-looking sedans and an old Volkswagen van with eyes painted all over it. Vickery parked away from the other vehicles,and when Castine climbed out she tried to comb her disordered hair with her fingers.

"You've got to get some plastic to cover those windows," she said, speaking for the first time in several minutes.

"Top of my list," said Vickery shortly. A green Dumpster stood beside a pile of cardboard file boxes at the back of the building, and he made a mental note to look through it all if the building were indeed unoccupied.

They walked around to the front, and through the glass doors they saw a wide bare floor and a split drywall partition and wires hanging out of a couple of holes in the walls. Vickery rattled the door, which was, unsurprisingly, locked.

"Let's look in the trash," he said, leading the way back to the parking lot side of the building.

He flipped a couple of file boxes aside when he saw they were empty and unlabeled—but he jumped backward and sat down hard on the pavement when a white-bearded man suddenly stood up in the Dumpster. Castine had only dropped a box and stepped back.

The old man in the Dumpster towered over Vickery, his shaggy, bearded head silhouetted against the blue sky. Blinking and scuttling back, Vickery was able to make out that the man was tall, even allowing for the elevation of the Dumpster floor, and his face was sun-darkened under a blowing fringe of white hair. A threadbare gray sportcoat was bunched over his shoulders, and Vickery could see that he wore another coat under that. The collars of both coats, and a blue shirt under them, were all turned up under his beard.

Vickery got to his feet, and carefully stepped around to the far side of the Dumpster and leaned forward to peer into it. Aside from the old man himself, whose eccentric outfit was completed by bulky corduroy trousers and worn sneakers, the rusty container was empty. The smell from it was like burnt plastic and rotten strawberries.

The old man had shifted around, his sneakers grating on the metal floor, and he said "I don't know you," then looked across at Castine. "Or you either."

"No," agreed Vickery, slapping dust off the seat of his jeans. "We're not from around here. Do you know where they went?" He waved at the building. "The people who ran ChakraSys?"

"They went thataway," said the old man, without moving at all. "You losers. Are your chakras out of order? Grip your heads with your Kegel muscles."

"Were you," Vickery persisted, "around when they were in business?"

"If they had a business," said the old man, "they didn't build that. They were munchkins standing on the shoulders of giant ants."

Vickery tried once more. "What did their business *do*?"

The old man stood up straight and squared his shoulders as he glared at Vickery, who took a step back from the Dumpster.

"*Do*?" the man rumbled. "What does it look like they did? They ran. Have you made a *deal* with those people? Do you think I can't fly away? Hah!" He gripped the rim of the Dumpster and began scuffing the inner wall of it with a shoe, apparently intending to climb out.

Vickery caught Castine's eye and nodded toward the car. "Uh, thanks anyway!" he called to the struggling old man as he and Castine began walking across the asphalt toward the Saturn.

Behind them the old man was singing now: "*We left behind the old gray shore, climbed to the sky . . .* "

Back in the car, Vickery started the engine as Castine pulled her door closed. He steered around the colorful old van to a driveway, and made a left turn onto Sepulveda; a few blocks ahead was an onramp onto the 405 freeway, which would take them north to connect to the eastbound 10. Neither of them spoke as he drove past a Subway and a Carl's Jr.

Finally, feeling that he ought to say it before Castine did, Vickery said, sheepishly, "Former LAPD officer and Secret Service agent flees from unarmed old lunatic in trash bin."

Castine smiled. "He wasn't a *ghost*, was he?" she asked.

Vickery was startled. "Uh—no, his sneakers grated on the Dumpster floor. He was solid. Good thought, though—when he does become a ghost, he won't have to change much."

"I'm glad some of my thoughts are good."

Vickery made a right turn and sped up as the short lane curved to join the freeway. "I'm sorry, I've been . . . testy, haven't I? I just feel like this thing is rolling over us. And I don't even know what it is! Black holes, egregores, imps."

"One thing at a time. Right now, Boardner's, to meet Supergirl." She looked at her forty-dollar Target watch. "We'll be early for our appointment with her—we can sit in a back booth and look at the papers Ragotskie says he stole."

The wind had started fluttering through the back windows again, and Vickery spoke more loudly. "But then we've got to go to that freeway nest—"

Castine raised her voice too. "After we see what's in the papers, and after we hear whatever Supergirl might be able to tell us."

"Okay, yeah." He sighed. "You're right, one thing at a time." A distantly-remembered tune was playing in his mind, and he whistled a few bars of it.

Then he sang, softly, "*We left behind the old gray shore, climbed to the sky, until we all one burden bore, never to die.*" He looked at Castine. "Do you remember that song?"

"What song?"

He sang it again, louder.

She shook her head.

"It was from the '60s or '70s," he said, "a group called Fogwillow. They were like, I don't know, Iron Butterfly or Deep Purple. The song was called . . . 'Elegy in a Seaside Meadow.'"

"Before my time!"

"Hey, mine too. I grew up on Guns n' Roses and Radiohead. But I listened to the old stuff too."

"One burden bore," she said, leaning back. "That's a line in Poe's 'The Raven.' Gimme a minute." She moved her lips silently, one finger tapping out meter in the air. "*Caught from some unhappy master whose unmerciful disaster followed fast and followed faster, till his songs one burden bore . . .* something something, *nevermore.*"

"We recited that in the Labyrinth, last year," said Vickery; he shook his head at the memory, and went on, "to save our sanity."

"In that place," said Castine, "it was a step in the direction of sanity."

"Under the bridge last night," Vickery went on thoughtfully, "one of the ghosts said, 'Quoth the raven.'"

Castine inhaled audibly. "Good Lord, you're right. I forgot that."

"I thought the next word was nevermore, like in the poem, but it might have been—"

"Egregore," said Castine. "Maybe we should have talked to that old guy in the Dumpster."

"I tried to, remember? And anyway, it was a popular song back then—that old guy probably rotates it with 'Eve of Destruction' and 'Like A Rolling Stone.'"

Castine shrugged and shook her head.

"Songs of the time," explained Vickery. "I think I'll stay on freeways here, 10 to the 110 to the 101."

"Very binary sort of freeways," Castine observed.

Vickery laughed. "I wish. Ones and zeroes. But they're generally fractional, if not downright fractal. Sometimes there's a lot of free wills moving along them, fast, sometimes a few, sometimes a lot but slow. It's a bunch of unbalanced forces, fluctuating indeterminism, never in equilibrium. Even without the Labyrinth to fall into anymore, they're dicey."

Castine was gripping the seat belt that crossed her from shoulder to hip. "You figure you're okay driving? Fast?"

Vickery opened his mouth, then closed it. "I'd let you drive, but the old-house vision hits you too. We *have* to travel—if I start to sense two girls on a boat, I'll swerve straight to the median or the shoulder."

"That's—not a very good plan."

"What else is there? We've got to get around, and a taxi driver wouldn't do things we might need to do."

Castine was still holding onto the seat belt. "I wish I'd gone to Confession before we got into all this."

Vickery got off the 101 at Highland and drove down to make a left turn on Hollywood Boulevard, and he parked in a lot off Las Palmas. Boardner's was on Cherokee, on the other side of the parking lot. He and Castine rolled the front windows down to match the rear ones, San Francisco style, and he opened the trunk and lifted out Ragotskie's envelope.

He handed it to Castine and tucked the car keys between the envelope and her right hand.

"Wait here by the car," he said. "I don't trust Supergirl absolutely. I'm going to go in and order a beer. If I don't see any bad guys and nothing happens, I'll come out and salute. If I'm not out in three minutes, or if I step out and make any other gesture, or if anybody seems to pay attention to me and follows me in, toss that in the car and drive away. You know how to drive evasive if you have to, and the bloody sock is in the trunk, so they can't track you that way anymore. You remember how to get to my place outside Barstow?"

She nodded, tight-lipped.

"Go there—evasive!—and I'll catch up when I can. The trailer key's on the ring."

"I've got a gun and I'm trained," she said, "and we're allies. Friends, even."

She spread the fingers of her right hand, and the keys fell onto the asphalt.

Vickery stared at her expressionlessly for several seconds, then bent to pick up the keys.

"Okay," he said, straightening. "Both or none it is. Allies— friends." He gave her a grudging smile. "I won't forget again."

"Good."

He took the envelope from her and led the way across the parking lot. "Three-sixty," he said over his shoulder.

She was already glancing behind them and to the sides, and didn't reply. No cars slowed or sped up as they crossed the two lanes of Cherokee, and Vickery didn't see anybody sitting in the visible parked cars, and when he pulled open the door of Boardner's nobody at the bar showed any special alertness as they stepped into the dim interior and made their way down the row of booths to one at the far end. Scents of gin and leather floated on the cool air.

Vickery laid the envelope on the table between them, and looked up at the waitress who had walked to the booth. He recognized her from their visit the day before.

"Today I'll have a Kahlua and milk, please," Castine told her. "Caffeine," she explained to Vickery.

"Could I have the two Coorses together this time," Vickery said. "It's been that kind of day."

When the waitress had smiled sympathetically and moved away, Vickery slid the contents of the envelope out on the table. He picked up a booklet that was on top and riffled through it. It was old, the staples separating from the tanned pages.

"It's a coloring book," he said quietly after he had flipped half of the pages, "like Ragotskie told us. Caricatures, very '60s—Dylan, Ginsberg, Lenny Bruce."

"He said Harlowe printed one last year, and distributed it," said Castine, peering past Vickery's elbow at the thing. "With some picture from this old one reprinted in it."

"They're dumb pictures." He flipped to the back page.

"What's that supposed to be?" She touched the page. Printed on it was an intricate pattern of tightly curved lines.

"I don't know," said Vickery. "A maze?"

"No, look, there's a figure in the middle of it. It's a bird, like a hawk, with a human head. And it's got a little beard, like a goat."

Vickery felt a chill along his forearms. "It looks kind of like . . . " he began.

And Castine finished the thought: "An Egyptian hieroglyph." She slapped the coloring book closed, sending bits of brown paper flying. "Ragotskie said don't stare at it!"

Vickery sat back. "Does a picture in a coloring book count as an artifact?"

Castine slid a newer-looking pamphlet out of the sheaf of papers. "This must be the one Harlowe printed up." She opened several pages at random; it did appear to be a coloring book. "It's published by ChakraSys," she said, "all pictures of smiling people doing exercises or sitting on the floor eating bananas. Ah—but check out the back page."

On the back page was the same convoluted pattern they had seen in the old coloring book, with the same human-headed hawk figure at the center of it. As soon as Vickery nodded in recognition, she closed the book.

A sheet of paper was paper-clipped to the back of the coloring book, and Castine pulled it free and laid it on the table. Several curving lines had been drawn on it, with an X close to one line.

"A map," said Castine.

"With no orientation at all, not even an arrow to point north."

"Well, that's a street or highway," said Castine, touching a double line. "The single lines are smaller streets, probably."

Vickery shrugged and laid it aside. "It's no use unless you already know where it is."

The waitress walked up to their booth with a tray, and set the Kahlua-and-milk and the beers on their table.

When he had thanked her and she had walked back to the bar, Vickery said, "Ragotskie says we should figure out what went wrong with that egregore in '68, and make it happen again now."

"Probably Harlowe knows what went wrong then," said Castine.

She paused to take a sip of her drink, and pointed at the printout pages.

Vickery picked up the sheaf of typescript that had been under the coloring books and looked at the top page.

"*When DeMille learned what the set technician had done,*" he read quietly, "*he excavated a long trench and had the entire City of the Pharaoh set—walls, gates, sphinxes and all—pulled down and buried. His explanation was that he didn't want low-budget movie companies to come in later and use his costly sets in their own films—and in fact that probably was a factor in his decision. But his main purpose in obliterating the set was to be sure of burying the perilous image.*"

Vickery looked up. "It seems to start *in media res.*"

"'Perilous image' is suggestive," said Castine. "We'll have to—" She stopped talking, for a woman had walked up to their booth and stopped. Vickery laid the printout pages on top of the coloring books.

The woman had short-cropped dark hair, and wore a white blouse untucked over faded blue jeans. It occurred to Vickery that she could very believably dress as a short, wiry cowgirl, too, if a movie character like that should become popular.

"Hi, Rachel," he said. "In civvies today?"

"I'm not gonna sit," she said. "I phoned around and got hold of a guy. He used to live up in Laurel Canyon—he stayed at Frank Zappa's log cabin for a while, and Peter Tork's house—and I met him and showed him your picture. It scared him."

Rachel picked up Castine's glass. "What's this," she said, "chocolate milk?"

"Kahlua and milk," said Castine.

"Okay then." Rachel tilted it up to her mouth and swallowed till it was empty. "He said it looked like an old house that used to be down in Topanga Canyon," she went on. "Somebody filmed an indie movie there in the '60s, called *What's the Hex*? And a lot of famous people used to go to parties there, but it was all witchcraft rituals and drugs. Charles Manson stayed there for a few weeks, but it freaked him out and he left. It got wrecked in a flood and torn down in '69, but in '68 there was some kind of bad night there, and several people got shot. An L.A. biker gang was involved, he thinks they were called the Gardena Legion, and it may have been them that started the trouble, like the Hell's Angels did at Altamont."

She clanked Castine's emptied glass down on the table. The ice rattled.

"Are you sure you won't have a—another drink, Rachel?" said Vickery. "That all seems very long ago. Before any of us were born."

Rachel wiped her mouth on her sleeve. "Well, this old guy I talked to, he's a groundskeeper now at—at a place in L.A., and back in January a couple of guys came to him and said to call a number if he heard about anybody showing an interest in that place, or what happened there on that bad night in '68. The guys gave him a card and said he'd get big money if he should hear anything and tell them about it. After they left he just tore up the card, but he told me that there *is* a guy going around asking questions about it, an Egyptian, and he's got a gun. He's only maybe forty years old, but in '68 there was another Egyptian involved, a guy they called Booty, and he had some connection with the Gardena Legion. And my . . . source says he heard from a pal of his from the bad old days, who said *he* got a visit from these two guys too, also around January. It looks like they were finding everybody from that scene who's still alive, saying let us know if anybody's asking about that night. Which you sort of are."

Rachel picked up one of Vickery's beers and drank most of it in four big swallows.

She put the glass down and exhaled. "That's all I've got, and I'm not going to sell you out—I think it'd boomerang, for one thing. My source, who made me promise to forget his name, said I should forget about the house, too, and everything he told me. I only came here now because you paid me. That helps, because I'm going to stay off the boulevard for a while." She gave Vickery a taut smile and said, "It's been nice knowing you, on the whole."

Then she turned away, and there was just her rapidly receding back as she strode down the length of the bar to the street door.

Castine slowly picked up her glass, looked at it, and put it down. "Booty," she said.

"Omar Sharif's predecessor," said Vickery. "Also trying to retrieve—and destroy, I bet—that missing artifact."

Castine lifted they printout pages and looked at the two coloring books. "A tall order, to confiscate and destroy every copy of these things." She leaned back and sighed deeply. "What the heck?" When Vickery gave her a blank look, she added, "The title of the movie."

"Oh. Hex. *What's the Hex?* We should check it out. I wonder if it's on YouTube."

Castine shivered. "It would be . . . unsettling . . . to see that terrible old house in a video. Even though I've seen it *in person,* sort of, too many times."

"I'm just glad to hear it was torn down in '69. We've got to get to the library, look some things up."

"Too bad we can't just . . . stay off the boulevard for a while, like Supergirl." She lifted her glass, then sighed and put it down again. "But you're right," she said, "We've got to chase this stuff more effectively than it chases us. So let's read the rest of it. How doth the little crocodile improve his shining tail!"

"Uh." Vickery blinked at her. "What?"

She seemed disconcerted. "I—" She cleared her throat and hummed for a moment. "I don't know why I said that. It's from one of the *Alice in Wonderland* books. I'm tired, my mind's wandering!" She shook her head and waved at the papers. "Well?"

"Okay," said Vickery slowly. "It's kind of long—maybe you ought to have something to eat? They've got pretty good nachos here, chicken wings—"

"If I wanted a snack," said Castine impatiently, "I'd have had those French fries in your car. You said Philippe's."

"Right. Would you like a . . . whole drink, in the meantime? Or coffee?"

"I'm *fine.*" She got up and stepped around the table to slide into his side of the booth. "We can both read it."

"Let me know if I read too fast for you."

"As if." She squinted down at the printout.

Vickery nodded, then after a moment he too began scanning the paper.

The account in the printout proved to be fragmentary. After the mention of Cecil B. DeMille burying the set of a movie—Castine was sure it must have been *The Ten Commandments,* which was made sometime before talking pictures—the narrative spoke of a "sigil" that had been buried in 1927 down in San Pedro by the Port of Los Angeles, specifically on a street called Paseo del Mar. Over the next two years, according to the printout, the buried sigil had "moved toward the sea," and in 1929 it had pulled the whole clifftop neighborhood down to the sea with it, houses, streets, a hotel and all. The narrative jumped then to an account of an unnamed occult motorcycle gang in 1965 digging up the sigil from among those broken pavements and foundations on the San Pedro shore.

Castine tapped the page. "That'd be the—what did Supergirl say was the name of that biker club?"

"The Gardena Legion. Gardena's down in the South Bay area. By San Pedro, in fact."

The text began now to deal with a person, evidently a man, identified only as "the guru." The guru was a rock guitarist who, according to the printed pages, "*was one of the Laurel Canyon hangers-on in 1965, and had the dubious distinction of being banned from Cass Elliot's house on Woodrow Wilson Drive, apparently for having stolen some cash from her. the guru was already aware of the sigil that was in the possession of the biker club, and was making plans to steal it from their Topanga Canyon clubhouse. They were using it only to sustain the group identity of their club, including members who (with some frequency) died in highway accidents or clashes with the other violent, occult-inclined motorcycle clubs from Los Angeles and San Bernardino counties. the guru had grander, in fact world-spanning plans. He stole the sigil from the biker club's clubhouse, and soon printed the sigil in his coloring books, copies of which I was able to acquire in 2016 . . . *"

Vickery looked around, and lowered his voice. "Okay, the sigil is that complicated figure in the coloring books."

Castine nodded. "Obviously. And obviously this guy who the Elliot person didn't like is the hippie rock musician Ragotskie mentioned, who tried to start an egregore in the '60s."

"Obviously," echoed Vickery. He looked across at her. "Cass Elliot was in the Mamas and Papas." When she gave him a blank look, he added, "Jeez, Ingrid—*California dreamin', on such a winter's day*—"

"Whatever." She touched two words on the page. "That's twice he forgot to capitalize 'the' at the beginning of a sentence."

"Guy's careless," observed Vickery, pausing to take a sip of beer before leaning over they page again.

"*The biker club*, the printout went on, *fully the eponymous swine, attacked the guru's group when they were in the midst of consummating the birth of the guru's egregore, further down the canyon. Several people, including the guru's wife/woman/girlfriend, were apparently killed. The biker club suffered casualties as well, and subsequently disappears from the roster of Los Angeles cult groups."*

Vickery felt Castine shiver beside him. "*That's* how you kill an emerging egregore?" she said. "Kill the members? I don't see us doing that."

"There'll be another way. Omar Sharif didn't look like he'd do that. What do you bet," he added, flipping to the next page, "that we know the place where this attack happened?"

"What, that old house? Ugh—I do *not* want to see the rest of that day."

The next few pages of the printout dealt with Harlowe's acquisition of the ChakraSys business and the organization of his egregore-to-be, which he referred to as: "*the Singularity project—e pluribus unum. It was synthe guruity that I found ChakraSys just as I was ready to initiate the Singularity.*"

Castine frowned. "Synthe guruity? What's that mean, synthetic guruhood?"

"I guess so," said Vickery. "So what's he trying to say, that it was through being a fake guru that he found ChakraSys?"

Castine was silent, and when Vickery started to speak, she quickly raised her hand to stop him. He sat back and let his right hand slide into his jacket pocket, wondering if she had seen some sign of surveillance or imminent attack. He looked down at one of his beer glasses, trying to scrutinize the bar peripherally.

"Sorry," said Castine. "I think I—look." She tapped the page in front of them. "The word he wanted there was pretty clearly *synchronicity*. It was synchronicity that he found ChakraSys just when he had a use for it, right? Not . . . synthetic guruity. And on the other pages, the T isn't capitalized when 'the guru' is the beginning of a sentence."

"Okay," said Vickery, relaxing and looking at the words she was pointing at.

"So after his first draft of this file, before he printed it out, he did a quick find-and-replace on the whole file, see? In the first draft he must have used the actual name of this rock guitarist, but afterward he replaced the name with 'the guru.' And in the places where the guy's name was at the beginning of a sentence, find-and-replace substituted the replacement words—'the guru'—which of course started with a lower-case T!"

Vickery leaned forward excitedly. "So if the word should have been *synchronicity* but got changed to *synthe guruity,* then the replaced word was—"

"Chronic," said Castine.

"What kind of name is Chronic?"

She shrugged. "It *was* the '60s."

Vickery picked up his second glass of beer and took a gulp. "He did it before, too—" Putting the glass down, he pulled out a few of the pages they'd already read, and riffled through them. "Look. He says, '*The biker club, fully the eponymous swine, attacked the guru's group.*' According to Supergirl's friend, the club's name was the Gardena Legion. But what's swinish about Gardena? Her friend remembered it close, but wrong."

"Well, I've never been to Gardena."

"What does the name 'Legion' suggest? Along with 'swine'?"

Castine picked up her glass, noticed once again that it was empty, and put it down. She cocked her head. "Of course. 'My name is Legion, for we are many.' That's what the demons in the possessed guy told Jesus, in the gospels. And when Jesus cast the demons out of the guy, they went into a herd of pigs—swine—and they all ran off a cliff. The famous Gadarene Swine. Poor old pigs." She tapped the page. "Yes, Harlowe did another find-and-replace here, didn't he? The name of the biker club must have been the *Gadarene* Legion."

"Sure. Supergirl's friend apparently never heard the gospel story, and remembered it as Gardena. Like I said, close."

On the last page of the printout was what appeared to be a poem, but Vickery pointed out that it was the lyrics of the Fogwillow song, "Elegy in a Seaside Meadow."

"What the Dumpster man was singing," said Castine. "We *should* have talked to him."

Vickery remembered falling down in surprise when the old man had appeared in the Dumpster, and then scurrying away backward. "Oh well," he said shortly. He finished his second beer. "You sure you don't want a drink?"

"I'm fine. What's next?"

He slid the papers and booklets back into the envelope. "We

should look up a bunch of this stuff on a computer in the library," he said. "I've got a San Bernardino County library card, but it won't work here. Without a card, you only get fifteen minutes on the computers, so let's—"

Castine slid out of the booth. "I've got an L.A. County one that's still valid," she said; "well, not on me, but I remember my card number and PIN number. I'm sure I can get us on for a full hour." She waited till he had stood up, then said, "Are we going back to Barstow tonight, after we meet with Ragotskie?"

"And pours the waters of the Nile," said Vickery flatly, "on every golden scale." Then he gave her a look that must have expressed his sudden alarm, for she took a step back and her eyes were wide.

"You didn't mean to say that," she whispered, "did you?"

He shook his head, then cleared his throat and hummed briefly, confirming control of his own voice; just as, he recalled with a chill, Castine had done a few minutes earlier. "Was that," he said carefully, "from the *Alice* books too?" When she nodded, still wide-eyed, he went on, "Yes, Barstow tonight."

Castine took his black-nylon-clad elbow, careful not to touch his hand with hers, as they hurried toward the door.

"Pull over here," said Harlowe. "There she stands."

"And welcomes little fishes in," piped one of the twins in the back seat of the station wagon, "with gently smiling jaws!"

Agnes Loria spoke over them. "It's a church," she said flatly as she eyed the building at the corner of Fedora and Pico; indecipherable graffiti made black squiggles across the white wall facing the street, and two shopping carts stood on the over-long grass inside the fence. The next building to the west was a discount center with ATM and EBT signs in the window. The neon light over its doors was on already.

"It's my only other property in L.A.," said Harlowe, sounding nettled, "and it's vacant. Our stuff is mostly moved in already, the computers and furniture."

The twins were now peering out at the four-story Romanesque bell tower and the red-painted steps leading up to the wide, arched doors. Loria was already thinking about the trouble she would no doubt have in keeping them out of the tower.

"I don't go much for churches," she said. She had pulled to the curb, but had still not turned off the engine.

"It's what we *have*," said Harlowe. "Your damned rogue *boyfriend* made the Sepulveda place impossible."

The twins giggled in the back seat. Loria switched off the engine and opened her door. "You know he's not my boyfriend," she said tiredly. "Okay, just so it's not Catholic." The breeze from the west carried the smells of barbecue and cooling sidewalks. Loria looked across the street at a row of narrow, brightly lit shops behind luxuriant old curbside trees, then back, disapprovingly, at the church.

"No no," Harlowe assured her, getting out on his side and opening the back door for the twins, "some kind of Protestant sect." His burgundy-red hair fluttered in the breeze as he pulled a set of keys from his pocket and unlocked the gate. "You need to put your bourgeois childhood behind you, kid."

"Or sink it." Loria herded the twins ahead of her as Harlowe relocked the gate behind them and led the way up the walk to the steps and the tall, iron-bound wooden doors. The doors were unlocked, and he tugged one open and stood aside.

Inside the vast nave; fading daylight through the stained glass windows high up on the west wall was dimmed by a couple of standing lamps on the broad dais at the far end, on which several of the Singularity crew were busy stacking boxes on a wide table, no doubt the one-time altar. A pulpit off to the left was crowded with half a dozen more lamps. The still air smelled of mildew and damp plaster.

The twins scampered ahead down the central aisle between rows of wooden pews arranged in a herringbone pattern.

"There's a dozen or so cots set up downstairs," said Harlowe, stepping up beside Loria and waving vaguely. "though there's only two bathrooms down there—there's another up here, in the sacristy, for us senior staff—and there's a kitchen in a kind of meeting hall out back. And I had them set up a TV downstairs—DVDs in a box, get the girls set up down there, and then you've got to help me try to deal with Pratt."

"What, funeral arrangements? Couldn't one of the others . . ." The twins were in one of the pews now, kneeling, and Loria wondered where they could have picked that up.

"No," said Harlowe, "I've got to get his ghost into that copy of *The Secret Garden* that has Vickery's daughter in it! Together in there, contrarily paired, they should function as . . . ghost flypaper, able to catch and absorb any ghosts that are attracted to our vibrant, emerging egregore."

Loria had been listening with decreasingly concealed impatience, and now she burst out, "Oh for God's sake, Simon! There's no ghost in that book, and Pratt's dead and gone! You might as well try to—catch leprechauns with a box of Lucky Charms cereal!"

Harlowe leaned toward her until his face was just inches from hers, and she could feel the mental buzz as their auras overlapped. "Pratt's ghost," he hissed, "broke the window of my SUV a couple of hours ago, a mile north of here! And it's not a *ghost* in the book, it's a distinct person who paradoxically never existed, never got born! The juxtaposition, the incongruous overlap, the *impossibility* of the pairing must certainly distract any ghosts that . . . come fluttering around our flame."

Loria stepped back. "Get Pratt's ghost into the book," she said, nodding. "So I should scout up a funnel and a mallet, maybe?"

"I've got his toothbrush, it was back at the Sepulveda office. We cam summon him with that. His spit, his DNA will be all over it. I think one of us should lick it to catch his attention—"

"Yuck! That's you, that does that."

"Fine! And the other, you, hold open the book when I toss his ghost onto it, and you slap the book shut."

Loria stared at him. "You really think this is possible? Actually? *Ghosts*?"

"And never-born persons. Yes. It's implicit in the math, just as antimatter was implicit in Dirac's relativistic wave equation. Ours is a weirder sort of math, admittedly, but—*eppur si muove*. Listen, we may have to talk Pratt into cooperating. You always got along with him."

Loria knew that the Italian phrase meant something like, *Nevertheless, it moves*. She believed Galileo had said it about the solar system.

"Who?" she said. "Oh, Pratt. He was a puppy dog. And—like all of us—he wanted to be in the egregore. Doesn't this book business kind of exclude him from that?"

"He's excluded already, Agnes, because he died! He's a *ghost*! Think! I've got the book here now, in the sacristy—get the girls downstairs."

"This is—" Loria realized that she didn't want to finish the sentence. She turned away and began striding up the aisle toward where the twins knelt as if in prayer.

Ten minutes later she was standing beside Harlowe at a counter beside a stainless steel sink, looking down at a blue plastic toothbrush and an open trade paperback book. The sacristy was narrow, with a high, cobwebbed ceiling and a print of the Last Supper hung on the far wall; the only window was above the sink, and fogged with dirt. After clicking a light switch up and down for several seconds, Harlowe had struck a match to a couple of candles, and the smell of burning wicks dispelled the old reek of incense.

"Oh," he said, his hand now extended halfway to the toothbrush, "have you ever—excuse me—been intimate with somebody who died on, or very close to, a freeway?"

"What . . . the . . . *hell*?"

"If you haven't, then you probably won't be able to see Pratt's ghost. In that case, you'll have to—"

"Have *you*? I always got the idea you were seriously celibate. Now that we're getting personal."

Harlowe's eyes dulled and his face sagged, and the wrinkles around his mouth were more evident—the expression was vacuity, as if he had lost consciousness, but his voice was level: "No, but I, I killed a man once. A burglar, in my trailer in Salinas, in '83. It was only a hundred feet from the 101 freeway."

"Were you intimate with him before or after you killed him?"

Harlowe's face resumed animation, and he pressed his lips together in evident annoyance. "Sex," he said, picking up the toothbrush, "is not the only intimacy. Killing somebody unites the two of you even more indissolubly. When I nod to you, that will mean Pratt's ghost is here—tell him—"

"So this is going to be an *invisible* ghost." Loria had tried to sound sarcastic, but her voice had quavered; What would become of her if Harlowe were simply insane? Had she wasted nearly two years on a heartbreakingly attractive fantasy?—and driven away a man who loved her, and whom she might have loved?

Harlowe seemed to sense her misgivings. "You've experienced a bit of what the twins can do," he said quietly. "You've seen some edges of humanity begin to fall partway into our egregore already, the events you call black-hole phenomena. But the idea of a *ghost* is inconceivable?"

"Oh, shit, whatever." More than anything else, she felt all at once very depressed. "Let's do your trick."

Harlowe lifted the toothbrush. "When I nod to you, tell him why he should get into the book. Keep your eyes on the floor then, and try to break up your sentences. Apparently it's not a good idea to speak to ghosts in recognizably complete sentences."

"Why he *should*? What reasons do I give him?"

Harlowe waved the toothbrush impatiently. "Improvise. Here goes." And he licked the toothbrush and said, loudly, "Pratt! Come over here!"

Loria kept her eyes on Harlowe, waiting for his nod. *Why don't you just jump into that book there?* she thought. *There's a nice nonexistent girl in it, waiting for you.* She hoped nobody would come in while this crazy exercise was going on.

"Pratt!" called Harlowe again, and again he licked the toothbrush. Loria managed not to gag. "Pratt!" Harlowe repeated.

And then Loria jumped back, convinced for a moment that two birds had got into the sacristy and were swooping around her head; but when she focused on one of the flapping things, she numbly comprehended that it was bodiless human hand. The other one, also now visibly a hand, bounced off a cabinet, dropped several feet and hovered a yard above the linoleum floor.

Loria's shoulders thumped against the wall beside the nave door, for she had reflexively backed away fast from the spectacle; her face was stiff and the breath was stopped in her throat. Now, with a sound like cloth tearing, the churning gray silhouette of a man flipped into view between her and Harlowe, and when the darting hands fluttered to the smoky wrist stumps and clung there, the silhouette assumed color and three dimensions.

The figure was recognizably young David Pratt, though it rippled like a projection on an unmoored bedsheet. It appeared to be in pain—its chest was heaving as if it were panting, though it made no sounds, and at each spasmodic constriction a red vapor jetted from its gaping mouth.

"Look at the floor!" snapped Harlowe. "And talk to it!"

"Send it away!" said Loria hoarsely. "This isn't—"

"Tell it to get into the goddamn book! And look at the floor!"

Loria stared down at her shoes. "David," she said, emptying her lungs. She inhaled, and managed to croak, "get—in that book, you can—relax, forget everything. Good God."

"There's," whispered the thing that stood between her and Harlowe, "a nobody in the book."

"Wouldn't you," she faltered, "like to be with—a nobody? Instead of—somebodies?"

Still staring at the floor, in her peripheral vision she saw the Pratt ghost expand to enormous size and then shrink to a buzzing dot; and the dot wavered out of her sight toward the counter.

She heard Harlowe slam the book shut. A momentary wave of hot air swept past her.

"Got it myself," he said.

She looked up and saw the book, closed now, on the counter. It was distinctly shivering.

Harlowe lifted it in both hands. "You *saw* it," he said. "I doubt you've ever killed anyone, so some lover of yours must have died on or near a freeway in the last year or so. I hope it wasn't Elisha. He's still our Judas goat."

She had had only had two others. Dazedly she hoped it was Brad, who had moved away and stopped answering her texts when she had believed she was pregnant during her senior year at UCLA.

She looked at the book in Harlowe's hands, and realized that she was smiling. Pratt's ghost had been real after all, and Harlowe had trapped it in that battered paperback book, just as he had said he would. He wasn't insane, or if he was, it was a splendid and effective insanity. The egregore was *not* a delusion, and she *would* finally be able to dissolve her ignoble identity into the transcendent entity that would be God, or as good an approximation of the fabled Deity as there would ever be.

She looked at Harlowe, noting the habitual black turtleneck sweater, and the blatantly artificial dark-red color of the hair that curled around below his ears, and the high shine on his ridiculous red cowboy boots.

"*Are* you *resolutely* celibate?" she breathed, not sure what answer she hoped for.

Harlowe looked away from her, then took a step toward the door to the nave, clutching the paperback book. "People like us have better things to do than to form adhesions," he said, and then he was striding away toward the door.

The familiar six notes from Strauss' *Death and Transfiguration* sounded from her pocket, and she called, "Wait" to Harlowe as she pulled out her phone. She glanced at the screen and said, "It's Elisha."

Harlowe had stopped, and now he hurried back, gripping the book in both hands. "Find out where he is," he said.

Loria swiped the screen. "Elisha!" she said, "Where are you?"

"The St. James Infirmary," came Ragotskie's voice from the phone; and he went on to sing some old-sounding bluesy lyrics about a guy visiting his dead girlfriend in a hospital, and how she'd never find another man like him.

"Well no, not if she's dead, honey," said Loria. She covered the microphone slot with her thumb and whispered to Harlowe, "I can hear people chatting, and surf in the background." Lifting her thumb, she said, "I didn't know they meant to *kill* you, Elisha! I'm so sorry! Where are you? I need to see you."

She heard the distinctive clink of a bottle on a glass, and then Ragotskie said, "I hope you mean that, Agnes, for your own sake. I don't think your egregore is going to happen, and if not, it'd be nice if you walked away from the failure with a functioning conscience."

Now she heard a dog barking, not far from Ragotskie's phone.

Again she covered the microphone slot, and whispered, "I'm sure he's at the On the Waterfront Café, in Venice. We used to go there." She uncovered the slot.

Harlowe nodded and ran to the nave door, the heels of his cowboy boots knocking on the linoleum floor.

As he yanked it open and hurried out into the nave, Loria said into the phone, "Why do you think it's not going to happen, Elisha?"

"Well if I told you," he said, and his voice was constricted with bitterness and satisfaction, "you might be able to save it, and lose your—your poisonously lovely self. That was Harlowe's boots I heard, wasn't it? This is a burner phone, but I'm going to hang up now just in case your murdering Messiah can track it. Goodbye, Agnes. I really think some of these days . . . well, you never heard of Sophie Tucker, but," and then he sang, "*you're gonna miss me*."

The connection ended with a click, and Loria dropped the phone back into her pocket. That's okay, sweetie, she thought as she walked toward the nave door herself, just take your time over that beer.

Probably it was Brad who had died on a freeway. And good enough for him.

CHAPTER TEN:
What's the Hex?

Vickery took the 101 freeway to the 110 south, and the battering of wind in the open back windows discouraged conversation. Again they drove past the spot from which they had both exited the normal world last year—but it was on the northbound shoulder, and there was no other world to fall into now, and Castine didn't even look across the median. Vickery got off the freeway at Sixth Street, and drove slowly along the shadowed, tree-bordered floor of the canyon between the skyscrapers, the tops of which gleamed orange in the westering sunlight. The streets here were all one-way, so at Olive Street he turned left, then turned left again on Fifth and again on Flower, and then he was almost superstitiously wary to find an empty parking space right across the street from the library.

Only the library's tower was visible above a couple of jacaranda trees, but he remembered the long pools and the cypresses in front of the modernist Art Deco façade. He had often come here, in the days when he had been a Los Angeles police officer, just to stand under the murals in the high-ceilinged rotunda, and take the escalators up through the vast airy volume of the atrium to wander among the comforting shelves of literature on the third floor.

It seemed like someone else's life.

He and Castine crossed the street and stepped up the curb and between the trees, and then they were walking in the shadows of the cypresses, up the stepped levels beside the long blue-tiled ornamental pools. Vickery noticed new sculptures in the pools as he passed them—an iron lizard in one, and an iron lizard skeleton in the next. Ahead were the green copper doors below the remembered frieze of Greek horsemen.

Castine hopped up the last steps and pulled open one of the doors, then led the way down a brightly-lit hall to the Directory kiosk. Computer monitors and keyboards were arranged on a circular waist-high shelf around it, and she quickly tapped a keyboard, then entered her card and PIN numbers into spaces on the computer's screen.

"What time is it?" she asked, without looking away from the screen.

Vickery tilted his wrist. "Quarter of five."

"I'll make a reservation for five o'clock. Never mind, a computer's free right now. And—we've got an hour. It's at International Languages, one floor down." She lifted a couple of pencils and a sheaf of blank cards from slots on the shelf.

They took an escalator down one side of the atrium and stepped off at the next floor. On their right was a bank of windows and an open glass door and a sign that said *New Americans Center,* altogether looking like a little shop in a mall. Castine walked through the doorway, and Vickery followed her across the carpet to a polished wood booth; inside it were a low table with a computer monitor and keyboard and mouse, a shelf to the right, and a wooden chair. Castine sat down and Vickery stood beside her, leaning forward.

She clicked past the opening screen and said, "What?"

"Try Googling ChakraSys," said Vickery.

She found *chakrasys.com* on Google and clicked on it, and the page that appeared had CHAKRASYS in flowing blue letters along the top, above a stylized silhouette of a woman sitting in the yoga position with seven colored stars arranged vertically on her body from head to crotch. Below that was the address of the emptied building on Sepulveda, along with a phone number, and off in a sidebar was a photo of a florid man with wavy, dark red hair standing in front of a wall of variously colored glass jars on shelves. He wore a black turtleneck sweater and cut-off jeans, and one hand was raised in a gesture of something like benediction. The caption was *CEO Simon Harlowe.*

"Well, there's our guy," said Castine quietly.

The text below was apparently innocuous information about meditation and pranayama breathing and clearing energy blocks to align one's physical body with one's "subtle body." Diet and exercise were evidently important. There were no links or further pages.

"Note the phone number, at least," Vickery said, "and then let's get back to Google." He scratched his beard. "My passwords have all been changed since I was a cop, so I don't have access to sites like CLETS—That's the California Law Enforcement Telecommunications System—but let's try Pipl."

He spelled it for her, and after a few clicks she was at the Pipl website, and she entered Simon Harlowe. On the next screen she specified California, and only one name came up: Simon Harlowe, 61 years old, from San Francisco and Los Angeles. Harlowe's name was in blue, so she clicked on it.

The page that came up had the picture of Harlowe from the ChakraSys site at the top. Under "Career" was just the word "entrepreneur," and his listed education was Stanford University from 1973 to 1975.

"Pretty good," said Castine, "to get in when he was sixteen. But I doubt he got a degree in two years."

The phone number the site provided was the same as the one on the ChakraSys site, but under "Places," in addition to the familiar address on Sepulveda, was an address on Pico. Castine was already writing it down.

"Let's check out Mr. Chronic," she said. She typed in *chronic los angeles hippie 1968*, but though 170,000 sites were found, the ones on the first few Google pages either didn't include the word chronic or had to do with homelessness and bronchitis. Substituting *guitarist* for *hippie* got different sites, but none in which Chronic was a name.

"Oh well," said Castine. "What was the title of that movie that supposedly had the old house in it?"

"*What's the Hex?*"

Castine went to the International Movie Data Base site and entered the title.

"Here we are, *What's the Hex?*, 1966—Not Rated, 110 minutes, comedy drama."

Under the broad IMDb banner was a summary of the movie: *A beautiful witch raises the ghosts of dead surfers to compete in a surfing competition, with* SEE FULL SUMMARY >>

Castine clicked on the link, but the remainder of the summary was just: *unfortunate results.*

Someone named Leo Marlin was listed as both the writer and director, and under *Stars* were listed three names: Gale Reed, Dot Palmer and Van Conlon. The full cast and crew were listed in a column below—only Reed and Palmer were represented by thumbnail photographs, the rest just by default gray ovals.

Castine scrolled down through Company Credits and Technical Specs, and paused at Soundtracks. The only name in that category was Fogwillow.

Vickery was looking over her shoulder, and nodded when she pointed at the name. "See if Wikipedia has an article about the movie," and Castine exited IMDb and checked the movie title in Wikipedia. There was an article, but it was short, and provided nothing that they hadn't learned from IMDb.

Castine looked up Dot Palmer, Gale Reed, Leo Marlin and Van Conlon.

Dot Palmer, originally one of the Gazzari Dancers on the TV show "Hollywood A Go-Go" and later a promising young actress, "died of heart failure while hiking" in 1968. *What's the Hex?* was Leo Marlin's only film credit, though he had been in some TV ads; he was killed during a robbery of his home in 1968. The only information on Van Conlon was that he died of a heroin overdose in, unsurprisingly at this point, 1968.

Gale Reed, born in 1933, was apparently still alive, and had a fairly lengthy Wikipedia page. She had starred in a number of B-movies, most notably the 1957 romantic comedy *Catch That Blonde!* She was married twice, and her second husband, Stanley Ancona, had left her in 1968; she had evidently never remarried. After taking small parts in negligible movies in the '60s, she had eventually subsided into being one of the stars on the TV game show "Hollywood Squares" for many years, finally retiring to do fundraising for a number of animal rescue organizations. A link at the bottom of the page led to a 2014 Los Angeles *Times* article with a picture of Reed on one of "her annual visits" to the La Brea Tar Pits to hang a wreath on the fence around the lake, in memory of all the mastodons and saber-tooth tigers who had died there over the millennia.

"She probably lives in L.A.," mused Vickery, "if she can regularly visit the tar pits at age eighty-four."

"If she still does that."

"It'd be interesting to talk to her. See what Pipl has on her." But Pipl proved to have nothing at all under "Gale Reed."

Castine clicked back to Reed's name in Google, and then clicked on Images. The monitor screen filled with a long gallery of pictures, mostly glamorous publicity photos of Gale Reed from the '50s, or *Catch That Blonde!* movie posters, or shots of her in one of the brightly-lit cubes of the "Hollywood Squares" set. Scrolling down, Castine found more recent pictures of Reed, several taken as she was hanging wreaths on the fence around the La Brea Tar Pits. Her hair was still gold but her eyes were now obviously narrowed by face-lifts. Castine scrolled further down.

"Whoa." Vickery pointed at one image, a photo of a person on a gurney being wheeled by paramedics past a long hedge, with a brick-fronted Tudor-style house obliquely visible to the right.

"That doesn't look good," said Castine, clicking on the image and then on the Visit button. What came up was a 2015 article at the TMZ website, headed "Hollywood Squares Star Hospitalized."

Castine expanded the page, and Vickery leaned in to read the article with her. It appeared that—yes, it was her—Gale Reed had suffered a grazing bullet wound in the head; the explanation she had given to police was that she had been cleaning an old gun, and an overlooked round in the chamber had been discharged accidentally. Police had considered placing her on a 51-50 hold, involuntary 72-hour commitment to a psychiatric ward for evaluation, but she had apparently talked her way out of that.

Castine scratched at the old gunshot scar on her own scalp. "*I* should have been 51-50'd last year," she muttered, "for even getting myself into that . . . lethally crazy situation."

"I wouldn't be here if you hadn't got into it," remarked Vickery.

"Dear dead days." She leaned back in the wooden chair and tapped the monitor screen. "According to the L.A. *Times*, Reed was back to hanging wreaths at the tar pits the following year."

"Go back to that picture of her with the paramedics," said Vickery, "and expand it."

She clicked back, and he peered at the image. "That street sign in the background," he said, "white, with the raised section along the top—you can't read the street name, but they only have street signs shaped like that in Beverly Hills. And—that big white house on the hill in the distance, I know where that is, you can see it from lots of places along Sunset. Her house is in the Flats, just . . . a bit south of Sunset, and on the east side of some street."

"I wonder why she shot herself."

Vickery raised his eyebrows. "It was an accident, weren't you paying attention?"

"Oh yeah. You want to what, pay her a visit?"

"She was in the movie that was filmed at that house we see in the echo-visions. And she seems to be the only one involved in it that didn't die in '68."

"You think you can find her place, just from that picture?"

"In Google Maps we can sort of fly over the area in a virtual helicopter."

When Castine had got Google Maps up, Vickery took hold of the mouse and swept the perspective to the area of Los Angeles south of Sunset and north of Santa Monica Boulevard. Then he clicked on Satellite View and tapped on the + button until he could see individual houses. He moved the map sideways, tracing Sunset.

"Okay, there's that big white house on the hill, see? So let's look at the houses fairly south of that."

"There's a million of them! And I just see the roofs!"

"Nah, watch." Vickery zoomed in on one street, waited till the image had come into focus, then clicked on 3D, and the viewpoint dipped to show the fronts of the houses. He clicked on the curved arrow in the margin and the view rotated so that they could see the houses from a different angle.

For the next twenty minutes Vickery moved the view along one street after another, several times pausing to drag the little yellow-man icon to a spot in front of a likely-looking house and drop it to street-view; and finally they were looking at a Tudor-style house with a diagonal hedge out front. Vickery backed the viewpoint down the street a few yards, and the image was virtually identical to the TMZ picture.

Castine nodded, and he clicked out of street view and hit the – button several times to get a broader view of the area, and Castine wrote down the nearest cross streets.

Vickery stood back. "We should," he said, "try to verify that the house from our visions is actually in that movie. Supergirl's friend might have got it mixed up with some old 'Green Acres' episode."

"Oh. Right."

Castine shifted her chair back and looked—wistfully, Vickery thought—toward the ranks of end-on bookshelves on the other side of the long room, and the several visible people engaged in presumably normal pursuits. Then she slid her chair forward and resolutely faced the monitor again. "Okay. How?"

"YouTube."

Castine sighed heavily and clicked back to the Google screen and from it to YouTube. Slowly she typed in, *What's the Hex?*—and then even more slowly moused the pointer up to the question-mark icon and clicked it.

A stack of images appeared on the left side of the screen, with captions off to the right; and in among a lot of videos about Hex Girls and Hex Color Codes, there was a picture of a surfer and the caption *What's the Hex? Trailer*. Castine spread the fingers of both hands, then delicately clicked on it.

The trailer video was sixty seconds long, and the first twenty seconds were just shots of young people surfing, and then a bit of conversation, about ghosts, between two men in front of a ramshackle beachside restaurant called The Raft. But after that it cut to a follow shot of a motorcyclist riding down a dirt path between sparse trees and bare hills, and when the motorcycle rounded a curve, the view was of—the house.

Vickery heard Castine's hiss of indrawn breath, and he realized that he had winced and clenched his teeth.

It was the first time they had seen the place in normal daylight, but it was precisely the same building that had appeared in their visions: the gables, the wooden steps, the sharply sagging porch, the broken windows—and now Vickery could see that it was even more decrepit than he had been able to discern by echo-light in the visions. Sun-grayed paint remained only in patches, and the shingles of the roof were discolored and eroded.

The motorcyclist got off his bike and started toward the house just as a man in garish zombie makeup came lurching out of the front door. In a new camera angle from the side, the motorcyclist drew a gun and fired several shots at the creature, but it came plodding down the steps unfazed, and seized him by the throat, and his histrionic scream was the end of the video.

Castine clicked out of YouTube and sat back, and Vickery straightened up. For a moment neither of them spoke, then Vickery exhaled. "Oscar caliber, for sure."

"Oh shut up. Don't be flippant right now." She was looking away from him, and he suspected it was because she didn't want him to see tears in her eyes. "This makes it *real*."

"I know. Sorry."

She wiped her eyes on her sleeve and looked around at the booth as if it had been tainted by what the monitor had shown them. "Our hour's about up. I'd like to be moving. Anywhere, just moving."

Philippe's is the oldest continuously operating restaurant in Los Angeles—a big, noisy, brightly-lit place with long red wooden tables on a floor scattered with drifts of sawdust. The warm air is always redolent of bacon and roast beef. Castine and Vickery waited in one of the lines at the long counter and eventually ordered beef dip sandwiches and cole slaw, with a glass of Frog's Leap merlot for Castine and a bottle of Dos XX beer for Vickery, who also ordered a purple pickled egg. They carried their trays to the far end of one of the tables, several yards away from the nearest of their fellow diners.

"It's been a long time since breakfast," commented Castine, taking a bite of the broth-dipped end of her sandwich. "I might have another of these—I bet it'll be cold up in that clearing by the freeway."

"And Ragotskie might very well not show up," said Vickery. He drank some beer and took a bite of his pickled egg. "I don't know how much more he can tell us anyway, and I don't know how he imagines we might help him get his girl away from . . . " He glanced aside at the family sitting down the table from them.

"Quoth the raven," said Castine. "Yeah, best not to drop keywords carelessly. You might set off a black hole." She had a sip of her wine. "I think we should help him if we can. He seems like a decent sort."

Vickery had tipped up his beer mug for another swallow, and nearly choked on it. "A great guy," he agreed, setting the mug down and wiping his mouth, "aside from having tried to poison you and shoot you yesterday."

"He was doing it to save this girl he loves," said Castine. She gave him a tired, rueful smile. "I don't know, you're right—as gallantry goes, it is a bit extreme."

"If he can get an advantage with her by setting up a trap for us, he will." Vickery bit off the end of his sandwich. "So," he said, chewing, "we enter from above, by way of the freeway shoulder. That way—"

Castine had been glancing around the long, high-ceilinged room, and she now caught Vickery's eye and said, "Look straight down at your plate till I tell you something."

Vickery was tense as he stared at his sandwich. "What's up?"

"*Don't* meet his eye if he looks around, but check out the guy at he table behind you. The one with the backward baseball cap."

Like that narrows it down, thought Vickery. But her tone had been wary, not alarmed, so he picked up his beer again and hiked around on his stool and let his gaze range generally across the crowd; and he let it stop when he was facing the undershirt-clad back of a man at the next table.

Beneath the reversed baseball cap the man's hair was white—and as Vickery watched, it darkened to brown, and then faded back to white. The man's bare, pale right arm was extended sideways, and his hand was snatching at the remains of a sandwich in front of the woman next to him, but she was talking to a companion and they both seemed unaware of it, and anyway the man's fingers weren't succeeding in moving the sandwich at all. In fact, Vickery noted with a chill, the man's fingers were *passing through* the sandwich, without jiggling it at all.

Vickery turned back to face Castine, and nodded. "They're not uncommon," he said, keeping his voice steady, "in a big city. It'll dissipate soon."

"I should tell her not to eat that sandwich. It's probably got all kinds of ghost germs on it."

Vickery smiled. "She'd probably—"

He stopped talking, for a man behind Castine, an older man in a wool coat with wire-rimmed glasses perched on his patrician nose, was giving him a conspiratorial smile.

Seeing Vickery's fixed expression, Castine turned around to look at the man too.

He looked from Vickery to Castine, and past them at the back of the apparently hungry ghost, and then he winked and nodded. In a cultured voice he said softly, "And we're none of us in prison!" and gave them an ironic thumbs-up. Then he pushed his stool back, bowed and strode unhurriedly away toward the Alameda Street exit.

"He—!" began Castine; then she went on just loud enough for Vickery to hear, leaning across the table toward him, "he's a killer! And he thinks we are too!"

Vickery spoke quietly. "Well we *are*, Ingrid. He knew that's why we—and he—could see our friend behind me trying to pick up a sandwich."

"I know, last year, when I—and you—but those were self-defense! He obviously thought we were *murderers*! Uncaught! Like him!" She stared in the direction the man had gone. "You were a cop—catch him!"

"Sure, citizen's arrest. 'This guy, whoever he is, evidently killed somebody somewhere, sometime!'"

Castine's shoulders slumped. "You're right. But let's move on. I feel all creepy now, like he gave us his . . . unblessing."

"Finish your sandwich," said Vickery, picking up his own. "And your wine. God knows when we'll eat and drink next."

He heard a faint thump and glanced behind him. The ghost had disappeared, and no one else seemed to have been able to see it. He shrugged and took another bite of his sandwich.

"Poor old ghost," muttered Castine. "If they sold ghost sandwiches here, I'd have got him one."

Lateef Fakhouri had parked his rented Nissan in the back lot of the discount center beside the church to which Simon Harlowe had apparently relocated his operation. The air inside the car was uncomfortably warm and smelled of motor oil, and it had been a relief, an hour ago, to get out into the cool evening breeze and step to the torn section of the chain-link fence that surrounded the narrow church grounds.

It seemed unlikely that Harlowe's people had had time to set up any security measures outside yet, and he had crouched through the gap in the fence and made his way silently through tall weeds and around a couple of old shopping carts to a back door. It was locked, but a narrow window in it gave him a dust-fogged view of a lighted stairway inside. He had been about to investigate the added-on building at the back of the church when he had seen people descending the stairway; he had stepped back then, to be in shadow, but watched intently.

It had been the woman and the two girls whom he had followed from the Manhattan Beach parking lot yesterday evening: Harlowe's evident Girl Friday, and his two nieces, who were pretty certainly destined to be the communication nexus of his egregore.

All three of them had continued down the stairs, out of sight, and a few moments later Fakhouri had been startled by a light coming on beside his ankles; glancing down, he'd seen that it came from a long, narrow window set only a few inches above the dirt, with close-set iron bars over the glass—clearly in the wall of a basement.

The glass was frosted, and he had gingerly lain down prone on the weedy dirt with his ear only inches from the glass.

There had been conversation, but to his annoyance he had only been able to hear the woman say loudly, "I don't want to hear a goddamn peep out of either one of you!" and then the light had gone out.

That had been an hour ago. Fakhouri had quietly got to his feet and gone back to his car, and sat in the driver's seat in the gathering darkness and sweated and smoked up an entire pack of costly Cleopatra cigarettes, crushing each one out after only a few inhalations. His eyes stung now with smoke and sweat and possibly tears.

If this scheme succeeded, and he managed to spirit away Harlowe's nieces—kidnap them, to put it plainly—he would simply be taking them in order to stop the egregore. He could not, in all honesty, tell himself that he was doing it to rescue them, to make up for having left those two Coptic girls in the garbage district of Cairo.

Still, he *would* be rescuing them. And it *might* put and end to the nightmares that he still suffered.

He peered out through the fogged windshield at the sky. The night was about as dark now as it was going to get.

"*Damn* it," he said, and picked up the flashlight and the sheet of paper from the seat beside him. He got out of the car, and the night breeze was cold on his wet face.

He carried the flashlight and the paper back through the gap in the chain-link fence to the low basement window, which was still dark, and again he lay prone on the dirt beside it. On the sheet of paper was a felt-pen tracing of the *Nu* hieroglyph from Khalid Boutros' old photograph, and Fakhouri now slid the sheet between the bars and pressed it against the frosted-glass window, careful to have the inked side against the glass. Holding it there with one hand, he rapped the flashlight against the glass, then drew it back and switched it on, illuminating the paper.

To the extent that the girls were initiated into the *Ba* hieroglyph, they should be drawn to this one, even as he would lead them, Pied Piper style, back to his car. That was his plan, but he wasn't cheered to hear exclamations and activity start up now in the basement beyond the glass. After a few seconds it became quiet, but through his fingers on the paper he felt fingers brushing the glass on the other side.

Leaning close to the glass, he said, quietly but clearly, "Come outside."

There were no further sounds from behind the glass, and no light came on. After several anxious seconds, Fakhouri got to his feet and stepped away from the building, folding the sheet of paper and ready to run back through the hole in the fence if one of the adults were to appear in the door window.

But soon it was two bobbing heads that blocked the light in the lower third of the glass, and a moment later Fakhouri winced at a distressingly echoing snap, and the door swung open, its bottom edge slithering over weeds. He quickly shoved the paper into his coat pocket.

The two girls he had seen at the beach yesterday morning shuffled outside, their disordered hair backlit against the open doorway. They were both wearing overalls and white sneakers.

"What was that picture, please?" asked one.

"Are you from out of the ocean?" the other one asked, and added, "All we got for dinner was—" and then they both spoke in unison, "—green bean casserole!"

"And we rolled it up our napkins and flushed them down the toilet."

"Hush!" whispered Fakhouri, backing toward the fence and beckoning. "The picture was a hieroglyph." He had to repeat the word for them. "Listen! You must come with me, to be safe from— I—ah—you had no dinner? I can get you dinner. But you must—"

At least the girls were following him. One of them said, "Can you get—" and pronounced something that sounded like *poyo loco*. Possibly some Hawaiian food.

Fakhouri had backed into the chain-link fence, nodding furiously. "In Los Angeles I'm sure it can be found. Whisper, can't you?" He looked around and saw the hole in the fence a yard to his right, and he crouched through it.

One of the girls followed him. "The toilet turned into a volcano," she said solemnly. "We've met that *hie-ro-glyph*," she added, "under the sea. Its name is Nu."

"It's too big and empty to have a *name*," Fakhouri replied distractedly, helping the other girl through the fence. "But—you must lift your foot!—but yes, people have called it *Nu*."

"We need to meet it again, in person," said one of the girls, "to close Uncle Simon's app. It makes our heads buzz all the time."

"I can do that," said Fakhouri. "I can make it stop."

When both girls had got through the fence, Fakhouri led them across the discount center parking lot to his rented Nissan, and opened a back door for them.

When they were in and he had closed the door and got behind the wheel, he glanced to the left, toward the church—and he saw a figure silhouetted against the bright rectangle of the open doorway. A man's voice shouted syllables that Fakhouri knew must be *Lexi* and *Amber*.

He hastily started the car and backed it in a curve to face the street, and winced when the back bumper collided noisily with what sounded like a row of trash cans.

Clicking the car into drive, he sped out of the lot and made a left turn onto Pico.

There's only night staff at the consulate, he thought, I can hardly bring them there until the full complement of personnel arrives in th morning, and even then it will be a sad confusion. But the boy Santiago mentioned a place . . .

In the rear view mirror he saw a pair of headlights swing into view and quickly begin closing the distance between them and his car. Fakhouri pressed harder on the gas pedal, but the following headlights only drew closer.

"Fasten your seatbelts!" he croaked.

Instead of doing as he had asked, both girls knelt on the back seat to peer out the rear window.

"Who is it?" asked one, and then answered herself: "Uncle Don and Mr. Nunez are out running errands, and Uncle John's hand is all shot off. Let's see." The other girl reached out and touched the slant of glass. "It's that one that looks like Severus Snape," said the girl who had spoken first, "and one of our stupid *guards*." She hiked around on the seat and gave Fakhouri a piercing look in the rear view mirror. "Don't let them take us back."

The pursuing driver began to angle out to the left, clearly intending to pass the Nissan.

"I don't know what I can do—" Fakhouri began.

The girl turned back to look out the rear window. "That's okay."

Abruptly the car behind them swerved sharply to the right, its tires screeching and its headlights momentarily lighting the interior of Fakhouri's car; then Fakhouri heard a hard metallic bam, and in his rear-view mirror glimpsed a power pole rotate from vertical like the second-hand of a clock. Whatever noise it might have made in striking the street was lost in the roar of the Nissan's engine.

CHAPTER ELEVEN:
She's Still Agnes

"He's still riding his idiot bicycle east on Washington," came a voice from the phone Agnes Loria was holding to her ear as she drove. It was Chino Nunez, who had been in charge of security at ChakraSys, and who was now standing in for the injured Taitz. "Maybe he's aiming for Nevada. He's made three stops, at a Subway sandwich place and a liquor store and a sportin goods store. He's got a couple of bags now in the saddlebags on his bike, and he's got a new puffy jacket."

"I can't be there," Loria said, "if you're going to take his blood pressure." She was driving north on the 101 freeway, just passing the Alvarado exit.

"No," Nunez assured her, "it looks like he's got a destination, and if it's the Vickery and Castine couple, you can just turn around and go back to the church, and we'll delete them all from the situation. But if he goes another hour without meeting them, then the boss will want your help in asking him about them."

My help, thought Loria. Her right hand was slick on the steering wheel of her station wagon, and she was furious at herself for caring that, one way or another, Elisha Ragotskie was going to die tonight.

People like us have better things to do, Harlowe had told her back at the church, *than to form adhesions.*

Washington Boulevard, up which Elisha was reportedly riding his bicycle—all the way from the On the Waterfront Café in Venice!—was down by the 10 freeway; evidently he was not heading for their

Echo Park apartment, as she had thought he might. she'd have to get off this freeway and get on again heading south, and take the 110 down to the 10. She lowered the phone to click the turn signal lever up with her little finger, and merged into the right lane to get off at Rampart.

Adhesions, she thought. Like when abdominal organs get stuck together, and you get intestinal obstructions and ectopic pregnancies. Is that what human sexual relations amount to? Souls sticking together to their detriment?

She steered one-handed through the Ramparts offramp. "Can't Elisha tell," she said irritably into the phone, "that you're following him?"

"I don't think so. He's done a couple of evasions, like riding his bike around parking barriers, but it's seemed like just precaution; and we're in two cars, Baldy Foster's in the other one. There's other bicyclists riding east from the beach, but we can easily keep our eyes on him."

A moment later Nunez added, "Now he's turned south on Estes. Probably just another precaution, Estes just dead-ends at the 10 freeway."

Elisha, you idiot, thought Loria, didn't it occur to you that I would recognize the sounds of that café? Or did you imagine that I wouldn't pass your location on to Harlowe? Did you still, after everything, *trust* me? *Idiot.*

Nunez spoke up again. "I don't think this is an evasion. He's gone two blocks. But this *does* dead-end up ahead."

He's going to meet Vickery and Castine, Loria thought. Harlowe says he's with them now, damn him.

I'll get down to the 10, she thought, and get off at Vermont; that's the offramp before Estes. Taitz and Foster will wait, to make sure. I might get there before they make their move, but I won't warn Elisha. I won't.

"Wait for me," she said, and laid the phone on the seat.

Traffic was heavier on the 110 now, and it took Vickery twenty minutes to drive down to the 10 interchange; and when he had merged with the westbound 10 freeway, he drove slowly in the far right lane. A dull red streak in the sky ahead of them was all that was left of the sunset, and he had to squint to see the trees and low bushes beyond the shoulder guard rail.

"Along here," he said, "after the Vermont exit and before Normandie."

"Not much shoulder," said Castine.

"I'll write a note and hang it on the antenna. 'Dead battery, went to find a phone.'"

"Everybody's got their own phone."

"I'll say mine's in therapy."

He swerved into the narrow shoulder lane, which was marked with diagonal white lines and was barely wide enough to let him get the car out of traffic. The passenger-side door scraped the guard rail.

"You'll have to climb out on my side," he said, lifting a pen and notepad from the console, "and look behind before you open the door or step out."

"Duh," said Castine, already drawing her legs up.

Vickery, and then Castine, climbed hastily out of the car and hurried around the front bumper to the convex steel strip of guard rail. Vickery scribbled a few words on a page of the notebook, tore it off, and speared it on the antenna.

"Crouch out of sight now," he said, "and over the rail into the bushes."

In the waxing and waning shadow of the car's bulk, they rolled over the guard rail and, moving diagonally to stay as much as possible in the car's shadow, crawled into the mass of bushes that fronted the shoulder. A few yards further they reached a cluster of trees, and were able to stand up in the deeper shadows.

Vickery watched through intervening branches while a dozen cars rushed past his parked Saturn without swerving or braking. Satisfied that the car was safely out of traffic, he turned to peer into the shrubbery, then caught Castine's eye and patted his jacket pocket. She nodded and slid her right hand into her coat pocket.

The night sky over central Los Angeles was never as dark as what Vickery was used to in Barstow, and even when the peripheral glow of rushing headlights behind them wasn't making the surrounding leaves glitter, he was able to lead the way between the close-set trees and bushes to the edge of the slope that led down to surface streets.

He and Castine paused at the crest. Below them, the bright lines of boulevards seemed to spread apart as they swept from the remote dark foothills and, closer, became individual spots of colored light. Vickery let his gaze follow their expanding grid down to the base of the freeway shoulder slope, where the dark rectangles of the bowling alley and thrift store sat behind pools of streetlight radiance.

"A bit further west," he whispered to Castine.

After they had picked their way for several yards through the overhanging greenery along the shoulder crest—while Vickery became aware of the incongruous scents of vinegar and onions on the otherwise diesel-tainted breeze—he pushed a branch aside and paused.

The gypsy nest clearing was directly ahead. By the dim ambient light he could see four plastic web chairs and several beer cans, and he knew that the little pale flecks on the packed dirt were old cigarette butts. This was the freeway gypsy nest, evidently unoccupied.

"Vickery," he said, just loudly enough to be heard for a few yards, "a driver for Galvan." It was an identification most freeway gypsies would recognize.

Leaves thrashed behind an oleander bush on the far side of the clearing, and Elisha Ragotskie stepped out of the deeper shadows.

He wore a bulky nylon jacket now, and he was holding a hunting knife with a six-inch blade; after a moment he seemed to become aware of the knife, and he quickly slid it into a sheath at his belt.

"Sorry!" he said. "I didn't know who might be crashing around up here. Were you able to find out anything?"

"In seven hours?" said Vickery. "Well, a little. You were careful coming here? Watched your back?"

"Sure," said Ragotskie, stepping to one of the chairs. He waved toward the street-side slope. "I'm on a bicycle, and I rode around a lot of barriers where cars couldn't follow me, stuff like that." He started to sit down, paused to push the knife sheath out of the way, then carefully lowered himself into the chair. "I brought sandwiches and a six-pack of beer, but there's nobody around. So you found out something?"

Vickery looked carefully into the surrounding shadows, listening, then sat down in one of the chairs. "We got an address to check out. What, you bought a knife?"

"I couldn't get a gun." He took off his glasses, peered around, and then put them on again. "What kind of address? You've only got one day."

Castine was holding the back of another chair but hadn't sat down. "What happens in one day?"

Ragotskie looked up at her. "What do you think? Halloween. Tomorrow at midnight Harlowe launches his egregore, if you haven't found a way to short it out. What address have you got? I rode my bike out to the ChakraSys office on Sepulveda, and it's been cleaned out, like I thought."

"One day!" whispered Castine. "That's less than *a few.*"

Vickery cocked his head, momentarily certain that he had heard someone singing some distance away; but the wind blew away the faint sound and might have been the sole source of it.

He returned his attention to the shadowy figure of Ragotskie. "The place on Sepulveda," he said. "We stopped by it earlier. Was there an old guy hanging around? Talking crazy?"

"Huh? No, nobody was there, just some kid on a bike going through the trash. After that I rode down Venice Boulevard to a place Agnes and I used to go to, and had a few beers." He blinked around defensively. "I called her on the phone, in fact." When Vickery frowned and started to get up, Ragotskie was quick to add, "I used a burner phone! And I was only on for less than a minute."

Vickery subsided in his chair, but cast a wary glance toward the descending northward slope and the city beyond. "Not smart anyway," he said gruffly.

"Well, I needed to tell her some things. Goodbye, mainly."

"Good." Vickery leaned forward. "So we can forget about her? If you can—"

"No," said Ragotskie hastily, "no, you've still got to help me get her away from them! Did you guys find out anything about the '68 egregore? I called the—"

"If you're done with her," said Vickery, "why does it matter what she does?"

In the dimness, Vickery saw the young man spread his hands and shrug. "She's still Agnes."

Castine nodded.

"So what's this other address?" persisted Ragotskie.

"It's on Pico." Vickery hesitated, then told him the street number. "I don't know what it is, but it's the only other property listed for Harlowe, besides the place on Sepulveda. So he's going to launch this thing *tomorrow night*? Damn. Do you know where?"

"It's got to be done at the same place where it was tried in '68, and on an anniversary of it—the fifty-year anniversary, as it turns out—when the stars are more-or-less the same again, because really Harlowe's egregore is just a reprise of that one, coloring books and all, though he doesn't like to talk about that. It's someplace in Topanga Canyon; he won't say where, but he wants the *Black Sheep* to be anchored just offshore, that's his boat, so I think it's down at the bottom of the canyon, by Pacific Coast Highway." He sniffed and looked behind him. "You guys want a sandwich?"

"We just ate," said Castine.

"Is he," said Vickery, "using my book, in some way? Has he ever said anything about—"

"Oh, *fuck* your book! I'm sorry, Ms. Castine." Facing Vickery, Ragotskie said, "I'll get you another copy, shit, sorry, I'll get you a signed damned first *edition* of it, if you can just manage to *stop Harlowe* and get Agnes *away* from him."

Vickery's hand darted to the gun in his pocket then, for a branch behind Ragotskie had been pushed aside and somebody—somebody not tall—was stepping into the dark clearing.

The figure spoke, and even after a year and a half, Vickery recognized the boy's voice. "I think I don't have to kill anybody tonight," said Santiago. "I'm glad." He crossed the packed dirt and sat down in the fourth chair. "A guy told you to get out of town," he said to Vickery. "I told him you wouldn't."

"An Egyptian," said Castine. "You've spoken to him?"

"Harlowe's scared an Egyptian might show up," put in Ragotskie, who had started to get to his feet and now sank back in the chair. "He says there was one hanging around in '68, trying to wreck everything."

Vickery could make out Santiago's unruly dark hair and narrow face. The boy was wearing a sweatshirt that was probably a hoodie, and one pocket of it sagged so heavily that Vickery was sure the boy was carrying a gun—possibly the .40 caliber Sig Sauer he had stolen last year. Vickery could see a dark line below one of the sleeve cuffs, and remembered that Santiago wore a leather band on each wrist.

"Mr. Laquedem is dead," said Santiago. "These people," and he waved toward Ragotskie, "killed him, because he wanted to stop the Harlowe man."

"I don't know anything about this," squeaked Ragotskie.

Santiago went on, "Laquedem said these people were going to make a *desastre* worse than what almost happened last year, a poison that would destroy *almas*—souls. He wanted to stop them, but Harlowe's people killed him." Through the shadows, Vickery could see Santiago look up. "We were back here in L.A.," the boy went on. "I was with him, we were walking beside a gas station, and I could do nothing—he—he just fell down, with blood on his face, and then I heard the gunshot. I pulled out my gun, but there was no one to see."

"I'm sorry," said Castine. She reached a hand toward the boy, then hesitated and let it drop. "But it might have been—"

"It was them," said Santiago.

"It probably was," said Ragotskie miserably. "Harlowe doesn't like free radicals."

"I've been watching the ChakraSys store," said Santiago, "taking turns with a couple of the gypsies, and one of them saw a man and a woman talk to the old *brujo* there, this afternoon. That was you two."

Vickery nodded. *Brujo?* he thought. Spanish for wizard. We certainly should have talked to that crazy old man.

"And I was there when this man came," Santiago went on, turning toward Ragotskie. "I knew you were one of Harlowe's people, mister, I've seen you at that place before. And I followed you here, meaning you no good. But—what, you quit? You got fired?"

Ragotskie mumbled, as if to himself, "Okay, maybe somebody on a *bicycle* could have followed me . . . " He looked at Santiago. "Both. I quit and I got fired. I tried to—" He glanced warily toward Vickery and Castine. "Yesterday I tried to do something that would stop Harlowe's, uh, project—"

Santiago nodded. "Egregore."

"Right. But it didn't work. So I'm hoping these two can help me find another way to stop it."

"And," the boy said, "it wasn't you who killed Isaac Laquedem."

"I didn't know anything about it. I've never killed anybody!"

"Not near a freeway, anyway," put in Vickery. To Santiago he added, "He can't see ghosts."

"What is your name?" Santiago asked Ragotskie.

"I don't think you need—"

Castine said, "He just now refrained from killing you, remember."

Ragotskie slumped in the chair. "Oh—Elisha Ragotskie."

Santiago nodded acknowledgment. "I was listening, here, just now," he said with a wave behind him. "I think it's maybe a good thing you two didn't leave town, like Mr. Fakhouri told you to."

"Fakhouri?" said Castine. "That's the Egyptian? You know him? He told us he was going to take care of it all himself."

"Try, sure," said Santiago, "but he doesn't know everything. I been moving around the city, finding things out for him. He will try to stop the egregore monster, but I think it's good that you be working too. Laquedem wanted it stopped." He looked at Vickery. "Driver for Galvan? Not lately, I think."

"No," agreed Vickery. "Galvan wants to sell us to Harlowe, in fact."

"Sell you to him? Why does he want you?"

"It seems we'd be a perfect part for his damned egregore," said Castine.

"An essential part," said Ragotskie.

Santiago stared at Castine and Vickery. "So maybe Fakhouri is right. Maybe you should leave town."

"We've thought about it," Castine said.

Again Vickery caught a faint sound like singing on the wind, and he opened his mouth to hear it better; it was more than one voice, and the song was—yes, definitely—"What a Wonderful World."

Rustling among the leaves didn't seem to be caused by the wind, nor by people either.

The clearing was so dark now that Vickery knew that Santiago had stood up only because he heard the aluminum-frame chair flex. Vickery guessed that he had heard the singing too, and knew what ectoplasmic throats it came from. And he would have heard the closer noises among the leaves too. "I'll find you again," the boy said, and then he had disappeared among the dark trees. A whisper came back: "I'm taking your sandwiches, mister."

"Let's us go too," said Castine; her voice was tense, and she was uselessly looking around at the shadows under and between the trees.

"Yes," said Vickery, getting to his feet. He kept his voice level as he added, "My car's probably got a ticket, if it hasn't been towed. Ragotskie, what's the number of your burner?"

"Uh, okay," said Ragotskie, and recited the phone number. "But what, are we through here? When do we meet again? There's not much time, and you'll need my help with Agnes—"

Clearly he had not heard the singing, or even the agitation among the leaves.

"We'll call you tomorrow." Vickery started to reach for Castine's hand to help her up, then remembered catching her hand last night beside the freeway bridge outside of Barstow, and he pulled his hand back.

But she was standing up anyway, and the two of them hurried through the bushes back toward the freeway shoulder where they had left his car. The frail singing voices were soon drowned out by the mundane roar of rushing car engines.

Just as Agnes Loria was merging onto the westbound 10 freeway, she heard Nunez's voice on the phone say, "There's some kind of activity up the slope, on the freeway shoulder. Can't wait, we're gonna go in."

Loria didn't curse because Nunez would hear it, but she hit the steering wheel with her fist.

I'm too late, she thought, to exit on Vermont and hope to get past Nunez and Foster down on Estes.

But if Elisha is up on the freeway shoulder—well, so am I, in about five seconds.

She sped past the Vermont exit, then braked hard and swerved into the narrow shoulder lane, where a white Saturn was already parked against the guard rail, and she brought her station wagon to a halt a dozen yards behind it and switched off her engine and headlights.

Nunez and Foster will come up cautiously, she thought. I can hop over the guard rail and probably get to Elisha before they make their way up the slope—and then—what, tell him to run? Tell him I'm sorry?

She was about to open her door and get out when two people, a man and a woman, emerged from the shoulder-side trees ahead and stepped over the guard rail and stood by the rear bumper of the parked Saturn; they were looking her way, past her car, clearly waiting for a gap in traffic that would allow them to get into their car on the driver's side, since the passenger-side door was blocked. Their faces were intermittently illuminated as cars swept past, and Loria recognized the woman from photographs Harlowe had distributed back at the Sepulveda office.

It was Ingrid Castine, and the man with her must be Sebastian Vickery. And Elisha wasn't with them!

She snatched up her phone and said "Nunez, wait, get back to your car!"

Castine, and then Vickery, had scrambled around and lunged into the Saturn, and Vickery yanked the door shut just before a big semi swooped past. The Saturn's taillights came on.

"You nearby, Loria?" came Nunez' voice from her phone. "We've waited long enough—"

"Vickery and Castine are up here on the 10 shoulder," she interrupted, speaking rapidly, "above you, just got into a white Saturn with an Anaheim dealer's plate—he's in gear, moving west toward Normandie, I'm going to let a car or two get between us—"

"Don't lose him!" shouted Nunez. "We'll get on at Normandie." From the phone on the seat Loria heard a squeal of tires, then, "Foster stays here for Ragotskie."

The white Saturn accelerated away up the shoulder lane and merged with traffic. Loria hastily started the engine of her station wagon and clicked it in gear, switched on the headlights, and stepped on the gas pedal. By the time she was able to merge with the right lane, at least three cars were between her and the Saturn, and she moved to the faster lane on her left to keep the Saturn in sight among all the swaying and weaving taillights ahead of her.

"He's passing Arlington," she yelled without looking away from the traffic ahead. "Now he's signaling—I think he's gonna get off at Crenshaw. Yeah, shit, he's braking, still signaling."

"I'll be there," gasped Nunez' voice.

Loria gritted her teeth and swerved to the right, cutting off a pickup truck and getting an angry four-second blast of its horn; and then she swept across the blessedly empty right lane into the Crenshaw exit lane. Now there was one car between her and the Saturn.

"We're on Washington," came Nunez' voice from the phone on the seat beside her. "He might get right back on the freeway, to see if anybody's following him."

"He's still got his right turn signal going," said Loria. "And he's in the right-turn lane. I think he's definitely gonna head north on Crenshaw."

The Saturn halted at a red light at the bottom of the exit ramp and then turned right, and Loria waited impatiently for the next car to do the same. When it was her turn she rolled through with barely a glance to the left.

The Saturn was now proceeding north along Crenshaw at a reasonable thirty-miles-per-hour in the slow lane, past glowing windows in the old apartment buildings and fenced-in craftsman houses, and the car ahead of Loria passed the slower-moving vehicle; Loria was now right behind the Saturn.

"I'm on his tail," she said. "I'm gonna pass him so he doesn't get spooked. You at Crenshaw yet?"

"Any second now," said Nunez. "Go ahead and pass him, but keep him in sight."

Loria flipped her turn signal and moved into the left lane—and as she passed the Saturn she couldn't help glancing to her right.

When they had got into the freeway exit lane, Vickery had flicked a look at the rear view mirror and said, "There was a yellow station wagon parked on the freeway shoulder behind us, remember?—and it's getting off with us here." And it had stayed behind them.

Now it was passing him, and he looked at the driver. For a moment he saw her profile, then she turned to face him.

And he stepped on the gas pedal and yanked the steering wheel to the left, smashing his rear door against the station wagon's front bumper. The station wagon spun sideways across the dividing line, and the headlights of several oncoming cars dipped as the drivers hit the brakes.

Vickery straightened the wheel and kept accelerating.

"It was the woman who was pushing the baby carriage," he said tightly, "in February." He pulled the gun out of his pocket and laid it on his lap.

Castine didn't ask him if he was sure. She licked her upper lip and nodded, glancing around at the other cars. "Ragotskie was careless." She had drawn the .38 revolver from her coat pocket.

Washington Boulevard was coming up fast, but just short of it Vickery swerved across the oncoming lanes into the side alley of a brightly lit Mobil station—just as a black BMW sedan made a fast left turn from Washington and then rocked up a driveway into the station on the other side.

Vickery braked to a sudden stop when the BMW's high-beam headlights swung around the station's convenience store and halted a couple of yards from his front bumper, and he and Castine both ducked below the dashboard as he pushed the gear shift lever into reverse with his left hand.

Four loud gunshots shook the air almost simultaneously, and Vickery felt the Saturn shudder as little cubes of windshield glass peppered the back of his head; then he stamped on the gas pedal, and as the Saturn surged backward he straightened up and fired four shots through his crazed windshield at the vaguely perceptible shape of the BMW. Castine had fired three shots through the windshield at the same time, and when the Saturn had bumped down onto the Crenshaw pavement she leaned forward and smashed at the riddled windshield in front of Vickery with the butt of her revolver. When she pulled the gun back, a flap of window glass pulled away with it, and Vickery dropped his gun and reached up to push more of the glass aside with his left hand as he grabbed the wheel with his right.

They were moving fast in reverse down the southbound lanes of Crenshaw, and Vickery corrected the car's back-and-forth swerving; a single headlight steered into sight in their wake, and a blink of white light just above it was probably the flash of another gunshot; all he could hear was the Saturn's engine roar through the torn windshield.

He stomped on the brake and spun the wheel, and when the Saturn had screechingly rotated a hundred-and-eighty degrees he shifted to drive and pressed the gas pedal to the floor. The Saturn was under control and facing forward now, and he smoothly passed a couple of slow-moving cars. His nostrils twitched at the metallic smell of coolant steam on the headwind through the ruptured windshield.

"He *can't* shoot anymore," said Castine tensely. "He'll hit another car!" She leaned forward again to grip the edge of the widened hole in the windshield, and pulled another section of crackling glass aside.

Vickery hardly heard her. In his mind he was back on the night-training course at the Rowley Training Center in Maryland, and all the cars on the street were vector lines in a rapidly changing calculus problem.

The yellow station wagon no longer straddled the center line, and when the one-headlight BMW switched to the passing lane, Vickery saw that the crosswalk signal ahead had turned red, and he pivoted the Saturn into a screeching turn to the right, across the front of a big Stater Bros. delivery truck, and continued the turn right around, to bounce up into the parking lot of a strip mall.

He drove straight through it to the other driveway and swerved back onto Crenshaw, driving north now in the southbound lanes; and even as he heard Castine squeak in alarm as the headlights of a couple of cars rapidly bore down on them, he yanked the wheel to the left and the Saturn went bucking up over the curb and slewed into the driveway of an apartment building.

Vickery braked, then drove up the inclined cement track into a small parking lot behind the building. A sodium vapor light on a pole cast a white radiance over the pavement and the other cars in the lot, and, peering through the ragged hole in the Saturn's windshield, he could see steam curling up from under the hood. He was relieved to see that a row of rose bushes ahead was lit by both of his headlights.

He switched off the engine and the lights, then twisted the key back to the on position to keep the fans going.

He looked sideways at Castine. "You okay?"

"Yes." Her eyes were wide and she was biting her lower lip. "You?"

"Not a scratch. Unlike the car."

He hiked around to peer through the starred back window at the driveway.

"I—think I'm gonna throw up," said Castine, looking at her hand. There was blood on her shaking fingers, doubtless from tugging at the broken windshield. "I *don't like* this!"

"You can't park here!" came a call from a back door of the

building, and Vickery saw a woman silhouetted against an interior light, waving at him.

Vickery just waved back, keeping his attention on the driveway as she repeated her statement in Spanish—but no other car came surging up from the street, and after sixty seconds he opened his door. It creaked, and some part of the lock fell out onto the pavement. He climbed out stiffly, holding his gun down by his thigh where the woman in the doorway wouldn't see it.

He quickly bent down to glance under the car, and was relieved to see only a small puddle of green coolant splashing and steaming under the engine; a bullet had evidently torn the top radiator hose, not the bottom one or the radiator itself.

Looking back toward the driveway, he called to the woman, "Busted radiator hose is all, I'll tape it up and be out of here in twenty minutes."

He walked to the corner of the building and crouched to peer around it, but there was nobody on the sidewalk and no BMW in sight.

Sliding the gun into his jacket pocket as he stood up, he turned and trudged back to the Saturn. Castine had got out and was leaning against the right front fender, possibly to conceal bullet holes. Her hands were in the pockets of her coat. The woman in the doorway hadn't moved, and Vickery was glad the car was turned partly away from her, so she couldn't readily see what was left of the windshield; though the rear window had at least a couple of suspicious-looking holes in its web-cracked expanse.

He leaned in through the open driver's side door and tugged at the hood release lever. Castine stepped back, but nothing happened.

The yellow blanket was still in the back seat, and Vickery took it and walked around to the front bumper. He pounded on the hood and it seemed to click, so he draped the cloth around his hands and yanked up on the hood. It popped up an inch, and another piece of metal clinked to the pavement. He groped under the edge and pushed the catch, and then he leaned back and hoisted the hood up. He squinted against a billow of hot, damp air, and by the sodium vapor glare he could see steam jetting from a ragged rip in the top radiator hose.

"Fixable," he told Castine. "It can't have got too hot in the short time we were driving, and it's only been a minute leaking. I've got coolant and duct tape in the trunk. Once it cools down a bit, I think I can get us moving again."

The woman in the doorway contented herself with saying, "See that you do!" and retreated inside and slammed the door.

Castine walked back to the trunk. "Will it get us back to Barstow?"

"Not across the desert without a new hose." More quietly, he went on, "And even when I can get one, I'll have to bust out what's left of the windshield and rear window, and," he said, glancing at his watch, "the glass shops I know of are closed now. It's illegal to drive without a windshield, as I recall, unless you stay under thirty-five miles per hour. Even then, you've got to have eye protection and working windshield wipers."

In a lowered voice, Castine said, "Windshield wipers for no windshield?" When Vickery shrugged and nodded, she said, "So— what, a motel?"

"I don't think so. We can put tape patches over the bullet holes, but it'll still look awful Bonnie and Clyde. Even at a real lowlife motel, it's too likely the manager would call the cops."

"Are we scared of the cops?"

"I'm sure several people reported the gun-battle behind the Mobil station. We'd be detained, at least."

Castine spread her hands. "Sleep in the car somewhere?"

Vickery touched the radiator cap, trying to guess how long it would be before he dared twist it. He leaned into the car and switched the key to the off position.

"Like in a Walmart parking lot?" he said, straightening up. "Still risky." He wiped his face and gave her a crooked grin. "It'll take a while, just on surface streets, but I've got sunglasses, and I think we can make it up Mulholland."

"Mulholland?" She gave him a blank look, then her eyes widened. "Not—not *Hipple's* old place?"

Vickery rocked his head, acknowledging her reluctance. The small-time blackmailer, extortionist and ghostmonger known as Jack Hipple had lived in an eccentric house down a hillside from Mulholland Drive, and neither he nor Castine had pleasant memories of time spent there.

"His house would never pass a code inspection," Vickery pointed out, "especially with that back door, so I bet it's vacant, and I doubt anybody's bothered to tear it down. Anyway, that clearing with his mailbox is out of sight of the highway. Nobody'll see the car."

"You *did* hear that singing, right? Up in the freeway nest there?" When he nodded again, Castine went on, "that was ghosts, wasn't it?"

Vickery poked at the ruptured hose. "Most likely."

"And," Castine went on, "we saw—how many ghosts at Hipple's place, last year?"

"Uh, four. No, five, counting Hipple's own, on that last visit."

"The first time I spent the night with you, it was in a tomb. This is worse."

"At least we're chaste," Vickery observed drily.

"I hope it counts for something."

Twenty minutes later Vickery had taped up the torn hose and refilled the radiator and the coolant reservoir, and when he started the engine the tape didn't leak and the needle on the temperature gauge quickly moved to a point comfortably left of vertical. He and Castine got in, and the woman in the apartment didn't reappear to complain about the puddle of coolant on the pavement as he backed carefully down to the street.

CHAPTER TWELVE:
Likewise, I'm Sure

Vickery cut over to Western Avenue and then drove north in the slow lane, and though the Saturn drew some amused looks from other drivers, it was only passed by two police cars, and both times Vickery switched on the windshield wipers in the hope that the metal arms and rubber strips flapping back and forth in mid-air in front of his face and noisily striking the top of the dashboard would give the illusion of a windshield behind them; and in fact neither of the police cars slowed. Castine, bundled up in the yellow blanket against the chilly headwind, was several times reduced to helpless, anxious laughter. The fan belt whined now every time he started forward from a stop light, and he hoped he wasn't losing the alternator; the car wouldn't go far working off the battery alone, especially with the headlights on.

At Franklin Vickery turned left, and then for a dozen blocks he was mostly driving down the narrower street between quiet apartment buildings; at Highland he turned right, and after passing the Hollywood Bowl parking lot they were driving up Cahuenga Boulevard, with the sparsely lit darkness of the Hollywood hills looming at their left and the rushing headlights of the 101 freeway beyond a fence to their right.

Finally he made a left-hand loop onto Mulholland Drive, and they were away from city streets. Except for widely-spaced streetlights, the only illumination was from the Saturn's headlights, which showed occasional reflector posts and driveways and clusters of momentarily-vivid red bougainvillea flowers in the otherwise featureless darkness; twice Vickery glimpsed For Sale signs swinging on one-armed frames, and he wished they didn't suggest gallows.

The road was all curves and sharp switchbacks, and the moon seemed to swoop capriciously around in the sky. The headwind through the empty windshield frame was much colder up here in the hills, and Vickery was about to ask Castine to share the blanket when he braked suddenly, fairly certain that the headlight beams had swept the familiar driveway on the left.

He saw no glow of reflected headlights behind him, so he quickly reversed and then steered into the driveway.

The Saturn's right headlight had begun to blink on and off in response to bumps in the road, and before Vickery had driven halfway down the curved, descending track, the light gave a final extra-bright flash and went out with evident finality.

By the remaining headlight he saw the clearing at the bottom of the driveway, and a broken post where the mailbox had once stood— and, partly hidden behind a big rosemary bush, a white compact sedan.

"Oh shit," said Castine. "Somebody's here. Let's go."

Vickery slid the gear shift to park and turned off the remaining headlight. "We were lucky to get here without a curious cop pulling us over because of no windshield," he said. "Driving with one headlight too would make it impossible. And I don't like the noise from the fan belt." He sighed and switched off the engine. "Let's at least take a look."

"Furtively," suggested Castine, opening her door and stepping out onto the packed dirt.

Moonlight frosted the border of webbed glass around the windshield frame and threw deep black shadows under the clustered trees that bordered the south end of the clearing. Vickery pulled the key out of the ignition and got out of the car, closing the door quietly. Castine shook out her hair, and Vickery heard the patter of glass fragments hitting the dirt.

He led the way to the south edge of the clearing and into the weeds beyond, and then he was scuffing down a dirt slope with his arms held out in front of him to catch any branches in his path. He could hear Castine hopping and sliding along behind him. The air down among the trees was even colder than it had been up in the clearing,and was sharp with the smell of pine.

The darkness was relieved by occasional flickering patches of moonlight, but Vickery had to grope his way, and he tried to grab tree trunks or branches for balance—though several times he wound up sitting down and sliding. Hipple had hung hooded robes with oval mirrors for faces on several of the trees, but if any were still in place, they were invisible now.

The wooded slope, he knew, extended all the way down Franklin Canyon to Sunset Boulevard three or four miles away; he recalled that the one-time actress Gale Reed apparently now lived just below Sunset, and if his view weren't blocked by trees bending in the wind, a light at her house might have been part of the boulevard's blurry bright line.

He was expecting the first of two concrete trenches that crossed the hillside, and so he didn't fall over it. He bent to feel the bottom of it, and it was full of dry leaves. When Hipple had been alive, water had flowed through it.

"Trench here," he whispered back to Castine, "with another a few yards further down."

"I remember," came her exasperated whisper.

When they had both crossed the second dry trench, Vickery paused to look around for the short statue that had stood nearby, but it wasn't visible either. But Hipple's house, he recalled, was not far below this point.

He and Castine both tried to move more quietly now, though they still slipped and fell from time to time, sliding through drifts of leaves and sending pebbles rolling ahead of them. At last they halted, panting, for just beyond a wide oak trunk they could see the one-story clapboard house in a level moonlit clearing. The roof bristled with TV antennas, and the house's eaves extended well out past the walls, and in their deep shadow Vickery could see faint, flickering light in the dozens of tiny windows.

Then he noticed that a vertical shape on the front step was a person standing there. A gasp from Castine let him know that she had seen it too.

"A ghost?" she whispered, almost too faintly for him to hear.

The figure stepped out into the moonlight. It was a young girl, perhaps twelve years old, in overalls; and with the suggestion of a ghost fresh in his mind, Vickery's first, irrational thought was that it was Mary, his never-conceived daughter. But this girl had dark hair, and was taller . . . and she cast a distinct shadow in the moonlight.

"Welcome, little fishes!" she called cheerfully.

Vickery clasped his hands together to stop them shaking, then wiped his chilled forehead. Mary is gone, he told himself. She was never anything *but* gone.

He heard the distinctive metallic creak of a screen door opening, and another girl came out of the house. She too was dark-haired and wore overalls.

A voice from inside the house said, "Is someone there? Get back inside!"

The girls giggled and retreated into the house, and a man emerged; a gun gleamed in his half-raised hand, and Vickery recognized him by his moustache and his sport coat, which even in the moonlight was visibly plaid.

Castine had recognized him too. "It's Omar Sharif!" she whispered.

Vickery spread his hands and walked out from behind the tree. He cleared his throat and called, "We've met," as Castine shuffled up beside him.

"Oh!" said Lateef Fakhouri. "You two!" He didn't raise the gun to eye level, but he didn't lower it either. "You told me you would fly away. Did you follow us here?"

"No," said Vickery, "we—"

"What makes you come here?"

"Good question," muttered Castine.

"Harlowe's men tried to kill us an hour ago," Vickery said. "If you walk up to the mailbox clearing, you'll see my car with bullet holes in it, and the windshield shot out." He ventured to lower his hands. "We couldn't drive back to where I live, and both of us have been here before—it seemed like a good, hidden place to spend the night."

"This is true?" said Fakhouri. "I can kill you both, be sure of it."

Castine spoke up. "If you want to walk back up the hill, we can show you the car."

After a brief hesitation, Fakhouri muttered, "I think you had better come in. Did you know this man who lived here, Jack Hipple?"

After a moment's hesitation, Vickery and Castine walked across the clearing and followed Fakhouri into the house. The air inside was a few degrees warmer, and at least they were out of the wind.

The front room was softly lit by the flickering glow of a dozen candles on windowsills and otherwise empty shelves, and the flames resumed their steady teardrop shapes after Fakhouri closed the door. The couch and table and chairs and the old analog TV set were where Vickery remembered them, but the computer was gone, along with the paintings that had hung on the walls and everything that had been on the shelves. The remembered smell of latakia tobacco was replaced now by the aroma of barbecued chicken, and Vickery noticed a Pollo Loco bag and three styrofoam trays and cups on the table. A dark hallway opened on the left, and the two girls stood there, staring with evident interest at Vickery and Castine.

Fakhouri seemed distracted, but he had not put down the gun. "They're just normal candle flames," he said, then waved toward the couch. "I think it's best if you sit down. This house is abandoned, there is no electricity or water. Candles, luckily."

Castine had looked from the two girls to Fakhouri, raising her eyebrows and clearly expecting an introduction; but Fakhouri had ignored her look, and she was now peering around at the bare walls and the cobwebby television set and, warily, at the door in the south wall. She and Vickery remained standing, and for several seconds no one spoke.

"Why wouldn't they be normal flames?" Castine asked finally.

"I mean they are not grafts from the Baba Gurgur fire." Fakhouri looked from Castine to Vickery, then closed his mouth and looked chagrined at having answered her question.

"You lost me," said Vickery. "And yes, we did know Hipple, though not as friends. Uh . . . did you know him?"

"No. You knew he is dead?"

"Yes." Hipple's ghost, thought Vickery, is even now in a pinecone at the hub of a pinwheel on the roof of my trailer, back in Barstow. "There's probably still some bloodstains on the floor behind the couch there."

The girls both hurried around the couch and peered uselessly into the deep shadows. "Blood?" said one.

"Did you kill him?" asked the other. "We can't watch the TV without electricity."

"No," said Vickery. Could these girls, he wondered, be the twins Ragotskie had mentioned? Harlowe's nieces? Why are they with Fakhouri? "We found his body," he added, "some time afterward."

The girls had quit looking behind the couch and now stood beside the table. "We know you," said one of them. "You saw the woman get shot on the porch."

Castine nodded and said, "The two little girls on a boat. We both sensed you."

"Likewise, I'm sure," said the other. She bobbed in what might have been a curtsy. "We're Lexi and Amber."

Fakhouri exhaled and rolled his eyes. "Yes, tell everyone." He sat down in a chair by the television and rubbed his forehead. "Girls, our visitors are—"

"Betty Boop and Colonel Bleep, if you don't mind," said Castine.

Fakhouri nodded. "Yes. Better so."

"You two," said Castine, "pushed us into that vision, yesterday morning. We nearly crashed our car."

"We didn't mean to push you," said one of the girls. "Just touch you. But when we did, it popped out."

The other girl nodded solemnly. "It made Uncle Simon fall down, and Miss Loria said a bad word."

"So did I, as I recall," said Castine, remembering Vickery's car spinning off onto the shoulder on the drive south from Barstow. "Harlowe saw it too? Your Uncle Simon?"

"Only because you did," said the first girl.

Vickery looked away from the twins to Fakhouri. "What brings *your* party here?"

"Endless trouble of a serious kind!" Fakhouri shifted awkwardly in his chair. "But this place? The man Hipple has been mentioned several times when I've spoken to people about the many local . . . er, unnatural situations, and this derelict house was described by a young person I spoke to. It seemed, as you say, a safely hidden refuge, involving no explanations—nor credit cards!—nor, I had hoped, visitors." He nodded toward the bare shelves and added, "It has evidently been selectively looted at some time, but there is dust over all, now."

The girls had sat down on the carpet. One of them picked up a styrofoam cup from the table and began slurping through a straw.

Vickery looked at Castine and shrugged, and they both stepped around the table and sat on the couch.

"We had to stop at a—a *fast-food outlet*," said Fakhouri, "after witnessing what may have been a fatal car crash! And then—do you know about the door back there?" he added, nodding toward the south wall. "Was there a balcony there once? I nearly walked out through it!"

Vickery recalled that the door opened on a sheer hundred-foot drop. "No. Hipple was a blackmailer, as much as anything, and he often got information from ghosts . . . who seemed to prefer a door that didn't need to be walked up to."

"Car crash?" said Castine.

Fakhouri frowned moodily at her, then shrugged. "I am about *rescuing* these . . . Amber and Lexi," he said, "these girls. Excuse me, it has been a dreadful evening. From a church on Pico Boulevard. From their uncle, who has plans to put their poor minds in a blender! To make a spiritual kind of Godzilla, if I may speak frankly."

"And they chased us!" exclaimed one of the girls. "But we fixed 'em."

Fakhouri was staring at the low beamed ceiling. "Harlowe's associates saw us leave, and pursued us in a car. And Lexi and Amber guessed which person was probably driving, and—and the car turned into a telegraph pole. That is, it *struck* a telegraph pole. I am afraid people in the car must have died."

"They wanted to take us back to the church," explained one of the girls, "or the boat in the new marina."

"But Mr. Fakhouri showed us something—*new*," said the other. "A *hier-o-glyph*."

"We looked at it real hard," agreed the other girl, "and now *we're* new."

"Sometimes," amended her sister. "When we are, it feels like jumping off the edge of the world into the big ocean outside. Other times, our uncle's app is still open."

Fakhouri waved sharply at them to be quiet, then gave Vickery a look that was at once defiant and apologetic. "Pardon," he said, "I almost entirely believe you are not working with Harlowe, but nevertheless if he should capture you . . . and interrogate . . . "

"Likewise, I'm sure," said Castine.

"We know about a hieroglyph," said Vickery, not looking at the twins. *We fixed 'em,* he thought with an inward shudder. "If it's the same one, it's showed up in some coloring books, and it's supposed to be dangerous to look at."

"That is the *other* hieroglyph," said Fakhouri. He added, with evident new worry, "Have you seen one of these coloring books?"

"We've got a couple," said Vickery. "We've only glanced quickly at the hieroglyph." Castine frowned at him, and he told her, "I'm revealing none of our plans. And Santiago trusts him."

"And you trust Santiago?" Castine said. "Seb—uh, Colonel Bleep—" She rolled her eyes and went on, "For one thing, I think Santiago has probably killed people, at least one person." When Vickery raised his eyebrows, she said, "He saw the spirit of your . . . your personal ghost, if you recall, outside that Catholic church last year."

That's true, thought Vickery, Santiago saw the ultra-frail ghost of my never-was daughter—and the only people who can see ghosts are people who have been intimate with someone who died within the possibility-widening field generated by the freeways; and though Santiago is surely too young to have had sex with anybody, "Ending someone's earthly life for him is about as intimate as you can get," as Jack Hipple himself had once said.

The twins were listening avidly. "You have a personal ghost?" asked one; and the other said, "I think it's who cuts his hair."

The three adults might not have heard them. "It is conceivable," said Fakhouri slowly, leaning forward and clasping his hands, "that the boy has killed a person. If so, I make no doubt that it was justified. But if he has the ability to see ghosts, it is from the deaths of his father and mother. They were killed on the San Diego freeway three years ago, trying to cross it. He was with them, but was not himself struck by any car."

"Oh," said Vickery; then, "He'd have been about ten years old."

"Last year he told us," said Castine in a softened voice, "that the leather bands he wears on his wrists contain the subsumed—fossilized—ghosts of his mother and father." She looked across the table at Fakhouri. "He didn't tell us how they died. You must inspire confidence."

"We share a common outweighing purpose," said Fakhouri. "It was he who told me of this house. He is loyal to the wishes of his old mentor, who was also killed. I—" Fakhouri paused, considering, and he glanced cautiously at the twins. "I want to stop an Egyptian thing from destroying innocent people, as a fellow civil servant did, fifty years ago."

"Booty," said Castine.

Fakhouri sighed. "You know more than I would like. Yes, that's what the *hippies* of the time called him."

"I'd like to ask these girls some questions," said Vickery.

"No," said Fakhouri. "I think you do mean to help—but the best way is for you both to go away. You can provide only hindrance to me."

"To you and Santiago," said Vickery. "He thinks we should hang around."

"The boy should have more faith. You must not . . . *hang around.* You put yourself and this woman in mortal danger—*immortal* danger!—by remaining in Los Angeles."

"What is the . . . Gurgur fire?" asked Castine.

"You have the name wrong," Fakhouri told her, "and I will not correct you. And it is nothing of importance."

One of the girls tipped her styrofoam cup to her mouth and caught a chunk of ice, and began crunching it.

"We got that from you," exclaimed Castine, "didn't we? You're why we've found ourselves chewing ice cubes!"

The twins suddenly looked distressed. "Did we hurt your teeth?" said one in a near wail. "Sorry!"

Vickery remembered the things he and Castine had found themselves involuntarily saying at Boardner's, six hours ago. "And the 'little crocodile' line," he said, "and the thing about pouring the waters of the Nile on every golden scale. The bits from *Alice in Wonderland.* Those were from you two?"

"We hear you sometimes," explained the other, earnestly, "and reach out and touch you. You're the other IMPs, we can't help it."

"None of you will be IMPs," Fakhouri burst out. "And even if this Harlowe chooses another pair, I will see to it that the egregore fails again, as it did fifty years ago."

"That was a different one," said Castine. " . . . Wasn't it?"

"That October night in 1968," said Fakhouri, "is in a, a time-bubble, un . . . unpopped?"

"A fifty-year time-spike," said Vickery.

"Just so. It is the work of another, but Harlowe intends to—" Fakhouri paused for a brief, humorless smile, "—to take over the long-dormant account, as it were. He has already set in motion the opening of the bubble or time-spike, the release of the enduring potential of that night. Already people are falling in and out of the emerging mind. Without IMPs, the mind would be a vast idiot, and that is marginally better than that it should have intelligence and purpose. But you must trust that I will choke it into utter oblivion, by means of—"

"Something *new*, I bet," said Lexi or Amber.

"Do hush, child!" Fakhouri pleaded. "If Harlowe were to learn—"

He paused, listening; and Vickery had heard it too: a faint knocking.

Castine had jumped at the sound. Now she took a shuddering breath, and whispered, "It's somebody at the back door."

The twins started to get up, but Fakhouri raised a hand and in a harsh whisper said, "Halt!" He threw Vickery a tense, questioning look.

Vickery thought about the ghost repellers that Hipple had kept in a box on a nearby shelf—but even if they had still been there, a ghost had to be induced to look at them, and there wasn't nearly enough light in the room for them to be effective.

"It's probably that Pratt boy again!" whispered Castine.

Vickery's chest felt suddenly hollow.

"His jaw got pushed into his brain," said one of the twins. Fakhouri waved sharply at her and she clapped her hands over her mouth.

The knocking sounded again, no louder but somehow more forceful.

"'*Tis* the *wind*," whispered the other twin, "and nothing more."

Vickery slowly turned his head to look toward the door, the frame of which was dimly discernible in the candle light.

Pratt, he thought, I killed you, and now here you are, knocking at a door. Can I apologize, explain? Do you have something to say to me? Can I refuse to hear it, after putting you where you are?

"Think up some math," he told Castine, and got to his feet. "I better . . . oh hell, I have to see what he wants. Don't anybody look it in the eye, or talk to it." He gave the twins a sharp glare. "Understand?"

Castine looked up at him, wide-eyed. "Sebastian," she said, "why? It'll probably go away if we ignore it."

Now a low groan sounded from outside the door.

"If it's Pratt, he's come for me," Vickery said. "I'll listen to him. I owe him that."

"*It*," said Castine, "it's not a person, it's not who he was."

"It's some part of him."

He walked around the couch to the back door. He took a deep breath, then reached for the doorknob, twisted it, and pulled the door open.

A cold, pine-scented breeze rushed into the house, and Vickery was squinting out at the remote glow of Beverly Hills in the darkness to the south; but the view rippled, as if with impossible heat waves, and he stepped back when he realized that the distortion was caused by some nearly invisible thing hanging in mid-air only a few feet out from the doorway.

It was an upright shape, and it darkened into the outlines of a man and stepped forward across the threshold and into the room.

Now it was nearly as solid-seeming as a real person, though blurry around the edges. Vickery got an impression of a light-colored shirt and dark pants. Its face was in shadow.

"Is Agnes here?" the ghost wheezed then, as it moved forward.

Vickery heard Castine say, hoarsely, "*Ragotskie*?"

"The whole world is lit up," said the ghost, "I hear babies crying, I watch them glow, the tar's bubbling, and the Legion are gunning their Harleys and Harlowe's afraid they'll catch him with his Shantihs down. We've got to get Agnes away from there!" It stretched one arm behind it, and when its wobbly fingers touched the door, it slammed shut, shaking the house.

The ghost peered around the room, and Vickery was glad to see the twins and Castine and Fakhouri look away from it. Fakhouri's fists were clenched, and Vickery thought it was not from fear, but from a wish that the ghost would shut up.

"Where," said Vickery, then glanced at Castine. Don't talk to them in complete sentences, he thought.

She nodded in comprehension. "Is," she said.

"She?" finished Vickery.

"She's at the church," said the ghost, clearly struggling to speak distinctly, "looking at me on the floor. She had to do it, I stuck my knife into Foster." The thing bobbed its hands up and down its torso, then let them drift loose. "I left it there, I guess. It was pretty heavy. I'd like to get it back—it's in Foster's stomach, okay?"

"Okay," breathed Vickery.

"Let," said Castine, and with one hand she made a quick lifting gesture toward Vickery.

"Un," he said, "Agnes?"

Castine rocked her head back in evident impatience, then said, "Be our."

Ragotskie's ghost was looking from one of them to the other, seeming to listen.

"Concern," said Vickery with assurance.

Castine nodded. "You."

Vickery shrugged. "Can?"

"Go gently."

The ghost was leaning forward, with its head cocked, apparently attentive.

"Into that good night," finished Vickery in one breath.

"Poor creature," added Castine.

"Not," said the ghost. It groaned and clutched at its head. "Not till . . . Agnes! . . . is just Agnes. The world is lit up. But I can't see. I can't find her."

The thing opened its mouth, and Vickery crouched, ready to jump to one side if its tongue should come springing out; but it seemed to want to say more.

Before it could speak, if it had even meant to, it spun around in a circle; and rotated again, and again, faster and faster but silently, and then it simply wasn't present anymore, and the candle flames fluttered in a quick buffet of imploding air.

A chorus of exhaled breaths followed it.

Castine sat back and dragged her fingers through her hair. "I don't think she deserved him," she said.

"Does that door lock?" Fakhouri asked. When Vickery shrugged, he said, "At least brace a chair against it."

Vickery crossed to the door and brushed a hand along the frame, and felt a dead-bolt knob. He twisted it, and heard a bolt thump.

Castine hiked around on the couch to look in his direction. "I hope you're not disappointed . . . ?"

"That it wasn't Pratt?" Vickery returned to the couch and let himself collapse onto it. "No. No, that's not a meeting I'd wish for." He leaned back to look toward the kitchen. "I know where Hipple hid a bottle of brandy. It might still be there."

Castine nodded emphatically, but Fakhouri just picked up one of the styrofoam cups and swirled the remaining ice in it. "I'll abstain," he said. "But prepare your refreshments. And then," he added, glancing at the twins, "we can sit together and keep silent on many important subjects."

An extension cord had been run into the sacristy, and a clamp light was now attached to a cabinet door, pointing upward. In the reflected glow, an elderly member of the Singularity team who Loria knew only as Scooter was on his knees, mopping up the last of the blood with a big car-wash sponge. Simon Harlowe paced back and forth in front of the sink counter, overseeing the clean-up. His cowboy boots were a brighter red than the blood. Loria leaned against the wall by the nave door, puffing on a cigarette.

"You didn't have to," Harlowe said to her. "We could have questioned him."

"You weren't here." She took a last, deep drag on the cigarette and tossed it toward the sink; it bounced off the cabinet and landed on the floor in front of Scooter, who wordlessly scooped it up with his sponge.

You weren't here, Loria thought.

The fast confrontation that had occurred an hour and a half ago was still painfully vivid in Loria's mind.

She had only been back at the church for half an hour, still shaky from having nearly been hit head-on by several cars after Vickery had knocked her car sideways on Crenshaw; and she had been alone in the sacristy when she had heard scratching at the back door. Peering out through the little window, she had seen Elisha Ragotskie waving and mouthing something.

She closed her eyes now, remembering.

The door had squeaked when she unbolted it and pulled it open, and Ragotskie had winced behind the lenses of his silly Harry Potter glasses. "Shh! Agnes, the egregore *is* going to fail, just like it did in '68—I *know* this! People are probably going to die, down in Topanga Canyon tomorrow night, and you mustn't be one of them! I may not like you or trust you, but I love you, and I do want you to live. You've got your car—you and I have got to get away from—" he waved around, apparently at everything, "—all this."

"Elisha!" said Loria in a shrill whisper. "Did *you* take Amber and Lexi?"

"The twins? No—they're gone? That's good. Come *with* me!"

Loria gave a jerky wave and shook her head—and she wondered if the egregore *could* succeed, with neither Vickery and Castine nor the twins. What if that whole self-renouncing apotheosis simply *didn't happen,* tomorrow night? What would she be left with?

Elisha, for all his vanities and foolishness, clearly cared about the identity that was Agnes Loria, found Agnes Loria worth taking huge risks for—what if his opinion of her was truer than her own dismissive one?

"My car," she had told him, "won't drive right. A fender is rubbing a wheel now. And anyway—damn it, Elisha,—"

And then Foster had stepped up out of the darkness behind Ragotskie and grabbed his right arm and twisted it behind his back. Ragotskie exhaled through clenched teeth and with his free hand groped around at his belt.

Loria pulled Harlowe's .22 from her jacket pocket and pointed it at the struggling pair.

"Stop it!" she cried. "Foster, let go of him! Look, I've got a gun!"

She stepped aside as Foster and Ragotskie reeled into the room. Ragotskie was gripping a knife in his left hand now, a lethal-looking length of gleaming steel, and he jerked it down and sideways. Foster grunted and bent forward.

And the gun in her hand sprang upward with a flash of blue light and a loud *snap.* Both men tumbled to the floor, and both seemed for a few moments to be trying to get up again, then sagged in final relaxation.

Loria dropped the gun and hurried to them, and she crouched

beside Elisha. His glasses were broken and had fallen off, and in the clamplight's reflected glow she saw lines of bright red blood criss-crossed down his cheek from a little round puncture in his temple. His eyes were open, but empty.

Her own head was ringing, and she sat down and pushed herself away from him. "Oh, Elisha!" she whispered, "I'm sorry! You damned idiot, I'm so sorry!"

Curious about the noise, several of the Singularity staff had come in from the nave then, and it wasn't until they rolled Foster's body over that she saw the knife hilt standing up from his solar plexus. Loria had gone out into the nave and sat down in one of the pews.

Then Harlowe had burst into the church through the front doors with the news that Nunez's ear had been shot nearly off of his head, and that the car pursuing the twins' kidnapper had crashed, and Castine and Vickery were still in the wind; and when he had made his way to the sacristy and stridently demanded an explanation for the bodies on the floor, Loria had managed to recount what had happened. He'd had to be told twice more before he had believed it. Then he had knelt down and roughly searched Ragotskie's body, looking for the bloody sock, but found only $360 and receipts for a six-pack of beer, half a dozen sandwiches, a quilted jacket and a Smith and Wesson hunting knife. Harlowe had ordered several of the Singularity staff to drag the bodies out to the meeting hall at the back of the church.

The sacristy floor was now clean, to the eye at least, and Scooter got to his feet and turned to the sink to wring out the sponge under running water.

Harlowe gave Loria a baleful look and said again, "We could have questioned him." His forehead was misted with sweat. "This night has been a rout."

"I was *trying* to save *Foster*," said Loria; knowing that in fact she hadn't meant to fire the gun at all, and certainly not at Elisha. "Can it still be done?" she asked urgently, "the egregore?" Don't, she thought, tell me I'm condemned to this distinct Agnes Loria identity, with the memory of having . . . taken Elisha's blood pressure!

"Yes." Harlowe nodded firmly. "Yes, one way or, or another. And we'll cover this incident, don't worry."

Loria felt her shoulders begin to relax, and she tried to push out of her mind the image of Ragotskie's slack, blood-streaked face. "Nunez got shot? What happened?"

"Oh—following your directions, he cornered Vickery and Castine, and shot at them. I warned him that Taitz said they seemed pro! They shot back, and now Nunez needs to have his ear sewed back on! One of us must do it. He tried to give chase anyway, but they evaded him and drove away, God knows where. Are they quick, or what? You were right yesterday, I was too hasty in ordering them killed." He raised both fists, then let them fall to his sides. "Damn, but they could be good IMPs, in spite of their link to the past! That could even be a strength, turned in the right direction."

"Still? How? The sock is gone."

"We have," Harlowe said, glancing at his watch, "twenty-six hours in which to find *them*—and I've set out some trip wires that might still yield something. And I believe we do still have Lexi and Amber."

"Simon," Loria said hesitantly, "no we don't. Somebody took them, remember?"

"I'm not *senile*, Agnes! I mean I'm pretty sure we still have them *spiritually*. They colored in the *Ba* image again yesterday, do *you* remember? Renewed their initiation, *opened the apps* again after closing them with their dip in the ocean. It won't matter where their *bodies* are, they don't need to be present when the rest of us hold hands and launch the egregore tomorrow night—it will sweep up all initiated members when it ascends." He raised a hand and then waved it off to the side, as if acknowledging and dismissing an objection; and he added, hesitantly, "Their thoughts, my awareness of their thoughts, *has* been . . . flickering for a couple of hours now—but that's probably just because I'm so very tired."

"Flickering?" Loria had been relieved to hear that the twins were still candidates to be the egregore's switchboard, its IMPs, its thalamus, but Harlowe's evident uncertainty and exhaustion revived her worries. "Like what, like they're jumping in and out of the ocean again, from time to time?"

Harlowe squinted at the ceiling; and after several seconds, during which Loria wondered if he had heard her, he said, softly, "As if they're jumping off the edge of the world into the big ocean outside." He shook his head sharply and exhaled. "And back. They're still with us, mostly. They're still initiated. The, uh, *app* is still open . . . mostly."

"Mostly." For a moment Loria was consciously aware of the faint vibration that was always going on in her mental background; it was a promise of immortality without awareness of self, and she clung to it. "Okay. But Simon, whoever took them wants to stop the egregore. He might *kill* them. What then?"

Harlowe seemed to sag, and for a moment it was very evident that he was in fact over sixty years old; his red hair and cowboy boots seemed all at once ludicrous, even pathetic. "Then," he said hollowly, "we go to plan C."

Loria blinked at him. "I didn't know we had a plan C."

"We didn't," said Harlowe, "until tonight."

Loria opened her mouth to ask what it was, but reconsidered when she saw the evident suffering in Harlowe's face. "I'll go downstairs," she said instead, "and see how Taitz is doing."

Harlowe had forcefully vetoed the proposal to take Taitz to an emergency room with aan obvious gunshot wound. Loria had cleaned, disinfected and bandaged the deep gashes on his right hand, but she was afraid he might lose a couple of fingers—including his trigger finger. And now it looked as if she might have to sew Nunez's ear back on!

"Hm?" Harlowe's attention returned from far away. "Oh, yes, do that. I'm—I think I'm going to spend a bit of time reading *The Secret Garden.*" Harlowe gave her a rictus smile and shambled toward the door.

Loria nodded. She was standing perfectly still, but she felt as if she were rushing in darkness downhill, past briefly glimpsed and scarcely known faces, toward a precipice, with no idea whether she would fall when she reached it, or take flight.

CHAPTER THIRTEEN:
Would You Prevent God?

Bluejays calling to one another in the trees outside woke Vickery.

The selective looting Fakhouri had referred to had not extended to Hipple's bed or closet, though the paintings that had hung on the bedroom wall were gone. The twins had slept in the bed, Castine had slept on the couch, and Vickery and Fakhouri had found places on the floor. There had been enough blankets, on the bed and in the closet, for everybody to have one.

Vickery sat up when the twins began bumping around in the bedroom. Gray daylight shone in the many tiny windows on the far wall, and he was surprised to see Castine already awake, hunched in her blanket and looking at him.

"Not through eastern windows only," she said, "when daylight comes, comes in the light." She spread the fingers of her left hand, squinting at the cuts where her fingers had gripped the broken windshield in the flight from the assassins in the BMW; she had cleaned the cuts with some of Hipple's brandy last night, and seemed satisfied that they weren't getting infected.

"Hark hark, the lark at Heaven's gate sings," muttered Vickery, "and Phoebus 'gins arise." The air in the room was stale with the smells of old barbecued chicken and guttered-out candles.

Fakhouri sat up abruptly and darted a glance toward the ceiling. Last night Vickery had opened the actions on his automatic and Castine's and Fakhouri's revolvers and run a lamp cord through the barrels, and then hung them, together with several wind-chimes, from a convenient hook in a ceiling beam. The magazine and bullets were on a shelf.

Vickery had been uneasy about making the guns difficult to get to, but he wasn't sure Fakhouri wanted to let Castine and himself continue meddling in "an Egyptian thing," as he had put it last night; and Vickery had made sure both doors were solidly locked, and he had known that he would awaken at any sound. And the guns were still there.

He threw his blanket aside and got to his feet, then climbed up on the table and freed the angular steel bundle from the hook. The wind-chimes made a jangling racket that got briefly louder when he jumped down to the floor.

The twins came scurrying up the hall, dressed in their overalls again, or still.

"The rhyming and the chiming of the bells!" exclaimed one.

Vickery was untying the knotted electrical cord, and the other girl said, as if he had asked her, "We didn't hear any gun-wind during the night." She looked at the paper bag on the floor. "We should have got more Pollo Loco."

"I'd open that back door and yell," said Castine, swinging her feet to the floor and reaching for her coat, "if I thought a ghost would bring me coffee."

Vickery freed Castine's revolver and loaded it. He turned around and put it in her outstretched hand, then worked his own gun loose. He crossed to the shelf and slid the magazine into the grip and worked the slide once, chambering a round, then popped the magazine out and pushed the last round into the top of it.

Turning to Fakhouri as he slid the magazine into the grip, he said, "And now I'm afraid I really have to beg your pardon." He passed Fakhouri his revolver, still tangled in the electrical cord and the wind chimes. "It's like this—Harlowe wants to kill, uh, Betty Boop and me, and my car isn't driveable, and we've got no means to rent a car." He grimaced and shook his head, aware that he was not the good guy in this moment. "The fact is, we've got to take yours. We'll drop you and the girls anywhere you like—the Egyptian Consulate?"

Fakhouri looked at him sadly for several seconds, then glanced at the gun in Vickery's hand and said, "You are *resolute* in this?"

"I'm afraid I am, yes. I am sorry."

Castine was frowning at Vickery, but after a moment she got to her feet and faced Fakhouri. "We do sincerely apologize!"

Fakhouri looked toward the twins, but they were just watching with interest. He shook his head in evident disappointment, then said to Vickery, "You have a plan?"

Vickery shrugged. "A goal."

Fakhouri spread one hand in a gesture of philosophical resignation. "As I do too. If there is a God, may He grant success to at least one of us. I can rent another car—from a different agency, I suppose. And as a representative of the General Intelligence Directorate, I can probably concoct a basis for giving these girls some species of temporary asylum at the Consulate. *Ma hadhih alfawdaa!* You don't want me to report the Nissan as stolen."

"No," agreed Vickery. "Not till midnight, anyway." He recalled that the Arabic phrase had meant something like, *What a mess!*

"Yes, midnight." Fakhouri got to his feet. He had untangled his own gun from the wire and wind-chimes, and he crossed to the shelf and began dropping bullets into the chambers in the open cylinder.

Castine was standing by the old TV set with her hand in her coat pocket. When Fakhouri snapped the cylinder into place, he reached into his pocket with his free hand and pulled out a key on a ring. He held both hands out in front of himself as if weighing the key against the gun, then tossed the key to Vickery.

"I hope we may all still be individuals after that," he said.

"Thanks," said Vickery. "We're allies, more or less." He crossed to the front door and unbolted it. The twins crowded up, but he pushed them back. "Go sit on the couch," he told them sternly, and when they had retreated and sat down he glanced at Castine, who had now drawn her gun and was holding it pointed at the ceiling. He opened the door cautiously, keeping behind it. A cold wind angled in, chilling his nostrils with the scent of damp earth.

We weren't followed, he thought, but what about Fakhouri? Could Harlowe have snipers among the trees on the slope? I shouldn't have made so much noise with the wind chimes.

"I'm going to go up the slope to where the cars are," he said to Castine. "If there's nobody around, I'll come back and fetch everybody."

"I'll go with you," she said, stepping up beside him. "Mutual cover, like Butch Cassidy and the Sundance Kid. I trust Fakhouri not to shoot us in the back."

Vickery looked at her in the wedge of daylight. Her auburn hair was disarranged from sleeping on the couch, and he could see the little bald patch over her right ear. There was anxiety in the narrowing of her eyes, but determination too.

"Okay," he said. "Thanks."

But when they sprang over the threshold and sprinted to a couple of widely-spaced trees at the edge of the clearing, no rifle shots echoed and there hadn't even been a startled rustling of leaves, and Vickery relaxed and tucked his gun into his jacket pocket.

He began to climb the slope, crouching forward on the steeper patches to pull himself up by grabbing roots or jutting rocks. Castine angled toward him across the leaf-strewn unevenness, her suede coat already bristly with twigs and pine-needles, and soon they were within a couple of yards of each other.

"We shouldn't be so close," he whispered across to her. The steam of his breath whisked away on the cold breeze.

"We had a chaperone," she answered with a quiet laugh. "And anyway, if there were bad guys around, they'd have acted by now."

"They probably know we'd think that," he said, but in fact he agreed with her.

When they had worked their way up to the lower of the two cement trenches, Castine sat down on the coping and pushed her damp hair back from her forehead. "Coffee and a long hot shower," she said, then looked up at Vickery. "It sounded like Ragotskie's girl Agnes killed him."

"Yeah, it did." Vickery perched beside her. "But he still wants us to get her away from Harlowe. His ghost does, anyway."

"Do we owe him?"

"Well, let's see," said Vickery. "He tried to poison you and shoot you on Monday . . . and last night he led Harlowe's assassins to us, though they only managed to wreck my car. What we owe him wouldn't be nice to say."

"That girl with the bicycle then, at MacArthur Park on Monday. Remember? She was being subjected to that black-hole channeling, just briefly then, but at midnight she might fall into it for good, lose herself, whoever she is. And a lot of other people will do the same. Do we owe them?"

"Am I my stranger's keeper?"

"Well, according to what Ragotskie said, it'll be us too, eventually. After the egregore 'comes online.'"

Vickery looked over his shoulder at the extent of wooded slope still above them. He could hear bluejays chattering away up there, evidently not disturbed by any unusual activity; though of course snipers would lie motionless.

"How's your cut hand?" he asked.

"No problem. We can pick up band-aids and Neosporin someplace."

"I've got a first-aid kit in the car." He nodded and got to his feet. "Onward. Watchfully."

Soon they reached the uphill trench, and stepped over it.

"Fakhouri got alarmed," panted Castine, "every time the girls referred to some new thing. Part of his plan that he didn't want us to know about, I was thinking; some new factor that old Booty didn't know about?"

Vickery gripped a low branch to pull himself over a pile of loose leaves. "I noticed that. And they pronounced *new* differently—in the remarks that made Fakhouri anxious, they said *noo*, like moo or two. But when one of them said the boat was at a new marina, she said *nyew*, like few, or cue ball—and he didn't have a problem with what she said."

"I didn't catch that."

"I notice accents," he said. "Like, a lot of people under thirty pronounce *which* and *where* the same as *witch* and *wear*. No *huh* in them anymore."

"I suppose soon we'll just have one word for everything. Just different inflections."

"I hate to think what the word will be."

They climbed a few more yards in silence. Then, "We're coming to the top of the slope," Vickery whispered. The incline was shallow enough for them to stand up, and they placed their feet carefully as they walked.

But the clearing at the top of the slope was empty except for the devastated Saturn and the partly hidden Nissan and the stump where

Hipple's mailbox had once stood. The birds had gone quiet, but unseen cars whooshed past on Mulholland Drive at the top of the long driveway.

Vickery walked across the dirt to Fakhouri's Nissan and pushed a button on the key fob to pop open the trunk. The only thing on the trunk's carpeted floor was a canvas Trader Joe's shopping bag with pictures of fruit printed on it. Vickery shook two packages of dried Turkish apricots out of it and carried the empty bag across the clearing to the Saturn.

The Saturn's back bumper was dented, and the trunk popped open when Vickery simply slid the key into the lock. Castine lifted out the two bags of clothes they had bought in Hesperia the day before, and Vickery tucked a flat metal box into the pocket of her coat. "Band-aids and Neosporin," he explained.

He slid Ragotskie's envelope into the shopping bag, and tossed the old brown-spotted sock into the bag too.

"Couldn't you just, I don't know, *bury* that damn thing?" asked Castine.

"It's a mobile hotspot, or something," said Vickery as he lifted the bag. "It spontaneously drew Platt's ghost yesterday afternoon, and maybe Ragotskie's last night, even up here on the hill, and it's—"

"A sock with some of my year-and-a-half-old blood on it. Yuck."

"It's the blood of somebody who no longer quite fits flush in this reality. It's a link to you, but I think it's also a . . . a threadbare spot, in the sane world."

"Where's the sane world?" Castine asked as she followed him around to the front of the Saturn. "I used to live there. I think I still have pictures."

Vickery opened the passenger door and hoisted out the old yellow blanket and draped it around Castine's shoulders, then opened the glove compartment and pulled out all the papers, as well as a screwdriver. The papers he dropped into the shopping bag. He carried the screwdriver around to the driver's side and leaned in through the gap where the windshield had been, and wedged the blade of the screwdriver under the metal VIN strip on the dashboard; the strip broke free when he twisted the screwdriver, and threw it out over the slope.

Castine carried the bags of clothing across the clearing toward the open trunk of the Nissan. The blanket flapped around her like a cape.

Vickery stepped back and took a moment to look at the Saturn. It was a 1998 model that he'd bought eight months ago in Barstow, for cash, and it had been a reliable car. Shortly after getting it, he had prepared the disguising styrofoam blocks and blue plastic sheeting, and three days ago, in preparation for his trip to Canter's, he had laboriously glued it all onto the car; and the next day he and Castine had pulled it all off again in a hurry, in that alley off Fairfax. Now the car looked as if it had been abandoned for years—the primer-red driver's side door had a six-inch strip of duct tape across it, covering the groove and puncture of an obliquely striking bullet, the windshield and rear window were pretty much gone, and the right side rear door was concave and streaked with yellow.

He shrugged and turned away, but Castine had walked back, and she caught his arm. "There's a firing pin in the ashtray."

"Oh. Right." He pulled open the door and leaned in. The ashtray was open, and he quickly found the little firing pin from Ragotskie's gun and dropped it too into the shopping bag. Straightening up, he said, "Let's get the others up here and go. We've got to drop them off at the Egyptian Consulate."

She eyed him curiously. "And then what?"

"Breakfast somewhere."

"And *then* what?"

"Oh hell. Go talk to Gale Reed, I suppose, if she lives at that house we identified on Google Maps. Fakhouri can work his *noo* thing, but—"

Castine gave a quick, nervous nod. "It'd be nice if there was a second front. Our strangers' keepers—I think we're stuck with it."

"Within reason."

Castine laughed shortly. "As if *reason* has anything to do with any of this."

A couple of joggers had thumped and panted across the grass, but no car engines punctuated the slow rumble and big exhalations of the surf. Santiago had locked his bicycle to a fence railing, and now waited in the shadow of a wide oak tree in Point Fermin Park until nobody was near him but a young couple walking back toward the cars parked along the shortened length of Paseo Del Mar. The street ended at a fence made of iron bars that curled outward at the tops, but an older, narrower extent of the street could be seen past the fence. Santiago knew that the fenced-off pavement stopped abruptly at the edge of a cliff.

He walked unhurriedly across the grass to the chest-high white wall at the south end of the park and rested his hands on it for a moment, looking out over the broad, wave-streaked face of the Pacific Ocean, deep blue in the morning sunlight; then he fitted a sneakered foot into one of the decorative openings in the wall and swung a leg over the top and dropped to the narrow pavement on the other side.

He stepped off the pavement onto a slanting surface of loose dirt. The sea wind was cold, and he zipped up his hoodie. Below him now was a deep crevasse in the seaside cliff, and he shuffled carefully past it to the downward-slanting end of the iron bar fence; the tops of the bars still curved forbiddingly outward, but the dirt had gullied away below the bottom ends, and he easily ducked under them. Here a path leveled out, and he strode past a No Trespassing sign that was nearly illegible with graffiti. To his right a steep slope descended to the stony beach, and already he could see canted slabs of old concrete down there at the surf line.

The path soon curved left to join the fenced-off length of Paseo Del Mar, and Santiago followed the broken old street pavement for six hundred feet to the edge of the cliff.

Below him now was an uneven, colorful ruin, where in 1929 a forty-thousand-foot section of San Pedro had slid down to the sea. Paths wound irregularly among palm trees and big, tilted sections of old pavement, covered now with brightly colored graffiti designs. Even at this early hour, Santiago could see a few people down there, perched on pavement fragments on the tower-like promontories or, beyond those, picking their way among the black rocks of the shore. He tried to identify the particular concrete block that Lateef Fakhouri had described—"the cement table by the old Red Car tracks"—but even viewed from above like this, the crumpled landscape was a snakes-and-ladders maze of precipices and chance-formed corridors and tilted foundation slabs, and Santiago couldn't see any railroad tracks at all.

Fakhouri had told him that a man named Wystan had once got hold of an image, a *sigil*, that rightfully belonged to Egypt; Wystan had damaged his eyesight by drinking illegal liquor—and serve him right, according to Fakhouri—and the sigil had been buried in the yard of an old woman named Haas, who had lived on the now-fallen section of Paseo Del Mar. This had all been back in the 1920s. The sigil had wanted to go into the sea, and in 1929 it had nearly got there—and pulled down a whole section of San Pedro in the attempt.

In the '60s the sigil had been dug up from the landslide ruins by some motorcycle gang, and taken away; but when it had still been down in the ruins here, in the '30s, blind Wystan had reportedly climbed down the new cliff to the broken streets one night—daylight meaning nothing to him by that point—and had then swum out to sea, and drowned himself.

And according to a couple of very old men who spent afternoons playing chess in Point Fermin Park, the story they had heard when growing up was that a symbol etched into a particular cement slab down in the ruins had been cut by Wystan himself, with a hammer and chisel, just before he embarked on his fatal swim. They had described the slab, but they couldn't recall what the symbol had been—"A cross, I think," said one—and neither of them had ventured down into "that damned Atlantis" in decades.

Fakhouri hadn't wanted to climb down there either, and had asked Santiago to do it. He had given the boy a notepad and pencil with which to copy the symbol Wystan had chiseled into the slab, if he could find it.

Santiago now began trudging along the rim of the collapsed area, for he could see a path ahead and to his right that appeared to slant down into the ruins. A cement table, he thought. By some railroad tracks, the man said.

This might be a waste of a couple of hours, when there were hardly sixteen hours left.

He reminded himself that Fakhouri was working toward the same goal that Isaac Laquedem had been pursuing, and therefore Santiago wanted him to succeed. And, more importantly, Fakhouri was in conflict with the people who had killed Laquedem.

Under his sweatshirt Santiago could feel the medallion that had belonged to Laquedem. He even felt that old Laquedem's ghost was with him sometimes—not communicating anything, just . . . watching over him. And that wasn't impossible, since Laquedem, like Vickery and Castine, had once been to the Labyrinth afterworld and back, alive, and had not been the same as ordinary people after that. The difference had shown up in odd insights the old man had sometimes had—like knowing who had been in a room an hour earlier, or what the headline on a newspaper had been even when the newspaper machine was empty. The insights generally followed brief interludes when Laquedem had seemed to be blind and deaf, and Santiago had worried about the old man's health.

Laquedem had been able to sense Vickery and Castine, since they too had fallen into the Labyrinth and come out again, and so their souls were torqued in the same way as his; he had known that Vickery was up around Barstow, and that Castine was somewhere back east. But after a while he had stopped being able to sense them—he had still sometimes seemed to lose consciousness briefly, but when he recovered he had just muttered about some *mezurgag* house, and refused to elaborate. Santiago had heard the old man use that term before, and had gathered that it meant something like *rotten*.

When Laquedem became aware of what Harlowe was trying to do, he had tried to find Vickery for help in stopping it—*He owes me,* the old man had said—but Harlowe's people had killed Laquedem before he had been able to locate Vickery.

Santiago shied away now from the memory of Laquedem suddenly pitching forward on a Santa Monica Boulevard sidewalk, hitting the pavement face-down, with blood pooling out around his head and the gunshot echoing back from nearby storefronts.

Santiago kicked a pebble over the edge of the cliff and took a deep breath of the cold sea air.

Three years ago Laquedem had found Santiago hiding in a packing crate behind a Home Depot on Figueroa. The boy's parents had been killed by a speeding car down near San Diego only a month or so earlier, and he had made his way, mostly alone, to the perilous streets of Los Angeles; and by the time Laquedem had found him he had been sick and nearly starving. Laquedem had given him food and money and employment, and, more than that, the equivalent of a living father.

Santiago had now reached the path that led down to the ruins and the sea. It wasn't steep, and he was able to look around at the weird landscape as he walked down the slope. The wild, garish graffiti on all the tumbled cement slabs was what first caught his eye—sprawling stylized letters spelling out incomprehensible words or names, the bright blobs of color seeming to dim the natural tans and blacks of the dirt and rocks.

The slabs were scattered everywhere down here, some of them still fairly lined up in the order they'd had when they'd been streets—Santiago could see the curbs along the interrupted edges, and wondered what cars had parked there, before 1929; and whether by moonlight the shadows of those long-gone cars might show up on the old pavement sections. He shivered in the chilly wind and moved faster.

The path broadened out as it curved around to the west, and to his left an eroded ridge stood between him and the sea; it was impossible to tell whether the crooked striations in the ridge wall were sedimentary rock or buried masonry.

In the same moment that he heard someone up ahead singing, Santiago saw the twelve-foot long steel bar that stretched in a shallow arc from a fragment of broken stone to a dirt bank; and a few steps further he saw the person who was singing. It was a tall, white-bearded old man on a nearby tilted slab, in a ragged gray sportcoat and baggy corduroy trousers and worn sneakers, and at first Santiago thought the man was doing a dance on the slab.

The wind was whistling in the bare branches of a tree growing sideways behind the old man, but Santiago caught some words of what he was singing: "*We left behind the old gray shore, climbed to the sky . . .*"

And Santiago recognized the man. This was the *brujo* who had been in the ChakraSys Dumpster yesterday afternoon, when Vickery and Castine had been there . . . and in the past year Santiago had occasionally seen him talking to solitary figures on the little islands in the L.A. River by Dodger Stadium, and Santiago knew that ghosts often found their way to those islands.

The *brujo* noticed him, and stopped singing and scuffing the cement block.

"You wear two people," the old man grated, "on your wrists. Do they control your hands, are you a puppet?"

It jarred Santiago that this old derelict was able to sense the subsumed ghosts of his parents in his leather wristbands, and he pushed away the memory of their tumbled and broken bodies on the 5 freeway shoulder.

"Who are those you talk to," Santiago countered, "on the islands in the river?"

Behind a blowing fringe of white hair, he old *brujo*'s blue eyes were bright in his tanned face. "The shadows of men who have missed the train," he said, more softly. He glanced down at the slab he was standing on. "And I think you're a puppet for a man who wants to derail it."

Santiago waved toward the single derelict Red Car rail that arched for a short distance over the uneven dirt, and laughed. "It's been derailed since 1929."

"You know the train I mean, I think." The old man rearranged his feet on the graffiti-vivid slab. "Would you prevent God?"

"I want to look at that cement block you're standing on."

The old man stood up straight, and squared his shoulders. Up on that slab he seemed as tall as the palm trees. "Your puppet hands can't move me."

Santiago thought for a moment, then stepped back and reached into the sagging pocket of his hoodie and pulled out the gun he had scavenged last year, a .40 caliber Sig-Sauer semi-automatic. He lifted it to point at the ragged base of the slab. "You might miss the train yourself," he said.

The old man twisted his head like a bird, looking with one eye and then the other. "A boy," he said thoughtfully, "but boys younger than you kill people. And you can see ghosts, on the islands." He stepped back and hopped down off the slab. "It means nothing anyway. Wystan was blind by the time he put a chisel to that stone, did you know that? He was only trying to cut his name, memorialize himself, but he failed even in that."

Santiago moved forward and waved the gun; the old man backed away another couple of yards.

The surface of the stone was streaked with red and blue lines that formed broad, stylized letters—presumably someone's more recent try at memorializing a name—but the slanting morning sun cast shadows in old grooves that had not been quite filled in with layers of paint. Wystan had cut deeply with his chisel.

Santiago could see the outlines of an inverted T, and below that, two parallel lines that seemed to be just sawtooth zig-zags.

"A cross," said the old man, "or a blind man's best attempt at one. And then his fucked up cursive signature. You can't read it. They don't teach cursive writing in school anymore, do they?"

"I wouldn't know," said Santiago, stepping back.

For several seconds the old brujo just stared across the slab at the boy, his white mane tossing in the wind. "Tell your puppeteer," he said finally, "to kill the messenger, not the message. One burden to be borne, never to die."

Santiago shoved the gun back into his hoodie pocket, then, without replying, turned and ran back the way he had come. He was all for killing the messenger, but Laquedem had wanted to kill the message too, and Santiago was determined to carry out Laquedem's intentions.

Vickery steered into the drive-through lane at a McDonald's on Wilshire to get Sausage McMuffins for the girls and hotcakes for Fakhouri, then dropped them off a block further east at the Chase Bank Building, where the Consulate General of the Arab Republic of Egypt occupied the eighteenth floor. Before ruefully relinquishing his car, Fakhouri had taken the girls' hands and then paused on the sidewalk to look back at Vickery and sigh heavily. "Stymie them, if you can," he said, "and I'll be working at doing the same."

Vickery had nodded, waved to the two girls, and pressed the accelerator.

"Fairfax is the next street," he told Castine as he shifted lanes. "You want to try Canter's again?"

"Hah. Sure, why not? I can clean up a bit and change in the ladies' room." She sat back and nodded. "I hardly got to look at the menu on Monday."

Vickery turned left on Fairfax, then stopped for a red light at Sixth Street. His window was down, and a young woman in the crosswalk halted to give him a blank look and say, "Do you *enjoy* doing things like going to the bathroom?"

She sneezed then, and resumed walking. Vickery and Castine both stared after her.

Castine opened her mouth, but before she could speak, Vickery said, "Don't say 'Only in L.A.'"

"That wasn't what I was going to say." When Vickery raised his eyebrows inquiringly she just shook her head.

The light turned green and he sped up and caught the light at the next intersection; and within minutes he was turning in to the Canter's parking lot.

When they had got out of the car and Vickery had locked it, the parking attendant walked up. "Or spending a third of your life unconscious?" the man remarked as he handed Vickery a green validation ticket.

"What?" said Castine.

The man blinked and looked at her. "I didn't say anything."

Castine seemed ready to argue, but Vickery took her arm and led her toward the sidewalk. "I don't think he did," he told her.

They walked quickly up the sidewalk toward the door of Canter's, but two pedestrians spoke to them before they reached it: a woman leading two children paused to remark, "Evolution moved on from unicellular life," and a young man looked away from his phone to add, "and intelligent life on earth is about to move on from isolated, conflicted individuals." Both speakers seemed uneasy immediately afterward, and hurried away.

Castine gave Vickery a haggard look. "This is like what happened day before yesterday, with that girl in MacArthur Park. With the bicycle."

"Join me," said an overweight man just stepping out of Canter's. "Know everything, live forever." He gave an embarrassed cough and walked quickly away.

"Yes," Vickery said to Castine. He was absently snapping his fingers, thinking. "It's the black hole thing Ragotskie mentioned. Random people saying what the egregore people are thinking."

Castine had stepped to the curb and was looking fearfully from one passing pedestrian to the next, clearly expecting more enigmatic, helpless statements. "It's Harlowe himself," she said. "He's talking to *us*, isn't he? Does that mean he knows where we *are*?"

"I don't . . . *think* so," said Vickery. "It seems more like a radio broadcast, and we're like FM radios—with varying frequencies— while everybody else is AM. That's what Ragotskie said, remember? These people are involuntary radios. But just in case—I bet we could knock down the transmitter."

A teenage boy on a skateboard skidded to an awkward halt beside Castine. "All your guilts will vanish," he said, and a woman getting out of a car at the curb added, "Be loved by everyone, which is yourself."

Castine turned a haunted look on Vickery. "Knock it down how?"

He wiped his hand across his mouth and looked up and down the street, then back toward the parking lot. "You won't like it."

"Sebastian!" Castine began shrilly; then went on more quietly, "I haven't liked one bit of this!"

"Okay. Last night when you told the twins that they pushed us into that vision—when I nearly wrecked the car yesterday on the 15 freeway—one of them said, 'It made Uncle Simon fall down,' and the other one said Harlowe experienced the vision, because *we* did. I think those girls, in touch with us and with Harlowe, opened him up to our vision of the old house in the canyon. Maybe if we broadcast *that*, it'll break his transmitter, or at least disrupt this broadcast."

"You want to—do you mean we should deliberately see that old-house vision again?"

"It doesn't *hurt* us, Ingrid! That we know of." He waved back toward the parking lot. "I think we should sit in the car while we do it. We won't be able to see or hear anything that's going on here and now, but I'll leave the door unlocked, and if anybody shakes my shoulder I'll feel it and say we're just meditating, leave us alone."

"But—I don't *want* to see that house again."

"You want everybody on the street to keep telling us what a great thing the egregore is?"

Castine shook her head bewilderedly, but walked back with Vickery toward the parking lot.

"The old mythological God," said a woman in shorts and sunglasses as she passed them, "consisted of only three persons."

A bearded man seated against the wall looked up from his *HOMELESS* sign as they hurried past and growled, "—but the new, real God will have billions of persons! Be Him! Own the universe!"

In the parking lot, Vickery opened the car's passenger side door for Castine and waved at the parking attendant. "Just going to meditate a bit before breakfast!" he called, not wanting the man to come over and tell them something else about the egregore god.

When he had got in on the driver's side and closed the door,

Vickery raised his right hand. "At this point," he said, "I bet we don't even have to focus past the immediate moment anymore—I bet it'll happen if we just hold hands, like by the freeway bridge Monday night."

"Shit. Okay." Castine lifted her left hand, which had band-aids on three fingertips now, and clasped his.

The world was suddenly dark and silent. Vickery could see three bright dots in a line, bobbing and crossing in front of one another; they were growing brighter and bigger. In the moment before they swung around out of his view, he recognized them as motorcycle headlights.

Now he saw glowing copper rectangles—a tall one in front of him and two smaller ones flanking it at the level of its mid-point. A moment later they sprang into perspective, and Vickery recognized them as an open door with a window on either side; and he realized that they weren't actually expanding and descending—they were growing closer, and his viewpoint was incrementally rising.

He was mounting a set of steps, and then the sides of the open doorway disappeared in his peripheral vision as he moved into the house. The doorway was narrow, and he was disoriented to feel Castine's hand still clasping his as his viewpoint passed across the threshold.

A long room filled his vision now, lit by bare light bulbs swinging on cords from a cracked plaster ceiling, and on the far wall he glimpsed a yard-tall wooden board with the carved figure of a man-headed hawk attached to it; and though Vickery's viewpoint stayed horizontal, he was peripherally able to see that the floor was uneven rippled sand. A number of people were dimly visible, standing by a glassless window to the right or sitting on a couple of tilted couches on the sand straight ahead, but Vickery's involuntary gaze swiveled so quickly to the left that he caught only an impression of beards and beads and a couple of people apparently smeared with black mud.

His view now was of a spiral staircase with incongruous metal-tubing banisters; a woman who appeared to be in her mid-30s was hurrying down the stairs, her face starkly lit by the swinging light bulbs, and a moment later Vickery saw the familiar lean-faced man in the open Nehru jacket coming down behind her. The man's mouth was opening and closing, and he slapped the woman's shoulder, but he stopped halfway down the stairs and looked directly into Vickery's viewpoint. His eyes narrowed and he pulled the revolver from his belt.

He quickly raised it, and the flare of the gunshot became bright morning daylight as the view of the Canter's parking lot and the rhythm of traffic on Fairfax flooded back into Vickery's perception.

He was slumped against the door in Fakhouri's Nissan, and Castine, beside him, slowly unclasped her hand from his. He realized he'd been holding his breath, and exhaled.

"Jesus," Castine whispered,and it sounded like prayer. She cleared her throat and went on, "He *shot* us, didn't he?"

"He shot *at* us, at least," said Vickery. He straightened up in the seat and rubbed one hand over his face. "I wonder who the hell we *are*, in those visions!"

"Maybe that was the end of them," said Castine. "Maybe our . . . *host* got killed, there."

"That'd be nice, I guess." Vickery pressed the button to roll down the window, but the key wasn't in the ignition, so he opened the door and breathed rapidly in the cold fresh air.

"You saw that board," she said, "hanging on the wall? That carved figure on it must have been the image in the coloring books," he said, "without the distracting lines around it. Harlowe's sigil."

Vickery suppressed a shiver and nodded. "I think what we've been seeing is Halloween, 1968."

"Yes." Castine opened her door, but didn't step out yet. "Yes, I think it must be. Everything old is new again. Did you recognize the woman on the stairs?" When Vickery shook his head, she said, "You weren't looking closely enough at the monitor when we Goggled her yesterday. It was Gale Reed, star of *Catch That Blonde!* And yeah, she looked about the right age, for 1968."

Vickery swung his legs out and stood up on the pavement and stretched. When Castine had got out too, and shut her door, he dug out the keyring and pushed the fob-button to lock the doors.

"I'm going to have a Denver omelette," he said.

Simon Harlowe rolled over on the floor of the sacristy, sweating and clutching his elbow. "Bastards!" he hissed. "They threw that damned old vision at us again!" He scuffed at the floor with his boots, but got no traction. "Right before it happened, I had a sense of two people in a car, holding hands. Did you get that?"

"Uh . . . yes, I think I did." Loria had only sat down, though probably fairly hard, when the old-house vision had exploded into their senses.

"That was Vickery and Castine! They did it on purpose!"

"Your nieces," said Loria, wincing and getting to her feeet, "opened us up to it. We should see if Tony's all right. He was on the boat with us when it happened yesterday."

"Fuck Tony." Harlowe stood up, in stages, awkwardly. He saw that Loria was looking at him in surprise, and he guessed it was because he seldom used profanity. "Excuse me, but I may have broken my elbow."

"The guy on the stairs, in the vision," said Loria, "who pointed a gun at . . . us? is the same guy we saw in the vision yesterday, who had shot that woman on the porch . . . of the same house? Who is he? I think you know."

Harlowe almost said *Conrad Chronic,* but he stopped himself. Speaking that old name out loud, or the name *Sandstrom of the Gadarene Legion,* seemed like profoundly bad luck on this day of all days.

"It doesn't matter," he said. He wiggled his fingers and made a fist and gingerly bent his arm, and decided that his elbow wasn't actually broken. "He failed, fifty years ago, and we're going to finish what he started."

Loria's eyes were wide. "That was the *guy,* the hippie musician guru? Was that *the night,* that we just saw, in 1968? Who was that woman?"

"I don't know who she was. None of that matters." Harlowe looked around at the walls and cabinets and ceiling of the sacristy. More than ever he felt isolated and small and enclosed. "If Castine and Vickery give it some thought, they'll contact me. Ragotskie knew how to get to this place, so they probably do too. And I still sense Lexi and Amber's thoughts."

"Steadily, like before they started to flicker in and out last night?"

"No," he admitted irritably. "It's still irregular, like . . . a rock that gets covered and uncovered by waves. But one way or another we will have our IMP function."

"By midnight tonight?" Loria raised one eyebrow and shook her head. "You better warm up Plan C."

"Plan C." Harlowe suppressed a shudder. "Yes. Excuse me, I—I think I'll lie down for a bit."

He hurried out of the sacristy without looking back at her, and crossed the altar dais to the stairs. Down in his room with the door shut, he stretched out on his cot and tried to read *The Secret Garden*, but the book jiggled in his hands—perhaps because he was trembling, perhaps not—and a memory from 1983 kept intruding.

He had been twenty-six, living in a trailer a mile or so south of the Salinas city limits, and one midnight a vagrant had broken the lock on the door and come blundering in; Harlowe, in a panic, had killed the man with a knife, and the district attorney had ruled it a justifiable homicide . . . but the dreadful intimacy of that encounter with the man had profoundly shaken him. For weeks afterward he had been unable to sleep for more than a couple of hours at a time, and even then he was plagued by visions of the man's close, wide-eyed, hotly-panting face. Finally one night he had opened his old copy of Burroughs and Ginsberg's *The Yage Letters* and retrieved from between the pages a square-inch piece of paper with an R. Crumb drawing of Janis Joplin on it; it was blotter LSD, and he swallowed half of it. Later he estimated that he had taken roughly a 100-microgram dose.

It was the first and only time he had taken LSD. After lying on his narrow bunk for an hour, he had been able to see individual photons spraying from the electric light, and when he had moved his hand in front of his face, it had been outlined with a rainbow aura, and left a glowing streak in the air behind it that was slow to fade; and then the elaborate accumulated structure that was Simon Harlowe's identity had simply fallen apart, evaporated, and all that existed anywhere was a barren plain without any entity at all to perceive it.

After subjective eons he had become aware of his body, and the trailer, and he had slept; and in the days that followed he had resumed his place in the cycle of eating and sleeping and working odd jobs. He was very nearly entirely the Simon Harlowe he had been before—but the part of his soul that was capable of intimacy was gone; and he knew that his identity was a provisional, cobbled-together artifice, adrift and alone in an infinite vacuum.

Now he could hear people walking around on the church floor overhead. He tried to imagine that someone might have brought news about Vickery and Castine, and he found that he couldn't imagine it. Mentally he strained to perceive the faint twittering of the twins' thoughts, but it was once again absent. *In the big ocean outside.*

Plan C.

Harlowe sat up and put *The Secret Garden* aside, then stood and crossed to the box that held his few personal belongings. Crouching, he lifted out his copy of *Alice's Adventures in Wonderland,* and Blake's *The Marriage of Heaven and Hell,* and then found *The Yage Letters.*

He carried the little book back to the bed, and flipped to the page where the top half of the blotter-acid tab sat like a bookmark. All that was left of the Janis Joplin image was her wavy hair and her closed eyes, with exaggerated tears on her cheeks.

If his people failed to find Vickery and Castine—and if Lexi and Amber's initiated presence continued to be sporadic and unreliable— then a dissolved mind, a living human brain with all identity washed out of it, might serve the IMP function. It could be an unconfined relay center, shunting impulses with no *self* boundaries to get in the way.

And this time his identity wouldn't come back. If Plan C worked, his personal ego death would be subsumed in the ego deaths of all the members of the egregore.

He sat staring at Janis Joplin's closed, weeping eyes, while the copy of *The Secret Garden* jiggled all by itself on the floor beside his cot.

He prayed to the void that did not yet contain a God: Let this tab pass away . . .

CHAPTER FOURTEEN:
In Some Times

Their food had arrived on the table by the time Castine came clumping down the stairs from the restrooms. She slid grumpily into the booth, across from Vickery. It was the same booth she had briefly occupied on Monday.

"It *would* be nice not to have to go to the bathroom," she said as she picked up her fork and regarded her pork chops and fried eggs. "Along with all the other maintenance chores—bathing, brushing your teeth—" She poked an egg yolk. "Even eating. You do all this stuff one day, and the next day it's like you never did it, and you've got to do it all again."

"'The routines of our proud and angry dust,'" said Vickery, rephrasing a line from A.E. Housman as he shook Tabasco onto his omelette, "'are from eternity, and shall not fail.'"

"They may be *from* eternity, but they're not *to* eternity. Eventually we just die. I'm half tempted to dig out that damned coloring book and look hard at the picture."

Vickery forced a laugh. "Sure, that's a *good* idea. Like poor old Ragotskie said, soon enough you'd be one of the egregore's discarded cells, wandering around crazy and starving." He took a forkful of his omelette, chewed it, and washed it down with a gulp of beer.

"Maybe. But by then I'd be in the Long Island Iced Tea that's God. That starving body shambling around would no more be *me* than my ghost would." She looked away from him, around the dining room. "Have we done such great things with our particular lives?"

Vickery decided to let that one go. "So God doesn't exist, yet?" he said. "How'd we all get here? You should go to Mass more often."

"God can time-travel," she said, at last taking a bite of her egg and beginning to cut her pork chop. "He goes back in time and kicks off the Big Bang, to make all this, and us."

Vickery nodded. "You do know—right?—that everything you're saying is total crap."

She forked a piece of pork chop into her mouth and rocked her head thoughtfully as she chewed. She swallowed and took a sip of coffee. "Yes. But wouldn't it be nice to leave all the guilty memories behind? The old gray shore? I killed a fellow TUA agent last year . . . and got my fiancee killed by getting him involved in all that." She raised her fork like a crossing-guard's stop sign. "Yes, he turned out to be a shallow coward, but I did get him killed."

And I killed a man too, last year, Vickery thought. It was to save Ingrid, but he was a living person with memories and tastes and maybe a wife or girlfriend, and I did kill him. And on Monday I killed this Platt kid.

"Our guilts are what make us us," he said.

"Well exactly. Creepy old usses."

"We sound like Ragotskie and his Agnes." He thought of telling her that he didn't want her to disappear, but realized that that would be, at best, irrelevant.

Castine laughed. "You're right. And this pork chop is good, I'm glad to be able to eat it. And really, you and I aren't that creepy, considering."

"Comparatively," agreed Vickery, hiding his relief and assuring himself that she'd just been irritable and contrary.

"So Gale Reed," he said, happy to change the subject, "was there for the first attempt at the egregore."

"If that's what we saw. Okay, yeah, the sigil did seem to be on the wall there."

"So she's probably actually an eyewitness to how it failed then. And if that was her house the paramedics were taking her out of, three years ago, we might be able to talk to her."

Castine was making short work of her breakfast. "What's our cover story?" she asked around a mouthful.

"We're reporters doing a story on romantic comedies of the 1950s.

Do we know enough about that genre, or about being reporters, to fake it? Maybe not. Okay, we're grandchildren of Leo Marlin—he was the writer and director of *What's the Hex?*—and we've been trying to find out about him. He was killed during a burglary of his home in '68, you recall. Or we're screenwriters hoping she'll agree to do a cameo in a script we're writing—we imagine that having a famous actress like her agreeing to be in it will make our screenplay more attractive to an agent."

"We sound pathetic."

"Pathetic's okay. Or we're movie memorabilia collectors, and we've found a cache of old publicity stills and lobby cards from *Catch That Blonde!* and we're hoping she'll autograph some, or buy some."

"What if she wants to see them?"

"Well, we didn't presume to bring them—we wanted to see if she was amenable—"

Castine slid the last piece of pork chop around in the remains of the egg yolk. "I think the Leo Marlin angle would be a more natural way to bring the conversation around to Halloween of '68. We could say our mom told us Reed was there."

"We can figure it out on the drive. You about ready?"

"We should both get some clothes out of the car and change, first! And wash off, as much as one can with wet paper towels." She shook her head glumly. "More coffee before anything. This is my first taste of it since I got two sips at your girl Galvan's lot yesterday."

Vickery turned left off Sunset onto Lomitas Avenue, and then he was driving Fakhouri's rented Nissan through the turns he remembered from looking at Google Maps in the library yesterday evening. The houses that weren't hidden behind ivied walls were mostly two-story Moorish or Spanish or Colonial styles, with long, perfectly cropped green lawns and lots of arches and balconies.

Castine's lips were pursed. "I wish we didn't look like such bums." In the Canter's lady's room she had changed into khaki pants and a tan blouse, and had brushed most of the pine needles off the suede coat; Vickery was now wearing a new pair of blue jeans, a flannel shirt, and a black denim jacket.

"We've looked worse," he said. "She's seen worse. That's it on the left there."

Past a long, shoulder-high hedge, the two-story house they'd seen on Google Maps swung into view. Its steeply slanted gable roof, spiral brick chimneys, and half-timbered front with exposed wood framing around sections of white stucco, gave it a fairy-tale look, and Castine remarked, "She really ought to have a whole bunch of garden gnomes out front."

"We can pretend we're selling those."

Vickery turned in to the long, curved driveway and switched off the engine. Birds chattered in the overhanging jacaranda trees, and when he opened the door the breeze smelled of jasmine.

Vickery and Castine walked up to the iron-banded front door, and Vickery pressed a button in a brass plate on the door frame. He looked at Castine and held up crossed fingers, but lowered his hand when footsteps could be heard approaching inside.

A bolt clanked, and the door was pulled open by an elderly woman in a blue linen skirt and jacket, with a small gold cross on a gold chain hanging at the front of her white blouse. She didn't seem to be Gale Reed.

"Ms. Reed?" said Vickery.

The woman smiled in evident bafflement. "I'm sorry, I think you must have the wrong address."

"We're trying to reach Gale Reed," said Castine.

Vickery was taller than the old woman, and at the far end of the long, tiled entry hall behind her he saw a white-sleeved elbow briefly emerge from behind a corner, and withdraw.

"The actress?" said the woman. "I remember her—she was on that show with everybody stacked in boxes, with Paul Lynde. He was gay, you know."

"She knew our grandfather," said Castine, "Leo Marlin. He directed a movie she was in, in 1966. We've been looking up people who knew him, and we were talking yesterday to a guy named Chronic, and he gave us this address—"

A metallic clatter sounded from further back in the house, and the woman looked over her shoulder in alarm. "Oh, she's fallen! Help me."

Vickery and Castine stepped into the house and hurried after the woman. The ivory-white entry hall was bare gray tile except for a couple of ornate console tables with mirrors above them, and a passage at the end of it opened to the left into a broad sunlit kitchen. And on the tile floor lay a capsized aluminum walker and, partially under it, a frail-looking old woman in a bathrobe. Her disordered, thinning hair was an unrealistic shade of gold. She was moving her legs and fumbling weakly with the poles of the walker.

Vickery crouched beside her and slid his hands under her arms and knees and lifted her—she could hardly have weighed more than a hundred pounds—while Castine picked up the walker.

"Carry her in here and lay her on the bed," said the woman who had opened the door. "And thank you."

Vickery followed the woman away from the kitchen, down a corridor to the open door of a bedroom. The walls were all hung with bright tapestries between inset bookshelves, and Vickery carried the old woman to a baroque four-poster bed and laid her on the bedspread. The entry hall had smelled of floor polish, but the bedroom only carried a eucalyptus whiff of Ben-Gay.

"Are you hurt, dear?" asked the woman who had followed him in. Castine had left the walker standing in the kitchen and was now peering over the woman's shoulder.

"Nothing broken," croaked the old woman on the bed. For several seconds she just inhaled and exhaled and rolled her head back and forth on the pillow. Finally she said, "You can go, Beatrice," and waved at a small silver bell on the beside table. "I'll ring if I—need help."

"I think I should stay," said Beatrice.

"It's all right. These people—you heard, I knew their grandfather."

Beatrice spread her hands, then nodded. To Vickery she said, "I'll be in the kitchen. Come get me if she needs attention, *any* attention, do you understand?"

"Yes," Vickery told her.

Castine stepped past Beatrice into the bedroom. "We understand."

Beatrice walked away, and when her footsteps were echoing in the kitchen, Gale Reed stared at Castine. The old woman's eyes were uptilted slits in a face that seemed partially collapsed, but she fairly radiated alarm.

"Chronic," she said huskily, "isn't dead? Are you *sure* it was him?"

"You misunderstood," said Castine gently. "we were talking to someone *about* this Chronic person. Who probably is dead, yes." She glanced questioningly at Vickery, then went on, "But somebody is now trying to fire up Chronic's egregore again."

For several seconds Gale Reed just blinked at her like a wary old cat. "I heard you clearly," she said finally. "Leo Marlin wasn't your grandfather, was he?"

"No, ma'am," said Vickery. "We want to talk to you about—"

"He was a male chauvinist pig," Reed said, still talking to Castine. "You're lucky he wasn't your grandfather. How did you get this address? It's not in my name. Nothing is anymore."

Castine looked helplessly at Vickery, who just shrugged. "A picture of this house," Castine said, "in Google Images. And then a search for it in Google Maps."

"I'll have Beatrice delete the picture somehow." Reed turned to Vickery and said, "Is this some fandom project? Have you been grubbing around in bad old gossip? I can't imagine why you think I'd want to hear about it." She reached one spotted, skeletal hand toward the bell on the beside table.

"This man," said Vickery, "his name's Harlowe, has got the sigil, the hieroglyph, from Chronic's old coloring books, and people on the street are already speaking his thoughts, involuntarily. He's going to launch it again *tonight,* unless we can stop it. We're sorry to intrude on you here—but we need to know what made the egregore fail in '68."

"And we want to get a young woman out of it altogether," added Castine, which irritated Vickery. We never *promised* Ragotskie that we'd get his Agnes free, he thought. And he *is* dead.

Reed's hand faltered and fell.

"You do know what we're talking about," said Vickery.

"I," the old woman admitted hesitantly, "heard about it. Back then. This Chronic fellow was supposedly dangerous. He knew some people I knew, and they were scared of him. They're surely all dead by now." It was impossible to read the expression in her perpetually narrowed eyes. "And I heard he had some project, and yes, it was called *egregore,* whatever that means. But I didn't have anything to do with it."

"You were there," said Castine flatly, "in that house in Topanga Canyon, on that night. You were standing beside Chronic on the spiral staircase when he shot somebody."

"We saw you," said Vickery. "The past hasn't always receded out of sight."

For fully half a minute, during which Vickery heard the front door open and close, none of them spoke. Finally Reed bowed her head and ran her bony old fingers through her thinning, vividly blonde hair.

"All these years later," Reed said, as if to herself, "here come da judge." She squinted at her two clearly unwelcome visitors. "I've fled it, down the nights and down the days. For years I could still feel that faint, damned, maddening buzz in my head! Three years ago I managed to silence it, by nearly silencing myself."

We read about that on the TMZ website, thought Vickery.

Reed sighed deeply. "Do you young folks remember *Hollywood Squares*? That TV game show was a bright, blessed haven for years, even though I had to climb a little . . . *spiral staircase* to get up to my square, every time!" She coughed and cleared her throat. "But I can't help you. It was just a very bad time in L.A., spiritually. *Something* went wrong with Chronic's new god, that terrible night—I really think some people disappeared, or appeared out of nowhere! Thin air! Sandstorm's gang of motorcyclists rode up and there was a fight, with guns!—but Chronic was more scared of some fellow outside with a lantern, I remember. People were actually *killed,* though it never made the papers . . . I don't *know* what went wrong, besides everything."

She was silent, and Vickery wondered if this was all she would say. Finally Reed's marionette mouth opened again.

"My husband knew it would fail," she said in a soft, quavering voice. "He and I were supposed to be the egregore's switchboard, because of . . . what we were. But Stanley did a lot of historical research on olden-days egregores," she said, nodding toward the bookshelves, "and he found some problem. It was something scary, he wouldn't tell me what it was because we were already grafted into the egregore, such as it was—but he tried to get Chronic to stop the project."

She waved one frail hand. "It was too late. Stanley never really recovered from the disaster, and I couldn't guide him back to sanity; he nearly took me down there with him." She closed her eyes. "He spoke in complete sentences, that night, to . . . the wrong sort of person."

"A ghost," said Castine.

Reed just stared at her.

Vickery recalled that Reed's husband, Stanley Ancona, had left her in 1968. "Would it be possible to talk to your husband?"

"Stanley," whispered the old woman, "had to hide from the spirits, like a Pharaoh, after that. They wanted to *take* him, he said, take his place, and he didn't want to be one of them, ever. Dot Palmer, you remember her? She was in *Billy the Kid Versus Dracula*, with John Carradine. Chronic told us he killed her that day." Her voice strengthened. "Heart failure while hiking, the papers said! Yes indeed, nothing stops your heart like a bullet does!"

"On the porch of that house," ventured Castine.

"That awful old house full of sand, yes, her blood was still on the steps when we arrived there that evening. And then Sandstorm's bikers rode up, and it was just . . . bedlam, bloody murder!" She frowned and closed her eyes. "His name was Sand*strom,* but we all called him Sandstorm, he was the leader of the motorcycle gang, the, uh . . . "

"Gadarene Legion," said Vickery.

"Yes!" Reed shivered and opened her eyes. "I remember! Yes, Chronic shot *him,* too, in the arm. He'd know what it was that went wrong that night—I think he was it."

"Is Sandstorm still alive?" asked Castine.

"I doubt it. Who is, besides me?" Reed was staring at the wall now; or, thought Vickery, through it, to the past. "The Legion had a clubhouse," Reed went on, sounding mildly surprised at the recollection, "in Topanga Canyon, below Camp Wildwood— Sandstorm kept the Egyptian sigil at the clubhouse, until Chronic stole it and reproduced it in his coloring books. Sandstorm said it kept all the members of the club together, in allegiance to the club, allegiance to the Legion! . . . even the ones who had died."

"Do you know where the clubhouse was," asked Castine, "exactly?"

"I certainly never went there!" Reed scowled at Castine for a few heartbeats, then shrugged. "Dot did, poor girl. She said the path to it was right across from a rock that looked like . . . somebody."

Vickery heard the front door open, and footsteps approaching through the entry hall. Beatrice appeared in the bedroom doorway and said, "No paper yet." She looked from Vickery to Castine and added, "I think it's time you two left."

Castine turned back to Reed. "Who did the rock look like?"

"I don't remember, child. Beatrice, call the *Times* and complain. They're always late. Do it right now, before you forget."

Beatrice blinked. "I'll call them on the landline. My phone's in my room, charging."

"Inefficiency everywhere." Reed looked back at Vickery.

"You two don't come back, I've told you everything I remember. It's all I can do to help." She laid back and closed her eyes.

Vickery glanced uncertainly at Castine, then shrugged. He nodded to Beatrice, and he and Castine walked out of the bedroom. They were halfway down the entry hall when they heard Reed's frail voice behind them: "Wait!"

They hurried back up the hall and around the corner to the bedroom.

Beatrice was standing tight-lipped beside the bedroom door, and Gale Reed was sitting up in bed and pointing an unsteady finger at a bookshelf. "There was a book my husband thought was important. You can take it, it's the one with black tape over the back of it. I've never opened it, and it seemed wrong to dispose of any of his things—but—giving it up to you, on this day—I believe it's all that's left that I can do, to pay him what I owe. Finally."

Vickery nodded and reached up to the high shelf. The book was heavy, and a drift of dust came down with it when he pulled it free. He opened his mouth, but the old woman in the bed made a chopping motion to silence him.

"If it has a title," she said, "Don't read it to me. Now take yourselves, and it, at long last forever out of my sight."

Vickery made a sort of bow, and he and Castine left the room again and walked down the hall to the front door.

When they had stepped outside into the chilly morning breeze and pulled the door closed, Castine said, "What's the book?"

Vickery opened the dusty old volume, and the first leaf was the age-tanned title page. "Wow, published in 1837! It's, uh, *The Epidemics of the Middle Ages. No. 1. The Black Death in the Fourteenth Century. No. 2. The Dancing Mania.* And Stanley wrote his name in the top margin. I don't know, we'll have to look at it later."

"Where to now?"

"There's the address on Pico," Vickery said as they walked down the driveway to the car. "That's probably where Ragotskie's Agnes killed him. I gave him the address last night in the freeway nest, and he was headed there, and the next time we saw him—well, we *didn't* see him, we saw his ghost."

He opened the trunk and slid the book into Fakhouri's Trader Joe's shopping bag. Castine was already in the car, and he got in on the driver's side and started the engine.

Castine glanced at her watch. "It's early yet."

"Sure. Okay, let's try for the rock that looks like somebody. We might find something, even after all this time."

Harlowe had told the Singularity crew in the church nave to lock the front door, sit down in the pews, and not make a sound. He and Agnes Loria sat in two chairs in the sacristy, staring wordlessly at Harlowe's iPhone, which sat on the counter by the sink. A fly was looping around in a slanting beam of morning sunlight, and Harlowe had to keep reassuring himself that its buzz was too faint to be picked up by the phone's microphone. He had thought of putting a strip of tape over the microphone slot, but he wasn't certain it would stop sound, and in any case he didn't want to jiggle the phone at all.

He leaned to the side and breathed into Loria's ear, "What's the rock that looks like somebody?"

Loria, holding her own phone and watching the screen of the iPad in her lap, just shrugged. She pointed at the map on the iPad screen, which showed a green dot on Sunset Boulevard, not far from Beverly.

Harlowe hoped Beatrice Kittredge kept her phone fully charged. And he was glad that Taitz and Foster had been so very thorough in tracking down everybody who had been involved with the Chronic egregore fifty years ago, and in offering each of them ten thousand dollars if they could reliably report anybody showing new interest in it. Taitz said he hadn't been able to talk to Gale Reed, but had given Harlowe's number to Reed's housekeeper companion . . . who had called the number only a few minutes ago.

Beatrice had carried her phone outside while "a man with a gray beard and a woman with reddish hair" talked to Gale Reed about things that had happened in 1968, and for the renewed promise of ten thousand dollars, she had given Harlowe the license number of the couple's car; and then, for the emphatic promise of an additional ten thousand, she had reluctantly given Harlowe her Apple ID and password and agreed to hide her phone in their car without ending the call.

Harlowe had got the idea from Ragotskie. Loria had found a phone with a dead battery in a map pocket of her car, and guessed that Ragotskie had hidden it there on Monday night to listen to directions from the Waze app on her iPad.

Immediately after talking to Beatrice, Loria had gone to iCloud.com and entered the woman's data, and now she and Harlowe could watch the green dot which was Beatrice's phone moving west on the screen's representation of Sunset Boulevard.

Harlowe was running short of action-qualified personnel. Two fingers of Taitz's right hand had turned black, and Nunez's torn ear, cleaned and smeared with Neosporin and bandaged back onto his head, had nevertheless got infected, and he was running a fever; and the car Nunez had been driving last night needed a new headlight, windshield and rear window, and Loria's station wagon couldn't be driven without abrading a tire against a fender. The car that had pursued the twins' kidnapper was totalled.

Harlowe had sent Tony and Biloxi, the former ChakraSys sales manager, out in Biloxi's prized Camaro, and Loria was texting them directions so that they could follow Vickery and Castine. Harlowe had not trusted either of them with the monitoring iPad.

As soon as Vickery and Castine stopped somewhere and looked likely to stay a while, like for lunch, Harlowe and Loria would drive there in the Tahoe, join Tony and Biloxi, and, one way or another, get Vickery and Castine into the Tahoe and restrained. In the meantime, Harlowe wanted to hear what they might say.

A woman's voice, presumably Ingrid Castine's, came out of the phone's speaker: "You said there's dried apricots in the trunk? We should have got 'em out."

"You just had pork chops and eggs!" said a voice that must have been Vickery's.

The phone relayed a creaking which was probably Castine shifting on her seat, and she said, "Peril seems to make me hungry."

The phone was silent then. That exchange had been worthless.

Harlowe glanced down at the iPad in Loria's lap, and saw that the green dot had turned south on Beverly Drive.

A fluttering started up at the other end of the counter, on the far side of the sink; Harlowe's first horrified thought as he leaped up from his chair was that one or both of Pratt's disembodied hands had escaped the *Secret Garden* book—but it was the book itself making the noise. Its pages were fluttering wildly, as if in a high wind.

"You hear that?" came Vickery's voice from the phone. When the woman murmured an apparent negative, he went on, "Something funny with the exhaust, maybe?"

Harlowe shut the book and pressed both hands onto it, holding it closed—against palpable resistance!

"I don't hear it now," said Vickery.

Harlowe could hear a faint, muffled voice coming from the book; he could feel the vibration of it in his sweating palms. With a wild glance at Loria, he picked up the book and shuffled to the nave door; but it was closed, and he didn't have a free hand.

Holding the vibrating book shut in one tightly-gripping hand, he opened the door with the other. And as soon as he had stepped out onto the altar dais and closed the door behind him, the book squirmed out of his grasp and went flapping to the floor.

And, very faintly, he heard a little girl's voice saying, "When the sky began to roar, 'twas like a lion at my door; when my door began to crack, 'twas like a stick across my back . . . "

For a moment Harlowe just gaped down at the thing in horror. Had the infusion of Pratt's ghost revitalized the little-girl wraith? Unfossilized her?

He bent down and made himself pick up the book—a dozen members of the Singularity team, sitting in the church pews, were staring at him—and he hurried to the stairway door.

Down in his room, he locked the book in a trunk under his cot; and when he had hurried back upstairs and quietly opened the door to the sacristy behind the altar, Loria looked up at him and shook her head. The phone was emitting only a low roaring sound.

When he closed the door and crossed to where she was sitting, and leaned down, she whispered, "They've turned on the car's heater, and I guess it's aimed straight at wherever Gale Reed's companion hid her phone."

"Keep listening," whispered Harlowe. "I'm going to go downstairs and . . . worry about that damned book. I'm—I'm not sure it was a good idea, after all, to put Pratt's ghost into it."

Vickery turned west on Santa Monica Boulevard, and after they crossed Wilshire the broad green lawns and sunlit white Romanesque church towers of Beverly Hills gave way to a less intimidating Starbuck's and a Walgreen's drugstore and a McDonald's. After several miles Santa Monica Boulevard ended at Ocean Avenue, with nothing ahead but the wide green median and its bending palm trees, and the glittering blue band of ocean beyond. Vickery made a right turn and drove for half a mile with tall white geometrical hotels on his right and bicycle paths and palm trees on his left, and then he turned left onto the California Incline, the street that slants down across the face of the ocean-fronting bluff to beach level at Pacific Coast Highway. The sky was a bright clear blue, but there was a wind from the sea, and he left the heater on.

As he drove north on PCH, the beach and the ever-folding surf swept past steadily on his left, but after the first couple of miles the steep slope on his right was hidden behind a high, stout wooden fence, presumably holding back potential landslides. After another mile, the fence gave way to four-foot-tall concrete Jersey barriers, which disappeared in turn after another quarter mile, leaving the weedy, rocky slope crowding right up to the highway shoulder.

The road curved to the west along the coast toward Malibu, and at Topanga Canyon Boulevard he turned right, inland, leaving the sea to dwindle away in the rear-view mirror as the road wound between wooded slopes.

"Watch for a rock that looks like somebody," Vickery told Castine. "I've got to keep my eyes on the road."

She peered around. "I don't see any rocks, just bushes and trees— sycamore and oak, mostly. I guess we left all the palm trees behind at the beach."

Vickery swung the steering wheel back and forth as the road curled up through the canyon and passed in and out of shadow. After a while he noticed a number of oddly shaped rock outcrops flanking the pavement, but Castine didn't remark on any of them. When they had driven several more curving miles, he said, "I think we're coming up on Wildwood. Still nothing?"

"I haven't seen—" she began; then she pointed ahead and exclaimed, "There's Freddie Mercury! See that rock?"

Vickery slowed and peered ahead. A rock in the cliff face to the left did look vaguely like a head.

"Freddie Mercury wasn't around when Dot Palmer was alive," he said.

"Well maybe she thought it looked like Valentino or somebody, but it's the only face we've seen."

A dirt track bent away between two steep slopes on the opposite side of the road.

On this side a weedy bank was just wide enough for Vickery to pull the car over, out of the way of other vehicles. He edged up onto it, slid the gearshift into park and looked across the road. The car was tilted, and Castine had to bend down over the steering wheel to look in the same direction.

"Worth a try?" Vickery asked.

"If it's the right place, there might still be something up there. Gale Reed thought the Sandstrom biker guy was what went wrong with the egregore."

"Okay," Vickery clicked the engine into gear and steered the Nissan across both lanes, and started up the rutted bumpy path. "I bet nobody's been up here for years."

"May as well keep going. You can't turn around."

The track climbed sharply, and Vickery shifted to low gear; and after a dozen yards of slow, swaying progress the trail leveled out, and on a narrow, uneven plateau, walled on three sides by rugged slopes, he saw a structure like an abandoned barn. A big wood-frame door at the front of it was slid halfway open and looked as if it hadn't been moved from that position in decades.

But a shiny black panhead Harley Davidson motorcycle leaned on its kickstand a few yards in front of the barn.

"Good lord," whispered Castine.

Vickery braked to a halt.

"Have your gun handy," he told Castine as he opened his door. The smell of motor oil tainted the juniper and tree bark scent on the cold breeze.

Castine got out, and she and Vickery walked cautiously toward the incongruous barn. Vickery noticed that the motorcycle had no clutch or front-brake levers, nor rear-wheel shock absorbers. A real old-school hardtail chopper, he thought.

They halted when a bald old man in boots and jeans and a ragged, once-white T-shirt stepped out of the building into the sunlight. His face and arms were tanned almost purple, and his left hand was behind his back.

"I bet you thought this was the Café Mimosa," he said, in a high, nasal voice like a nailed-shut box being pried open. "That's another mile up the road."

Vickery cleared his throat and said, "We were told a man named Sandstrom used to hang out here." His hands were in his jacket pockets.

"He's dead," said the old man. "I'm watching his place till he gets back."

Vickery nodded uncertainly, wondering if they were dealing with a lunatic—but the well-maintained antique motorcycle was evidence that the man might actually know something about the old days of Sandstrom and the Gadarene Legion.

"It has to do with some things that happened in 1968," Vickery said.

"A lot of things happed in the canyon in '68," said the old man. "If this old bike could talk, it could tell you some strange stories."

"Somebody's trying to restart Chronic's egregore!" Castine burst out; she paused, then nodded. "With the coloring books and all."

For several seconds none of them spoke, and the wind in the hillside trees was the only sound.

The old man spat. "Sure. It's been hanging fire for a long time. You think the ghosts don't know about it? Shit."

It occurred to Vickery that this figure might itself be a ghost—and he and Castine had spoken to it in complete sentences!—but the sun had risen above the hills surrounding this notch, and the old man was casting a clearly delineated shadow on the leaf-strewn dirt.

Struck with a sudden conviction, Vickery said, "Mr. Sandstrom, can you tell us what made it fail, in '68?"

The old man's jaw worked as if he were chewing something, and finally he shrugged and nodded. "Cops wouldn't know or care about that stuff. Yeah, I'm him. What do you want?"

"We want to know how to stop it again," said Vickery.

"All you gotta do is kill somebody."

To Vickery's surprise, Castine said, "We've both done that."

"Have you now! Sweet little chick like you. Well, old ones don't count. Who did you kill?"

She stared straight at the old man. "A federal agent. Last year."

Sandstrom turned his reptilian gaze on Vickery, who rolled his eyes, hesitated, and then said, "Another federal agent. Likewise last year."

"You two desperadoes. Why don't you be good little outlaws and just—" He paused, and peered narrow-eyed at Vickery and Castine. "Hah!" The old man rocked on his heels and grinned, exposing several teeth. "If you're the pair I think you just might be, tell me what you brought back."

Vickery waved his free hand. "Brought back where?" he asked. "From where?"

But Castine had caught her breath and then shakily exhaled. "He means from the afterworld," she said to Vickery, "the Labyrinth." Facing the bald old man, she said, "A hang-glider. It wound up blocking a hole in a clearing off the Pasadena Freeway."

Sandstrom's eyebrows were halfway up his wrinkled forehead, and he had stopped chewing. "A hole to Hell, they say. Though sometimes the story is you had a hot-air balloon. After that, do you . . . live in *now,* all the time?"

Vickery pursed his lips. "Not *all* the time," he allowed.

"I should have guessed you two would be likely to show up this week." Sandstrom stared at them for a few heartbeats, then swung his left arm from behind his back and dropped the revolver he'd been holding hidden, and he nodded toward the open door of the barn. "Come inside, you can carry my gun. I'm sure the brothers will want to see you."

Vickery and Castine exchanged a wary glance, then Vickery crouched to pick up Sandstrom's revolver and they followed the old man across the uneven dirt to the half-open door of the barn.

The interior was lit by a couple of dusty skylights in the high roof, but after a moment Vickery's eyes had adjusted enough to see three flames in glass chimneys on a shelf at the far end of the big chamber; and then, in the shadows to his left, he noticed a cobwebbed tangle of haphazardly stacked old motorcycles. Wind whistled through gaps between the boards of the walls.

Sandstrom led the way across the rippled floor of square paving blocks to the shelf where the three flames stood upright above corroded gas jets, protected from the draft by the glass chimneys. Vickery noticed a fourth chimney at the end of the row, its gas jet unlit.

Irrationally, Vickery felt exposed in front of the flames, as if they were three malevolently senile old men staring at him. The flames weren't terribly bright, but when he looked away, their arrangement lingered in his vision for several seconds.

"I let 'em out for a while, most days," said Sandstrom, "to sit on the propane. The rest of the time they're in a lantern I got from old Booty, after it was all over. Lamp oil's my biggest expense these days." He waved at the unlit gas jet. "The dark one at the end is waiting for Coastal Eddie—he got shot off the porch that night, and just plain disappeared. But I'm holding his place for him." In a louder voice, he said, "Brothers, here's two more who don't live in this bullshit future!"

Vickery guessed that Sandstrom was addressing the flames; and when they all wavered at the same moment, it seemed that they were responding—acknowledging. A couple flared briefly, seeming to score Vickery's retinas, and he suppressed a shudder.

"They want to know did you die," said Sandstrom. "You can talk plain, they don't stir from the flames."

From their combustion wheelchairs, Vickery thought.

"Uh, no," said Castine nervously. "We went across in our bodies, and came back, still alive."

All the flames bobbed, and Sandstrom grinned. "They're not dead either, see, just in this fake 2018. It's still '68 in the way station down there at the bottom of the canyon, and they mean to go back." He looked up at an empty section of the wall. "And I'll get the *rest* of the old Legion here again, in their home place—they're in the sigil Chronic stole from us."

"The Egyptian hieroglyph," said Castine.

"Its name is *Ba*," said Sandstrom. His lean, deeply grooved face seemed best suited to express rage or ironic humor, but now he sounded almost reverent. "We found it back in '65, where it once tried to jump into the sea and took a big old part of San Pedro with it. That's how the club got its name, jumping off a cliff, dig?"

Castine nodded. "It makes sense. The Gadarene Legion."

"Sure. And we'll have our sigil again."

"In this bullshit future," ventured Vickery.

Sandstrom waved his left arm toward the three flames. "It's bullshit to them. Gas is still thirty-four cents a gallon where they are, two bucks gets you a six-pack of Bud and change, and Buck Owens is on the radio." He sighed. "I wish I could go back myself. Can I have my gun?"

"Oh, sure." Vickery handed it to him. "So what made Chronic's egregore fail?"

"I told you. People got killed there, when he was launching his *invitation* across the *nation*, at that crazy old house." Sandstrom looked from Vickery to Castine and added, speaking clearly, "Ghosts got in the mix. Ghosts are spaces shaped like somebody, but the somebody isn't there, they're like bubbles in a fuel line—the engine stalls."

"We heard he shot you," said Castine. "In the arm."

After a pause, Sandstrom nodded. He touched his right arm and stiffly flexed the fingers of that hand. "He was a punk. I went there that day to try to *negotiate* the return of our property, which the fucker stole. There was a movie actress there too, with some legal hassle for him, and he shot her. And then yeah, he shot me that night, when four of us rode back down there to just *take* the sigil back, right as I walked in the door."

With a sudden chill, Vickery realized that he and Castine had experienced that, three hours ago. It's this Sandstrom person, he thought, who must be the source of our visions!

Castine's mouth had dropped open, and she exclaimed, "He was on the stairway, right?—with Gale Reed, when he shot you."

In the ensuing silence the three flames were motionless.

Sandstrom cocked his head and squinted at her. "If you say so, doll."

"And that was your sigil, wasn't it," asked Vickery, "hanging on the wall over the couch?"

The flames jiggled furiously in their glass cylinders, and Sandstrom folded his arms with his gun hand out, the barrel pointed at the high ceiling planks; he smiled and said, "You tell me, Lazarus."

Vickery had the impression that in the last few seconds he and

Castine had stepped wrong, forfeited whatever degree of openness Sandstrom and his flaming companions had extended to them.

Perhaps sensing the same thing, Castine looked back toward the open doorway. "I think we've learned what we wanted to know. If you—all—will excuse us—" Then she looked back at Sandstrom. "Where was that wrecked house full of sand, the place where it all happened?"

Sandstrom let his arms fall to his sides. The gun was pointed at the floor now. "I told you. That's the way station. It's down at the bottom of the canyon. If you drove up from PCH, you went right by it."

"But it was torn down, right?" said Castine. "After the flood in '69?"

"In some times. Not in all."

Vickery asked, "Where exactly is . . . its place?"

"You don't need to be there."

"We'd like to watch."

"Come back here one day and I'll tell you about it."

"Right." The discussion was clearly ended. "Be seeing you." Vickery nodded toward the flames, from which the only response was flaring and sputtering, and took Castine's suede-sleeved elbow and led her back across the floor and out onto the sunlit dirt. Sandstrom followed, and watched from the doorway as they got in the car and Vickery started it up.

Vickery managed, on the narrow and tilted space in front of the barn, to twist the steering wheel and switch from drive to reverse enough times to get the car pointed back the way they'd come, and after inching his way down the bumpy track for several minutes he reached the two lanes of Topanga Canyon Boulevard.

He signaled for a right turn, and when no car was visible to the left, he swung into the lane and accelerated, heading back south.

Castine fastened her seatbelt and whistled a descending note. "I did *not* like the way those flames *looked* at me!" she said.

"Nasty old men," Vickery agreed. "I didn't like the way they looked at me, either."

The car's heater was still on, but Castine shivered and pulled her coat more tightly around herself. "You remember last night, when Fakhouri said the candles at Hipple's house just had normal flames?

I think we just saw *ab*normal flames." She turned in her seat to face him. "So!—damn it!—why should we have been experiencing *his memory* of that terrible day?"

Vickery shook his head, not taking his eyes from the curving road. "I don't think that weird purple tan on him is from the sun."

Castine raised one hand, palm up and fingers beckoning in a *go on* gesture.

"Those flames," Vickery said, "are out of synch with recommended retail time, just like we are—as Sandstrom said, it's still 1968 for them. So they're FM transmitters, in this world of AM. And Sandstrom's been standing in front of them for—what do you think, a million hours?"

"Say an hour a day, for fifty years. Call it eighteen thousand."

"Okay. I think they've lit him up, like an electric current through hydrogen gas. The hydrogen doesn't shine with the full spectrum, just a few frequency bands, and I think Sandstrom just shines—on what you might call their carrier wave—with his memories of that day fifty years ago. Laquedem probably saw the old house visions too, since he'd been to the Labyrinth afterworld, and got chronologically fractured same as us. He'd have been an FM receiver too."

"Sure, that old gag," said Castine, knotting her fingers together in her lap. "I don't want to see it—I don't want to *be* there!—when Gale Reed's bedlam starts up."

"It looks like that's the next installment," Vickery said, "since the gunshot didn't kill him."

"We need to check out the way station while the sun's still up," said Castine. When Vickery looked away from the road to give her a questioning look, she added, "It's got to be the X on that map in Ragotskie's papers."

Half an hour ago the iPad had lost the signal from Beatrice Kittredge's phone. The green dot had been moving west past Will Rogers State Beach when it disappeared, and Loria, free to talk in a normal voice, had said Vickery and Castine had probably driven up into Topanga Canyon, which famously had bad phone reception. Harlowe had insisted that GPS locating could still function, and Loria had explained that one needed a particular app for that, which Kittredge apparently didn't have.

CHAPTER FIFTEEN:
The Inverted Broken Ankh

The ragged old man stood at the top of the hill above PCH, his white beard blowing around his tanned face. Behind him was the Pacific Ocean, and below him to his right the colorful array of Oasis Imports outdoor furniture stretched up the road to the rambling red-and-white building that was the Malibu Feed Bin; but he was looking down the inland slope, past the terraced hill paths to the curving line of trees that marked the course of Topanga Creek.

Two people, a man and a woman, had parked a white car on the highway and gone walking up the path to the creek; and a few minutes later he had seen them again, through a gap in the trees, following the creek's westward curve. After several more minutes they had not reappeared in a clear area to the left. They had stopped, somewhere down there among the trees.

Very near whatever foundations of the house might be left.

Half a century ago the house's roof would have been visible from up here, the two gable windows on the rear side . . . and Cayenne would still have been alive. She had been twenty years old to his twenty-eight, generally in a feathered hat and wool shawl and big rainbow sunglasses, with a shy smile and a frank resolve to rid herself of a life she had never wanted. He had loved her, and had been a proxy for the egregore in wooing her toward a bigger, selfless existence—but in the end she had had to settle for her old goal of plain death, when a load of buckshot from a Gadarene Legion shotgun had caught her squarely in the chest, on that disastrous final night.

He shook off the memory of crouching over her broken body amid the melee, seeing the shock fade to infinite absence in her blue eyes.

The egregore had not manifested itself on that night, and none of the eager communicants had achieved the bigger, selfless existence.

He had been long gone by the time the 1969 flood knocked the place over and it was finally cleared away, decades after it had stopped measuring up to any municipal building code; but in the '60s, people hadn't cared about such things. He had met, and recruited, many prominent people in that crazy old place, with its non-vertical walls and ground floor drifted with sand—movie directors and stars, writers, politicians; Dot Palmer hadn't by any means been the most notable.

And treacherous Dot Palmer had threatened, on the very day of the intended consummation, to go to the police about a couple of underage runaway girls who were staying at the house.

He had not been able to afford any such delay.

And Palmer's ghost, only hours old by that time, had probably done its part in wrecking the egregore, though several more ghosts—including, intolerably, Cayenne's—had been created to join Palmer's before that night was out. Sandstorm had led a real scorched-earth assault, perversely unable to comprehend the benefits the sigil could offer to everybody, not just his gang of hoodlum bikers.

Conrad Chronic watched the trees along the creek banks, but nobody had appeared. He believed he had recognized the inquisitive couple, even seeing them at this distance of several hundred feet. They were the pair he had met yesterday afternoon, at Simon Harlowe's vacated ChakraSys office on Sepulveda. Chronic had driven his old VW van there to try to stop Harlowe, even kill him if necessary, but Harlowe and the whole ChakraSys crowd had abandoned the place, and he had been trying to find some clue to their new location when this pair had wandered up.

He had supposed then that they were just a couple of losers pursuing some dipshit spirituality . . . but here they were, at the site of the focus house itself.

The old man bent down and lifted the yard-long pine board with

Tony and Biloxi had just been turning onto PCH. Harlowe told them to get to Topanga Canyon Boulevard and head north. The signal had to reassert itself when Vickery and Castine got out of the canyon.

"And we've got to get out there," Harlowe told Loria. "Bring my phone and the iPad."

she was wearing Biloxi's hoodie. "Nobody's following us," he said, returning his attention to the traffic ahead, "and we've got our IMPs! Who cares if he was in the military?"

"I'd like to know where they were, up the canyon."

"It doesn't matter now. Do you have enough Narcan to give them another nose-squirt, if it wears off before the morphine does?"

"We got a bunch of it at Walgreens." She leaned forward over Castine's still-limp body and took hold of Vickery's chin. Turning his face toward her, she asked quietly, "What did Gale Reed tell you?"

"Tension apprehension and—" He blinked several times, then squinted directly at her. "I know you, don't I?" he said. "You—stopped a baby carriage in front of my car—in—February. And—you were in a car on Crenshaw—was it last night—?" His mouth worked. "Did you squirt something up my nose? It tastes like a stale menthol cigarette."

"Yay," said Castine, by Loria's right knee; she went on, indistinctly, "though I walk through the valley of the . . . shadow of death . . . "

"That's from the Bible," put in Biloxi, still leaning over the back of the rear seat.

"Shut up," Loria told him. "Yes," she said to Vickery, "that was me. You were working for that Mexican woman that first time, what was her name?" When Vickery didn't answer, she said, "Galvan, that was it. What were you doing before that?"

Vickery managed to sit up. He shook his head and said, "We haven't had lunch yet." He looked down at Castine, who had raised her arms and was blinking at the duct tape around her wrists. "Have we, Ingrid?"

"Wha-at?" Castine said. She looked up. "Sebastian? Jeez, tell 'em to turn up the heat." She licked her lips and exhaled through her nose. "Did I get sick? I don't feel good."

"Blood," said Harlowe from the front seat. He opened the console, then tossed a plastic bag back to Loria. "Quick, before they're awake enough to resist."

Loria unzipped the bag and shook out onto the floor two handkerchief-sized white altar cloths and a steak knife. Quickly she poked the knife-point into Vickery's forearm above the duct tape; he jumped and reflexively raised his bound arms.

Loria leaned down and cut Castine's arm the same way, and Castine grunted. "Careful with that thing!" she muttered groggily.

"Oh, did Biloxi cut you?" crooned Loria then, tossing the knife past Biloxi into the back of the vehicle. "Here, let me put something on that."

"*I* didn't—" began Biloxi, but he closed his mouth when Loria gave him a brief glare.

She pressed one of the altar cloths onto Vickery's cut arm and the other onto Castine's. The cloths quickly blotted with bright red blood.

"You got 'em?" called Harlowe, and when Loria said she did, he added, "Don't mix them up. If one of our IMPs should get away in the next few hours, *per impossibile,* we want to be sure we're using the right tracker."

"And we got plenty enough to triangulate it this time," said Loria, peeling off one of the wet cloths in each hand. To herself she muttered, "Vickery left, Castine right." She leaned back to see Harlowe. "We going to the church?"

Harlowe shook his head without taking his eyes from the highway. "We've got everything with us. Cabrillo Marina is only half an hour down PCH. We can take the *Black Sheep* out to where the chronocline is flat—get our IMPs securely initiated as soon as possible. But leave the bloody cloths here, in the vehicle, just in case."

Loria nodded, then turned to the back seat and carefully wedged herself between Vickery's bloody right arm and Castine's knees. To Tony and Biloxi she said, "Move all the weapons to the front seat," she said, "then lift Vickery over the seat and into the back. Even with their wrists bound, I don't want to risk them touching each other."

Harlowe and I don't need another dose of the old house vision right now, she thought, especially with him driving.

Santiago was perched on a tree branch projecting out over a white-painted picnic table, peering through the leaves at the dirt track below the slope. The old *brujo* had watched two men chase Vickery and Castine, and had then retreated into the greenery, probably to walk back up the winding path to the top of the highway-facing hill. Santiago had seen Vickery and Castine run toward the gate by PCH, and had seen the gray SUV turn in and block them; the boy had heard a couple of what sounded like .22 shots, and then four rapid shots from the carved wooden figure of a man-headed hawk glued onto it. Over the decades he had several times had to re-gue the figure, but exposure to weather and ground water—and marijuana smoke, when it had hung on the wall of the filthy Gadarene Legion clubhouse— had long since silhouetted the place where Claude Wystan had originally glued it.

Chronic had reproduced the image in the *Groan* coloring book in '66, and had distributed copies as widely as he could—at the UCLA and USC campuses, at one of the "acid tests" hosted by Ken Kesey's Merry Pranksters in the Cinema Theater on Western, and even, briefly, at Disneyland—and the egregore, he believed, had very nearly come to life.

Tonight at midnight this Harlowe guy meant to awaken and hijack it. But I'll take it back, thought Chronic, and in that fragmented hour I'll find Cayenne, young and alive, and this time we'll all leave behind the old gray shore, climb to the sky.

I suppose Harlowe knows that he needs a couple of switchboard operators. I had Stanley and Gale, my telepathic twin brother and sister pair, who had fled their home state, changed their names, and got married because it was only with each other that they could really communicate—all of it a closely held secret.

A faint reminiscent smile deepened the wrinkles in Conrad Chronic's cheeks.

But Chronic had been the guru of the idealistic egregore group, their Messiah, in fact, ready to lead them all to transcendent immortality . . . and so it had been natural, one stoned night, for Gale to confide in him her deep but illegal relationship with Stanley. And private knowledge had always been a useful lever in getting people to do what he told them.

Stanley had rebelled, come up with some crazy historically-based reasons why the egregore would fail. And it did fail, but almost certainly because of the inclusion of fresh ghosts, not Stanley's predicted psychological perils. And after that disastrous night, Stanley had simply disappeared.

Chronic clasped the weathered board to his chest. He still couldn't see the man and woman down there by the creek. Why *had* they come sniffing around Harlowe's vacated place on Sepulveda yesterday? And what had brought them *here*, on this day of all days?

Down on Topanga Canyon Boulevard, a green Camaro convertible had pulled up behind the white car the couple had arrived in; and now two men got out of it and started up the dirt path, moving purposefully. Chronic gripped the board under his arm and began walking along the zig-zag path that led down the hill to the creekside trees.

He glanced at the clear blue sky. O moon, grow bright, he thought. Cayenne, only a few hours more until we're together forever.

Vickery had parked on the Topanga Boulevard shoulder well short of PCH, and taken Fakhouri's shopping bag out of the trunk and carried it along as Castine led the way around a chained road-blocking gate and up a dirt path toward a hill that stood between this four-acre field and the coast highway. They were in a little wilderness of trees and weeds and curling paths, but Castine had dug around in the shopping bag and pulled the map from among the papers Ragotskie had given them, and insisted that the paths and a nearby creek corresponded to lines on it.

After a few minutes of walking, and pausing to peer at the map and squint around at their surroundings, she came to a halt. She looked south between two luxuriant willows at the hill, and breathed, "My God, look at that slope! Don't you recognize it?"

Vickery did. It was the slope he had seen many times behind the house, in the visions that were Sandstrom's memories. "These bricks must be where it was," he said, pointing to a low wall mostly hidden by white calla lilies that bobbed in the breeze. "It looks like they once tried to shore it up a bit." He realized, with a wave of vertigo that he knew Castine must share, that they were standing where Sandstrom had stood when Chronic had shot Dot Palmer, fifty years ago. We're here in person at last, he thought.

Castine pointed a trembling finger at a rosemarybush above the low wall. "That would be where the porch was, where Dot Palmer was killed." She raised her hand and moved it to the right. "And that's where the staircase was. This morning we saw Gale Reed walk down those stairs when she was—uh, born in '33—she'd have been thirty-five. And an hour later we talked to her when she was *eighty*-five."

Vickery stepped back, his hands in his pockets. "She deteriorated a lot in that hour."

"She was still hanging wreaths at the La Brea Tar Pits as recently as four years ago," Castine pointed out; then her face went blank. "Egyptian mummies were preserved in bitumen," she said quietly, perhaps to herself.

Vickery glanced at her in alarm, wondering if this was another of the *Alice in Wonderland* quotes projected from Lexi and Amber, like the "pours the waters of the Nile" line; but Castine waved impatiently. "Gale Reed told us that her husband Stanley hid from the spirits like a Pharaoh, remember? He didn't want to become a ghost."

"Bitumen is asphalt," said Vickery slowly, "tar. And—"

"And she hangs a wreath annually at the La Brea Tar Pits! It's *not* in honor of the mastodons and giant sloths that died there a million years ago."

Vickery whistled softly. "You hop over the fence after the place is closed, put rocks in your pockets and wade out. And then you're down there in the tar, with the saber-tooth tigers and all." He nodded judiciously. "It probably is a good way to keep from becoming a vagrant ghost."

"I bet it's his birthday," said Castine, "or their anniversary, when she hangs the wreaths."

She and Vickery both jumped when grating voice intruded from the slope above them: "Oh, Br'er Fox, whatever you do, don't throw me in de tar pits! Hah! So now he *is* the tar baby!"

Vickery heard a slithering rattle of leaves and gravel higher up the slope, and he and Castine quickly stepped away from each other; Vickery's hand was on his gun in his pocket, and Castine's was in the pocket of her jacket.

And they recognized the white-bearded old man who now limped out from behind an oak trunk and sat down on the knee-high wall. He was holding a weathered board carefully in both hands—like, it occurred to Vickery, Moses carrying the Ten Commandments down from Mount Sinai.

"As if anybody'd want his crappy incestuous old ghost anyway," the old man said, hiking himself forward and standing up.

"You were in that Dumpster behind the ChakraSys place yesterday," said Vickery.

"Incestuous?" said Castine.

"They were brother and sister," the old man said, "him and Gale.

Part of what made 'em a likely switchboard. Blood under the bridge, a dead guy under the tar. I know, I know, you got guns. Big deal." He squinted from Vickery to Castine over the top of his board. "You saw Gale Reed come down those stairs this morning? What, an old home movie I didn't know about?"

"That's right," said Castine quickly.

"Huh. And here you are, since this place is listed in all the *tour books,* right? *Maybe* somebody filmed it. Or maybe you two *saw* her, *saw* this place. You got a date, tonight? With that Harlowe guy's crowd? You tell him, you hear? Tell him he's reaping what another man sowed."

"You're talking about Chronic," said Vickery; then he remembered the lean face of the man on the porch in the visions, and compared it to the face of the old man in front of them; the cheekbones and forehead were similar, but it was the eyes that he recognized.

In a hesitant, wondering voice, Vickery said, "You *are* Chronic."

"Chronic as a virus," the old man said, grinning, "in remission for fifty years but back again. And Chronic for Chronos, master of time, and the titan Cronus, who incorporated his children."

"Cronus *ate* his children," said Castine. "And we're not with Harlowe."

Chronic cocked his head, and locks of white hair trailed across his face. "Does he specially *want* you to be with him? Are you two— you see events from the past!—can you two be his desired switchboard?"

"You could say so," said Vickery. "But don't worry, we're not going to—"

Chronic opened his mouth and bellowed, "*Over here!*"

Vickery looked back toward the boulevard and saw two men walking on the path he and Castine had followed. At Chronic's shout, the men raised their heads and began sprinting this way.

"What do we do?" asked Castine quietly.

"Not a gunfight. Assume others. Run."

And then he and Castine were dodging tree trunks as they ran through patches of shade and sunlight, away from the old man and the two men on the path. The loops of the wildly swinging shopping bag jerked at Vickery's left hand, and when they passed a shoulder-high bank of bull-thistles he noted the location and pitched the bag onto the far side of the clustered green leaves, where it wouldn't be seen.

The creek curved to the left ahead of them, disappearing in the shadows among an impenetrable-looking stand of trees, but a makeshift wooden bridge spanned the water to their right, and they thumped across it to the open area on the other side. Now they were on a south-slanting footpath that widened out in a proper dirt road. A row of white cabins stood on a rise to their right beyond a couple of picnic tables, and Vickery was fairly confident that he and Castine, who was panting along right beside him, would reach Pacific Coast Highway before their pursuers could catch up.

When they rounded a corner and he saw a yellow road-blocking gate a couple of hundred feet ahead, he knew that they were at the other end of the unpaved lane that transected this untended area; and even as he and Castine exerted themselves in an extra burst of speed, a familiar gray SUV turned in from the highway and came to an abrupt stop on the other side of the gate.

The doors opened, and out stepped Simon Harlowe and the woman whose car Vickery had sideswiped on Crenshaw last night. Harlowe was raising a rifle to his shoulder.

Vickery and Castine dove to opposite sides of the dirt road, but Vickery heard a hard snap, and Castine yelped. He rolled to his feet and looked across the road—Castine was up and running toward a thicket by a big mesquite tree, but she stumbled and fell to her hands and knees in a drift of dry leaves. Vickery saw a dot of bright green on the shoulder of her coat even as he heard another snap and felt a hard punch to his thigh. He looked down.

A plastic cylinder with an identically green cap stood up from his leg, and through the clear barrel of it he could see that the syringe's plunger was right down by the needle housing.

He quickly yanked out the dart and drew his Glock, but the two figures by the gate had ducked out of sight around the front of a highway-facing shed, and Vickery was already dizzy with whatever the injection had been.

He lowered the gun and fired four rapid shots into the dirt, hoping that the loud bangs would draw strangers' attention; it occurred to him that he could have taken off his belt and tried to nake a tourniquet above the puncture, as for a snake-bite, but his fingers were already too numb even to hold onto the gun, and a remote pain in his knees let him know that he had fallen forward. His last thought was to wonder if the dart had contained a lethal or only a tranquilizing agent.

Tony and Biloxi came puffing along the path as Harlowe was tossing the Cap-Shure rifle into the SUV and glancing around nervously. Loria couldn't help thinking that his red boots and the burgundy-colored hair fluttering around his ears made him look like a clown.

"Biloxi," Harlowe called shrilly, "you and Agnes get Castine—Tony and I'll take Vickery."

Loria hurried to where the Castine woman lay face down in the dead leaves.

Biloxi scurried up and knelt beside Castine's body. He was skinny and bearded, wearing a black hoodie and gray yoga pants, and Loria hoped he'd be able to do his part in lifting Castine.

"Harlowe shot her?" he asked in a hoarse whisper. "Is she dead?"

"It was Vickery shooting," Loria told him. "She's just tranked. Roll her over, then you get her under the arms. And I'll tell Harlowe if I see you copping a feel."

Biloxi reared back now at the suggestion. "I'd never," he sputtered, "I respect—"

"Shut up. After tonight it won't matter who you were."

Together they rolled Castine over onto her back. Biloxi gripped her under the arms, and he lifted her limp body to a near-sitting position. Her head rolled loosely. He straightened up with a shrill grunt of effort, and Loria got between Castine's legs and lifted her knees; they shuffled around a side-post of the gate to the SUV and pushed her in onto the carpeted floor, then stepped aside so that Harlowe and Tony could step up. Tony had to climb in, avoiding stepping on Castine, and pull Vickery's limp body over the back seat arm-rest and lay him on the seat. Harlowe tossed Vickery's gun after the rifle.

"Was somebody shooting?" came a shout from behind the SUV.

Loria stepped back and saw two young men in colorful shorts and T-shirts shading their eyes and peering into the shadows of the dirt lane.

She glanced at the SUV and saw that Tony was even now swinging the door shut. "Backfire," she said. "Nitrous oxide additive in the fuel. You know."

"Oh," said one of the young men, nodding uncertainly. "Like in the *Fast and Furious* movies?"

"That's it," she said. She stepped to the back of the SUV and began unbuttoning her blouse, to their intense and focused interest; then she pulled it off and turned to tuck it around the rear license plate.

Above her jeans she was now wearing only her bra. She smiled and hurried around to get into the vehicle on the passenger side. Harlowe was already in the driver's seat and had started the engine.

He glanced at her and then stared. "Wha-what do you mean by—" he began.

"Go, will you?" As he spasmodically yanked the gear shift into reverse, she crawled between the seats and squatted by Castine. She leaned forward and patted the extent of Castine's slack body, and quickly found the revolver in her coat pocket. She handed it to Tony, then tilted Castine's head back. "Tony, the Narcan. You do Vickery."

Tony's eyes were wide, but he passed her a couple of little white plastic objects that looked to her like toy rocket launchers, and she quickly stuck the nozzle of one of them into Castine's left nostril and pressed the plunger; she tossed the emptied thing away and stuck the nozzle of the other one into Castine's right nostril and squirted its contents too into Castine's nose.

The vehicle accelerated forward now, throwing Loria against Vickery's yielding shoulder. Tony had just pulled the second narcan nozzle out of Vickery's nose.

"You're, uh, supposed to use two on each of them?" asked Tony, looking away from her bra.

"Are they all right?" yelled Harlowe from the front seat.

"Probably!" Loria called back.

Biloxi had climbed into the back, and he was simply staring over the back of the seat at her breasts.

"One's what they advise," Loria told Tony, "but what the hell." To Biloxi, she said, "Give me your hoodie." When he opened his mouth to protest or ask a question, she added, "Now, dipshit."

Biloxi's hurt expression disappeared under the black cotton fabric as he pulled it off over his head, exposing a red and black Che Guevara T-shirt. "What about my Camaro?" he asked.

"You're up on Topanga?" Loria said. "With luck you'll never see it again." She quickly put on the hoodie and leaned down to shake Castine's shoulder. "Hey, Ingrid? Speak to me, Ingrid."

Tony was crouched on the floor by Castine's feet; he stood up as best he could in the bobbing vehicle and slapped Vickery on the chest. "Hey, man, wake up."

"Are they all *right*?" demanded Harlowe again.

"*Probably!*" repeated Loria. "Biloxi," she said, "fetch me that roll of duct tape from the back." When the sulking young man had tossed it to her, she pulled the end of the tape free, then quickly bound Castine's wrists together, pulling the roll of tape around the joined wrists four times before tearing it off.

She gave the roll to Tony, who pulled Vickery's wrists together and bound them the same way.

He had barely torn it off and pressed the edge down when Vickery exhaled sharply and tried to sit up. On the floor, Castine was rolling her head back and forth and mumbling.

"Vickery!" said Loria.

"What," said Vickery hoarsely. He raised his hands as if to rub his eyes, then paused, squinting at his wrists. "Get this off."

"Soon." Loria looked down. "Ingrid, how're you doing?"

Castine sneezed, then said, "Lea' me alone." She was shivering.

"They're all right!" called Loria to Harlowe. Vickery's pupils were tiny and his face was slack and pale, and Loria knew he was only half awake at best. "Where were you for the last hour and a half?" she asked him. "We lost your signal in the hills. You started up the canyon, but then you came back down. Why?"

Vickery closed his eyes tight. "Tension apprehension and dissension have begun," he said distinctly. He was shivering.

"What do you mean?"

He only repeated the phrase.

Loria leaned back, between the front seats, and tilted her head toward Harlowe's intent profile. Quietly she asked him, "Has this guy been in the military or something? I'd almost think he's been trained in resisting interrogation."

Harlowe glanced down at her, and seemed reassured to see that she was wearing Biloxi's hoodie. "Nobody's following us," he said, returning his attention to the traffic ahead, "and we've got our IMPs! Who cares if he was in the military?"

"I'd like to know where they were, up the canyon."

"It doesn't matter now. Do you have enough Narcan to give them another nose-squirt, if it wears off before the morphine does?"

"We got a bunch of it at Walgreens." She leaned forward over Castine's still-limp body and took hold of Vickery's chin. Turning his face toward her, she asked quietly, "What did Gale Reed tell you?"

"Tension apprehension and—" He blinked several times, then squinted directly at her. "I know you, don't I?" he said. "You—stopped a baby carriage in front of my car—in—February. And—you were in a car on Crenshaw—was it last night—?" His mouth worked. "Did you squirt something up my nose? It tastes like a stale menthol cigarette."

"Yay," said Castine, by Loria's right knee; she went on, indistinctly, "though I walk through the valley of the . . . shadow of death . . . "

"That's from the Bible," put in Biloxi, still leaning over the back of the rear seat.

"Shut up," Loria told him. "Yes," she said to Vickery, "that was me. You were working for that Mexican woman that first time, what was her name?" When Vickery didn't answer, she said, "Galvan, that was it. What were you doing before that?"

Vickery managed to sit up. He shook his head and said, "We haven't had lunch yet." He looked down at Castine, who had raised her arms and was blinking at the duct tape around her wrists. "Have we, Ingrid?"

"Wha-at?" Castine said. She looked up. "Sebastian? Jeez, tell 'em to turn up the heat." She licked her lips and exhaled through her nose. "Did I get sick? I don't feel good."

"Blood," said Harlowe from the front seat. He opened the console, then tossed a plastic bag back to Loria. "Quick, before they're awake enough to resist."

Loria unzipped the bag and shook out onto the floor two handkerchief-sized white altar cloths and a steak knife. Quickly she poked the knife-point into Vickery's forearm above the duct tape; he jumped and reflexively raised his bound arms.

Loria leaned down and cut Castine's arm the same way, and Castine grunted. "Careful with that thing!" she muttered groggily.

"Oh, did Biloxi cut you?" crooned Loria then, tossing the knife past Biloxi into the back of the vehicle. "Here, let me put something on that."

"*I* didn't—" began Biloxi, but he closed his mouth when Loria gave him a brief glare.

She pressed one of the altar cloths onto Vickery's cut arm and the other onto Castine's. The cloths quickly blotted with bright red blood.

"You got 'em?" called Harlowe, and when Loria said she did, he added, "Don't mix them up. If one of our IMPs should get away in the next few hours, *per impossibile,* we want to be sure we're using the right tracker."

"And we got plenty enough to triangulate it this time," said Loria, peeling off one of the wet cloths in each hand. To herself she muttered, "Vickery left, Castine right." She leaned back to see Harlowe. "We going to the church?"

Harlowe shook his head without taking his eyes from the highway. "We've got everything with us. Cabrillo Marina is only half an hour down PCH. We can take the *Black Sheep* out to where the chronocline is flat—get our IMPs securely initiated as soon as possible. But leave the bloody cloths here, in the vehicle, just in case."

Loria nodded, then turned to the back seat and carefully wedged herself between Vickery's bloody right arm and Castine's knees. To Tony and Biloxi she said, "Move all the weapons to the front seat," she said, "then lift Vickery over the seat and into the back. Even with their wrists bound, I don't want to risk them touching each other."

Harlowe and I don't need another dose of the old house vision right now, she thought, especially with him driving.

Santiago was perched on a tree branch projecting out over a white-painted picnic table, peering through the leaves at the dirt track below the slope. The old *brujo* had watched two men chase Vickery and Castine, and had then retreated into the greenery, probably to walk back up the winding path to the top of the highway-facing hill. Santiago had seen Vickery and Castine run toward the gate by PCH, and had seen the gray SUV turn in and block them; the boy had heard a couple of what sounded like .22 shots, and then four rapid shots from a bigger caliber gun—and the two men who had been chasing them helped a couple of people from the SUV load the limp bodies of Castine and Vickery aboard, and the vehicle had driven off.

Santiago pulled one of the two cheap flip-phones from the less burdened pocket of his sweatshirt and tapped in a number. When a man's voice answered and repeated the number back, Santiago said, "Castine and Vickery were just here, and some people caught them and took them away in a van or something. It looked like maybe they got shot."

"*Kabar aswad!*" exclaimed Lateef Fakhouri's voice from the phone. "May God grant that they were shot dead—though I fear they were not." Santiago could hear the man breathing into the phone. "You must in any case stay where you are. I'll be there in a few hours, when I have acquired the necessary apparatus. Do you understand?"

For several seconds Santiago didn't answer; then, "I understand," he said.

The boy closed the phone and slid it into his pocket and leaned against the tree trunk. Through the branches he could now see the old *brujo* above the treetops, making his slow way back up the zig-zag path toward the top of the hill.

When Santiago had ridden his bicycle to the Long Beach parking lot where he'd agreed to meet Fakhouri, and told him what had happened below the cliffs in the collapsed section of San Pedro, Fakhouri had dismissed the boy's account of the old bearded man. "Just an insane alcoholic, one of many here," he had said. He had concentrated on Santiago's drawing of the symbol carved in the flat stone.

And after studying Santiago's sketch for a full minute, he had paced to the parking lot's chain-link fence and back, frowning.

"The inverted broken ankh must mean *not life, not identity*," Fakhouri had mused, "and the sawtooth lines mean the sea—a very sharp sea!—and the sea is *Nu*, the right arm of *Nu*, even on this around-the-world coast. He had snapped his fingers then. "Hah! You know what it is? It's a blind man's simplification of the Nu hieroglyph! It was meant to awaken the *Ba* hieroglyph and *propel* it directly into negation in the sea!" Fakhouri had not even seen Santiago's shrug, and had gone on, "I wish Wystan had succeeded, in that! But of course the hieroglyph remained buried there until 1965, when motorcyclists unearthed it."

Santiago had tried to say something, but Fakhouri had waved him to silence. "This is more than what Boutros knew. More than *I* knew! But we *should* have known!" He waved the boy's drawing. "Do you see? The *Nu* hieroglyph does *not* draw the *Ba* hieroglyph to *itself,* but to the actual *body* of *Nu*—the sea!"

Standing beside the car, Fakhouri had quickly given Santiago new instructions. Previously the man had planned to set up some kind of cardboard sign down in the field here tonight and shine a lantern on it, and only wanted Santiago to watch for possible interference by Harlowe's crew. That was simple enough, though it seemed pointless.

But now the plan was that Fakhouri would bring *two* lanterns, and an *extra* firebox, and Santiago would have a duplicate of the cardboard sign. And at midnight Santiago was to be standing at the top of the seaward hill, holding up one of the signs in the light of the second lantern.

Fakhouri himself would at the same time be standing knee-deep in the surf, out beyond PCH and the beach, holding the other lantern and cardboard sign. Fakhouri's only explanation was, *You will draw the* Ba *attention and relay it to me, in the sea.* Nu *is the eternal grave of identity, and this time there will be no half-awakened egregore left, afterward, to ever be quickened again. The coloring books will be inert, and what belongs to Egypt will not be used by others.*

Fakhouri had pulled car-keys from his pocket. "Get in the car. We have much to do."

Fakhouri had driven to a Staples office supply store and told Santiago to wait in the car; Fakhouri had taken a sheet of stiff cardboard from the trunk and hurried into the store, and when he emerged again ten minutes later he had been carrying two sheets, both now wrapped in brown paper. He had then driven Santiago down to PCH, and pulled over near the road-blocking gate where Vickery and Castine were captured a few minutes ago.

He had opened the trunk and given Santiago the two paper-wrapped cardboard sheets, and told him to take them to the top of the inland hill and wait for him there. Fakhouri had driven away then, "to get some fire."

▼▼▼

That had been nearly two hours ago.

Santiago had obediently carried the sheets up the path to the field between the hills—but with the old *brujo* standing at the top of the seaward hill, he had not wanted to be conspicuous standing at the top of the inland one. Instead, he had climbed up the side of this tree that faced away from the seaward hill, and the paper-wrapped sheets of cardboard were now wedged across three branches above his head.

He glanced up to make sure they were secure, then peered out through the branches and waving leaves. The old *brujo* had reached the top of the hill again.

Santiago shifted his position on the tree branch and touched the medallion on its string under his sweatshirt. Laquedem had always worn it, and the boy had tugged the string from around Laquedem's bloody broken head before running away. Some inches of the string were still stiff with the old man's blood.

I hope, he thought to the ghost of old Laquedem, that I am not wasting your purpose, doing what this Egyptian says.

The boy jumped, for a phone had begun vibrating in his pocket. It was the other phone, the one he'd been using for ordinary business during the past month.

Pulling it out and opening it, he said, "Santiago."

A voice that might have been of either sex said, "You're the boy who watches and runs errands, right?" When Santiago just listened, the voice went on, "The freeway gypsies say you know how to find Sebastian Vickery if anybody does, and one of 'em gave me this number. My name's Anita Galvan, and I'll pay you to tell me how to find him."

Santiago cocked his head and brushed the black hair out of his eyes. "The taco truck Galvan?" He had never heard her first name before. When she confirmed it, he said, "I think you want to sell Vickery to a man. And I think the man's got him now already."

"What? Shit." For a moment the woman didn't speak; then she said, "Do you know where they are?"

"I don't," said Santiago.

"Do you know somebody that does?" When Santiago didn't answer, Galvan went on in a rush, "I'm on Vickery's side now, damn it, I want to stop Harlowe! My nephew Carlos and the *niños,* their heads buzz now when they're together, and the freeway gypsies say it's because of coloring books Carlos got for them—made by ChakraSys, which I find is this man Harlowe. The gypsies say my family will plain lose their minds tonight, to a big vampire mind! I need to find Vickery!"

I'm on Vickery's side now, she had said. Which had been Laquedem's side too. It seemed likely that she was telling the truth, what with worrying about her family and all.

"I'll call you back," said Santiago, and he closed the phone.

Coloring books again! Maybe Fakhouri wasn't crazy.

Santiago reached into the neck of his sweatshirt and pulled out Laquedem's medallion, dangling on its string. It was a silver disk with a raised six-pointed star on it formed by two triangles, one upside-down on the other. He turned it over—on the other side was a candelabra holding seven candles in a row.

He squeezed the medallion in his fist, then dropped it back inside his sweatshirt. He thought for several seconds, then opened his phone again and touched Galvan's number.

CHAPTER SIXTEEN:
IMPs Don't Need Kneecaps

Palm trees lined the long parking lot, and when Vickery squinted through his watering eyes he could see blue sea and the decks and masts of boats beyond a railing ahead. Sun glare seemed to be reflecting off everything—the sea, the white boats, the very pavement under his shuffling feet. Harlowe and the woman walked ahead of Castine and himself, with a muscular young man in a white T-shirt and the skinny one called Biloxi bringing up the rear. Harlowe had told Vickery and Castine that all four of their captors carried stun-guns, and that any attempt to run or call attention would only result in an apparent medical emergency and great unpleasantness later. And he had given them each a big red five-kilogram fire extinguisher to carry in front of themselves, which made the positions of their wrists look awkward but not unnatural. "Either of you drop it," Harlowe had said, "the other one gets a zap."

Vickery had seen one of the stun-guns, and it was a Vipertek, able to deliver upward of fifty millions volts, with a lanyard connected to a kill-switch pin which would disable the weapon if it were pulled out of the man's hand.

Vickery was still nauseated from the morphine, which was probably also the cause of his excessive sweating and shivering in the cold sea breeze. He was fairly sure he could let go of the fire extinguisher and break the duct-tape binding and spin fast enough to disable the man behind him, but Castine would probably get a multimillion volt shock from the other man's stun-gun before Vickery could prevent it.

And there was Harlowe's remark, *We've got everything with us.* That might include Vickery's precious copy of *The Secret Garden,* and Harlowe was wearing a bulky nylon knapsack.

It would be better to postpone action until the effects of the drug had diminished, in both himself and Castine. Clearly Harlowe did not, after all, mean to kill them, and Vickery could free himself from the bindings at any time—Harlowe apparently didn't know that duct-tape around the wrists could easily be broken with a sharp downward jerk of the arms.

Vickery watched the pair walking along a few feet in front of him. Harlowe had a confident stride even with the knapsack riding on his back, and somehow, with boats visible beyond him, his burgundy-colored hair and red cowboy boots had a vaguely swashbuckling, piratical air. The woman was in jeans and a bulky blue nylon jacket, with a knitted green cap over her loose chestnut hair, and her step was springy with evident anticipation.

Guessing, Vickery said, "Agnes"—and she looked back over her shoulder.

Vickery smiled and said, "Ragotskie wanted us to get you out of this."

"Well, I got *him* out of it," she said tightly, turning back to face the direction in which they were walking.

"We did promise," put in Castine.

Without looking back, but sounding angry, Agnes said, "We're going to put you two *into* it."

"You'd thank us later," added Harlowe without looking around, "if you could."

The group reached the railing and turned right, down an open walkway. To their left was a forest of masts and rigging and horizontal booms wrapped in blue tarpaulins, above hulls that glittered with reflections from the water. At the end of the walkway the tight group stepped with elaborate caution through a gate, then made their way along a gently bobbing concrete floating dock that was wide enough for them to walk two abreast. On this Wednesday afternoon there were only a few people visible on the decks of the boats they walked past, and Harlowe's group drew nothing more than a couple of glances and polite nods. Vickery knew that he'd be flattened by millions of volts of electricity before he would be able to say more than one syllable of *Call the police.*

They halted beside a gleaming white boat with a high, railed foredeck and a fly-bridge above the cabin; the sheerline swept from the flared bow to a low freeboard cockpit. Vickery estimated that it was forty or fifty feet in length.

Harlowe and Agnes mounted the boarding steps, hopped down to the cockpit deck, and turned around to watch Vickery and Castine come aboard with Biloxi and the other man right behind them.

The door to the lounge was open, and Vickery and Castine were hustled inside.

An incongruous card table had been set up between a padded bench on one side and a long couch on the other. A doorway in the forward bulkhead led to stairs, presumably down to a galley and staterooms. Harlowe shrugged out of his knapsack and laid it carefully on the deck against the forward bulkhead, then waved his two captives to the bench while he and Agnes sat down on the starboard couch. Biloxi and the other man waited by the door.

"Tony," said Harlowe, "cast off the lines and get us out to the area we were at yesterday morning."

The young man in the white T-shirt pocketed his stun-gun and stepped back out onto the cockpit deck, and Vickery, sitting on the bench now and looking out the aft window, saw him untying a rope from a cleat on the dock. The other man, in what Vickery now saw was a red Che Guevara T-shirt, closed the door and held his own stun-gun ostentatiously ready.

Vickery glanced at Castine, who gave him a strained look. He knew she must find the awkward position of her wrists and the weight of the big red cylinder as uncomfortable as he did.

He looked at Harlowe and asked, "Can we put down the fire extinguishers?"

"Oh!" said Harlowe. "Sure, it doesn't matter now."

Vickery and Castine both bent forward and unclasped their cramping hands from the red cylinders, then sat back, flexing their fingers. Vickery heard Tony's sneakers thumping along the deck outside.

Agnes remarked, "We should get those stowed. They'll roll all over the place."

Harlowe nodded toward the young man in the red T-shirt. "Biloxi can do it afterward."

For several long minutes none of them spoke. Agnes opened a cabinet door in the forward bulkhead and pulled out a leather folder; she slid a sheaf of papers out of it and appeared to devote all her attention to them. Harlowe and Biloxi both stared fixedly at Vickery and Castine, Harlowe with a faint frown deepening the wrinkles around his eyes and Biloxi licking his lips nervously and switching the stun-gun from one hand to the other every few seconds.

At last the boat's engines started up, and when they were shifted into gear Vickery had to scuff his foot on the carpet to keep from toppling to his right as the bow lifted and the boat got under way. Castine braced herself against his left shoulder. The fire extinguishers fell over with heavy clanks.

"I think you have something of mine," Vickery remarked. When Harlowe raised his eyebrows, Vickery went on, "A copy of *The Secret Garden*. Frances Hodgson Burnett."

"Oh. Yes. It's serving the greater good these days."

Vickery knew Tony was busy steering the boat out of the marina, and both Harlowe and Biloxi took occasional glances out the windows; and he judged that when the boat leaned to port to clear the breakwater and follow the channel out of the harbor, he could leap up and break the duct-tape in one motion, and then in follow-through neutralize Biloxi while avoiding the stun-gun's electrodes.

But Harlowe hiked himself up on the couch and reached behind him, and when he sat back down he was holding a semi-automatic pistol aimed halfway between Vickery and Castine. The muzzle look like nine-millimeters.

"I wouldn't kill you," Harlowe said, "but IMPs don't need kneecaps."

Vickery let himself relax, and Castine nodded. "They've got wings, as I recall," she said.

Agnes looked up and smiled. "That's angels. Imps are little devils."

"That's us," said Castine.

Vickery realized with a hollow feeling in his chest that a moment for breaking free had passed. He wondered how the *initiation* was to be administered. Ragotskie had said it consisted of staring at the image in the hieroglyph, the hawk with a man's bearded head—

probably Harlowe had some plan for forcing him and Castine to stare at it. Vickery could think of several effective methods himself.

The boat leaned to port, as he'd expected. Through the window behind Harlowe, Vickery saw the squat Los Angeles Harbor Lighthouse slowly move past, and he knew they were clearing the breakwater and leaving the harbor for the open sea.

After another ten minutes the engines throttled down and shifted to neutral, and the steady rise and fall of the bow quickly became a random side-to-side rocking. Biloxi crouched, bracing himself against the aft bulkhead with one hand and holding the stun-gun with the other.

Agnes leaned forward and laid a sheet of paper on the card table. Vickery hardly needed to glance at it to recognize it as the hieroglyph image.

Agnes drew a small .22 revolver from the pocket of her bulky nylon jacket, and Biloxi edged closer to Vickery; the stun-gun electrodes were inches from his right cheek now.

Harlowe pointed his gun at Vickery. "Miss Castine," he said, "until I tell you to stop, you will look closely at the figure on that piece of paper—and then live forever as a part of the ultimate transcendent serenity. You'll do it right now, or I'll shoot Vickery's left kneecap off, in which case you'll do it after that, because Vickery has another kneecap . . . and hands, arms, et cetera. If he thrashes around, Biloxi will subdue him electrically and we'll carry on until you have done it."

Castine had been staring into Harlowe's eyes as he spoke, and now glanced down at the paper for a moment before turning her head to look at Vickery.

Her expression was apologetic. She spread her constricted hands for a moment if to say, *What else can I do?* but Vickery believed he saw relief in her eyes too, and he remembered what she had said at Canter's this morning: *I'm half tempted to dig out that damned coloring book and look hard at the picture.*

Creepy old usses.

Vickery glanced at Harlowe, who was now looking directly at him. The gun was pointed down, and Harlowe's finger was inside the trigger guard.

And Castine was already gazing intently down at the image.

For more than a minute, none of them moved except to lean slightly forward and back with the rocking of the boat.

At last Harlowe said, "Stop."

Castine shivered, and the fingers of her close-bound hands spread again, slowly, like an opening flower. She looked up, toward Harlowe, and nodded.

"Now, Mr. Vickery," Harlowe said, shifting the barrel of his gun toward Castine, "you'll look directly at it for a while, or I'll shoot Miss Castine in the knee. I'm not sure what a 9-millimeter round would do to a knee, but in any case it's not necessary that our IMPs each have two working legs."

Vickery looked into Harlowe's eyes for another few seconds. Then, seeing no way out, he let his gaze fall to the image on the piece of paper. The fingers of his joined hands were tightly interlaced, as if in prayer; and in fact he was mentally beginning to recite the Our Father. *Thy kingdom come* . . .

After half a minute, the lines of the hawk body seemed to shimmer, and it threw Vickery's prayer out of focus. It's a bird, he thought then, showing me a direction . . . like the robin in *The Secret Garden,* which showed Mary the key to the walled garden.

The garden to which this hawk offered him the key was to be a secret too, in that nobody outside would know about it—because there would be nobody outside it.

Then his thoughts just drained away like a turbulent ocean quickly receding far back from a shore, exposing sunken ruins that the surf had generally hidden—and he couldn't avoid awareness of Mary, the wraith of the daughter he should have had, and Pratt, the boy he had killed two days ago . . . and a man he had killed in a Los Angeles street last year, and two men in a desert arroyo north of Los Angeles five years ago . . . and his wife, Amanda, who had killed herself a year before that . . . and there was an implicit promise that the unnaturally withdrawing tide was just prelude to a returning tsunami that would cover all of these jagged black memories, obliterate them, and even himself, in its irresistible force.

And for a moment he felt that his hands were free—in fact he felt as though he had a thousand hands, holding forks, sliding through sleeves, typing on keyboards, touching other hands; and a thousand feet, walking on mountain paths, climbing stairs, pressing gas pedals—and in his vision was a kaleidoscopic confusion of unsynchronized glare and color and darkness and motion—

It all promised release from the myopic focus on individual identity and responsibility; the uncramping of needlessly constricted vision and experience, and he could feel the boundaries of his self beginning to relax—

"Stop," said Harlowe.

Vickery blinked and exhaled—perhaps he had been holding his breath. His arms were still bound and he was still looking at the image, and he was aware now of a faint agitation deep in his mind, like a weak electrical current. At last he looked away from the seductive image, into Harlowe's eyes, and saw cautious welcome there.

"Now I think you understand," Harlowe said.

"Yes," said Castine, and Vickery said, "Understand, yes."

The tension in the lounge had loosened like an unstrung bow. Agnes had at some point pocketed her little gun, and when Harlowe nodded to Biloxi he tucked the stun-gun into his pocket.

"You can get those stowed below now," Harlowe told Biloxi, and the young man picked up both of the fire extinguishers and clumped down the stairs with it.

Harlowe stood up and crossed to the cockpit door, and Vickery and Castine got slowly to their feet, holding their bound wrists in front of them as they swayed with the motion of the idling boat. Castine staggered, and when Vickery caught her shoulder with both hands he felt an increase in the buzzing in the depths of his mind.

Agnes was standing behind Castine. "You felt that, didn't you?" she said. "That'll happen whenever your aura overlaps another initiated soul's."

"Until tonight," said Harlowe, sliding the door open and stepping out. Cold, salt-smelling air beat its way into the lounge, tossing the paper from the table. "After tonight we'll all be *one* soul. One *world-soul*, soon."

"Could I," said Vickery, "see the book? My daughter?" He suspected that it was in the knapsack Harlowe had laid on the carpet.

And Harlowe glanced back into the lounge before replying. "You want to enter eternal life facing backward?" he asked.

"Just a look." Vickery smiled and quoted a line from Milton's *Comus*: "With backward mutters of dissevering power."

"Our ceremony tonight will provide infinite dissevering power, don't worry. Come out and view your future kingdom." Biloxi had reappeared, sweating, and Harlowe looked at him and shook his head with a smile, briefly raising his own two hands pressed together at the wrists. Clearly he was reassuring Biloxi that the new initiates would not jump overboard with their arms bound.

He stepped through the doorway, and Vickery and Castine sidled carefully out onto the wet white deck after him, followed by Agnes and Biloxi. Beyond the gunwales the blue sea stretched away to the Long Beach skyline on the horizon.

Harlowe's artificial-looking red hair was tossing about his head as he waved out at the coastline. "Every person in every one of those buildings," he said, speaking louder over the wind, "will eventually join us, be facets of the infinite jewel that will be God. Guiltless, because God is the definition of innocence, and joined only to everything."

He turned to Vickery and asked, "Where are my nieces?"

Vickery had smoked marijuana in his youth, and the faint buzz at the core of his mind reminded him of that. He remembered sometimes fearing that the effect would never wear off; it always had, and he told himself that this would too.

"I," he began, and though it was an effort not to say, *Probably still at the Egyptian Consulate on Wilshire*, he finished, "don't know."

"Huh. I'll ask you again soon." Harlowe turned and looked up. Vickery followed his gaze and saw Tony leaning on the rail of the fly bridge.

"Get us back in, Tony," Harlowe called. "We're whole."

Tony nodded and stepped back out of sight. As the engines gunned and the boat surged forward in a long turn, Vickery took the opportunity to exaggeratedly sway and catch his balance.

"A bit dizzy," he said, "maybe Ingrid and I should—"

"Yes, go back inside," said Harlowe. "Agnes, maybe get them some coffee."

"That'd be good," said Castine, incidentally or deliberately looking unsteady herself.

Vickery stood aside to let her shamble into the lounge first, and when she stepped inside he appeared to lose his balance and tip forward against her.

"When we're in the harbor," he whispered into her hair, "I'll wink. Follow my lead."

She shook her head sharply and stumbled toward the padded bench and sat down. Agnes and Biloxi had followed them in, leaving the sliding door open. Harlowe stayed out on the deck, looking over the transom at their curving wake and the unbroken western horizon.

To Agnes, Castine said, "Does this ringing in the ears stop? I can't think."

"After midnight you won't notice it at all," Agnes assured her.

"Coffee helps," said Biloxi.

Agnes nodded and gave Vickery and Castine an enquiring look.

"Black is fine," said Vickery.

"Sugar," said Castine, "but no cream."

Agnes crossed to the stairs and thumped down to the galley. Vickery heard clinking and water running in a metal sink. After a few minutes she came back up, carrying a ridged cardboard tray with four plastic cups fitted into it.

She swayed gracefully to the table and set down two cups. "We're out of cream," she told Castine, "so I made it with no milk." She set the tray on her side of the table and sat down on the couch, chuckling to herself.

Vickery picked up a cup, necessarily with both hands, and blew across the top of it. "When do we lose the duct-tape?" he asked, hoping it wouldn't be before they docked—he wanted to take their captors by surprise when he, and ideally only a moment later, Castine, broke free of the wrist-restraints.

"Elisha Ragotskie," said Agnes abruptly, "is dead."

"We know," said Castine. She picked up the other cup and took a tentative sip. "You've got mine," she said to Vickery. After they had set the cups down and awkwardly switched them and picked them up again, she added, "We talked to his ghost last night."

"You *did*?" said Agnes. "You did not. What did he say?"

Vickery hoped to note how she displayed anger. "He said you killed him."

Biloxi opened his mouth and blinked in surprise, but Agnes just sat back. "It's true, I did. It was an accident. And now he can't be part of the egregore, even though," and she waved toward the sheet of paper that was now on the floor beside Harlowe's knapsack, "he was initiated."

Vickery took the opportunity to note the exact position of the knapsack. Looking up, he told Agnes, "He still wanted us to get you away from all this."

"He loved you," added Castine.

"Tonight I won't care," said Agnes. "I don't care now. Shut up. Where did you see him, his ghost, I mean? What else did he say?"

"He said he killed somebody named Foster," said Vickery.

"And he said you were at a church," Castine added; possibly she too was trying to get some kind of rise out of Agnes, for she went on, "I think that's good, that you went to church."

"I didn't *go to church*," said Agnes, finally with some heat, "I was at a building that *used to be* a church. And it wasn't Catholic. I know you're Catholic, we know all about you." She turned her head to glare at Vickery. "You probably are too. I bet you both go to *Confession* all the time. Hah!"

Castine raised an eyebrow and smiled at her. "You were raised Catholic, weren't you?"

Agnes smiled back at her. "Where did you go, driving up Topanga Canyon? You started up, then came back down."

Castine shrugged, letting her own question go. "We were heading for the Mimosa Café," she said, "but the car was overheating."

Vickery had been worrying about Castine's possible susceptibility to the initiation, and was relieved to hear her answer deceptively.

"They've got good vegan muffins there," put in Biloxi. "And a koi pond."

Agnes gave him a look of utter contempt. Turning to Castine, she said, "He felt you up when you were unconscious."

"I never—!" sputtered Biloxi. "I—"

"After midnight, who cares?" said Castine. "Right?"

"Who cares about anything," said Agnes quietly, "even now."

None of them spoke after that. Vickery was unobtrusively flexing the muscles in his arms and legs and breathing deeply, to get his circulatory system to metabolize whatever morphine might still be in his bloodstream.

After a few minutes the fore-and-aft rocking of the boat became smoother, and he craned his neck to see out the window at his back—and he saw the harbor lighthouse at the end of the southern arm of the breakwater. They were in the harbor, and the marina was only minutes away. He sat back and waited, breathing slowly and letting his muscles relax.

When he heard the engines slow and saw the masts of boats outside, he turned and winked at Castine. She gave him a blank look, but that could have been for Agnes' benefit.

He stood up, and raised his arms to rub his hands across his face. "Where's," he said breathlessly, "the bathroom? I"—he paused to jerk his head forward, lifting his chin—"I think I'm gonna be sick—"

Agnes was on her feet too, and she waved toward the cockpit deck. "Outside," she said, "do it over the side. Not in here!"

To Castine, Vickery whispered, "Watch." Then he raised his hands higher, over his head, and jerked them down, hard, so that his elbows grazed his ribs—and the overlapped bands of duct-tape broke.

His right arm rebounded out and drove his fist, middle knuckle protruding, into Biloxi's solar plexus, and as the man jackknifed forward Vickery spun toward Agnes.

Her hand was already in the pocket of her jacket, but he slammed his left fist into the side of her head and yanked her hand free; her revolver went tumbling across the carpet, and he caught it in one hand and crouched to snatch up Harlowe's knapsack with the other.

Castine had stood up, but her wrists were still bound.

"Break the tape like I did!" Vickery said urgently. Agnes was lying across the couch, shaking her head, and Vickery spun and was out the door—

But Harlowe had evidently heard the scuffle, and his gun was extended, pointing at Vickery's legs; and even as Vickery raised Agnes' gun and pulled the trigger twice, with no sound or recoil, Harlowe was firing wildly, the loud pops nearly overlapping one another as ejected shells flew out of his gun in quick succession.

Bits of fiberglass were spinning in the air and Vickery felt a hot lash across his left thigh and a kick against his right heel, and he swerved and converted his rush toward Harlowe into a long flat dive over the transom. In mid-air he felt a thrum in the knapsack strap as a bullet hit it.

He plunged into the sea, and though the water's temperature was no colder than sixty degrees Fahrenheit, his mind went blank for a moment, and something seemed to shift in his head.

Then his thoughts rushed back in like air filling an opened

vacuum, and he saw that he was only a few feet below the surface of the water; he quickly swam deeper, then looked up at the long dark hull of the boat, its spreading wake chopping up the brightly rippling patch of westering sunlight. He had let go of Agnes' gun in the moment of mental absence, but a strap of Harlowe's bubbling knapsack was still looped over his elbow, and he took a firm grip on it and pulled it down against its diminishing buoyancy. In the moment of diving over the transom, he had glimpsed rows of moored boats alongside a long dock, and when he looked ahead through the sunlit water he could make out at least one hull.

He paused to bend double and pull off his shoes, wincing as the fabric of his jeans was pulled across the gunshot groove in his thigh, and then began swimming toward the dock, using the undulating dolphin stroke to conserve oxygen. The knapsack was now just an inert drag, no longer bobbing upward.

Harlowe would probably not shoot to kill, but Vickery didn't want him to know where he was, or even if he were still alive. He resisted the urge to surface and take a fresh breath.

And his lungs were tugging at his rigidly closed throat when he twisted to pull himself under a gritty black keel and then at last let himself bob to the surface in the shadow of a spreading bow, between hanging fenders that looked like black punching bags. He exhaled at last, and sucked in fresh air. At his back was a floating concrete dock, a narrow extension from one of the long main docks, its surface a foot over his head. His fast deep breaths echoed between the vertical face of the dock and the curved hull.

He hooked a couple of fingers into one of the boat's drains and hiked his leg up; through the new rip in his jeans he could see the long cut in his thigh. It wasn't deep, nor bleeding excessively.

He could hear the low rumble of a boat moving toward the marina entrance, and he swam to the stern and, submerged to his eyes, peered out from around the port corner.

The *Black Sheep* was moving slowly out there, and he could see Tony on the fly bridge scanning the water around the marina boats with binoculars. Below, on the transom deck, Harlowe was visibly doing the same.

Vickery retreated to the shadows between this boat and the dock. Harlowe's slip was just down at the end of this long dock, as he recalled, and the man might tie up the *Black Sheep* and come looking for him along the dock, with Tony and Biloxi checking parallel ones—though they could hardly hope to see a person hiding in the water between the dock and a boat's bow. Their best bet would be to have the three men take up widely separated posts on the shore, and watch for Vickery to emerge.

The Port of Los Angeles, with its cargo terminals and cranes and rail lines, lies behind a breakwater that stands three miles out and extends from Point Fermin east to a point a mile off Seal Beach; within that, several marinas and sport-fishing docks are encircled by an angular five-hundred-yard inner breakwater, and the eastern end of that was about a hundred yards from where Vickery treaded water and gripped Harlowe's knapsack.

When he had been a Secret Service agent, until five years ago, he had been able to swim 50 yards underwater without taking a breath; he doubted that he could still do that, but no one ashore was likely to notice it if, out there in that expanse of sun-glittering water, he just let his face surface to empty and refill his lungs along the way. And once he had rounded the point of the shorter breakwater, he could swim rapidly west to the beach by the Cabrillo Beach boat ramp.

He relaxed and for two minutes just breathed deeply and slowly, in and out. Then he took a deep breath, submerged, and kicked off from the keel of the boat.

Fifteen minutes later he had followed the breakwater's five-hundred yard extent all the way around the outside of the basin, and here it ended a hundred feet ahead of him as a plain dirt slope, which slanted down to his left and stretched away as a sandy beach.

He paused, treading water. On this end of the shore were a couple of bushy palm trees, and further away four tarpaulin-draped kayaks and a cluster of little rowboats were drawn up on the sand, and fifty yards past them a long pier projected out over the water. A couple of people were visible in that direction, sitting on a grassy patch above the sand, so he decided to come ashore by the palm trees directly ahead, where the breakwater ended. It would be best to minimize the likelihood of anyone being able to answer questions about a fully dressed man emerging from the sea.

He paddled forward until one stockinged foot touched sand—

—And he tensed as if suddenly in free fall, for the sunlight switched direction and he couldn't see the beach and the palm trees—instead he was bodilessly aware of an open door in a stone wall, and beside it a little girl in overalls and a straw hat. He recognized her—the daughter he had never fathered, whose wraith had several times saved him in the Labyrinth last year. And her voice spoke in his head: *I can't follow onto land. The sea has freed me. Goodbye, and thank you for reading me to me.*

"Mary," he said aloud, breathlessly, "wait! I—I baptize thee in the name of the Father, the Son, and the Holy Spirit!"

The fleeting vision faded, and he was again paddling in cold salt water, seeing the shore straight ahead and the breakwater a few yards to his right. He looked around wildly, as if hoping to see at least some diminishing blur over the low waves, but the voice had stopped, and, he knew, the never-born little girl who had spoken was now, at last, truly nonexistent. The garden door had closed behind her.

Perhaps his last-moment baptism of her . . .

Another and very different voice now twitched in his mind: *I'll wait for you in hell.* And then it too was gone.

Both were voices he had heard before, but never from people who were alive. The second one had been that of nineteen-year-old Pratt's ghost, and Vickery told himself that asking it for forgiveness would after all have been an empty gesture—Pratt himself was two days gone, and the ghost had only been a cast-off shell that had thought it was him.

Goodbye, Mary, he thought. Goodbye, Pratt. I'm sorry.

Alone, Vickery resumed swimming toward the palm trees, dragging Harlowe's knapsack through the water.

Anita Galvan made a sharp left turn from 22nd Street when Santiago called from the back seat, "Behind us again!" The Buick's tires chirruped on the pavement. She was heading south now between little fenced-in houses and old stuccoed apartment buildings, and she glanced impatiently into the rear-view mirror.

In the reflection, Santiago appeared to be alone back there, but when they had been stopped at a red light a few moments ago Galvan had shifted around on the front seat to look at him directly—and the apparition of an old man had still been sitting beside the boy, who was whispering to it. The thing looked like a water-color portrait that had been left out overnight in the rain, but in its insubstantial hands it held a silver medallion that shone with emphatic solidity in the afternoon sun-glare. Galvan was surprised that the old ghost could hold the object up against gravity. Santiago had called the silver disk the old ghost's handhold.

Galvan's main business was providing rides for people who wanted to avoid ghosts, and now she was chauffeuring one of the unnatural things. She didn't like it.

"He senses them again?" she asked now as she concentrated on an approaching intersection.

"Just the man, just Vickery, he thinks," said Santiago, "and he won't let me speak more than a couple of words at a time to him. It's . . . hard for him to be a compass. Even when he was alive, it was hard, and now it nearly uses him up."

"Well tell him to last till we find Vickery."

Galvan became aware that she was nervously humming a couple of random notes over and over again, and made herself stop. Vickery alone? Santiago had seen both Vickery and Castine captured, possibly shot, three hours ago. If Vickery was alone now, did that mean he had escaped, or did it just mean the woman who had been with him was dead? Surely it meant he had escaped! He was a clever old *sinverguenza*, a tricky scoundrel.

"Right or left?" she asked, for this street ended at a park half a block ahead.

"Left," said Santiago, "but still south. By the water."

Galvan was cautiously hopeful. For an hour or so Santiago's creepy old ghost-pal had been tracking the two souls who shared with it the consequence of having been to the Labyrinth afterlife and back: a vibration in their slots in sequential time, apparently, like cars with bad motor mounts. The old ghost had guided Galvan and Santiago down here to San Pedro, but then about an hour ago it had stopped being able to detect their identities.

Galvan had been afraid the astral silence meant that Harlowe had killed Vickery and Castine—in which case she was convinced that any real hope of saving her idiot nephew and the children was gone. Vickery had been her only real hope of tracking Harlowe—Santiago had said that Vickery had seemed to have a plan for derailing Harlowe's mysterious soul-eating project.

But now Vickery had reappeared on the old ghost's radar, possibly—probably!—free. Santiago had spoken of some Egyptian who also wanted to defeat Harlowe, but Galvan believed the ever-resourceful Vickery might still be able to do it, and she had no faith in some Egyptian. And whatever Vickery might try to do, he'd surely need help, being at core a hopeless fuckup. Galvan couldn't sit around and do nothing.

She turned left, then resumed her southward course on Pacific Avenue.

"Turn left again!" said Santiago, "he's by the water!"

But to the left was just the apparently endless extent of a gated community—for several blocks, all Galvan could see on that side was locked gates and red tile roofs behind a spike-topped wall. "I'm trying!" she yelled. "This car can't fly!"

At last she was able to steer left onto a street that curled around in an S, and then she could see the ocean on her right, beyond a row of eucalyptus trees and a line of picnic tables.

"Further up now," called Santiago, and Galvan gunned the Buick north, past parking lots and a fenced-off lagoon, and soon the boy yelled, "To your right!"

Galvan yanked the steering wheel and bounced up a driveway into a parking lot. Ahead was some wide multi-level building with arches and more red-tile roofs—some sort of community center.

Santiago leaned over the front seat and pointed at the far corner of the parking lot. "That way!"

The Buick sped diagonally across the parking lot and halted at the edge of the asphalt, where a tan cement walkway led down toward the beach.

And a man in a black denim jacket carrying a heavy-looking knapsack was trudging up the walkway. There was nobody visible behind him, and Galvan noticed that he was wearing socks but no shoes.

"That's him!" said Santiago, but Galvan had already recognized Vickery. She pushed the gear shift into park and opened her door.

Vickery froze when he saw her climbing out onto the pavement, and she waved both empty hands. "Where's Harlowe?" she called.

"We gotta stop him! I'll pay you—I'll—you can keep your damn book—anything!"

Vickery stared at her for several seconds, then pulled the knapsack around in front of him. Galvan swore and reached for the semi-automatic in a holster inside her khaki jacket, but when Vickery unstrapped the knapsack and dug around in whatever its contents might be—while Galvan's hand was closed firmly on the grip of her gun—what he pulled out was a sagging red and black lump that she recognized as a waterlogged book.

"I got it myself," he said thickly, and he opened his hand and let the thing fall and slap on the pavement. "It's empty now." He trudged forward, leaving the thing behind him.

Galvan remembered the night last year when they had bought the book, in some haste, to contain his daughter's frail spirit; it had cost five dollars, and now it was clearly worth nothing.

"Okay," she said, nodding and relaxing, "okay. But listen, my nephew Carlos colored in a picture in a coloring book! Some of the *niños* too! You know about that, right?" When he nodded, she shook back the sleeve of her khaki jacket and looked at her watch. "We got not much time. Where is Harlowe?"

Vickery cocked his head, considering her. "How long before you sell me out again?"

"Right now you're my family's only hope," said Galvan impatiently, "I don't sell out my family."

"That's . . . well, that's true, I know you don't. So I'm safe with you till at least midnight, right? Like Cinderella. Okay." Vickery hurried to the car, and she noticed that he was leaving wet footprints on the tan pavement, and that his clothes were sopping wet. She brushed aside an instinctive concern for her leather upholstery and said, "You better sit up front, stash your bag on the floor. This is an ordinary car, and we got a ghost in the back seat with that kid Santiago."

Vickery halted, the sodden knapsack swinging from his hand. "A ghost? Are you sure?" When she nodded vigorously and jerked a thumb at the car, he said, "They're damn dangerous."

"*Get in!*" Galvan said loudly. "It's—cooperating!"

"Cooperating." After a moment's hesitation, Vickery shrugged and stepped quickly around to the passenger side. "Whose is it?" he asked as he pulled open the door.

"Some old guy Santiago—" Galvan paused and bent to peer in the back window. She didn't see the silver disk floating in the air now.

"It was Mr. Laquedem," said Santiago from the back seat. He bent down and picked up the silver medallion from the floor. Galvan only noticed that a looped string ran through a hole in the thing when Santiago pulled it over his head so that the medallion lay on his chest.

Santiago stared at Vickery, who was now sitting in the passenger seat. "He spent himself to find you." Tears shone in the boy's eyes as he added, "You damn well better be worth it."

Galvan slid into the driver's seat and pulled her door closed. "Do you *know* where Harlowe *is*?" she asked Vickery, speaking very distinctly as she started the engine. "You got away from him, right?"

"He'll be at the Cabrillo Marina," said Vickery, nodding northward, "he's got a boat docked there, the *Black Sheep*. He and a couple of his guys are probably waiting along the docks right now, watching the water to see if I climb out."

Galvan shifted into reverse and stepped on the gas pedal, and Vickery grabbed the dashboard as she backed fast across the parking lot and then spun the car around to face the street. The tires screeched in protest and dust was flying as she shifted to drive.

She spared him a sideways glance. "He had you on this boat?" She turned right onto the street and sped up.

"Yes. I jumped overboard—I had to, he was shooting at me—" Vickery touched his left thigh, and Galvan noticed a long rip in the denim fabric and a raw cut in his skin, "at my legs, he wants me alive. Ingrid Castine is still aboard, that's Betty Boop, we've got to get her away from him. Damn. You got guns? I'm unarmed."

"I got a gun. You know you smell like an old pier?"

"Do you have a spare?"

"Not me," she said, "ask the boy."

Vickery looked over the back seat, and in the rear-view mirror Galvan saw Santiago shake his head.

The street ended in a T ahead, and Galvan steered to the right, and then had to drive in a long loop before she was able to enter the marina parking lot.

"His SUV is in the first row on your right," Vickery said, peering tensely ahead through the windshield. But when she had driven halfway down the row, he sagged and said, "It's gone. They must have been quick."

"You sure?" asked Galvan as she steered into a parking space further down and switched off the engine; and when Vickery nodded, she said, "How long were you in the water after you jumped overboard?"

"Not long, maybe a half hour or so . . . uh, but I did have a sort of *episode,* just before I came ashore."

She opened the door and stepped out, and when Vickery and Santiago had got out on the other side, she said, "What's an episode?"

"A hallucination, more or less," said Vickery. He seemed defensive. "Let's walk down the dock—carefully!—and try to get on the boat. Ingrid might still be aboard."

Galvan looked at her two companions. The right pocket of Santiago's sweatshirt sagged, clearly containing some sort of firearm, and Vickery was still visibly soaked, and just in his socks. Get on the boat, she thought. God help Carlos and the kids.

Vickery was scanning the few other people in the parking lot. "His car's gone, but I bet they didn't all leave," he said. "Watch for a young guy in a red T-shirt, or one with a buzz-cut in a white T-shirt. Harlowe's got red hair and red cowboy boots. They've got stun-guns—they want me alive."

"I'll use a real gun," said Galvan.

"Pray God there'll be no call for it," Vickery said. "At most you can hold them off till we get to the boat—"

"I'm gonna kill this red boots *joto.* Fucks up Carlos and the *niños.*"

Santiago nodded solemnly.

"What," said Vickery to both of them, "here? No! And then what, we all sprint back to your car and drive out? Without Ingrid? You've got to—"

"It's a Glock with a good silencer, just makes a snap," Galvan said, "and he's had dealings with me, he'll know me, he'll let me get close. If we see him, our story is that I captured you for him." She grinned. "Neat, huh?"

"Listen to me!" said Vickery. "Who says killing him will stop the egregore, and save your nephew and the kids? I get the idea it's rolling to birth on its own. What we've got to do is kill *it.*"

Galvan exhaled and glanced at him. "What are you scared of? His ghost would be on me."

"Damn it, Harlowe's not the *thing*, he's only the guy who's got a lot of people lined up for it. It's going to arrive with or without him, unless we kill it."

"That's what Fakhouri says," admitted Santiago.

Galvan recalled that Fakhouri was the Egyptian. "Okay. For now. Santiago says you know a way."

"I'm pretty sure. Right now let's see if we can get aboard the boat."

The three of them hurried to the seaward end of the parking lot, Vickery squinting in all directions, but the few people visible were clearly not the ones he was watching for.

They made their careful way then along the second floating dock, between gleaming bows of moored boats. Galvan had her hand on the gun inside her khaki jacket, and Santiago was gripping what must have been a gun in his sweatshirt pocket. Vickery was just walking lightly with his arms out from his sides and his fingers spread, clearly ready to jump in any direction—but halfway down the dock he stopped at an empty slip, staring blankly at the narrow expanse of lapping water below the dock.

"It was here?" asked Galvan, seeing his shoulders slump as he looked around at the clustered boats.

He nodded. "We've *got* to find *Ingrid*."

"We've got to *stop the thing*," Galvan corrected him. "Eleanor?"

"Eleanor? Oh, *egregore*. We need Ingrid's help to do it."

"Why, exactly?"

Vickery opened his mouth, then closed it and shrugged. "She's one of us."

Galvan ran her fingers through her mop of black hair, then let her hand drop to her side. Vickery was probably just in love with the silly woman. Go along to get along, for now. "So where do we *go*?" she asked, looking past him at the sea and the boats and the dock.

"Topanga Canyon Boulevard," Vickery told her.

"What, Malibu, Woodland Hills? You think she'll be there? Or Harlowe?"

"Unlikely. But we need go there."

Galvan sighed mightily and turned to walk back to the parking lot. Go along to get along, she thought—for now.

CHAPTER SEVENTEEN:
A Revival of His Show

As Anita Galvan accelerated onto the 110 north, Vickery was hiked around in the passenger seat to keep an eye on the traffic behind them—and they had been moving along in the fast lane for a couple of miles, sometimes speeding up but more often slowing as brake lights flashed ahead of them, when the freeway began to slope upward to bridge Highway 1. Squinting past Santiago through the back window, Vickery was able to see a dozen of the following vehicles. One of the furthest back was a gray SUV.

"I think Harlowe may be following us," he said, relaxing back into his seat. "Pretty far back."

Santiago didn't turn around, but his eyes narrowed and he squeezed the medallion in his fist.

"We weren't followed out of the marina," said Galvan, not even glancing in the rear view mirror. "If it's him, he probably put a GPS tracker on you. Search your clothes, your . . . well you don't have shoes." She exhaled through her nose, and Vickery knew she was restraining herself from remarking again about the waterfront smell of his clothes.

Vickery twisted around to look back again, but the lane had leveled out and he could no longer see the boxy gray vehicle back there.

He remembered struggling back to consciousness in Harlowe's SUV; and he touched the cut on his forearm where Agnes had stuck a knife point into him. She had cut Castine too. *Don't mix them up,* Harlowe had said right after that. *If one of our IMPs should get away in the next few hours,* per impossibile, *we want to be sure we're using the right tracker.*

"I'm carrying a tracker all right," he said hopelessly. "It's my bloodstream." Galvan gave him a quick, irritable look, and he went on, "They cut us both, and got our blood on a couple of handkerchiefs. Our blood, our whole bodies, Castine's and mine, are like FM radios, and everybody else is AM. Every bit of us resonates—"

"What the *fuck* are you—"

"A cloth with my blood on it will be drawn to me," Vickery interrupted loudly, "like a compass needle."

"Mr. Laquedem had that kind of blood too," put in Santiago.

Galvan rocked her head, considering it. "He wants you alive, you said." Her voice was thoughtful. "How bad does it mess him up if you're dead?"

Vickery choked out one syllable of a startled laugh. "The egregore would still happen, boss," he said. "I'm not *indispensible*—to him. I believe I am, to you."

"Sure, sorry, just looking at all my options. Okay. But *I'll drive,* understand? You always leave my vehicles in Hell. Now tell me exactly what it is you're going to do on Topanga Canyon Boulevard."

Vickery understood that she was proposing to drive to her yard on Eighth Street and switch to one of her supernatural-stealth cars—which, modified as they were with aura-damping and attention-deflecting measures, probably would block the otherwise betraying resonance of his blood.

Vickery was turned around in his seat again, trying without success to get a glimpse of the gray SUV. "I'm going to retrieve something I left there this afternoon," he said, "right before Harlowe shot us with trank darts. It'll let me find Castine."

"Anything else?" demanded Galvan. "Anything that helps us kill Harlowe's thing?"

"We need Castine's help."

"No, we don't," said Galvan in a reasonable, almost kindly tone. "You look for her after we stop the Eleanor thing from happening at midnight. My car, my rules—and you got no gun, or shoes, even. You're working for me again." She gave him a sidelong look. "So what are we doing instead? We've got to get you into my stealth car so they can't trace you, and we've got less than seven hours till midnight."

Vickery paused long enough before answering to make it seem that he was considering alternatives and then giving in. "Okay," he said gruffly, "but after midnight you help, right? I save Carlos and the kids, you help me save Ingrid."

"That works," said Galvan. "You have to win, at this, to get her back." She flexed her fingers on the steering wheel. "Now we gotta get to my yard before Harlowe catches up with us."

To Vickery's surprise, she didn't begin passing other cars, much less driving along the narrow shoulder, as he had half expected; she even shifted to a slower lane, and Vickery could again see the gray SUV half a dozen cars behind them.

At one point when Vickery was looking back, Santiago caught his eye. "Maybe," said the boy, "she figures he'll run out of gas."

But Galvan moved into the fast lane, and when she had driven north as far as the Carson district and was about to pass the exit lane that connected to the westbound 405 freeway, she yanked the wheel to the right, forcing a tour bus to slam on its brakes and begin to slide sideways; she crossed its lane and the next one, to a cacophony of honking horns, and sped along the diverging connector lane. The lane curved under the 405 and then straightened out as it joined that freeway, and they were heading due west. Traffic was lighter here on the 405, and she was able to get into the fast lane and maintain a steady sixty miles per hour.

Vickery realized that he had been holding his breath, and he exhaled now. "Pretty good," he said, "but they'll still follow us. Me."

"Not by *that* connector," said Galvan, "no way they followed us off. They'll probably get off up at Artesia to go west, but we're gonna exit up here at 182nd and scoot back east, and then maybe crank up Western to the 105 and get back on the 110." She laughed. "As soon as they start chasing us one way, we'll already have gone another."

And for the next half hour she crisscrossed through Downey and Compton and Vernon, from freeways to surface streets and onto freeways again, past used car lots and run-down vaguely-Christian churches and around landscaped freeway islands, with the westering sun glaring through the windshield one minute and out of the mirrors the next—and at last she steered the Buick up the driveway into her yard.

She drove quickly past the rows of cars and the Airstream trailer and braked to a stop in front of the long maintenance bay, and she was out of the car while it was still rocking.

"Tom!" she yelled, "keys in the Caddy? Get the cover off, quick."

The bald, heavy-set yard manager sprang nimbly to a covered vehicle parked beside the tan Honda that Vickery and Castine had been in yesterday; and when he had pulled the cover off of it, Vickery was able, after a few seconds, to recognize it as a new Cadillac sedan with a big front end and an air-intake vent on the hood . . . but the car body was entirely covered with gaudy vinyl decals of photo-realistic clown faces in vivid color, which made the car seem bulbous and misshapen. Vickery knew that this would be Galvan's main stealth car, with run-flat support rings inside the tires, which in turn would be filled with air brought in from Nevada, and an air-filter peppered with dust from Oregon, and, under the interior upholstery, wire netting connected to the battery and insulated with woven human hair. And lately Galvan generally had pig blood in vinegar added to the coolant of her stealth cars.

Vickery and Santiago got out of the Buick, and Vickery said quietly to the boy, "You want a ride?"

Santiago nodded, and Vickery said, "Be quick." By then Galvan was in the Cadillac and gunning the engine. "Get in," she yelled around the still-open door, "Harlowe will probably be along any minute."

Vickery stepped around the front bumper, then halted and leaned down to peer under the car. "You got a coolant leak, boss."

Galvan was immediately out of the car, glaring at Tom as she braced one hand on the hood to bend down and look—and as Vickery straightened up, he pushed off from his left foot and rolled his right shoulder and drove his fist very hard into the pit of Galvan's stomach. Even as she exhaled a hoarse whoop, folded backward and rolled away, he had scrambled around and got into the driver's seat and pulled the door closed.

Santiago was already in the passenger seat, and Vickery pulled the gear shift into drive and stomped on the accelerator, feeling the ridges on the pedal through his threadbare sock. The car roared out of the repair bay and past the trailer and the cars to the street, and Vickery yanked it into a hard right turn.

Santiago fastened his seat belt and pushed his unruly black hair back. "You want to find the Castine woman first," he said, sitting up straighter to see over the dashboard.

"She's part of getting it done," muttered Vickery, alternately glancing at the rear-view mirror and watching the traffic ahead and the little metronome on the dashboard.

All of Galvan's stealth cars were equipped with metronomes like this. The pendulums were capped with bits of leather or wood or bone into which ghosts had been fossilized, and the pendulums clicked very rapidly back and forth in strong fields of expanded possibility around freeways, or in response to supernatural attention being directed at the cars—but this one was swaying only with the motion of the car.

Santiago hiked up in his seat to look back, then sat down again. "*Yo creo* Galvan thinks you're in love with Castine."

Vickery quickly passed a bus and made a left turn onto Irolo, intending to get to the 10 freeway via Vermont, a few blocks east, while Galvan would expect that wherever he was heading, he would take the more direct Western Avenue. He was speeding between more rows of apartment buildings behind narrow lawns and low hedges, and he was wrinkling his nose—the car interior smelled of curry, possibly some *santeria* supernatural-evasion measure. No doubt his sea-soaked clothing would leave it smelling even more peculiar.

"Galvan's a romantic," he said, "under all the barnacles."

"She's gonna kill you."

Vickery swung left onto James Wood Boulevard, driving now no faster than the other cars in the lanes. He was peripherally aware of drivers turning to stare at the clown faces on the Cadillac, and he remembered driving this way with Castine, last May, in the taco truck they had stolen from Galvan.

"She'd want to kill me anyway," Vickery said, "for something, sooner or later. It's how she is."

He remembered Castine throwing a phone out the window of the taco truck, that day. "Oh yeah," he said now, "grope around under the seat, or in the console. There'll be a smart phone somewhere—Galvan can track it."

Santiago nodded, and when he pulled a cell phone from under the seat, he pushed the button to lower the window and threw the phone out. "Mr. Fakhouri will probably be there, where you're going," he said as the window hummed up again. "He'll be mad—I was supposed to stay there. But I think he may be only crazy. you have a plan—what is it?"

Vickery remembered what Sandstrom had said. "I'm going to introduce a ghost into the egregore. That—I'm told—will stall its engine."

"Introduce," echoed Santiago. "How will you do that? 'Egregore, this is a ghost. Ghost, meet Mr. Egregore.'"

"I'm not sure how," said Vickery. After a moment he added, "Holler if you see a thrift store. I've got to get a pair of shoes. And a coat and pants. And a pair of wire-cutters." He wondered how difficult it would be to peel apart the waterlogged bills in his pocket.

A nervous yawn tugged his jaw open and brought tears to his eyes—and he realized, belatedly, that the faint buzz or vibration in his mind had stopped at some point.

The sun had set more than an hour ago over the dark curve of the sea, but remote red and gold terraces of clouds still silhouetted the hill above Pacific Coast Highway and the lone figure standing at its crest.

Three hundred yards inland, on a broad stony slope that rose higher but nevertheless seemed dwarfed by that hill's placement against the sea and sky, Lateef Fakhouri sat shivering in the sea breeze. Beside him on the dirt sat two oil lanterns, unlit, and two closed iron boxes that trailed wisps of smoke in the wind.

Below him, between his slope and that stark hill with its lone sentry, the broad, amphitheater-like field was in shadow, and the length of Topanga Creek was only traceable by the trees that followed its curling length.

The boy Santiago was gone. Fakhouri had tried calling both of his phone numbers several times in the last hour, but had got no answer.

Perhaps the boy would return. Perhaps he had not lost the two placards with the *Nu* hieroglyph printed on them; on an empty counter at Staples, Fakhouri had restored them to full potency by gingerly filling in his obscuring Wite-Out streaks with a gray felt pen.

And now, after so much careful preparation, where were they? Fakhouri cursed himself. He should not have entrusted crucial tools to a feral boy.

Fakhouri's phone had chimed several times, but the calling number had been the consulate's, and he hadn't answered. Doubtless the consular authorities were wondering what on earth to do with the two little girls he had left with them. But even if some crisis had arisen, he wouldn't be able to deal with it until after midnight; and by then the girls' minds might very well be gone. He knew his felt-pen rendition of the Nu hieroglyph, viewed by the girls through frosted glass, had freed them only partially, intermittently; Fakhouri had taken the girls away from Harlowe physically, but their minds, their selves, were still at risk.

He sighed and glanced at the iron boxes beside him. The sticks of smoldering punkwood were still smoking. Without either of the *Nu* sigils, he would not be able even to achieve as much as Boutros had.

Could he simply walk into the midst of Harlowe's invocation, and *shoot* the man? He shook his head. Even if he did, even if he *could*, the egregore would not be stopped.

The frail identities of Lexi and Amber would be dissolved in it, blended away in the homogeneous mix of all the other initiated souls; and Fakhouri would surely continue to be plagued with the dream of the two little girls he had seen so long ago in the Manshiyat Naser district of Cairo, sitting on a high pile of garbage bags in the back of a pickup truck.

He closed his eyes.

In the dream, the two girls wandered away down the narrow streets where the walls were hidden by bales of refuse, and even the balconies overhead and the roofs above them were clogged with huge, stained sacks; and the *Zabaleen,* the people of Garbage City, crouched in the open archways, dividing piles of trash into categories—paper in one bin, broken glass in another, fragments of dirty cloth in still another. And when the two girls approached them, the *Zabaleen* began unemotionally dividing the girls into their various parts, legs in one bin, arms in another—

Fakhouri shook off the dream-memory of the two young, blank-faced heads being tossed into a bin already half full of heads.

He leaned back against a weed-cushioned rock and looked around the borders of the shadowed field below him—and he saw an odd-looking car pull over on the Topanga Canyon Boulevard shoulder a hundred yards away down to his left. In the twilight, the car seemed to be painted in camouflage, blobs of light and dark. Its headlights went out and the passenger side door opened.

Two people climbed out of it, a man and a boy, and as they began to walk away from the highway, along the path on the other side of the creek, he was sure they were Sebastian Vickery and Santiago.

Fakhouri stood up, breathless with sudden hope, and eagerly watched their progress. The boy wasn't carrying the placards, but *he had come back,* and probably he had hidden them in this natural amphitheater somewhere.

Fakhouri had climbed this inland hill from the north side, and he glanced anxiously at the figure at the top of the shore-side hill—but it was a remote silhouette against the fading light in the west, and he couldn't tell if it was aware of the two new arrivals on the scene.

Leaving his lanterns and fire-boxes on the slope, he hurried down a track that would take him to the amphitheater floor, but, wary of the figure on the seaward hill, he didn't call to Vickery and Santiago.

Vickery must have heard his scuffling progress, though, for he looked across the field to his right, and up, and when Santiago followed his gaze and said something, they both stopped.

Fakhouri's wingtip shoes were clumsy on the shadowed pebbly incline, but by flailing his arms for balance he managed to reach the plain in under a minute, and he hurried across the weedy dirt to where Vickery and the boy stood between two trees on the other side of the creek. Santiago was still in his sweatshirt and jeans, but Vickery was now wearing a tweed coat and gray trousers, and Fakhouri felt less foolish when he saw that Vickery too was wearing black dress shoes.

The darkly moving water was a good dozen feet across, and Fakhouri didn't want to shout. But from his elevated perch he had noticed a bridge back by the highway, and he waved to Vickery and then made a looping gesture back in that direction, and held up the spread fingers of one hand, hoping it conveyed, *five minutes.*

Vickery nodded, and he and Santiago resumed walking west through the trees along the far bank.

Fakhouri swore under his breath—they might have waited for him to catch up!—but began loping wearily toward the bridge, five hundred feet to the east.

When he had crossed the bridge and made his way back through the trees on the other side of the creek, and reached what he believed was the point where Vickery and Santiago had paused, he didn't see them ahead of him in the varying depths of shadow. He trotted on, heavily, his shirt coldly damp with sweat, the holstered revolver knocking against his ribs, and his heart thumping alarmingly under it all. What in the name of all that was holy could Vickery and Santiago be doing? There wasn't time for wandering about.

After another few yards he heard, above his own panting breath, shrubbery being agitated ahead; and within a few more paces he was finally able to halt, leaning forward and bracing his hands on his knees to catch his breath, for Santiago was standing in the path and Vickery was just straightening up from having been grubbing around in a stand of weeds. He was now holding a shopping bag.

"You didn't call to us," Vickery said, just loudly enough for Fakhouri to hear him. "Who else is around?"

Fakhouri lifted one hand to wave at the hill slope behind Vickery. "A man," he said. "At the top." He made himself stand up straight, and he tugged his cuffs back into place. "Santiago," he said, "where are the hieroglyph placards I entrusted to you?"

"Hidden up a tree," the boy said. "They're safe."

Fakhouri exhaled, feeling a good deal of the tension leave him. He turned to Vickery. "Where is the woman who was with you?"

After a long, wary look up toward the hilltop, Vickery turned his attention to the shopping bag, and felt around inside it. "Harlowe's still got her."

"Good," said Fakhouri. "I mean," he went on quickly, "it's good that you're separated, I wish no harm to her. But there are still some hours before midnight—you must get on an airplane to a place far away, a very different time-zone, so that we may hope at least that your internal circadian clocks will be at odds—"

"I'm going to find her, and free her," Vickery said. He started walking back toward the highway, and the other two fell into step on either side of him. "Do you know who that is, up on the hill?"

"It's the *brujo* you talked to here," Santiago told him, "this afternoon. He called to the men who caught you."

"Chronic," said Vickery. "Of course he'd stay for the event. It's a revival of his show, really."

Fakhouri stopped, then had to trot to catch up. "Not the same Chronic, surely," he said.

"The guy that tried to spark up an egregore in '68," confirmed Vickery, peering with evident unease back through the trees that now hid the top of the hill. "He's old, but he's spry."

Santiago nodded as he trudged along. "*Peligroso*, dangerous."

The sea wind was colder on Fakhouri's damp face, and he did not look back. Chronic, Khalid Boutros' old adversary, he thought—still *alive*? Khalid, you failure! All you did was postpone the crisis! And you left *me*, a branch office General Intelligence Directorate research clerk, to deal with the diabolical prophet who has outlived you and may prevail after all!

"You must *not* fly away to another country," Fakhouri said decisively now. "The boy and I will need your help in doing the exorcism. You are evidently familiar with . . . guns, trouble."

"So is Castine," said Vickery. "We need her with us."

"But we must all stay here! We cannot know when Harlowe will begin the conjuring of his *Shaytan*." Fakhouri peered anxiously at Vickery's resolute profile. "Do you even know where she *is*?"

"No," Vickery said, and he hefted the shopping bag as he strode along the path. "But I've got an old sock in here that'll lead me to her."

Fakhouri was sure he must have misunderstood, but he dismissed it. He considered drawing his revolver and pointing it at Vickery— but to what end? He could hardly hold the man at gunpoint here for several hours, much less force him to cooperate in placing the hieroglyph placards and the lanterns . . . and Vickery could probably take the gun away from him in any case.

Fakhouri looked past Vickery at Santiago. "You stay, at least. We must hope Mr. Vickery will come back here in time."

"Miss Castine still owes me ten dollars," Santiago said, matching Vickery's pace.

"She does not," Vickery told him.

Fakhouri groaned almost silently, and clenched his fists. He cast a glance to his left, at the slope beyond the creek and the plain, and prayed that no wandering vagrant would find the lamps and the fire-boxes—or climb a tree and find the sigils!—then said, hoarsely, "I think I must go with you, to be sure you return. I cannot do this thing alone."

"You stay here," Vickery told him. "We'll come back, don't worry."

"I will worry no matter what happens. But I will not worry about where you are. I shall come with you."

Vickery laughed quietly and looked at him. "You've still got your gun? Sure, come along."

Fakhouri sighed and put his chilled hands in his pockets. One way or another, he told himself firmly, I will see that the egregore dies, and Lexi and Amber are freed.

The car on the shoulder was visible ahead now, and as they hurried toward it Fakhouri noted, with what blunted surprise he was still capable of, that its body was covered with grotesque clown faces. Dignity was clearly a casualty in this insane undertaking.

Harlowe and one of the ChakraSys girls were off somewhere, trying to track Vickery by means of the cloth which Loria had blotted with his blood, but the rest of the ChakraSys personnel—the Singularity team, as they called themselves—had relocated from the church down on Pico to Don Foster's triangular white house on Easterly Terrace in the Silverlake district. Castine was in handcuffs now, but they were a good deal less constricting than the duct tape had been.

Foster, Castine now knew, had been one of the two men who had tried to capture them in the alley yesterday, and Ragotskie had indeed killed him with a knife last night, just as Ragotskie's ghost had said.

Members of the Singularity team were coming and going from the house on various errands—including, an hour ago, the fetching of a half a dozen pizzas—and, siting on a bright yellow couch that matched the living room's table and chairs, Castine was only able to estimate that there were at least ten of the *Singularities*, as she thought of them.

Track lighting on the ceiling cast a stark illumination on their faces, most of which variously reflected anxiety, muted excitement, or glowing serenity at the prospect of their imminent group apotheosis. Even the burly fellow standing by the kitchen counter, with a bandage taped around his head and dried blood streaking his neck and staining his shirt, was smiling benevolently, if vaguely, at everyone.

The man who had been introduced to Castine as John Taitz was an exception. His right hand was heavily bandaged, and a dew of sweat on his forehead told her that he was in pain. She heard one young man, and then a woman, assure him that in less than four hours he would have left his injured body behind, but his answering smiles had been forced.

Paintings on the living room walls were just streaks of evidently random colors, and the books in the one visible bookcase were arranged by height, so that their top edges formed a smooth descending slope, and their spines had all been painted the same shade of yellow as the furniture. Someone had taped cardboard cutouts of a black cat and a green-faced witch to the inside of the front door, presumably in a half-hearted acknowledgment of Halloween. The room was too hot, and smelled of pizza and trendy colognes and sweat.

The Singularities had greeted Castine warmly when Harlowe had delivered her to the church on Pico two hours ago, and several of the women had solicitously cut the duct tape from her wrists, and, with cheerful efficiency, replaced them with the handcuffs; and when any of them caught her eye now as they bustled from room to room, they smiled and sometimes even winked conspiratorially. Castine found herself smiling back.

For the past couple of hours she had been aware of a faint humming in her mind—something like the carrier wave on a radio tuned to a silent station. It became more perceptible whenever she was within a yard of one of these Singularities, and she had been assured that it was just "interference fringes" caused by the overlap of two people's auras; and that her sensitivity to it was a result of her "initiation," when she had looked at the image in the coloring book.

She wondered if Vickery or Fakhouri were having any success, out there in the world, at stopping the egregore. She knew she should be assessing her situation here, looking for ways to escape—but it wasn't easy to concentrate on complicated sequential thoughts in this crowd of noisy conversation and frequently intruding auras.

The couch sagged, and when she looked to her left she saw that Taitz had sat down at the other end of it. She was sure that the lines in his face weren't usually as deep as they were tonight.

"That guy in the kitchen?" he said to her. "With the surgical tape all over his head? That's Chino Nunez. You shot his ear off, last night. Or that Vickery guy did." He gingerly lifted his bandaged right hand. "And Vickery shot a couple of my fingers off. Well, they're going to have to come off, it looks like."

Several people, in pairs, had drifted away down a hallway; one young man approached Castine, then saw the handcuffs and moved on. She wondered if these were last-minute amorous trysts, and hoped there were at least several bedrooms.

She rolled her wrists in the handcuffs. "You were going to kill us," she said carefully to Taitz. Sweat glistening on his scalp under the buzz-cut gray hair. She could see the grip of a holstered semi-automatic under his open windbreaker.

Taitz sat back. "That's true," he said. "Other times, like now, we're *not* supposed to kill you." He looked around the crowded room with evident disapproval. "Like college kids on spring break. And I never liked Don Foster."

"I don't like his taste in furnishings—"

But Taitz talked over her. "I was worried his ghost would come after me—or Ragotskie's, or Pratt's again. Today I went to a thrift store and bought three cheap rings and a pair of pants and a shirt and shoes. All second-hand. I was—"

"Hiding from their ghosts," Castine interrupted now. "Making yourself unrecognizable behind other people's imprinted personalities on those things." She glanced at his shirt and left hand, and went on, "But you're not wearing the rings, and your shirt isn't on backward. And I bet those are *your* shoes, not second-hand."

Taitz had been visibly startled by her observations, but now he frowned and nodded. "You went to Hell last year, and came back, didn't you? It figures you'd know about things like that. No, after an hour I threw all that stuff away. Hiding from their ghosts like that, it was like—"

Castine remembered Vickery's willingness, albeit a reluctant willingness, to meet Pratt's ghost last night, though in fact it had turned out to be Ragotskie's ghost that had come knocking at Hipple's door over nothingness. "Like cowardice," she said.

"Okay," he said gruffly, "yes. I bought that stuff so if they came looking for me, they'd see, yeah, *imprints* of other people. Pratt's ghost scared me, yesterday." He looked around the room again, then scowled at her. "You got a problem with that?"

"It scared me too. All ghosts scare me."

"Well, you're a girl, that's fine. But me—I'm damned if I'll hide from 'em."

"Okay," said Castine.

He bared his teeth, possibly because of the pain in his hand. "But I'm *going* to, aren't I? Hide from them? And hide from my fucked-up hand—sorry. And from another ghost, God help me; I bumped my girl Hannah off the freeway in '86, up in Santa Clara." He blinked rapidly, looking at the bare fingers of his left hand, and Castine wondered if some of the dampness on his face might actually be tears. "Yeah, I'm going to hide in the big egregore cloud," he went on, "where even *I* won't have any imprint." Now he looked up at Castine. "And you'll be there too—or *not be*, there."

Castine thought of Agnes' remark: *We're out of cream, so I made it with no milk.* Yes, she thought, it is like that—all of us individuals who have been initiated with the hieroglyph will, in effect, *not be*, in the transcendent egregore. Not as individuals, anyway.

It startled her to see Agnes herself come hurrying over to the couch. She was tucking a cell phone into the pocket of her jeans. "Ingrid," she said, "Simon's having a bad time tracking Vickery. It seems Vickery lost his qualification when he jumped into the ocean—who knew? Hi, John," she added to Taitz. "Just a few more hours now, hon."

Taitz's sweating face lost all expression, and Castine guessed that he didn't like Agnes calling him *hon.*

"We've got to find him," Agnes went on, "and get him re-initiated, in like the next three hours. Simon was tracking him just fine at first, and he thinks Vickery went to that Galvan woman's garage, but then the signal stopped, and when Harlowe asked Galvan about it she got real angry and said she hadn't seen him. The signal started up again an hour or so later, from somewhere southwest, but stopped again after half an hour, and the bloody altar cloth hasn't wiggled since. Where would he go?"

He's in one of Galvan's stealth cars! thought Castine. That's why you can't track him. And Galvan didn't say so, even though it sounds as if he stole it. Can she be an *ally,* to some degree, now? Or does she just want her own revenge?

But why would Sebastian have been out of her car for half an hour? Southwest?

Well, of course. To fetch the sock with my blood on it.

So he'll find his way here. If I want to hide, like Taitz says—from the memories of the man I killed last year, and the fiancee whose death I was responsible for, and the whole accumulation of things I've done and things I've failed to do, which I've never worked up the nerve to take to a priest in Confession—then I'll warn Agnes that I've got to be taken away from here, and shifted from place to place evasively.

Or I can say nothing and let Vickery find me, in which case I'll probably end up keeping those guilts and shames . . . and one brave day uncover them, acknowledge them, to God. It would be a lot of sins! I haven't been to Confession in decades.

Putting off answering Agnes' question, Castine said, "He lost his initiation? When he jumped overboard?" Agnes nodded. "So he can think clearly again."

"We all think clearly," Agnes snapped; then after catching an ironic glance from Taitz, she added, grudgingly, "When we're not getting too close to one another, anyway. But when we're all together in the egregore, *it'll* think perfectly. So do you know where he might be?"

If I give a phony location, thought Castine, Agnes is likely to have me take her there. And that would impede Sebastian finding me.

Choose, she thought.

"No," she said, and the word was a long exhalation. "Maybe he took off—Las Vegas, San Francisco, Mexico, I don't know."

"I think you took too long to answer. John," Agnes said to Taitz, "I think she knows where he is. We've got to get him and initiate him again, very damn soon."

Taitz gave her a strained grin and reached up with his left hand to touch the grip of his holstered gun. "You want me to pistol-whip her? Shoot her in the hand maybe, like her pal did to me?"

"Oh," Agnes said, and shrugged spasmodically, "maybe!"

Taitz looked at Castine and rocked his head. "Well, I'd feel bad about that . . . but soon I won't feel anything at all, right?"

Castine flexed her forearms against the restraint of the cuffs, uselessly, and backed her heels against the base of the couch, ready to jackknife forward.

"Right!" Agnes gave Castine a wide-eyed excited look. "He'll do it! So tell me where Vickery is!"

"*Actually,*" said Taitz, drawing the word out, "I won't. Even just for a couple of hours, I don't need to carry one more guilt."

Agnes hissed in exasperation and looked around the room, perhaps assessing the capacity for brutality of the other Singularities. After a moment she clicked her tongue and leaned down over Taitz. The proximity made her frown in concentration.

"Nobody's had cause to take your blood pressure, John," she said. "But it could happen." She quickly took a step back and shook her head. "I'm sorry, that's not what I meant to say. I mean, if we have to go with the twins, wherever *they* are—"

"Maybe you weren't thinking clearly," said Taitz. "I got a buzz when you leaned in close. But if I die before midnight, you can bet my ghost'll find its way into the mix. Your god-machine'll get vapor lock."

"It's your *god-machine* too, John!" Agnes protested. She gave Castine an angry look, as if Castine must have said something to shake Taitz's faith. She went on to Taitz, "Vickery took that *Garden Secrets* book, or whatever it was, but Harlowe's now got an even better way to keep ghosts out of the assembly. He's got Biloxi out right now scouting up parts for it."

"Vickery got his book back?" said Castine, resolutely playing for time. "When?"

"It was in Harlowe's knapsack," said Agnes impatiently, "on the boat. Vickery took it over the side with him. Harlowe thinks the . . . baptism in the sea probably wiped the ghosts out of it."

"What's the better way to keep ghosts out?" Castine persisted. *Sebastian,* she thought, *I hope you're close!*

"What?" said Agnes. "Oh—it turns out ghosts are repelled by . . . certain sorts of pictures, images . . ."

"The uncanny valley," said Castine, nodding. When Agnes gave her a blank look, she went on, "People like realistic pictures of faces—paintings, statues—and the more realistic they are, the more everybody find them interesting. The approval line, like on a graph, goes up. But if the images get *too* realistic, they start to give people the creeps, and the approval line drops. That drop is the uncanny valley. It's when a face looks pretty much totally real, but you can just barely tell it's not a genuine human."

"That's right," said Agnes. "Harlowe sent Biloxi out to buy a whole bunch of such things—big stills from movies like that *Polar Express,* and any very realistic mannikins he can get hold of, even a sex robot or two if he can find any for sale. Harlowe's going to set them up around the site, so any curious ghosts that come wandering up will be repelled."

She had been speaking softly, almost absently, and now her hand darted forward to Taitz's chest and snatched the gun from his holster. He had reflexively tried to block her with his bandaged right hand, but it had rebounded uselessly from her wrist, and he was now sitting back, gasping, his face white.

Agnes was staring wide-eyed at Castine. "Last chance," she said, "to tell me where he is. The gun Vickery took into the sea with him wasn't loaded, because I couldn't bear to shoot anybody again. But this one's loaded, and I can bear it for a couple of hours if I have to. So—where is he?"

Castine opened her mouth to give a fake address at last, but at that moment the sound of breaking glass in the kitchen caused all the Singularities, including Agnes, to look in that direction—and on the other side of the room the front door was kicked open, and in walked Sebastian Vickery, in a tweed coat and wool trousers now, followed closely by Lateef Fakhouri still in his rumpled plaid sports coat. Both were holding guns.

"To your left!" shouted Castine, but Agnes was pointing Taitz' gun past Castine, at Taitz himself.

"Drop it!" yelled Vickery, and for a frozen moment the tableau held: Vickery's semi-automatic trained on Agnes, who was aiming squarely at Taitz' face with his own gun, and the Singularities in the kitchen end of the room gaping uncomprehendingly.

Then Agnes opened her hand and the gun fell to the carpet, and thumping and footsteps sounded in the hall and Vickery stepped wide to cover that corner of the room too. Fakhouri kept his own revolver pointed horizontally toward the middle of the group of Singularities. Fakhouri was squinting and grimacing as if against a bright light, but his gun was fairly steady.

"Ingrid," Vickery said, "up!" She stood up from the couch and hurried across the floor to him, and without looking away from the half-dozen people beyond the sights of his gun, Vickery called, "Who's got keys for the handcuffs?"

The group clustered by the kitchen, and the figures stopped in the hall, shifted and muttered, but none of them answered.

A voice behind Fakhouri said, "I can open 'em after we leave," and when the speaker stepped into the light Castine recognized Santiago; and when she noticed that the boy's hands were empty, she recognized the .40 caliber Sig Sauer that Vickery was holding, and she was glad Santiago had let him borrow it.

Looking back toward the couch, she saw Agnes glance quickly from the gun on the floor to Taitz, and there was urgency in the look she gave him; but Taitz shook his head.

"You've still got the twins," he said, and hiked himself forward on the couch to kick his gun across the carpet toward her. "Take my blood pressure, if you want—I bet I won't be scared off by your sex robots."

But Santiago darted in and snatched up the gun and then hurried back to the doorway as he tucked it into his sweatshirt pocket.

Then everyone jumped and several people screamed as Chino Nunez suddenly roared and came charging out of the kitchen into the living room. Fakhouri's gun went off with a stunning bang, and in the next second Taitz had swung a leg to the side and tripped Nunez, who crashed to the floor, the bandage taped over his ear quickly blotting red. Bits of paper were spinning in the air, and Castine saw a gash across the yellow spines of the books where Fakhouri's bullet had gone.

Her ears were ringing, but she heard Taitz say to her, "Get out of here, will you?"

She nodded jerkily and turned toward the door. Vickery had grabbed the white-faced Fakhouri and shoved him out onto the front step, and Santiago was already outside.

"Don't anybody poke your heads outside for five minutes," yelled

Vickery, "or the next shot won't be for show. You're all on the verge of immortality, right? So it'd be a shame to lose it now."

With his free hand he waved Castine behind him, and as she hurried down the walkway she looked around at the cars parked up and down the narrow street and the yellow school bus right out front. A streetlight shone on a car double-parked down to her left, blocking the street, and big full-color wide-eyed clown faces all over the car made it impossible to guess what make it might be.

An uncanny damned *abyss*, she thought.

Vickery grabbed the arm of her jacket and hustled her toward it. "That Cadillac," he said. Fakhouri and Santiago had already run to it and were hastily getting into the back seat.

When she was in the passenger seat and Vickery had got in and started the engine, she gingerly reached up with both hands and unknotted the dirty sock from behind the rear-view mirror post. She could feel that a handful of coins had been tucked into the toe of it so that it would work as a pendulum.

Vickery drove fast past the parked bus. When she waved the sock in his peripheral vision, he nodded and said, "Don't need it now. Just don't get lost again."

"You stole this car from Galvan?" Castine asked.

"Had to," he said, his eyes on the narrow, curving asphalt in the car's headlights. "She didn't want to detour to pick you up."

"Well, thanks." She pulled her seatbelt across and found the slot for it. "I'll want to hear about that."

"I'll want to hear why that guy won't be scared by sex robots," Vickery said. "I would be."

Castine laughed, probably for the first time since breakfast at Canter's this morning, if she had laughed at anything then.

From the back seat, Santiago said, "You got a paper clip?"

"A paper clip?" Vickery made a left turn onto Silver Lake Boulevard, heading south toward Sunset to get on the Glendale freeway. "Actually, we do," he said. "Ingrid, on the floor by your feet there's Mr. Fakhouri's shopping bag." He glanced at Fakhouri in the rear-view mirror. "We never did get you some more Turkish apricots, sorry!"

"You have behaved in a regrettably high-handed manner all along," said Fakhouri.

Vickery bobbed his head in rueful agreement, then went on to Castine, "Ragotskie's papers are in there, and there's a paper clip on the old coloring book." He reached up and turned on the dome light on her side.

Castine bent down and groped among the papers with her cuffed hands. After a few seconds she dragged the old coloring book out; it tore into limp fragments, but she found the paper clip and pulled it free, then turned around in her seat to hold it out to Santiago.

"Stay like you are," the boy said, and he began unbending the paper clip. When he had straightened half of it out, he pinched it half an inch from the end and pressed the end against the no-doubt-bulletproof window glass until it bent at right angles. Then he fitted the makeshift key into the keyhole of one of the cuffs and twisted, and the rotating arm sprang loose; a few moments later he had opened the second one too, and the cuffs clattered to the floor behind the front seat.

Now Santiago's hand stretched from the back seat, and in his palm was Taitz's semi-automatic. "You take this," he said to Vickery, "and give me my gun back."

"Whose?" asked Castine drily, for the boy had taken it from a dead government agent last year; but she took the Sig Sauer from Vickery when he pulled it out of his coat pocket and handed it across the seat-back to Santiago, and took from the boy's hand Taitz's gun.

After a moment of thought, she gave it to Vickery, and he put that in his pocket. Looking at her watch, she asked, "Where are we going now? The egregore is set to fire in only about three hours."

"We're going to call up a ghost," he said. "Try to, anyway."

Fakhouri muttered in the back seat, and when she glanced back she saw Santiago just finishing making the sign of the cross.

"I could have killed someone!" Fakhouri burst out.

"It was an effective move," Vickery assured him, "deliberate or not."

Castine turned to Vickery. "Were you thinking of going down there and sticking a ghost into Harlowe's fuel line? Agnes says he's going to keep ghosts back by setting up a bunch of uncanny valley images around the site."

"There was a guy," said Vickery, "who tried to warn Chronic about a *different* way an egregore might go wrong. We need to find out what that way was. Is. And," he added, "in that bag we've also got his signature, to call up his ghost with."

"Whose signature?" asked Castine; then, "Oh, in that book Gale Reed gave you. Her husband, Stanley Ancona." She rubbed her temples and nodded. "So we're going to the La Brea Tar Pits."

Fakhouri made an unhappy sound in the back seat.

CHAPTER EIGHTEEN:
The Night Is Breathing

"They're *both* gone now!" said the young lady in the passenger seat of Harlowe's Chevy Tahoe. Harlowe believed her name was Avalon.

"The Castine woman can't be gone," he said. "It's just the turns in this street making it look that way."

The two altar cloths, the blood on them still damp, hung from strings in a wire frame on the dashboard. A few moments ago the one with Vickery's blood on it had finally shown a response again, tilting forward parallel with Castine's, but now both of them did seem to be swinging loosely.

Harlowe pressed the gas pedal, and the glowing windows of the houses along Silver Lake Boulevard rushed past more quickly.

Cars were parked at the curbs, and he had to swerve carefully when headlights came sweeping down the boulevard in the other direction; and now he had to brake and partly turn in to a driveway when an oncoming car came fast around a curve ahead, pretty much taking up both lanes.

He honked angrily as it rushed past, and he got a glimpse of tinted windows and—of all things!—three or four huge clown faces printed on the body of the car.

"Halloween in L.A.," commented Avalon. "But your rags *are* just dangling, no tilt."

Harlowe's phone chirped, and he fumbled it out of his pocket as he straightened the SUV and sped up again.

"What?" he said when he had turned the phone on and swiped the screen.

"Vickery was just here," came Loria's tense voice, "with some kid and a guy who I think is the Egyptian, and they took Castine away with them. They're gone. They had guns, I couldn't do anything!"

"Damn it! Where the hell was Taitz? And Nunez?"

"They were useless. The kid, whoever he is, took Taitz's gun." Harlowe heard an angry voice in the background, and then Agnes again: "Are the twins online?"

Harlowe probed mentally for his awareness of the twins' mentation, but the once-constant incomprehensible rattling of their thoughts was again gone.

"No," he grated.

That clown car that passed us, he thought. It must have been them, or probably was. Vickery must have some way of blocking the psychic signature of his blood, and now he's extended it to Castine too. The blood cloths are no good. Can I turn around and chase that car, catch up with it? And even then, can this Avalon girl and I stop them and overpower them? They've got guns, and now they've got Taitz's gun too.

"No," he said again, and he let the vehicle slow down. Easterly Terrace was coming up soon anyway, and there was no longer any reason to hurry. "I'm afraid we—" and he paused to take a deep breath, "—go to Plan C."

From the phone, Loria's voice asked, "What is that, exactly?"

"Never mind," he said. Mind, he thought, never again.

He ended the call and hiked up in his seat to pull the copy of *The Yage Letters* from his jacket pocket. By touch he slid the half-tab of blotter acid from between the pages, and in the moment when the SUV was passing under a streetlight he glanced down at Janis Joplin's exaggeratedly weeping eyes.

Through tears in his own eyes he peered at the warmly lighted windows in the houses they were passing, imagining the rooms behind them and envying the lives of the people who lived in them.

He tried to call up fond images from his own life, but all he could think of was the trailer outside of Salinas in the '80s, and the homeless intruder he had killed with a knife.

He sighed and laid the strip of paper on his tongue.

"What was that?" asked Avalon.

"Never . . . mind."

Vickery found a parking space on Wilshire, in front of a Starbucks under the towering Screen Actors Guild building, across the face of which swirled projected cartoon ghosts and vampires. He shook out Castine's bloodstained sock for quarters to put in the parking meter. Castine took the sock and shoved it in her coat pocket.

Vickery recalled that Johnny's Pizzeria and Callender's Grill were further up the block to the west, and even at ten o'clock at night there were pedestrians wandering among the planters and walkways that separated the businesses from the street. Several people paused to stare and laugh uneasily at the Cadillac, and one little boy in a Batman costume, whom Vickery felt was out way past his bedtime, started crying at the sight of it and pulling his mother away.

Tucking Stanley's book into the side pocket of his coat beside his newly-bought wire cutters, Vickery led his mismatched group west along the sidewalk. Wilshire Boulevard glittered with white and blue headlights and red taillights and neon signs, but the wind was cold and blowing from straight ahead. He wished he'd bought a flannel shirt instead of this lightweight cotton one, at the thrift shop where he'd got the coat and trousers and shoes he was wearing, and he saw that Castine was shivering even in her suede coat. When they hurried past the Callender's Grill, where he had occasionally stopped for coffee and pie when he had worked out of the Los Angeles field office of the Secret Service, he saw that it was closed and out of business; and he was reminded again that the Los Angeles he knew was rapidly becoming a city that didn't exist anymore.

They crossed Curson Avenue, and Castine paused by the stylized copper panther poised above a sign that read, LA BREA TAR PITS & MUSEUM. She cocked her head dubiously at the brightly-lit padlocked gates, and at the tall, close-set iron bars that were the enclosing fence; but Vickery caught her eye and waved further down the sidewalk.

"I'll show you the way kids used to sneak in at night," he said, and kept walking. Castine followed, trailed by Fakhouri and Santiago. Headlights rushing past on their left pushed their shadows ahead and swept them aside.

"We can't stay out of the car for long," Castine said as she hurried to keep up with Vickery. "Harlowe's got some cloths with our blood on them, and when we're not in Galvan's stealth car they swing toward us."

"They can only have been swinging for a couple of minutes now," said Vickery. "We'll try to be quick here."

"You're limping," she pointed out.

"Harlowe shot at me when I was jumping out of the boat. Nicked my leg." He glanced at her. "I *had* to jump, he got his gun out too fast and he was shooting at me, and Agnes' damn gun wasn't loaded—"

"Good God, Sebastian, don't apologize! You found me again."

Vickery reached over and squeezed her shoulder.

Beyond the iron bars on their right they could now see spotlit statues of mastodons and, closer to the street, the wide black water that was perpetually agitated as bubbles of tar broke the surface. Already the breeze smelled like a newly topped asphalt road.

This at least is one part of Los Angeles, Vickery thought, that will still be here even after Los Angeles itself is gone. Gale Reed's husband, Stanley Ancona, found an enduring place to hide from spirits.

Tall eucalyptus trees and toyon bushes hid the view of the water for several hundred feet then, and Vickery stopped his group at a driveway where another pair of padlocked gates interrupted the fence. Two iron bollards flanked the driveway just outside the gates.

"We rest here," Vickery told his companions, "until there's no traffic near us, east or west." Turning away from the street, he pulled Taitz's gun out of his pocket; he popped the magazine out and hefted it, then pulled the gun's slide back far enough to see the base of a round in the chamber. He let the slide snap back and pushed the magazine back into the grip until it clicked. He put the gun back in his pocket.

Castine looked at her watch and pursed her lips.

Fakhouri was staring open-mouthed at the gate. "Do you propose," he asked hoarsely, "that we trespass? It would be certainly unwise."

He then looked ahead down the boulevard, and Vickery recalled that the Egyptian Consulate, where he and Castine had dropped off Fakhouri and the twins this morning, was only a block west of where they stood.

"You should wait for us here," Vickery told him. "If cops or somebody comes rattling at the gate, act confused and start shouting at them in Arabic. Okay? We'll hear you."

"I *will* be confused," said Fakhouri, clearly relieved at not being asked to climb over the gate. "And I *might* start shouting in Arabic."

Vickery turned to Santiago. "You want to wait?"

"I'll climb over," the boy said. "But if there's trouble I'll ditch you and go with Mr. Fakhouri. We got stuff we still gotta do."

"Understood." To Santiago and Castine, Vickery said, "You notice that the gates have flat top rails—no spikes. You hold onto a rail, put a foot on the top of one of those bollards, and then you hop up and straddle the gate and let yourself down on the other side. Santiago, you might be too—"

"I can do it," the boy said. He looked at the sky, but no stars could be seen in the charcoal scrim of ambient light, and he shrugged. "It must be getting late."

Vickery waited until a red light back at Curson stopped traffic from that direction; and Wilshire curved here, so that headlights from the other direction lit the median palm trees more directly than this recessed driveway.

He gripped the top rail and boosted himself up with a foot on the top of the bollard, wincing as the move tugged at the cut in his thigh, and a moment later he had dropped to the cement pavement on the other side. He hurried to the right to crouch beside the fence, hidden from the street by a row of yucca shrubs outside the bars.

Soon he heard the gate rattle and then shoes hit the pavement, and he hissed when Castine stepped away from the gate and looked around. She had just crouched beside him in the yucca shadows when Santiago joined them.

A cement walkway paralleled the fence, leading back toward the water. Vickery pointed across the walkway and down, indicating that there was a descending slope on the other side, then pointed to the right, in the direction of the entrance they had passed.

Bent low, the three of them hurried across the cement strip, and when they were out of sight of Wilshire Boulevard they moved quickly. The smell of tar was stronger now. Within a minute they had climbed through a thicket of toyon and stepped over another row of yuccas, and found themselves in a paved clearing beside the walkway. Between two widely-spaced metal benches was a tilted waist-high sign that doubtless had some facts about the tar pits printed on it, and beyond it was a wire grid fence, low reeds, and then the expanse of water reflecting the lights of the museum building on a prominence a hundred yards farther away.

Vickery tugged the book and the wire-cutters out of his pocket and handed the book to Castine as he stepped past the sign. He clipped through a vertical row of wires in the grid of the fence, and when he had clipped them all the way down, he pulled one side toward himself, dragging the bottom edge over mud and leaves. The bent section of fence sprang back a few inches when he let go of it, but there was a clear yard-wide gap now.

He edged through, followed by Castine and Santiago.

All three of them paused on the reed-fringed bank. Patches of the lagoon's surface were matte and didn't reflect the glow of the distant lights, and on the glassy areas ripples spread and crossed one another in silence. Vickery could see bubbles out there, and he knew they were methane from millennia-dead primordial animals . . . or conceivably from the fifty-year-old corpse of one tormented human.

Castine looked back, as if hoping to see headlights through the trees and reassure herself that she was still in 21st century Los Angeles. "Old isn't even the word," she breathed, turning back to look out over the lagoon. "*Eternal.*"

"Let me have the book," Vickery said. "I'll open it to the front page and touch his signature when I call him."

"I should do it," said Castine. "I'm still initiated, connected to the birthing egregore. His ghost and I are loosened in a similar way." Seeing his puzzled look, she explained, "Agnes said you lost your initiation, your membership, when you jumped into the ocean."

Vickery was reminded that he hadn't felt the elusive carrier wave in his mind for several hours now. "A dip in the ocean cancels it? I think our next stop after this is to get you a full-immersion baptism." She just stared at him, so he went on, "Okay. Maybe he'll respond better to a woman anyway."

"Maybe *it'll* respond better." She pulled the old sock out of her pocket and twisted it around her right wrist: "Mobile hotspot," she explained. Then she flipped the book open and touched the inked name on the front page. "Stanley Ancona," she called softly out over the water, "we need your help."

The wind sighed from distant Westwood and the eucalyptus leaves rattled overhead, and there was no disturbance in the black water aside from the constant ripples.

Castine repeated her summons three more times, to no perceptible result, and Vickery began, "Maybe I should—" but she waved him to silence.

"Let's not hold hands," she said, "but let's each be touching one part of his signature, and—dip the book."

Santiago was hugging himself in his sweatshirt, and shivering. "You're not supposed to get close to that stuff," he said. "It'll drag you down, like it did those elephants."

"Then you can pull us out, right?" said Vickery, and to Castine he said, "Let's try it."

They both started down the low bank, their shoes slipping in black mud or tar under the clustered reeds, and when they crouched by the edge of the water each of them had to brace one hand in the mud.

Castine held the book out in her free hand, and by the dim diffuse light Vickery was able to see that it was upside down, and that her thumb was on the scrawl which was *Ancona*. He reached out and took hold of the other side of the book, carefully laying his own thumb on the ink lines of *Stanley*, and then together they lowered the book until their fingers, and the inked name—and, Vickery noticed, one end of the sock—were in the water.

The whole lagoon seemed to shudder, and the ripples on the water stood still for a moment.

"Stanley," said Castine on a long, shaky exhalation, "We need to—"

She and Vickery both jumped then, for a bubble had burst on the surface only a yard away, and Vickery's nose was full of the smell of crude oil . . . and somehow of cigarette smoke too.

And the lights of the museum beyond the lagoon dimmed. Vickery looked up from the ring where the bubble had been and saw the translucent silhouette of a man hovering over the water.

Vickery heard a whisper, and even out here in the open night it seemed to echo: "And I should sleep, and I should sleep!"

A curl of distortion around the figure's head might have been its tongue, testing the breeze for a target.

"We," said Castine quickly.

"Need to," said Vickery.

"Stop Chronic."

"Again."

"How?" finished Castine.

The ghost flickered, and then it looked bigger. The water rippled audibly, as if some submerged bulk had moved closer to the shore.

"Ghosts," said Vickery hastily, hoping Castine had a way to continue the sentence.

"In the!" she gasped.

"Mix?"

"What."

"Happens?"

There was no reply. Vickery was sure the thing was about to shoot out its ectoplasmic tongue, or even that Stanley Ancona's tar-preserved body was about to stand up in the shallows, and he burst out, "*What*, dammit?"

Castine added, shrilly, "Answer!" and lost her hold on the book. It slid out from between Vickery's thumb and forefinger too, and fell into the water.

The thing shrank, perhaps bending down over the floating book.

"What," came the windy reply as it straightened again, "happens?" Its right arm merged into the blur of its body; perhaps it was extending its hand toward them. How close was the damned thing?

"Egregores," it sighed, "commit suicide, always."

"Huh?" was all Vickery could think to say.

"As soon as they're," came the ghost's voice, "what . . . *self-aware*, yes." Its arms spread out to the sides now. "Hey nonny nonny, its members go mad, then. In Europe, whole towns, 1518 . . . dancing for days, till they dropped. I was dreaming of giant ferns and warm seas. I should sleep."

"The egregore," said Vickery.

"Needs to be," ventured Castine.

"Stopped. *How?*"

"For God's sake!" added Castine desperately.

The thing was silent, and the lights of the museum were slightly brighter, as if the ghost were dissipating.

"You're," said Castine. She turned to Vickery and pointed two fingers at her eyes and then moved her hand away.

What, thought Vickery, looking at something? Castine impatiently held her hand out flat and stared at it. Vickery realized that she meant the thing *had* looked at something—he *Ba* image.

"Initiated!" he said.

And the thing darkened slightly, and spoke again. "This—speaking to you—is not. Stanley Ancona was."

"The egregore," Castine reminded it.

"Still?" The silhouette shivered. "The sigil was on the wall," it said, "the fresh ghosts *looked* at it. Perversion." For a moment its blurry head presented a profile. "I am desolate and sick of an old passion; I have been faithful to you, Gale Reed, in my fashion!"

Vickery's right hand was numb in the cold mud, and the wind was chilly on his sweating face. "How," he said hoarsely, and Castine finished, "Perversion?"

When the ghost spoke, its voice was slow and strained, as if it were struggling to marshall long-decayed thoughts and express them. "A man is initiated," it said, "but he's gone . . . when he dies, shuffled off this mortal toil! His ghost is not him—" It fell silent, then seemed to take a breath. "If *it* looks at the sigil, it becomes . . . part of, a *necrotic* member . . . "

We need a ghost, thought Vickery, to bring to Topanga Canyon tonight, and we need it to look at the sigil—become a necrotic member of the egregore. He glanced down at the book floating in the scummy water, wondering if it was out of reach.

"Can," he said, and Castine had evidently had the same idea, for she quickly said, "you come," and Vickery finished, "with us?"

The ghost diminished in size, or retreated. "The spirit is willing," it whispered, "but the spirit is weak. And I should sleep, and I should sleep."

And then Vickery couldn't see it anymore. He pushed his right hand down in the tarry mud to get to his feet—

—But cold fingers closed slimily around his wrist. Castine yiped and tried to straighten her legs, but wound up sitting in the muddy reeds and sliding toward the black water as she reached around to try to free her left wrist from whatever had seized it. Her coat was rucked up around her shoulders.

Shapes were humping up out of the water, some much too big to be human forms. Triangular heads between bulky shoulders broke the surface, the distant museum's light glistening on them as they stretched and twisted, and out across the lagoon Vickery saw a trunk uncoil near the statue of a mastodon standing in the lagoon. Over the scuffling sound of Santiago hurrying back to the cut fence, Vickery could hear Castine's rapid gasps.

Closer at hand, several silhouettes rose erect from the water, and when they stretched out their upper limbs Vickery saw hands with long, moving fingers. These had evidently once been men, or nearly.

The breath was whistling in his own throat as he tried with his free hand to pry off the wet bony fingers tugging at his wrist, but Castine pushed herself down to the water, and her legs slid below the surface as she stretched her right hand out and caught hold of the floating book.

One of the manlike forms out in the water threw back its head and bayed at the night sky. Its voice seemed to shake the leaves of the surrounding trees, and carried a note of enduring rage and despair.

Castine recoiled from it, then braced her submerged legs and swung her arm back toward Vickery. She was holding the dripping book, and he could see her teeth clenched with effort.

"Tear up the page!" she gasped.

Vickery let go of the fingers clutching his wrist and let his feet slide down through the reeds into the water; and as cold water filled his shoes he extended his left arm and took hold of the book's sodden cover; he flipped it aside, then closed his fist on the signed title page, crumpling it in his palm. It separated from the book and he rubbed it to wet fragments on the front of his tweed coat. Castine tossed the book out into the lagoon.

For a moment there was no change; shapes that might have been limbs and trunks and tusks waved in the wind, and the semi-human silhouettes reached out blindly. Vickery's right hand was spasmodically pulled deeper into the water.

Then the lagoon shuddered again, and the moving forms sank, shoulders to heads and then out of sight, beneath its bubbling surface. The fingers on Vickery's submerged wrist gripped more tightly for a moment and then flexed away, and the muddy water swirled as they withdrew.

Vickery and Castine dug their heels into the mud and tar under the water, but both of them had to roll prone in the muck and crawl to get back up to the bank. At last they were able to get to their feet, and they hurried through the gap in the fence to the pavement by the benches. There was no sign of Santiago.

After a nervous look back at the lagoon, Castine sank heavily onto one of the benches. Water dripped from her coat and puddled around her shoes. "We can't linger," she panted. "Harlowe might be on Wilshire already. He might be right outside the fence here." Her hair was disordered from crawling out through the reeds a few moments ago, and she raised a hand—then saw the tarry mud on her fingers and let it drop. She wearily untwisted the sock from her wrist and shoved it in her coat pocket. "Sebastian—those were *primitive men* out there, among the mastodons!"

"Ghosts of them," Sebastian said, breathing deeply. "We called up Stanley, and got a party line. I'm glad you figured out how to hang up, break the connection." He gingerly flicked fragments of wet paper from the front of his coat.

Castine looked back, toward the water. "Jesus," she said hoarsely, and it sounded like a prayer. "They all died in the tar, what, a million years ago?" She shivered visibly. "And one of them was able to give a cry that echoed on 21st century Wilshire Boulevard!"

Vickery nodded. "I bet it wouldn't have happened on any other night. Harlowe and Chronic have got the whole supernatural world lit up."

Castine sat back and looked down at herself in the dim light. She sighed,and brushed ineffectually at bits of reed stuck to her coat. "We always wind up a mess, don't we?"

"Come on, I'll give you a boost over the gate."

"Right. Out of here." She stood up and shook her head sharply. "That sure didn't help the damned mental buzz."

"Nor my leg." Vickery tried to grin. "I'm probably going to get some prehistoric mastodon virus now."

"Hush."

At the gate, they peered through the bars, watching impatiently for a break in traffic, and finally Vickery judged it safe to climb over. He linked his hands to make a stirrup for Castine to step into, and when he heaved up on her muddy shoe she caught the gate's top rail and lithely swung her legs over it and landed relaxed on the other side, her wet coat flapping. Vickery pulled himself up and rolled over the top and landed beside her.

When they stepped out onto the Wilshire Boulevard sidewalk, it was clear that Santiago and Fakhouri were gone.

"Watch for Harlowe's gray Chevy Tahoe," said Vickery as they began walking quickly back toward where he'd parked Galvan's Cadillac.

"I am, I am."

But in the glow of the streetlights and headlights, Castine took a moment to look sideways at him, and then down at herself. They were both smeared with gleaming black, and they were leaving splashy wet footprints on the sidewalk pavement.

Vickery caught her look, and glanced at her. "Your suede coat's wrecked," he observed.

"If anybody says anything—we can claim we're in zombie costumes."

"Trick or treating," agreed Vickery.

"Galvan," Castine panted as they hurried across the Curson intersection, "is going to be furious at the mess we'll make of her car, and it's a Cadillac? How much time do we have?"

The car was only a couple hundred feet ahead of them now. Pedestrians they passed looked after them in wonder. The projections of cartoon ghosts and vampires were still swooping across the tall expanse of the Screen Actors Guild building.

Vickery tugged back his sleeve as they walked rapidly past the dark façade of Callender's. "It's eleven," he said grimly, "and I think we've got to find a ghost who'll be willing to look at the sigil."

"And get it past Harlowe's uncanny valley images," she said breathlessly. "We want something like Stanley's book—or Laquedem's medallion—so we can call up the ghost—after we're past the images."

"A *cooperative* ghost." Vickery had the keyring out, and he pushed the button on the fob that unlocked the car's doors.

Several people were standing on the sidewalk staring at Galvan's garish car, but they stepped back hastily when Vickery and Castine came panting up to it. Three of them, two teenage girls and a middle-aged man with tattoos on his bare forearms, began speaking in unison: "The night is breathing, look at the stars!"

Vickery automatically glanced at the sky as he opened the driver's side door, but of course no stars were visible.

He started the car as Castine got in and fastened her seatbelt, and he accelerated away west on Wilshire. His hands were at once slippery and sticky on the steering wheel.

"The heater!" said Castine, and Vickery nodded and switched the heater on.

After he had sped past a couple of blocks, Castine said, "Those people were in that black hole state."

"Probably happening all over L.A. tonight."

"And at midnight they all get swallowed up." She shifted on the seat and tugged at her soggy coat. Giving up on finding a comfortable position, she slumped back; and then pointed at the dashboard.

"Uh," she said, "your metronome's clicking."

Vickery glanced at the little metronome. "No, it's just rocking with the motion of—" he began, then stopped speaking when he saw that the rocking of the four-inch pendulum was slow but regular, and the thing was ticking at each end of its swing.

Vickery had many times seen the metronome pendulums in Galvan's cars click rapidly back and forth in response to expanded possibility fields or supernatural attention, but this slow ticking, like a long-stroke grandfather clock, seemed to indicate nothing but a minimal interference.

Vickery realized with a sinking feeling that the metronome had probably been doing this for some time, unnoticed amid all the distractions.

"What the hell?" he said, watching traffic again. "It doesn't act *focused,* but—" He flicked a glance at her. "Have you got some kind of talisman on you? Maybe they slipped a, a voodoo charm or something into your pocket?"

Castine poked a finger in the pocket of her blouse, then worked her hands into her coat pockets. After a few seconds she pulled them out and patted her sodden khaki pants and bent forward to feel the hems of the cuffs. "I've got nothing but the damn sock," she said, then sat up. "Wait. What did you do with the firing pin from Ragotskie's gun?"

"I, uh—yeah, I dropped it in Fakhouri's Trader Joe's bag, along with all the stuff from the Saturn's glove compartment." He nodded toward the bag on the floor by her feet.

She reached into the bag, and after a lot of crumpling of paper he could hear her fingers scraping the bottom.

At last she straightened up, holding the tiny metal rod between he black thumb and forefinger.

"Got it," she said.

"You think *that's* making the metronome move?"

"What else? The metronome is registering supernatural intrusion, but weak, barely enough to make it move at all. And I think if Ragotskie's ghost tried to cling to us, the firing pin from his gun is the only handhold it'd be able to reach." She held it out, and when Vickery extended his palm she disattached the thing from her sticky fingers. He scraped it off of his hand in his shirt pocket.

He returned his hand to the steering wheel. "Why would he— it!—want to cling—" Vickery paused, then nodded. "Oh."

"Right," said Castine. "He still wants us to save Agnes."

"In spite of the fact that she killed him."

"In spite of that," agreed Castine. "He loved her. His ghost still does." She sat back, watching as Vickery wove through the traffic. "I don't think he did the right thing when he tried to poison me or shoot me, but—" She shrugged. "You've got to admire his devotion to her. Even after he's dead."

Vickery contented himself with just saying, "I'm gonna take Santa Monica Boulevard all the way down to PCH."

CHAPTER NINETEEN:
Ground Zero

Beyond a scanty, scarcely glimpsed fringe of parking lots and lifeguard station that rushed past on their left, the dark sea was an unmoving boundary of the world. Vickery didn't bother looking at his watch since he was driving as fast as he could, edging around slower cars and catching the last moments of yellow traffic lights, and when he had passed the brightly lit Arco station at Topanga Canyon Boulevard he cut sharply left, across oncoming traffic, and braked to a rocking halt in front of a yellow gate blocking cars from Topanga Beach Drive.

"You're on the wrong side of PCH," said Castine. "And," she added, looking at the instrument panel clock, "it's twenty till apocalypse."

"The ocean's on this side," he said, opening his door and stepping out of the warm car interior into the cold sea wind, "and you've got to lose your initiation."

"Shouldn't we deal with the egregore . . . first?" she said as she got out. "Or even uninitiate me tomorrow? It's freezing out here!"

Vickery stepped around the seaward side of the gate. A wire fence blocked the way down a slope to the beach, but the fence extended only about twenty feet past the gate. "We need you fully yourself," he said. "And if we fail, and the egregore does take off, you don't want to still be one of the initiates."

"No, I—I don't," she said resignedly. She closed her door and followed him to the downward-sloping pavement on the other side of the gate. "Aren't you cold? My pants are soaked!"

"Mine too," said Vickery with some sympathy.

At the far end end of the fence he stepped off the pavement onto a weedy slope. The overcast sky provided a dim glow, by which he could see a narrow path below, and beyond it, surf breaking on a wide, pebbled beach. He started to reach out his hand to help her down, but she shook her head.

"I'm not touching you," she said as she followed him in a hopping, sliding descent. "All we need is another echo vision, now."

At the bottom of the slope, Castine paused and rubbed her hand across her mouth as she looked at the breakers. The crash and roar of the surf was louder here. "You're diving in too, right?"

"I can't, I've got Ragotskie's firing pin in my pocket. Sea water would probably wipe him out of it."

"Huh. *You* got to dive in when the *sun* was up." Castine took a deep breath and let it out, then shrugged out of her coat and handed it to him. "Sometimes I wish I'd never placed that ad in the *Times*." She kicked off her shoes and, after a moment's hesitation, began unbuckling her belt. "And I suppose I've—"

From up on the highway came a screech of brakes and a slam of metal on metal; Castine and Vickery both paused, looking up the slope.

And Vickery heard shoes slithering on wet pebbles to his left.

He spun in that direction and saw a man hurrying toward them across the beach by the surf line; he was carrying a swinging lantern and a rectangular object that flapped in the wind, and after a tense moment Vickery relaxed, recognizing Fakhouri.

Soon the man had trudged to within a couple of yards of them. Vickery noticed that a small metal box swung on a chain below the lantern, and smoke was wisping away from it on the wind.

"I do hope," Fakhouri panted, "that was not my new rental car."

Vickery spread his open hands.

"What are you," Fakhouri went on, "doing down here?" He took a deep breath and said, "Go make sure the boy Santiago is on top of the hill!—with his own lantern!"

"Ingrid needs baptism first," said Vickery. He looked back up the slope, doubtful that the car crash could be unrelated to the occult events of this night, and he saw two small figures on the road up there, making their way along the fence.

When they began sliding down the slope, Vickery recognized them. They were Harlowe's twin nieces, still wearing their overalls.

"*Ya rab!*" cried Fakhouri, "it is the girls!" He called, "Why are you here, disobedient children?"

The girls came scampering up across the crunching pebbles, and one of them said, "We're *supposed* to be here, our uncle said so."

"Well," added the other, "we're supposed to be over by the hill, but we want to close all the apps first." She smiled at Vickery and Castine and added, "We could tell you were down here, so we made the man in the car stop."

"He kind of crashed, we made him stop so fast," admitted her sister.

"Was it one of the Consulate staff?" asked Fakhouri, rocking his head back to look at the sky. "One of the people I left you with?"

"No, we made them let us leave. This was a man driving on the street. He said a lot of mean things to us!"

"But he drove us here anyway," said the other girl. "*Topanga Beach,*" she added, evidently proud of remembering the name.

Castine crouched beside them. "What do you mean, close the apps?"

"It'll be cold," said one of the girls, and she pointed past Castine at the surf. "We've got to get all the way under."

Castine nodded. "That makes sense. I'll go with you, okay?" When the girls nodded gratefully, Castine straightened up and turned to Vickery and Fakhouri. "We'll leave our . . . outer clothing, at least, up here. You gentlemen may stare up the slope till we rejoin you."

Vickery looked up and down the dark beach; there was no one else in sight. "Okay. Be quick—and just go out far enough so you can submerge, like waist deep. Your mind goes blank for a few seconds when the—" He paused to glance at the girls, "—when the effect happens."

Fakhouri was muttering under his breath, but he and Vickery obediently shuffled around to face inland.

"I left them in some degree of safety!" Fakhouri burst out, just loudly enough to be heard over the surf and the chilly breeze. "Now they have crashed another car, and with some innocent in it this time!"

Not at all confident that they would accomplish anything here tonight, Vickery was surprised to realize that he was feeling an odd, bleak exhilaration. He nodded and looked down at lantern and the cardboard placard the other man was holding. "Whaddaya got?"

"This," said Fakhouri, waving the cardboard, "is an image of the *Nu* hieroglyph, which will extinguish Harlowe's—Chronic's!—*Ba* hieroglyph, if I am standing in the sea and the Santiago boy is properly equipped on the hill."

"And you've got coals in the little box there, to light the lantern with?"

"Punkwood embers, with combustion descended from the Baba Gurgur fire. A long story." He gave Vickery a mournful look. "What is your own plan?"

"We're aiming to get a ghost to look at Chronic's hieroglyph."

Fakhouri sighed, clearly restraining himself from turning around to see how Castine and the girls were faring. "You and I, my friend, sound—and behave!—like lunatics."

"Only game in town. Listen, I don't care what Ingrid said, I'm going to—" He turned back toward the sea, but saw a flurry of clothing and heard a protesting squeak, so he faced the slope again; and less than a minute later, Castine and Lexi and Amber came hurrying up to where he and Fakhouri stood. All three were shivering, and their hair was sopping wet.

"The g-girls saved me," said Castine. "I think I—passed out."

"We've done it before," said perhaps Lexi.

"Couple of times," added the one who might have been Amber.

Looking at the bedraggled girls and Castine, Vickery's momentary exhiliration blew away in the cold wind. "Let's," he said, eyeing the slope and imagining the hill and the dark field beyond the highway, "get to the other side."

Santiago had crossed the bridge over the creek silently in the deep shadows of the surrounding trees, but just as he started toward the path whose zig-zag course would have led him to the top of the hill, a hard impact between his shoulders knocked him off his feet. His unlit lantern with its attached tinderbox flew out of his hand and disappeared in the shrubbery, and he landed on his belly, lying on his gun and Fakhouri's cardboard placard.

Before he could roll over, two strong hands clamped on his wrists and drew them together, and then he felt a plastic cable-tie zipped tight around them. Next moment the hands grabbed his upper arms and hoisted him to his feet and then patted him down. The pistol was pulled from his pocket and a man's voice said, "Whoa! Let's see what the boss says about you."

The man slid the gun into the waistband of his pants; then, gripping Santiago's bound wrists in one hand and the placard in the other, he marched the boy back across the unsteady bridge and across a patch of dirt toward one of several small tents that had been set up in the field between the two hills and Topanga Canyon Boulevard. Strings of lights glowed around the tent roofs, and a generator purred in the distance. A couple of dozen people were milling around, their smiling or troubled faces visible when they drifted close to the tents. Santiago looked longingly at the tree branch from which he had watched the capture of Vickery and Castine this afternoon.

He was being shoved toward a picnic table under one of the tents, where two women sat on either side of a man in a black turtleneck sweater; they seemed to be trying to calm him down.

"Nobody's going to interrupt it," one of the women was telling him, her voice tight with evident impatience, "we're entirely above-board—we've got the general liability insurance and the Temporary Special Events permit from the cops. Tony and Biloxi are—"

"Who's the fellow with the officer's hat, then?" the man demanded, rubbing his eyes. "Everywhere I look, Agnes, there he is! He's *really there*."

Agnes shrugged, but the other woman said, "Oh—that's a train conductor's hat. It's a computer-generated image of Tom Hanks, from the movie *Polar Express*. Biloxi got a dozen posters of him and put 'em up all around the site, to scare off ghosts. It's not *real*."

"But does it really speak?" The man dropped his hands. "The sky is breathing!" he said. "I can hear it!" He looked past Agnes at Santiago and his captor. "What's this?"

"Tony," said Agnes, "I don't think this is—"

"I caught this kid," said the man who was marching Santiago forward by jerking upward on his wrists. "I took a gun from him, and he was carrying this." Tony's hand extended from behind

Santiago, holding out the cardboard sheet with Fakhouri's hieroglyph printed on it.

The man in the turtleneck sweater reared back, his eyes wide. "It's the sea, crowding up!" he yelled. "Tony—if anyone can still hear me!—take this fish away and kill it, and bury its contrary sigil." Harlowe was now looking frantically back and forth at his hands on the table, as if he couldn't see them.

"Mr. Harlowe," said the other woman hastily, "It's a boy. Just lock him in the—"

Harlowe looked up. "Kill it, kill it!" he shrilled, and Tony shoved Santiago away from the table, away from the lighted tents.

"Outside the perimeter!" called Agnes. "We can't have a ghost in here."

Pushed from behind, Santiago had to walk or fall. He trudged ahead, away from the lights, and was directed between two of a row of signs—looking back as he passed them, he saw that each bore the image Harlowe must have been talking about, a moustached man in an official-looking hat.

Santiago knew that Tony still had his gun; but the man would probably look around after he halted at a good place for an execution, well away from the lights, and Santiago was mentally rehearsing a backward stomp on the man's instep and a quick whirl to . . . well, to kick him in the balls and then head-butt him if he bent forward, or kick the gun out of his hand, or something. Maybe lunge backward and knock him over, and then hope to get teeth to his throat? Santiago's heart was pounding in his chest, and he found he was counting his paces, hoping for a high number.

Footsteps thudded behind them—and not the heavy impacts of adult feet. A moment later two little girls had overtaken them and were walking through the weeds alongside Santiago. He noticed that their hair clung damply to their foreheads.

"You're walking the wrong way," said one. "You'll miss the show."

"Lexi, Amber," said Tony, his voice sounding strained, "you girls go on back to your uncle. This is none of your business."

"Get help," said Santiago tightly. "This man means to kill me with that gun he's got in his belt."

The girls let their shoulders slump and stared past Santiago. He heard Tony yelp, and the cardboard sheet dropped, and then he heard something thump on the dirt. Tony's hand released his bound wrists.

Animation returned to the girls' faces, and one of them giggled. "He doesn't have a gun."

"He has a knife, though," said the other. "Tony, cut that ribbon off him. What are you being so mean for?" Her voice became louder: "Cut it off him!"

Tony grunted and his feet scuffed on the dirt, but after a few seconds Santiago heard a click, and then felt the cold spine of a knife blade pass between his wrists, and his hands sprang apart. He stepped quickly away from Tony and turned to eye him warily. The man looked angry and scared.

"Go back to where Uncle Simon is," one of the girls advised Tony. "You're only getting into trouble out here."

Tony opened his mouth, but it shut abruptly, rocking his head back. He swiveled around, flailing his arms, and hopped forward, then began running back toward the tent.

The girls went running away after him without a glance at Santiago. He considered calling out to thank them, then just crouched to pick up the gun and the placard.

He shivered. *Those girls made Tony drop the gun and let me go,* he thought. *Without touching him! What the hell is that?*

He was glad they had done it, and glad they were gone.

He peered back toward the tent where Harlowe, apparently insane now, sat with the two women; and when Tony and the girls ran up to it, the Agnes woman stood up and glared out into the darkness in Santiago's direction.

He slid the gun back into his sweatshirt pocket and hurried away, sidling between the groups of restless people toward the waving trees by the creek. He intended to quickly work his way back west along the bank to the bridge, retrieve his lantern and tinderbox—which he prayed had not broken open—and then climb the hill. He wasn't sure he would have time, before imminent midnight, to follow the widely diverging doglegs of the hill path, and decided to simply climb straight up the slope, thrashing his way though the irregular areas of shrubbery and crossing segments of the ascending path as he came to them.

Another row of signs stood ahead of him, each of these also

bearing the image of the man in the hat. He stepped between two of them and hurried on, and when he reached the clustered trees and bushes that flanked the creek, he looked back—and for a moment Agnes was clearly visible in the light from one of the tents. She was moving in his direction, and he was pretty sure she was holding a gun.

He ducked into the deep shadows around the trees. The wind was rustling the leaves in the branches overhead, and the creek provided a steady rippling whisper, and he didn't worry about the fainter sounds his sneakers made, brushing through weeds and scuffing over rocks. He was very aware of the weight of his own gun swinging at his side. When he passed a gap in the trees he glanced out across the narrow plain, but didn't see Agnes among the people around the lighted tents. He listened intently for any sounds of someone coming along the bank behind him, but heard only the wind and the creek.

He reached the bridge, and when he crossed it he stopped and looked up toward the top of the hill. A dark spot was moving laterally across the pale hillside, and Santiago realized that it was the head of a man walking along the dogleg path. The man had a beard, and was descending.

Santiago knew it must be the old *brujo* who he had confronted in the ruins below the San Pedro cliffs this morning, the one Vickery had called Chronic. Santiago had seen him walk up this hill this afternoon—and now he was walking down. The boy quickly swept his gaze over the steep, bumpy slope, trying to estimate a route that would take him to the top without intersecting Chronic's looping descent.

Then Santiago crouched and gripped the gun in his pocket, for two figures were picking their way along the path ahead of him. They were a man and a woman, and the man turned and looked back.

"Santiago!" he whispered, and the boy recognized the figures of Vickery and then Castine.

Vickery let his hand fall out of his pocket. The overcast sky and the lights on the tents beyond the creek provided enough diffuse illumination for him to have recognized Santiago in the dimness. The boy was carrying what appeared to be a sheet of cardboard.

Santiago was clearly reassured to see them, and to hear Vickery's shoes scuff in the dirt.

"You're not ghosts!" Santiago whispered. "You got away from the tar and the monsters!"

"No thanks to—" began Castine, but Vickery waved her to silence. Santiago had, after all, told them that he'd leave with Fakhouri if there was trouble at the tar pits.

Santiago jerked his head back toward the bridge. "There's a woman maybe coming behind me with a gun." He turned to the side and crouched beside a clump of tall weeds, and when he straightened up he was holding a duplicate of the lantern Fakhouri had, right down to the metal box swinging from it on a chain. The boy held the unlit lantern up, and was visibly relieved to see a wisp of smoke trailing from the box.

All three of them jumped then, for a screech of electronic audio feedback sounded from the field on the other side of the creek, and then an amplified voice that Vickery recognized as Harlowe's boomed out: "*How doth the little crocodile—*" A loud clattering followed, and then another man's voice echoed through the trees: "All of you are supposed to get in a line now, come on—it's almost time, folks—" The voice was interrupted by "*And pour the waters of the Nile on every golden scale!*" and then resumed, "Damn it, line up, please! Shit, can you get him back—?"

The megaphone was turned off with an echoing snap, and Vickery heard cursing and splashing in the creek, some distance behind Santiago. It seemed clear that the woman who had been pursuing the boy found it more urgent to take her place in the line over there.

Santiago glanced up the hill and without any further word began scrambling through the weeds, up the slope. The sheet of cardboard he carried flapped in the wind.

Vickery took Castine's elbow, and they turned and resumed their previous course along the dark path. "I think Santiago's woman abandoned the chase, but heads up." He drew Taitz's gun.

Castine nodded. "Where are we, uh, going?"

"Where else?"

She made a soft *khaa* sound that expressed both fear and resignation, but she followed him as he led the way along the creek bank.

At one pont he leaned back to get a view of the hill through a gap in the overhanging branches, and then stepped to the side and looked more carefully. "There's . . . a guy walking down, along the path," he said. "It's got to be Chronic."

"Then hurry. You still got Ragotskie?"

Vickery's left hand darted to his pocket and kneaded the fabric, and he exhaled through clenched teeth. "Got him."

This creek-side path was a curl of lesser darkness between the trees. They moved along quickly, and after a dozen paces Vickery didn't need to waste breath asking Castine if she heard the inorganic singing that had started up, lilting from the treetops and the dense wild bushes. "What's that one?" she panted. "That's *ghosts* singing, isn't it?"

"Yes." The night seemed colder,and hostile. "That's 'House of the Rising Sun.' Hold up," he added then, for dimly in the shadows he could see the low brick wall they had noted this afternoon. The calla lilies were pale beacons in the shadows.

This was where the terrible old house had stood, and he was sure that Harlowe and his lined-up followers would shortly march across the creek and come here, to the same spot where the egregore had been partially awakened in '68.

"We're at ground zero," he said.

Vickery had seen a row of signs standing out on the plain, and apparently each one had the image of a man's face on it; probably those were intended to provoke the uncanny valley effect in ghosts drawn to the event. It was clear that there were ghosts on this side of the creek, in the trees and underbrush, but Harlowe must mean to have his people carry the repelliing signs across with them.

Castine had slid to a stop in the darkness. "Ghosts are awake and singing. Let's call Ragotskie."

Vickery stepped up onto the low brick embankment, wincing as the damp fabric of his trousers slid across the gash in his thigh, and he and moved a few yards up the slope. When Castine had followed and was standing beside him, he dug in his shirt pocket and carefully took out the little firing pin. He raised it, then looked at Castine. "What's his first name?"

"Elisha. I'll do it. Drop it into my hand without touching me. Carefully!"

Vickery squinted at the pale oval of her face, then followed the line of her throat and arm until he could make out her upturned, tar-spotted palm. He lowered his own hand over hers and let go of the firing pin.

She closed her fist and stepped back. "Good." Holding the thing between thumb and forefinger now, she lifted it, and with her free hand she pulled the old sock from her coat pocket. She took a deep breath, glanced nervously at Vickery, then called, "Elisha, we need your help to free Agnes." She and Vickery both waited, but the only sounds were the ghost voices singing.

"Elisha Ragotskie," Castine went on, "Agnes needs you now." She gave Vickery an anxious look. "Where's the damn sigil? Ragotskie's ghost has to look at it!"

At that moment the amplified voice boomed again from out there among the tents: "When I count to three, all hold hands, and the two on the ends raise your free hands—they'll clasp together when we become God! And—" More thumping and feedback followed, and then Harlowe's voice rang out, singing, "*We'll leave behind this old gray shore, climb to the sky!*"

Vickery looked up in alarm. "God," he whispered, "Harlowe's doing it *out there*, not here where the house was! How the hell do we get into the middle of them?"

"Cross the creek, quick," said Castine breathlessly, "we've got to do it before they all—"

"*One!*" called the amplified voice.

"But the face on those signs—!"

"*Two!*"

Vickery heard heavy footsteps in the brush above him, and when he turned he saw the shape of a tall man striding down the last loop of the terraced slope as if down a stairway.

"*Three, hold hands!*" boomed the amplified voice from the plain.

And the branches overhead suddenly thrashed, and Vickery and Castine both involuntarily exhaled as the air was sucked out of their lungs; a moment later a gust of wind rocked them back on their heels, and when they inhaled they both coughed at the harsh metallic scent of ozone.

For an instant Vickery squinted against sudden, relatively bright yellow light—he glimpsed a stained plaster wall in front of him, and a window, and sand under his feet—

—And the night closed in again. He opened his mouth to ask Castine if she had experienced the flash vision too, but a silhouette figure was now standing between her and himself. It was rocking forward, bending over, as if it had stomach cramps. Vickery could hear Harlowe's people shouting in rapid unison now, out on the plain.

"Where is Agnes?" the close figure said in a groaning voice.

"She—damn it—needs you," said Castine, with a nervous glance past Vickery, "we just need to wade—"

"No," said Vickery, "a bridge—"

Again the vision of a shabby, sand-floored room intruded on Vickery's senses.

He stepped back from the window, which showed only featureless black night, and turned around.

By the sickly yellow glow of bare light bulbs dangling on cords, he saw Castine standing a few feet away, her coat and trousers streaked with tar and mud; the form of Elisha Ragotskie, looking solid and three-dimensional here, was hunched and bracing itself on the wall beside her. It wore round black-frame glasses and a white shirt and red suspenders, just as Ragotskie had when they'd first seen him. The ghost singing wasn't audible now, and music was playing from speakers somewhere—Vickery recognized the eerie guitar of Jimi Hendrix's "And the Wind Cries Mary."

A dozen other people were in the room—men in robes or worn denim, young women in cut-off shorts or long skirts, faces with beards, arms with tattoos, amid smells of incense and marijuana and sweat and patchouli oil—several of them were sitting on a couch against the far wall, a couple by the window to Vickery's right, and a cluster around the foot of a spiral staircase to his left. The conversations were loud, but overlapping and indistinct. A man carrying a bottle of Mateus rosé wine blundered into Vickery and lurched away across the sand toward the staircase, with a mumble that might have been an apology.

And hanging on the wall across from Vickery, above the couch, was the wooden board with the carved man-headed hawk figure on it.

Vickery shuddered and turned to Ragotskie's ghost. "You need to—"

"You said save Agnes," the thing croaked. Its face was pale and misted with sweat. "Where have all the flowers gone?"

"You need to look at the image on that board," said Vickery, pointing, "to save Agnes."

A couple of the people on the couch were now staring in evident puzzlement toward the newly-materialized trio. One young woman wearing a feathered hat and a woolen shawl took off a pair of rainbow sunglasses and called something Vickery didn't hear, and pointed past him. Glancing behind, Vickery saw nothing but an open door and several people standing on a porch outside . . . and two or three lights bobbing in the distance. He returned his attention to Ragotskie's ghost.

Castine was wringing her hands. "You need to be initiated!"

"I'm initiated already," the thing said, peering around past its shoulder at her.

No, you're not, thought Vickery. Elisha Ragotskie was, but you're not him, even if you think you are. God help you, you're not even a *you*.

"You'll be a toxin in the egregore!" whispered Castine. "Look at it again!"

"I'm the opposite of naked," the thing said wonderingly, looking down at itself. "I've got clothes, but there's nobody in them."

Vickery thought he heard the sound of engines over the music now, but a movement on his left caught his attention.

Chronic had continued walking down the hill path, but now he was stepping down the spiral staircase, and Vickery only recognized him because he had seen the man in the echo visions. Just as he had appeared in them, as he had looked in 1968—just as he had looked when he'd shot Dot Palmer on the porch right outside—Chronic was young and clean-shaven, wearing a green paisley Nehru jacket, with tangled brown hair hanging to his shoulders. This was the first time Vickery had seen him thus in full color.

And walking down the stairs in front of him was a woman who appeared to be in her mid-30s, in an embroidered linen blouse and black Capri pants.

A huff of breath from Castine made Vickery turn his head.

"That's Gale Reed!" she whispered. "Her ghost, I mean! Did we make her die this morning?"

"Maybe not," muttered Vickery. "It's 1968 here."

The sound of engines outside was louder now.

Chronic was speaking, though Vickery couldn't hear what he said over the music, and he slapped the shoulder of the woman below him on the stairs. Then he paused and looked past her, toward the doorway.

Vickery turned in that direction, and stepped back, for a big, dark-haired man in a leather jacket had stepped in. He appeared to be in his late 20s, but Vickery knew it must be Sandstrom.

Castine must have realized it too, for she called, "Look out!" in the moment before Chronic pulled the revolver from under his jacket and pointed it at Sandstrom.

The gunshot was loud in the confined space of the room, and for a stunned moment Vickery saw Sandstrom as a double exposure; the young man tumbled to the piled sand at Vickery's feet, while the bald-headed old Sandstrom whose barn Vickery and Castine had visited this afternoon was still standing; and Vickery realized that they had experienced this moment, from Sandstrom's point of view, while sitting in the Nissan in the Canter's parking lot this morning.

And now half a dozen angrily shouting men crowded in through the doorway, and pushed past the elderly Sandstrom as if they didn't see him. Vickery got a quick impression of beards and leather jackets, but he saw pistols and shotguns in their hands—he spun to knock Castine backward onto the sand as his own hand slid into his jacket pocket and closed on the grip of Taitz' gun.

He threw himself down on top of Castine, and when he turned his head he had to peer past the ankles of the Ragotskie ghost, which was still standing. The members of the Gadarene Legion who had stumbled out across the drifted sand began shooting,and the battering hammer-strokes of the guns was punctuated by screams; Vickery saw bodies jerk and fall, and he had the gun out now, ready to kill any of the berserk intruders who might turn their attention toward himself or Castine. Plaster chips were flying, and the air was suddenly sharp with the sulfur smell of burnt gunpowder and the copper smell of blood.

From the staircase Chronic fired repeatedly into the Gadarene Legion group, and Vickery saw one of them punched right back out through the doorway. The young woman in the feathered hat had got to her feet, but a blast from one of the Gadarene shotguns spun her around and threw her face-down onto the sand.

Over the screams and the gunshots, Vickery heard Chronic wail, "*Cayenne!*"

Castine stretched out her right arm and tugged at the cuff of Ragotskie's pants; the ghost tumbled down as if she had snapped a string it had been suspended from. Its face was toward her, gaping through the round glasses in horrified incomprehension.

She pointed past it at the board on the far wall. "*Look at the sigil!*"

"Will the wind ever remember?" the ghost mumbled. "But for her, yes." It obediently rotated its head, and Vickery thought the board on the wall seemed to shake—though that might have been just the effect of stray shot pellets hitting it in the resounding bedlam.

The Ragotskie ghost was crumpling inward like a deflating balloon, and the sigil on the wall was definitely changing now. It shrank, and became dimmer—

And all the light was extinguished, and Vickery and Castine were lying on the dirt above the low brick wall in the sudden darkness; one spot of lesser darkness in Vickery's sight was a rectangle above him and a few yards away, and when he forced his eyes to focus on it, he saw that it was the sigil board that white-bearded Chronic was now holding over his head, and again Vickery was reminded of Moses carrying the tablets down from Mount Sinai.

People were splashing and chanting now in the creek behind Vickery, and someone was standing to his left; and when the person stepped back he fell off the low brick wall and sprawled onto an inert body lying in the path.

Sandstrom rolled to his feet and stared down at the body.

"It's Coastal Eddie!" Sandstrom barked, and Vickery recalled that the unlit lamp in Sandstrom's barn was reserved for the arrival of Coastal Eddie's ghost.

Sandstrom looked up from the body toward old Chronic, who was standing a few yards up the slope, and Sandstrom's bared teeth seemed to catch all the glimmering light as he pulled a gun from his belt.

But now a crowd of people came stamping and panting up from the creek bank behind him, chanting in fast unison, and they shouldered the bald old man aside as they crossed the path and scrambled up over the low brick wall, all facing Chronic and the board he held up in both hands. Many of them were waving the *Polar*

Express signs, and Vickery was glad that Castine had already got Ragotskie's ghost to look at the sigil and surrender to initiation.

The air seemed to shiver with a powerful but subsonic roar, and again Vickery caught the oily-metal smell of ozone.

He saw threads or webs that seemed to be blown in on the wind, but they thickened and began to glow, and in moments the crowd was enmeshed in a rippling incandescent grid that curved up along the hill and to the sides, possibly enveloping the field beyond the creek and even Pacific Coast Highway on the other side of the hill—

And it was alive, and the breath stopped in Vickery's throat as its transcendent attention simultaneously focused on each person. Vickery felt that it was aware of every proton and neutron and electron in his body, and every neural spark in his brain. His small identity was being crushed by its nearly infinite one.

The flexing grid was unfolding in more directions than there were, from its unfathomable entirety down to scales far below human comprehension, and it formed Klein-bottle funnels that snaked out and attached themselves to the heads of Harlowe's followers; no funnel warped out toward Vickery's head, nor—he registered as he recoiled away from the psychic drainings—toward Castine's.

He was distantly aware of something like a jellyfish lying in the dirt beside him, and when one end of it managed to hike itself up, he saw its tiny wobbling head—eyeless, blind but struggling—and the little slack ribbons that had once resembled red suspenders.

A golden filigree funnel bent out of the grid, or out of the treetops or the sky, and touched Ragotskie's diminished ghost.

And the grid sprang apart there, and then in other places, and a leprous, pewtery sheen spread out across the fractal web and dimmed its golden luminosity—and through its fading, wounded gray fabric Vickery saw a lantern flare at the top of the hill. The egregore web folded from everywhere and receded toward the light.

The crushing weight was abruptly lifted from Vickery's mind. An irregular drumbeat of feet stamping the ground made him get up even as Castine was pushing at his chest.

People were crowded around them in the darkness, all furiously contorting and hopping now; over their grunting gasps he heard ghosts singing again, more loudly than before, and it was some familiar song. Vickery gripped the shoulder of Castine's coat and pulled her to her feet.

Looking around tensely, he thought of Stanley Ancona's words—*dancing for days, till they dropped*. The egregore hadn't had time to commit suicide, but it had clearly died; been killed. He noticed that some of the figures around him were not dancing, but singing—and the elbows and ducking heads of the dancers passed through those.

"Half of these are ghosts!" whispered Castine.

Vickery pushed her toward the creek bank. "Cross running water," he told her, "and look at your feet, not at them." It occurred to him that the song the ghosts were singing was now Fogwillow's "Elegy in a Seaside Meadow."

Vickery and Castine shoved and ducked their way through the crowd of dancing or singing figures, and as they splashed into the cold, rushing water of the creek, Vickery glanced back.

For a moment a gap in the churning crowd let him see Sandstrom, who had climbed back up onto the brick wall; Chronic was standing a few yards higher up the slope, uselessly gesticulating now, and the old Gadarene Legionnaire raised his pistol and fired it at him. The sound of the shot was muffled by singing and stamping feet, but the muzzle flash made a stark strobe-light tableau of the moment, fixing in Vickery's memory the image of a torn black dot between Chronic's white eyebrows.

CHAPTER TWENTY:
Thanks a Lot, Girl, Just the Same

For several ecstatic seconds Agnes Loria had felt her self dissolving in the multidimensional golden matrix of the egregore, all her memories fading like dreams as she awakened to an infinitely vaster universe; she was a massless and unaware virtual particle in instant interactions among identical particles—

And then the matrix broke, curdled, folded away, and she was aware of dirt against her physical cheek and pain in a joint that was inescapably a part of her individual body. Nerves in limbs that were her own twitched with the impulse to get up and jump and stomp her feet, but the pain in—yes, it was her knee—quelled it.

She rolled over and forced her arms and legs to lie still. Breathing deeply, she tried to remember what had happened.

She had seen the crooked old house appear among the trees on the other side of the creek, its windows lit and its open door spilling out ascending chords from an electric guitar—and then she had watched in bewilderment as a motorcycle, and then three more, rode from the direction of Topanga Canyon Boulevard across the flat field between the hills. She got a quick impression of extended front forks and low back ends as the wild-haired leather-clad bikers swerved between trees—and sometimes seemed to ride straight *through* trees!—and then they stood up on the footpegs to ride right across the creek.

Yes, and she had leaned over the distracted figure of Harlowe and gripped his shoulder in the same moment that gunfire had begun popping and booming over there, and Harlowe's four-foot image of the sigil had torn free of its frame and gone scything away in the direction of the impossible house.

She had slapped Harlowe's face and yelled, "It's happening *over there!*"

Harlowe had looked around in confusion, but by the time he faced the creek, the house had disappeared and his followers were racing away in that direction.

Then, for a brief few seconds, the egregore had been alive—all-forgiving, inclusive.

And after those few precious seconds it had died and been pulled away.

Agnes sat up now, clenching her fists against the rhythmic twitching in her muscles, and she pulled herself up onto the picnic bench. She blinked in the glare of the light bulbs strung along the fringe of the tent roof, and saw that Harlowe was still sitting on the other side of the table.

Blood streaked his mouth and chin, and he was gripping the edges of the table as his feet clopped and scuffed under it. His gaze was fixed toward the hill beyond the creek, and when Loria looked in that direction she saw the bright yellow dot of a lantern at the top of the hill.

"The night has been choked," he said hoarsely, pointing one spasming finger toward the hill. "That boy with the contrary sigil—he threw God into the sea."

Choked, thought Loria. We had nirvana—we were God!—and then it was snatched away.

I'd rather never have had it at all, she thought dazedly, than to have it experience me, accept and engulf me, and then go away and leave me intolerably stranded here and now.

She sighed, emptying her lungs, and made herself take notice of here and now.

She knew that most of Harlowe's people were still on the other side of the creek; she couldn't see them through the impenetrable blackness of the clustered trees, but she could hear their fast, imbecilic chanting and the drumroll of their stamping feet. Even out here, a couple of hundred feet from the concentration of that mob, Loria could feel the impulse in her muscles to get up and dance—clumsily, mindlessly. Clearly it was affecting Harlowe too.

One figure was only a hundred feet away, gyrating and flailing, but headed this way. Its spasms lessened as it moved closer to the table, away from the creek. She focused her despicably limited eyesight on it, and when the person reeled up into the tent's light, she recognized Tony. He was carrying an old wooden board.

"It was here," Tony said, frowning and still helplessly bobbing in place. His face was wet, possibly from having splashed through the creek. "I was in it!"

Harlowe blinked up at him. "Did you see it fly to the light on the hill? It's *banished*, gone forever. All fled, all done, the sea has won."

"But I have its sigil," Tony said, "look!" He held up the board, and Loria saw that a carved wooden image of the familiar man-headed hawk was attached the front of it. "And old guy over there had it, but somebody shot him."

"That looks to me," said Harlowe—carefully, as if choosing words were like picking up pieces of broken glass—"like a null set, containing nothing now." He took a deep breath and went on, "How many boys did I tell you to kill, only Tony?"

"The twins are here somewhere," Tony protested, "they made me cut him loose and let him go." He looked past the table and added, "Here they are, you can ask them."

Agnes was peering at two small figures who were hurrying up from the perimeter, each carrying one of the *Polar Express* signs—but at a sudden gunshot she jumped and whipped her head around.

Tony was tumbling backward to the dirt, and Harlowe was lowering a pistol that had kicked up in recoil.

He swiveled around on the bench, and Loria flinched as the line of the gun barrel swept across her.

But it was pointing now at the twins. "You let him drown it!" he said. "You—*reptiles*—I'm alone forever now, look!"

The girls dropped their signs. Loria saw that their hair was wet, and they were shivering. "Don't yell at us," warned one.

"Our mom and dad used to yell at us," added the other, hugging herself. "*You* told us yourself what to do about that."

Harlowe's weirdly disorganized mind must have recalled that the twins were capable of making him drop the gun, or even turn it on himself, for he quickly raised it.

Loria tried to lunge across the table, but her twitching arm slipped on the wooden surface and her face was down when the gunshot cracked the air; but when she looked up, Harlowe was leaning back, his hand empty. It took several blinking seconds for Loria to realize that the gleam on the shoulder of his torn black pullover was blood, from a fresh bullet wound.

Someone had shot him; Loria understood that much. But when she squinted out at the darkness surrounding the tent, she saw at least half a dozen people backing away and muttering, and none of them seemed to be armed. She was tensed, but no more shots followed.

Harlowe's left hand was tentatively touching the bloody rip in his sweater; his mouth was opening and closing but producing no detectable sound.

Loria got unsteadily to her feet. Briefly she thought about putting some sort of makeshift bandage on Harlowe's wound; then she just stepped around him and looked down at Tony. His eyes were open, staring emptily at the night sky, and she didn't see any rise and fall of his chest, and she didn't care anyway. Harlowe's gun must have fallen under the bench, but she bent down and, with both hands, lifted the board Tony had dropped.

One figure was running this way, and Loria looked up. The person who came puffing up to the table was the moustached man who had burst into Foster's house with Vickery, three hours ago—his pants and shoes were sopping wet below a plaid sport coat, and he held a revolver still pointed at Harlowe.

In an oddly accented voice, he said, "Girls, you must come away with me," and Lexi and Amber hurried around the table to him. The gun was wobbling in his hand now, and he lowered it to point at the dirt.

"You shot Uncle Simon," observed one of the girls. "Is it over?"

"Let's get Pollo Loco again," the other said brightly. Then, looking past the stranger, she called, "Not at that house with no TV!"

Loria had to squint at the blackly-smeared couple who had pushed their way through the cluster of bystanders into the light, and she recognized Sebastian Vickery and Ingrid Castine.

The two of them hurried to the table, though Vickery seemed to be limping. Loria noted their filthy clothes and Castine's wet hair. What on earth had they all been doing?

Castine looked from Harlowe, pale and mumbling and gingerly touching his bleeding shoulder, to Tony's body sprawled motionless on the dirt, then turned to the man who had shot Harlowe. "Get these girls out of here," she said.

The man nodded and muttered something to her. He dropped his revolver into his coat pocket, then took the girls' hands and hustled them away toward the path that led back to Pacific Coast Highway.

They were passed by another short figure that came loping up toward the tent—a boy, holding a gun that looked too big for his hand. When he stepped into the ring of light and brushed a lock of black hair away from his face, Loria saw that it was the boy who had brought what Harlowe had called the contrary sigil, and who, it seemed, had somehow caused the egregore to fail and vanish.

The boy quickly took in the situation and then said to Castine, "You still owe me ten dollars."

"What?" Castine looked exhausted. "Oh God, I do not, shut up." To Vickery, she said, "The girls are all right, let's go."

He nodded. "Right, back the way we—"

Still holding the board Tony had dropped, Loria stepped back to face Castine and Vickery and the boy. "Look at him," she cried, nodding toward the withdrawn figure of Harlowe. "He's nothing now—I have nothing now!" She raised the inert sigil board and shook it. "This is dead now. But what *happened*? What did you *do*?"

Santiago looked back in the direction Fakhouri and the girls had gone, clearly not sure himself what had been done here tonight.

Vickery was tugging at the shoulder of Castine's muddy coat, but she pulled free and stepped up to Loria. "*We* didn't do it," she said harshly. "Maybe Fakhouri and Santiago helped—disposed of the damned thing into the sea—but Elisha Ragotskie's ghost raised up its poor ruined head and sacrificed itself—to *p-poison* the thing—!" She took a deep breath, then shook her head and turned away. To Vickery she said, "Yes, let's get back to the world."

"I hate him, you know!" said Loria loudly, "I—"

Fast stamping footsteps sounded now from the direction of the creek, and Loria turned that way. A flash and ear-stunning pop were simultaneous with a hard knock against the board she was holding.

She stepped back to catch her balance, dropping the board, and then Ingrid Castine slammed into her from the side. Both of them tumbled to the dirt as a second shot split the air where Loria had been standing.

"They're all gone, lost!" yelled the shooter, who she now saw was a bald-headed old man in a ragged leather jacket. "But the *sigil* is *mine!*" The gun was in his left hand, and moving to aim at her again.

Vickery had to step around Santiago to get a clear shot, and when Sandstrom swung the gun down toward the two women on the ground, Vickery fired two fast shots into the man's chest; and even as Sandstrom tumbled forward, Harlowe suddenly bent down and groped under the bench. When he straightened up he was holding a small-caliber revolver.

He raised it toward Santiago, and two simultaneous gunshots battered the air; Harlowe was kicked sideways across the bench and rolled off it onto the dirt, face down.

In the moment of ringing silence that followed, Vickery looked at Santiago, and saw the boy slowly lower the semi-automatic that he was holding now in both hands. Vickery tipped his own gun up.

"My shot hit him first," the boy said loudly. "For Mr. Laquedem."

"Okay," said Vickery.

Sandstrom's right hand was moving, and Vickery swung his gun down to point again at the man; but Sandstrom was extending his arm across the dirt to touch the fallen board. Breath was hitching in the old man's throat, but he managed to pronounce, hoarsely, "In some times." He coughed, and went on, "Not all." His body shivered then, and he was still.

Vickery turned toward the two women. Castine and Agnes were both getting to their feet. A number of people were hanging back in the darkness outside the reach of the lights, clearly wary of the gunfire.

"We need to be somewhere else, *right now*," Vickery said to Castine. He turned to Santiago. "You too—get lost, quick."

The boy nodded and sprinted away toward the row of upright signs and the inland hill.

Agnes was staring down at Harlowe's body. After a few moments she kicked one of his red cowboy boots. The foot rocked loosely.

She squinted up at Castine. "I wish you hadn't knocked me out of the way of that bullet."

"I didn't do it for you," Castine said. She brushed her disordered hair back with a tar-spotted hand, and exhaled. "We promised Ragotskie that we'd save you. I got to deliver on it."

"Save *me*," said Agnes scornfully. She turned and began plodding away in the direction of Topanga Canyon Boulevard, where Vickery supposed they had parked the bus.

"We're out of here," he said to Castine, stepping out of the light in the direction Fakhouri and the girls had gone, and he instinctively took her hand.

Castine gasped, and he felt her hand twitch in his—but no vision intruded on them, and they were simply striding quickly across the dark field.

"Do we just," said Castine, waving back with her free hand, "leave them? All . . . that?"

"You want to stay and talk to the police?"

In spite of the pain in his leg that impeded his stride, she had to release his hand and hurry to keep up with him. They skirted wide around the creek, and Vickery glanced across it toward the spot where the spiral staircase house had intruded into 2018 from 1968, and where a lot of Harlowe's people were still grunting and spastically dancing in the shadows under the trees.

In less than a minute they had reached the dirt road where they had been shot with tranquilizer darts almost twelve hours earlier, and Vickery caught Castine's shoulder and slowed their pace; but there was no sound of sirens on the wind, and he didn't see any reflections of police car lightbars.

It wasn't until they had stepped around the posts of the traffic-blocking gate and hurried to the edge of the Pacific Coast Highway pavement that Vickery saw two patrol cars approaching at high speed a hundred yards to his left, and now the night was pierced with flashing red and blue LED lights. The cars turned left onto Topanga Canyon Boulevard, and he could see more approaching from the same direciton.

No other headlights were visible at the moment. He took Castine's hand again—again with no psychic consequence—and they sprinted across the highway.

They stepped between two low wooden barriers on the other side, onto a driveway that paralleled the highway—and then Vickery saw a man plodding along it in their direction.

Walk on by, Vickery told himself—but the man stopped when they were about to pass him. Vickery slid his hand into his pocket and closed it on the grip of his gun.

Two more police cars turned north on Topanga Canyon Boulevard.

"I saw it jump the hill," the man said, his voice barely audible above the crash of the surf, "and ground itself in the sea." Vickery noticed that he had left a trail of wet footprints that gleamed in the white radiance of a streetlight behind him.

Castine stopped too, and peered at him. Hesitantly, she said, "Taitz?"

Taitz! thought Vickery. A surge of adrenalin coursed through his weary muscles, and he drew his gun and raised it in the man's direction.

Castine said, "You—went into the water?"

Taitz lifted his empty hands, one of which was heavily bandaged, and even in the shadows Vickery saw the man's tired, ironic smile. "I'm damned if I'll hide," he said to Castine. "Damned if I don't, too, but at least I'll still be me. With all my own sins." To Vickery he added, "I believe that's my gun you've got."

Vickery just nodded.

"You," said Castine hesitantly, "want a ride?"

Vickery gave her a quick, incredulous look, but Taitz shook his head.

"Thanks a lot, girl, just the same." And he trudged past them along the pavement.

For several seconds Vickery and Castine looked back, watching him recede in the night; then Vickery took Castine's elbow firmly, and they began walking back east along the highway shoulder.

"Sorry," she said. "I just thought—"

"It worked out."

They strode from one pool of streetlight to the next, and then doggedly on to the one after that. Vickery looked back several times, but Taitz was no longer visible. The wind from the sea on their right was cold, and even Vickery was shivering. He took off his tweed coat and draped it over the shoulders of Castine's suede coat, though really it could only add weight. But she nodded, walking fast.

A flatbed tow truck with yellow lights flashing sat in the entry to the side road where he had parked Galvan's Cadillac, and a red sports car with a smashed front end had been winched up onto the bed of it.

Now what, Vickery thought. He stepped around the rumbling grille of the truck, and as he pulled the Cadillac's keys from his pocket a young man in a sweatsuit strode around from the other side.

"That your car," he demanded, "with goddamn clowns all over it?" When Vickery nodded and pressed the fob button to unlock the Cadillac's doors, the man went on, "Two little girls hijacked me, that's my fucked-up car on the tow truck, and they made me drive into oncoming traffic! Another car already got towed away, it's a miracle nobody got killed! Your damn *clown* car made 'em think there was a carnival or something down on the beach!"

Castine had opened the passenger side door, but turned to look back at the man. She was squinting against the tow truck's lights. "Two little girls had guns? Knives?"

"No," the man said, "they were—hypnotists!"

"Gotta expect that on Halloween," said Vickery with a shrug, opening the driver's side door and getting in, wincing as he flexed his cut thigh. Castine was already huddled in the passenger seat. There was room to the right of the tow truck, and Vickery started the engine and carefully backed past it, turning the steering wheel to the left, until his back bumper tapped a stop sign post. He shifted to drive, steered onto PCH and accelerated east. Two more police cars passed him, going the other way.

"Turn on the heater," Castine said.

"It's already on. It'll be hot in a minute."

She sat back and closed her eyes. "The police are going to find . . . *one unholy mess* back there. But I *am* glad that Taitz uninitiated himself, and didn't turn all spazzy like the rest of them."

"Great guy," said Vickery, his eyes on the lanes ahead. "Only tried to kill us yesterday."

"Nobody's perfect." She shifted her feet on the carpeted floor. "When's this heater going to get *hot*?"

"Any second," said Vickery, breathing deeply. He had started shaking, and he gripped the wheel tightly and glanced at the rear view mirror. "I think," he said, but his voice was unsteady; "I think," he went on carefully, "we got away." The shaking gradually abated as he watched the lane-divider lines flash past under the tires, and he felt himself slowly relax, muscle by muscle.

"A mess," he said finally. "Yeah, you could say so. At least three people shot, ejected shell casings—"

Hot air was blowing from the vents now, but Castine was still shivering and hugging herself. "Fingerprints on those?"

"I didn't load this one, and I doubt Santiago has ever been fingerprinted. He may never even have popped the magazine out of that gun." He yawned, creaking his jaw and squeezing tears from his eyes. He blinked them away and added, "Oh, and they'll find a lot of pictures of Tom Hanks from *Polar Express.*"

"Good thing Biloxi didn't manage to score a sex robot."

Vickery managed to grin. "Maybe he did, that's why we didn't see him there."

Castine laughed weakly, then choked it off.

For several rushing miles neither of them spoke. Then Castine stirred and said, "Are you going to return this car to Galvan? I think there's a lot of tar on the upholstery."

"Sure. At least we didn't leave it in some other world this time, and we did save her nephew and the *niños.*"

"Return it tonight?"

"Tomorrow sometime, or Friday. If we stop for a lot of hot coffee somewhere, I can drive a couple more hours tonight. Back to Barstow."

"Better get it at a drive-through window. Nobody'll let us sit in a booth."

"Oh—yeah, good point."

She yawned too. "Barstow sounds fine. Second star to the right, and straight on till morning." Vickery nodded, acknowledging the quote from *Peter Pan.* "I can spell you," Castine went on, "driving, if I get enough coffee too." She stetched out and turned to look at him. "You okay? I don't mean just to drive."

"Oh—yeah." He took a deep breath and let it out. "I'm responsible for a couple more ghosts now—"

"You share Harlowe's with Santiago."

"—But," and he remembered something he'd told himself last year, "they killed themselves, in a way, by putting me in a position where I had no choice." He spread his fingers for a moment on the steering wheel, and cleared his throat. "It wasn't—damn it, it wasn't *my* idea."

She touched his shoulder, then clasped her hands in her lap. "Your neighbors in the trailer park are going to remark on this car."

"S'all right. Galvan never reports cars that get stolen."

"You should take the bed tonight."

"You're still the guest. I'm still on the couch."

"Sleep till noon, anyway."

"I've got to get to Mass sometime. Tomorrow—today!—is All Saints' Day. Holy day of obligation."

"Oh. That's right, I remember." She rearranged herself on the seat. "Okay if I sleep for a bit here? Wake me up if you get tired."

"Sure."

Traffic was light at this hour of the night, and Santa Monica Boulevard would be coming up in about five minutes. There would certainly be an open MacDonald's or something.

He glanced at Castine. Her chin was on her chest and she was softly snoring, and the slow whisper of surf rushing past a couple of hundred feet away to his right seemed to echo her. He smiled; as a Secret Service agent he had gone much longer than this without sleep, and in fact he felt wide awake. Maybe he'd drive straight on till morning.

EPILOGUE:
All Saints Day

Vickery turned the volume down on the radio when he heard the squeak of the trailer's bedroom door. He had opened all the windows an hour ago, but left the air conditioner turned off; Autumn had finally caught up with Barstow's weather, and the thermometer that hung outside the kitchen window read sixty-eight degrees. Beyond it, the desert stretched away to the distant railroad tracks under a silver sky.

He stepped away from the radio and poured coffee into a cup, and stirred two spoonfuls of sugar into it. It was on the table when Castine came blinking into the kitchen.

She sat down in one of the two chairs and nodded toward the radio as she took hold of the cup with both hands. "Turn it up."

"Just an ad right now." Vickery poured a cup for himself and sat down in the other chair. "But—Gale Reed did die, yesterday afternoon. Natural causes."

Castine bared her teeth. "Ugh. Then that *was* her ghost, on the staircase. Did we—I suppose we must have caused it."

"I think we, what, gave her a chance to . . . " Vickery paused to take a sip of the coffee. "To finally help undo what she helped to do, fifty years ago."

"Good of us."

Vickery let that go. He looked at her face and hands. "It looks like you got just about all the tar off."

"It took a while. You probably had a cold shower—I bet I used up all the hot water."

He waved it aside. Last night a cold shower had not been unwelcome. "And there was a report about a New Age Halloween celebration gone wrong at Topanga Beach. Seven people dead, including the ChakraSys guru, five of them from gunshot wounds."

"Five?" Castine spread the fingers of one hand. "Harlowe, that guy Tony, and Sandstrom . . . oh, and he shot old Chronic . . . "

"And Sandstrom's pal, Coastal Eddie. He was shot in '68, but it took him fifty years to finally fall off the porch."

Castine shivered. "It's done now, right? The egregore, the old house visions? We were getting Sandstrom's view, in them, and he's gone now." She looked over the rim of her cup at the low sky outside the window.

"A lot of things are done. You said yesterday that I've been living out here as if I were . . . what was it?"

"Marking time," said Castine. "Waiting." He nodded and didn't say anything more. She went on hesitantly, "Agnes said you got your *Secret Garden* book. And she said it probably—" She didn't finish the sentence.

Vickery nodded. "The sea water washed Mary's spirit out of it. Pratt's ghost too. But—" He had been holding his coffee cup, and now put it down. He didn't meet Castine's eyes. "I baptized her, pronounced the words while I think she was still there, anyway, and we were in salt water."

Three chords had been playing in his memory all morning; he remembered now that he had heard them last night in the phantom house—the heavy guitar interlude in Hendrix's "And The Wind Cries Mary."

Castine reached out as if to touch his hand, then just spread her fingers and let her hand fall to the table. "*Can* you—?"

"Baptize a spirit that never lived? I don't know. I'm sure a priest would say the whole thing's nonsense. *Sacrilegious* nonsense. But she's . . . at some kind of peace now." He looked at the ceiling and then gave Castine a tired smile. "I think I'll take down the pinwheels from the roof and throw them in the ocean too."

"A clean sweep," agreed Castine. "I suppose I've been marking time too, this past year—waiting!—staying on at the Transportation

Utility Agency." She sipped her coffee and nodded toward the radio. "The news didn't have anything about a couple who fled the scene in a car covered with clown pictures?"

"No." He sat back and sighed. "They're talking to some of the event organizers—Biloxi, and Avalon somebody—but I don't think any of them will be eager to say much. Blame it all on the dead guys would be the best bet. The news did say the place was a weird mess, with pictures of Tom Hanks on signs everywhere. And they said four old-style Harley Davidson motorcycles were found at the scene, one of them in pristine condition and the other three just rusted-out wrecks."

"Well, that's what sort of bikes ghosts would ride, isn't it? The last run of the Gadarene Legion. The last rerun." She stretched. "What if the cops talk to us?"

"Well, you'll be back in Maryland soon. And Sebastian Vickery was an identity that never existed anyway. If anybody ever fingerprints me, I'm Herbert Woods, onetime LAPD cop and Secret Service agent. And in the meantime I'm Bill Ardmore."

"Bill Ardmore the saucer nut. How's your leg?"

"UFOlogist. I cleaned it and put a bandage on it. I'll live."

"And we can finally burn that old blood-stained sock of mine, right? It's still in my coat pocket."

"Burn it and bury the ashes," Vickery assured her.

"What do you suppose will become of those girls? Amber and Lexi?"

"Oh—I suppose Fakhouri and the Egyptian Consulate will get in touch with the U.S. authorities, if they haven't already—see that they're sent to any family they may have, or at least put someplace where they'll get . . . foster care, therapy?"

Castine nodded. "I think Fakhouri hopes to get them away from L.A. altogether. Just before they took off last night, he told me he was finally rescuing the two girls from Garbage City."

Vickery blinked. "That's a bit harsh."

Castine stood up and crossed to the stove. As she refilled her cup from the coffee pot, she said, "When were you thinking of returning Galvan's car?"

Vickery looked at his watch. "It's only noon. I thought I'd drive you to the airport, then drop off her car. And, if she doesn't kill me, catch the 5 PM Mass at Blessed Sacrament on Sunset and take a bus back up here."

"Blessed Sacrament," she said, carrying her cup back to the table. "I remember that church. I can get a flight tomorrow—how about if I come along? All Saints Day—it is a holy day of obligation, after all. And if we stop at Hesperia and get my stuff, my credit cards, I might still be able to rent a car, to drive you back here."

"You don't mind meeting Galvan? I don't think she'd actually kill us, but she won't be happy. I punched her in the stomach yesterday."

"You did?" Castine laughed softly. "All things considered—no, I won't mind."